# R I O T

By

STEPHEN JAYDELL

ISBN: 9798720521622

**Riot:**

*/Noun:*

*Law. A disturbance of the public peace by three or more persons acting together in a disrupting and tumultuous manner.*

**Public Order Act 1936:**

Section 3: Sub-section 1:

*"If the police have reasonable grounds for believing any event or occasion may lead to serious public disorder, they may give directions as necessary for the preservation of said public disorder, including conditions prohibiting individuals from entering any public place."*

Section 3: Sub-section 4:

*"Any person who knowingly fails to comply with any directions given or conditions imposed or incites any person to take part in such event, shall be guilty of an offence."*

Section 5:

*"Any person in a public place using threatening, abusive or insulting words or behavior with intent to provoke a breach of the peace shall be guilty of an offence."*

**Vagrancy Act 1824, (Section 4):**

*"Every suspected person frequenting any public place with an intent to commit an arrestable offence shall be deemed a rogue and vagabond, and guilty of an offence, liable to be imprisoned for up to three months."*

LONDON, 1981.

Intense stop and search activity spread over five days and nights, effecting more than one thousand citizens, preceded the 1981 Brixton Riots. The riot resulted in over two hundred and fifty injuries to members of the Metropolitan Police, damage to fifty-six Police vehicles and over one hundred and fifty buildings being burned or destroyed. Reports suggest around five thousand people were involved in the rioting, with only eighty-three arrested for public order offences.

Four weeks after what was widely reported as the "worst outbreak of civil unrest" on the British mainland, Lord Scarman began a seven-month inquest into the events surrounding the "disorder". The inquest found unquestionable evidence of the disproportionate and indiscriminate use of "stop and search" powers by the Police, concluding complex political, social and economic factors created a disposition toward violent protest. The inquest found the disorders were not planned nor orchestrated, but a spontaneous outburst of built-up resentment sparked by particular localised incidents, and a loss of confidence in the Police. Lord Scarman recommended a new code of conduct for the Police within the 1984 Police and Criminal Evidence Act and the creation of an independent Police Complaints Authority, established in 1985, in an attempt to restore public confidence in the Police.

British Broadcasting Corporation,
'On this Day'

# Episode 1.
# "Riot"

Scanning across the void of rubble, broken glass and burning puddles a thunderous roar engulfs him. The smouldering scorched shell of a burnt-out Ford Cortina lays dying in the middle of the road as putrid petrol-stained air fills his lungs. Thoughts racing, a scribble of confusion, perhaps even fear, engulfs his exhausted mind. Head ducking, he struggles to control the urge to run as a molotov-cocktail sears the air above painting bright orange blaze across the dusky sky. Edging forward, a thousand ideas ricochet through his mind as burning red flames dance around his ankles. 'Oh god, why me, why now,' he whispers, knowing his thoughts are utterly futile and his questions rhetoric. Another step forward, he feels the dull pressure of half-bricks and broken bottles bouncing off the perspex shield, a fragile membrane separating him from those who want to tear him limb from limb. Three steps forward, glancing to his left, he can't help but stare at his colleague and friend, Andrew, driving on fearlessly, his face contorting and angry, his lips stretching across his gritting teeth.

'Charge!'

As the venomous hum increases velocity, palpable fear fills the air. Gathering pace, his eyes narrow, he knows this is it. Adrenalin pumping, heart racing, this close he looks into the eyes of the angry mob for the very first time, a discordant mess of violence, pointless aggression and prejudicial hate.

Stomach churning, he realises there's no turning back.

No. Turning. Back.

Not now.

'Keep pushing,' Sergeant Smith yells, urging the team of sixteen Special Operations Officers forward.

Toes digging deep into his standard issue boots, he flinches as bricks smash into the top of his shield. Not looking up to face his fear, he dips his head and pushes on. He's pretty sure they won't kill him, but, if they aren't pushed back, he'll be on the receiving end of a good beating at the very least.

Then…

At last, the aerosol driven foghorn echoes up and down the street-come-warzone. Bent double, he crouches in a foetal position. Thank God it's over, he whispers as an eerie echo of silence fills the breeze-block-make-believe houses masquerading as a South London battlefield. The baying mob fades seamlessly into the urban scenery and the Special Operations Team follow Sergeant Smith away from the wreckage.

'Good work out there, immediate appraisal?' Smithy nods.

'Sir, we, erm, kept our shape, stayed together and made good progress,' John nods, adrenalin subsiding as calmness resumes.

'Yes, I agree,' Smithy smiles, patting him on the back. 'I'll get a full debrief from the observers later, but for now, good work John, very good work indeed.'

Struggling to accept praise, he blushes.

'I'll tell you what though, they get into character a bit too easily for me,' Smithy chortles, nodding toward the mob standing around the tea van who, a matter of minutes earlier, were on the verge of anarchy, simulating a full-scale inner-city riot. The "mob", otherwise known as first term cadets, will later in the year endure the very same ordeal John and his team have just been through. Standard "Riot Control" as it's commonly known, had been introduced eleven months ago year in response to growing political resentment and social tensions in the inner cities. The make-believe street at the Metropolitan Police Training Centre, Hendon, represents a typical inner-city environment, even more so when filled with exploding petrol bombs, burnt out cars and a baying crowd.

After a handshake with Sergeant Smith, John follows his team-mates back to the changing rooms. The nineteen-fifties, flat roof prefab structure is filthy and, at this time of year, absolutely freezing. Most of the other cadets, still pumped-up and joking between themselves, are already in the lukewarm showers bantering and slapping each other. Even now, after all this time, he feels a little intimidated by the pack and struggles to clear his throat. 'Erm, guys,' he suggests, raising his voice above the frivolity. 'Superb work today, the Sarge is impressed.'

'Fucking loved it boss,' Donnie yells, who, in a single slow-motion action, performs an upper cut, tensing his pronounced bicep. Older than the others, a classic "late recruit", his added years show in his fuller physicality. At just under six feet tall, he's lean and toned, his face dominated by bony cheeks and a large angular nose.

'You would, you psycho,' Andrew bellows, standing unashamedly bollock-naked applying Head and Shoulders to his "number-two" buzz cut.

'What's that, ye-cockney shite-so-y'are?'

'You heard me-yah, you skirt wearing Jock.'

'It's a kilt, yah-dunderheaded-cunt-ye.' Donnies accent grows stronger under stress, John had observed, a caricature verging on a cliché he thinks.

'Sow, big-man, what ye'ginne do?'

'I'll show you what, you haggis-shagging-twat-yah.'

'Guys, remember who we are,' John cuts in, standing between them both before banging the shower and waiting for the water to trickle. Confident he's avoided world war three, his eyes close as the first lukewarm drops splash onto his face. Mind wandering, he considers how these two pumped up future-coppers will react in real life situations, no doubt handing out their own rough justice to anyone unlucky enough to cross their paths. He suspects this is an inevitable outcome of their inner city, working class upbringing and a warped view on social justice and authority mechanisms. He's different though, holding a fundamental determination to make a difference, a real difference, be part of the solution, not the problem. Never really feeling part of the team, his softly spoken middle-england accent and polite mannerisms alone are enough to turn most of them against him. While not surprised, he's disappointed, even now, they seem a little suspicious of his motives, and that their class-prejudice is so apparent. As the filth of the riot drill washes away through the Victorian sewage system, he towels himself dry before buttoning up his freshly pressed, clinically white shirt.

'Swift one, guv?' Andrew looks up, pulling on his blue and white Adidas Gazelles.

'Erm, no, don't think so Andy, I have to write up a report on today's drill.' Although he understands the social need for post-work bonding and the performance enhancing morale boost this brings, he finds the boisterous nature of such gatherings tedious and a tad draining. While appreciating the popular culture and humorous male dominated chit-chat, especially between Donnie and Andrew, he secretly longs for an evening of solitude, a good book with an even better bottle of burgundy and the emotive melodies of Brahms symphony number one.

'All work and no play makes Johnny-boy dull and boring!'

'Erm…'

'Oh, come on boss, the chaps will be gutted if you don't make one in. Perhaps demonstrate some of that "leadership" you keep going on about.'

'I really do need to sort that report,' John sighs, not reacting to Andrews crude attempt at satire.

'Report, right, of course you do,' Andrew smiles, mock punching his arm. 'A quick pint can't harm though.'

'Oh-okay, a quick half then,' John smiles. Even though

Andrew holds deep rooted racial prejudices about what he refers to as "ethnics", he's become a surprising confidant during the past year or so. When alone and not influenced by the bantering pack, John finds they speak on more than just a superficial, football-and-sex-and-alcohol level. After much deliberation, beneath the East End barrow-boy façade and extreme bar-room banter when in wider company, John concludes he has promise.

Friday, 16 January, 4:52pm
Dog and Duck Public House
Hendon, London

With green ceramic tiles surrounding a narrow wooden swing door, this typical London pub can, at best, be described as a dive. However, for some unfathomable reason, it's become the teams regular haunt for after-work socialising. John can't accurately determine the attraction of this particular establishment, although, according to Donnie and Andrew, it's local, cheap and every Friday lunchtime a stripper performs erotic dances to Blondie or Lips Inc. Taking a deep breath before stepping inside the cigarette smoke filled lounge, John finds a spot at the bar next to Donnie. Patiently holding two crisp ten pound notes, he asks the barmaid for twelve pints. Already toward the end of his second, Donnie sways. 'Aye, a bonny beauty,' he slurs, deliberately loud enough for the barmaid to hear while throwing John an overly theatrical wink.

John finds the taunting of any female, especially one who must take this type of humiliation day in, day out for very little pay, distasteful and completely disgusting he dislikes drunkenness nearly as much as misogyny. 'Stop it, Donnie,' he says assertively, pushing another pint into his hand.

'Okay-boss, calm down. probably an auld-lesbo anyway.'

Although disgusted with his behaviour, John is secretly fascinated by Donnie. In the time they've spent together at Hendon, he has never once talked about his family, nor why he left Glasgow or why he joined the Police in his late twenties, which is late compared to most other recruits. For all his bravado and muscular manliness, John see's Donnie as an intensely private person, probably the most private of the entire intake, and, as such, extremely interesting and worthy of further observation.

Having already delivered three pints, John precariously balances the remaining eight on a rectangular metal tray as he navigates the tables and chairs. The last thing he wants to do is fumble, fall and become the focus of ridicule.

'Look at those wankers over there-yah,' Andrew nods toward three mid to late teen males sitting at the other side of the pool table. John noticed them too as he entered, probably under-age and probably up to no good, however, he'd rather they drink in here, fall home legless and vomit at the side of their beds than be out causing havoc on the streets of London.

'Fucking little pricks.' Andrews face hardens.

'Taking the piss big man, a fucking liberty,' Donnie teases, finding his seat. He loves winding Andrew up.

'Too right, too fucking right,' Andrew growls. 'They can see this is our place, a coppers pub-yah.'

Having thought deeply about this ritual many times, John sighs a long deep sigh. Showering, drinking, perving over barmaids, more drinking and more often than not fisty-cuffs followed by a curry, is all part of the re-humanising process after policing the streets of London. A little boisterous behaviour might be okay, he supposes, good for team morale perhaps, as long it remains within the bounds of the laws of the land they've sworn to protect. He'll have to have his wits about him to stop this particular situation escalating.

'Oi, you three, do one,' Andrew yells.

Looking up, the faces of all three teenagers drop, realising they are drawing the attention of a group of inebriated coppers, including the man-mountain of aggression yelling over toward them.

'That's right-yah, go on, down the road,' Andrew seethes,

tensing his broad chest. Even sitting down, he has a huge physical presence and his posture, screwed up face and broad cockney accent only adds to his menace.

The youth in the middle looks left, then right, before standing up. 'What?' he shouts as his comrades stifle their giggles. 'Me?'

'I'll give you fucking "what-me", you little shit.' On his feet and instinctively into his fighting stance, Andrews top lip pulls against his snarling teeth. 'Go on, piss off or I'll fucking do you me-self-yah.' He yearns for them to disobey.

'Pack it in, Andy.' John grabs at his forearm.

Placing his lighter down on top of his freshly opened pack of Silk-Cut, Donnie shuffles into a more comfortable position. Leaning back, he blows a smoke-ring above his head. Oh yes, he'll enjoy this, at best there'll be a tear up, and he loves a tear up, at worst, he'll see Andy getting a bollocking from the boss. Everyone's a winner, perfect.

Noticing the smoke halo hovering angelically above Donnie's head, John struggles not to smile. What a wonderfully beautiful irony, he thinks.

'They're taking the piss, this is our pub-yah,' Andrew whispers through gritting teeth.

'A di-ab-ol-ic-al liberty big man,' Donnie suggests, exaggerating every syllable.

Fearing the worst, his two mates grab the youth back to the safety of the small round table they occupy. 'Fucking coppers,' he mouths, slumping back into the chair.

Reading his file, John is all too aware of Andrews formative teenage years growing up in Canning Town, East London. By all accounts, he suffered hideous brutality at the hands of his Father and Uncle, who brought him up to be what they referred to as a "real man". His adolescent upbringing, John thinks, is no excuse for poor behaviour as an adult. A grown man aspiring to be a Police Officer, he should be acutely aware of what's right and wrong and socially acceptable. Even so, John has witnessed first-hand the ultra-violence Andrew is capable of dishing out, and, as such, is fearful for the youths, especially the brave but stupid one in the middle. Gazing at Andrew snarling like a vicious dog straining on a tensing leash, John stares through his minds-eye into the future, picturing how this will play out…

In super-slow-motion Andrew leaps the corner of the pool table while grabbing the adjacent chair, simultaneously launching it toward the youths. The youth to the right tries unsuccessfully to turn away, raising his right arm over his head, but the chair connects and splinters all around him as blood splatters on the velvet velour wallpaper behind. The mouthy youth in the middle is grabbed by the neck and Andrews forehead smashes into his face, crushing his nose and detonating an explosion of deep red blood all around the pub. In a flash, Donnie's beside him, the heels of his boots pounding the head of the other youth to the left while the ("lesbo") barmaid is screaming above the sound of crashing wood and breaking glass. Then, the whole pub erupts, smashing chairs, throwing punches and loving the tear-up. John eventually gets involved, peeling away body after body from the mound of aggression, before grabbing Andrew around the neck with the vee of his forearm…

Shaking the images from his head, he returns to the reality of the pub. 'Andrew, I'm telling you formally, back off,' he whispers sternly, pulling Andrew back to the table. 'Are they really worth the trouble?'

Adrenalin subsiding, heart rate normalising, much to the annoyance of Donnie, Andrew glares at the youths before retaking his seat. Tension easing, the cadets embark on more drinking, tall tale telling and fantasising about graduating.

'Nice easy number,' Donnie proposes romantically before blowing smoke into the rafters. 'Something in vice I think.'

'Free blue movies, that's what you're after,' John chips in, trying his best to go with the flow. The group erupts into laughter while John sighs a huge sigh of relief.

'What about you John?' Andrew smiles.

'Erm, what about me?'

'Where next, after passing out boss?' Donnie adds.

'Oh,' John nods, thankfully. 'I'm really not sure.' He lied, of course he knew, he's already held several conversations with Sergeant Smith about his career development, in particular, a role in the Criminal Investigations Department. 'Maybe something at the 'Yard?' he shrugs.

The entire group nod in complete agreement.

'Couple of years on the beat for me,' Andrew cuts-in. 'After that, off to the countryside, middle of nowhere, out in the sticks. Local plod, nice and easy.'

'Countryside, you sure pal?' Donnie quizzes.

John looks on, intrigued as to where Donnies heading.

'Oh, hang on, aye, I get it big man,' he nods slowly. 'Virginal sheep for ye' to shag!'

Disappointed, John shakes his head.

Friday, 16 January, 10:09pm
Taste of India Restaurant
Hendon, London

As the majority of cadets stay in lodgings local to the college, they often share their evening meals together at one of the many eating establishments in North West London. Friday night is usually Indian, with Chinese on Saturdays. Through the window of the empty restaurant John observes a swarm of waiters pulling three tables together in preparation.

'Table for twelve,' Andrew yells, pushing the door open.

Even though they all know exactly what they'll order, eleven drunken coppers and a slightly inebriated Cambridge graduate find their seats and study the laminated menus. Hot, very hot and ultra-hot. Vindaloos washed down with several pints of lager is the unanimous order of the day.

'Poppadum, Sir?' the young waiter suggests tentatively.

'Too right Poppadums,' Donnie shouts from the far end. 'And don't forget the sweet-jammy-shite.'

The young waiter smiles. 'Oh-kay, twelve Poppadum and…' he nods at Donnie. 'Plenty of mango chutney, Sir.'

'Mangos aye, from the motherland,' Donnie belly laughs.

Closing his eyes, John shakes his head. He's become accustom to the tiresome poorly attempted and bad tasting joke every week, the same boring, disgustingly racist rubbish. Looking toward the young waiter, embarrassment etching across his face and indignation in his eyes, John takes a deep intake of breath. The cliché of the scene isn't lost on him and he feels equally embarrassed, ashamed even. As the young waiter turns toward the kitchen, John catches his eye and touches his arm. 'Erm,' he struggles to think of something non-patronising to say. 'Sorry,' he whispers. The waiter smiles before vanishing behind the multi-colour beaded curtain into the kitchen.

As the tea-light candles beneath the plate warmers are ignited and the main meals manoeuvred into the centre of the tables, the team become even more boisterous. At the same time, John feels more and more detached from the group so decides to expedite his exit as soon as possible.

Wiping the remains of his curry with a Chapatti, he stands and finishes the tail end of his pint. Dropping a five-pound note into the centre of the table, he makes his excuses before grabbing his jacket from the communal coat-stand. Opening the door, he's greeted by a stiff coldness. Glancing over his shoulder, the group appear not to have noticed his departure, which, he thinks, is more than acceptable.

# Episode 2.
# "Windsor"

Saturday, 17 January, 5:10pm
47 Saltoun Road
Brixton, London

Spark, burn, inhale.

Yeah man.

Relax.

'This is the life,' he sighs, re-igniting his deftly constructed five-skin spliff. Surrounded by a warm glow, a sense of peace fills his mind as every muscle relaxes. Turning the hot tap with his foot, he feels the warmness flow around him, nice man, nice. Mommas rules mean the emersion heater is switched on just once per day, meaning one bath per day between the whole house. He's lucky, today is his day.

Television on full blast downstairs, the action reaches a crescendo with the commentator eagerly describing Big Daddy belly-splashing Kendo Nagasaki. After the inevitable three-count victory, Dickie Davis reads through a round-up of the football scores on World of Sport. Saturday afternoon is Pops television watching afternoon. After a long week driving a London Underground train, he spends much of his rest-day in the betting shop, placing a one-pound bet on a six-horse accumulator, and another pound doing the football pools before heading home with a light-ale to watch his wagers unfold.

Twisting the hot tap again, his thoughts drift to what might be in store later tonight, when he and his two best friends will head to the West End for a big night out. West End clubs are very different to the moody, watch-your-back-or-get-stabbed-up clubs in South London. No hassle, lots of customers to sell to and, most importantly, lots of fine girls looking for fine men, men just like him, yeah man. Black or white, fat or thin, blonde, brunet or afro, he loves all the girls up West. Another pre-bath-assembled spliff later, he pulls the small chain attached to the black plastic plug and watches the water swirl down the plug-hole before reaching for the towel.

The room he shares with his younger brother is small, too small for a grown man and a shit-for-brains-pickney-youth teenager. Two single beds along each wall, both with brown woollen blankets covering soft cotton pink, yellow and cream striped sheets. A heavy oak dressing table with a large mirror sits in between, just in front of the single net curtain covering the window. A double wardrobe rests opposite the door to the landing, the left-hand door painted black, green and yellow while a topless picture of the latest Page-Three girl is stuck to the right-hand door with yellowing-at-the-edges sticky tape. Pressing the play button on his tape-deck, the cassette reels turn and a rumbling baseline bounces off the walls. Closing his eyes, he nods in time with the echo-chamber driven snares, the tunes magnifying his feel-good vibe as the sound waves ripple through his ribcage.

A minute or so later he drops to the floor and grunts out thirty push-ups followed by fifty sit ups before a quick sparing session with Apollo Creed through the mirror. 'Good-gosh, you is looking fine tonight Dev-on,' he smiles to himself with a wink. Delving into the drawers of the dressing table, searching with his fingers, he eventually pulls out clean Y-front briefs. On goes his Gabicci t-shirt, yellow with brown trim, then his grey Farrah trousers and dark green crocodile skin shoes. His gold bracelet, gold necklace worn outside the shirt and gold watch finishes the look.

Then.
Slam!
In a flash, the bedroom door bursts open.
Momma?
Police?
Skinheads?
Heartrate jumping, panic surges.
Swinging around, he pulls his right arm back while jabbing out his left, slapping the intruder on the top of his head. Ducking, the intruder offers a swift upper cut, just missing. Stepping back, he shimmies right before aiming a low right hook into the intruders ribs. Rolling onto the bed, the intruder covers up, ready to receive further blows. 'Leave off Dev,' he pleads.
'What you up to, sneaking around?' Devon snarls.
'Catch you at it, yeah?'
'Catch me at it, you'd be lucky, shit-for-brains.'
'Least I got brains, even if they're made of shit.'
'T'cha, not got time for you today,' Devon tuts, returning to the mirror.
'Come on, don't be like that, where we off to tonight?'
'We, we nothing, be serious,' Devon smiles. 'You're just a kid, a lickle pickney with a serious dose of ugly disease.'
'Nah-nah, serious man, I wanna get some pussy action.'
Laughing, Devon bends double at the thought of his little brother talking like a rude-boy. 'Pussy action, come on, you wouldn't know what to do with it.'
'Yeah, I would,' Marlon rolls off the bed before bursting into song Michael Jackson style. 'Don't stop till you get enough… keep on, keep sucking me off,' he sings, dancing around theatrically.
'You give me jokes man.'
'Come on Dev, let me come yeah.'
'Not tonight dred, soon though, soon.'
Appearing older than his fifteen years, Devon knows Marlon can easily pass for eighteen, maybe even twenty and would have no problem getting into the West End clubs.

But, same way, he can't have his little brother following him around, especially up West, that wouldn't be right.

'T'cha!' Marlon kisses his teeth.

'Anyway, you'll be going to the disco thing at the Youth-Centre, yeah, with your duppy-boy-lemon bum-chum.'

'Dickhead,' Marlon yells, storming downstairs.

Forty minutes later…

Devon grows impatient waiting at the foot of the stairs outside the family home. Even though he's nearly always late, Paul does have a car, (just about), a seven-year old two litre Triumph Dolomite, gold with a black vinyl roof and rusty rear wheel arches. At last, he says to himself as he spots the car turning into his road and gliding to stop at the foot of the curb. 'You're late, again,' he says, through the half open window.

'Needed to get the cash, yeah.'

'Tell me you got it though?' Devon looks sideways before climbing in.

'Come on, of course I have, no problem.' Paul says, pressing the accelerator.

Wheels spinning, they set off.

Two minutes later…

The car turns into Leeson Road.

'Just here nah-man,' Devon points to the pavement twenty feet from the front door of the Windsor Public House. 'Wait here yeah, dis no place for you.'

Heading toward the pub, he allows his right shoulder to dip ever so slightly lower than the other and adds an extra little bounce to his sway. Yeah man, he looks and feels every part the rude-boy man about town.

Saturday, 17 January, 6:23pm
Triumph Dolomite Sprint
Leeson Road, Brixton, London

'No place for the likes of me?' he tuts. Even though he's been hanging around here for fifteen years, ever since they became friends in the first year of secondary school, it's true, he still feels out of place. The Frontline, as it's locally known, is the area around Atlantic and Railton Roads, not far from the tube and train stations in the centre of Brixton including convenience stores, pubs, taxi-shops, fast food take-away restaurants and pool halls. Surrounded by a maze of small narrow streets, alleyways and railway tracks, the area is a magnet for all types including rude-boys, gangsters, punters looking for business and drugged up dirty skagg-heads who'll stab you up or suck you off for a five-pound fix. More recently two new threats have emerged. Firstly, the National Front who specifically seek out guys like Paul and secondly, the Metropolitan Police otherwise known as Beast or Babylon, on the lookout for suspicious youths to stop and search and generally harass.

Waiting for Devon to return, fingers strumming on the steering wheel, Paul watches life on the Frontline unfold. In the distance he spots a couple of rude-boys hustling at the corner while a few kids on BMX bikes zoom up and down the road avoiding the odd car cruising by. Still early evening, the Frontline comes alive on Saturday nights with urban hustle and bustle, deals being dealt, rumbles with fellow rude-boys or all-night blues parties hosted by one of the many local sound systems competing for supremacy.

Knock, knock!

Head spinning, he looks through the passenger window and a young girl staring in. Lank, greasy hair with bad teeth and terrible acne, she's god-damn ugly as sin and no doubt a skagg-head hooked on heroin. Nose pushing against the window, her breath forms a veil of condensation.

'Oi mate, mate' she whispers, motioning with her hand to wind the window down. 'Just for a second, go on mate.'

'Do one, yeah.' With his best mate returning any second with a hundred pounds worth of weed, he doesn't need this.

'Come on, open up,' she sings. 'Just a little bit.'

'For fuck sake,' he sighs, leaning over to wind the window a third of the way down. 'What the fuck do you want?'

‘Seen you around here a few times,’ she says slowly, running her finger along the edge of the window while slowly linking her lips. ‘Looking for anything special?’

Paul looks to the pub, still no sign of Devon. ‘Listen, do I look like a fella who needs a whore, and dirty one at that?’

‘What?’ she says, seemingly hurt by Pauls suggestion.

‘Do yourself a favour and get lost.’

‘But, I can be special,’ she says, forcing a sad smile while gripping the window. ‘Twenty quid, anything you want.’

‘Let go you slag.’ Paul hisses, winding the window up.

‘A tenner then,’ she pleads.

With the window wound up, Paul pushes the locking mechanism down and shakes his head.

Running around to the front of the car she puts both hands on the bonnet. ‘Five quid for a hand job?’

‘Fucking hell,’ he sighs, flinging his door open.

She looks around him to the end of the street and a skinny long-haired guy in a dirty denim jacket leaning against a wall.

‘Listen you fucking skagg-head-slag, I don’t give a fuck what you’re selling, or who’s pimping you down the road or your tragic backstory about your uncle shagging you or your parents dying when you were a baby.’

‘What, why?’ she says, hurt in her eyes.

‘I’m not asking but telling, fuck the fuck off.’

‘Lend me a couple of quid then?’ she backs away, fear filling her watery eyes. ‘Please.’

‘In two minutes time, a mother-fucker-rude-boy will be back, and if you’re still here he’ll kick the living shit out of your boyfriend pimp, then stripe your skinny ugly face.’

Shimmying her way around the other side of the car, she turns and shouts ‘wanker’ before skipping merrily back toward her boyfriend already walking away.

Saturday, 17 January, 6:22pm
The Windsor Public House
Leeson Road, Brixton, London

On the corner of a row of three-story terraced town

houses the Windsor Pub dates back to the late 1800's. Surviving the Second World War blitz, it sits adjacent to waste ground surrounded by half corrugated iron half wire mesh fencing. Devon glances through the rusting sheets of iron toward the plumbers merchants on Mayall Road. Smiling, he remembers selling lead flashing there as a kid, which he'd robbed from the local Catholic Church roof.

Yeah man, those were the days.

Pushing through the narrow double saloon doors, he enters the pub and the fragrant aroma of burning weed mixing with the stained smell of yeasty beer hits his flaring nostrils. It's small, with a u-shaped bar set in the middle and a dozen or so small circular tables dotted around, each with three or four stools. The regular clientele are in their usual seats, playing cards or backgammon or dominos as they sup their light ale or dark rum. Through the haze he spots Crissy sitting in the corner furthest from the door with two others with him. To his right, quite literally Crissys right-hand man, Claude, the Frontline enforcer who'll fuck you up as soon as look at you, the more brutal and bloody the better. He doesn't recognise the other chap, but he looks equally deranged.

'Wha-gwan rude bwai,' Crissy greets him in his deep, gravelly tone, removing his thick black rimmed glasses, placing them in between the two pints of Guinness.

'Easy nah-man,' Devon replies, pushing a rolled-up bundle of notes across the table.

He doesn't know much about Crissy, aka Cristobal Campbell, other than he's in his mid-fifties, maybe older and came to England twenty years ago. Rumour is, and there are lots of rumours, he competed in boxing or judo or something in the nineteen sixty-six Empire Games. Apparently, he accidentally killed an opponent and never competed again then moved to England. A living legend on the Frontline, Crissy commands respect because he doesn't blatantly sell on the street, he's discreet and subtle.

'Sa-breddah, wha-me provide?'

'Two quarts, man,' Devon nods, glancing around.

Grabbing the notes, Crissy looks to Claude who reaches under the table, producing a large handful of bushy-weed. Tearing off a large portion, he stuffs it into a NatWest Bank plastic coin bag then pushes it across the table. Looking either way, Devon picks it up and shoves it into his inside breast pocket.

'Where you-ah-ed tonight-man?' Crissy asks.

'Up west, some soul and funk club or something.'

'Soul and funk, nah-man, roots man, roots,' Crissy kisses his teeth, shaking his head.

'Hmm, der-be puntang inna-de-dance?' Claude says, shifting himself forward, excited by his train of thought.

'Yeah man, hopefully,' Devon smiles.

'Yo, yeh-need any-ting else?' the other, up till now silent guy grunts. Momma has a broad accent for sure, but this guy is ultra-broad and speaks really quickly.

'Yah-nah-some-ting a lickle more 'ard-core?'

Devon looks at Crissy, then back. 'Nah-man-nah, safe yeah.' Just like Crissy, Devon doesn't deal with anything other than weed, he doesn't agree with chemicals.

'T'cha!' the other guy mutters, kissing his teeth in disgust.

'Don't worry-bout Snakehead here,' Crissy interjects. 'He just landed and still a bit raw, yah-naw.'

'Right, right,' Devon nods.

Crissy moves closer. 'Listen, hear me now, Babylon not as tolerant as dey-are. All man-a-man pickney steeling from old ladies and ting, bring down rumpus and tribulation-on-a-da-whole-neighbourhood, seen?'

'True-say man,' Devon wonders where this is going.

'You and yours got to be discreet wit-yah dealings-star, yah-ear what I'm saying?'

'Yeah man, course-course.'

Nodding, Crissy motions to the door.

Devon exchanges nods with Crissy and then Claude, but Snakehead blanks him. Avoiding any eye contact, he can't help but stare. Snakehead has what looks to be a fresh three-inch-long over-pronounced pink scar across his cheek. Practically on the sides of his head, his eyes are discoloured yellow and too far apart, hence the name 'Snakehead' he supposes. Exiting the pub, he acts as normal as possible while looking both ways up and down the road. He spots Paul getting back into his car and a young girl running away. 'What the fuck's he up to now,' Devon whispers, maintaining the ever-so-cool bounce.

'Who-dat-den?' Devon asks, flinging open the passenger door and climbing back in.

'No-one, just a Tom looking for business.'

'We don't have no time for you getting no blow-job.'

'As if, I told her to do one,' Paul shakes his head, turning the ignition key and setting off.

'Beggars can't be choosers my friend,' Devon teases.

'Oh-shit,' Paul sighs through the rear-view mirror, his eyes locking on to the Police transit van following behind. 'SPG up my arse.'

'T'cha, we don't need no shit from Beasts tonight man,' Devon says, quickly pushing the bag of weed under his seat.

'Mate, if I get nicked I can kiss my job goodbye,' Paul tuts, gently pressing the brake, indicating left.

As the bonnet of van pulls up underneath the rear window four Officers climb out. Surrounding the car, they give it the once over, kicking the tyres and pulling at the body work. A man-mountain of an Officer taps Pauls window.

'Evening Officer,' Paul smiles, winding the window down.

The Officer looks in. 'Your car?'

'Yes Officer, it is. I have all the relevant paperwork.'

'Right, right, I see. You better get out then, both of you,' Man-Mountain Officer nods.

'Stay cool,' Paul mouths.

'You stay cool, fool,' Devon whispers. What does he think I'll do, jump up and down shouting, "sorry boss, de drugs pon de seat, please lock me up and beat my arse red raw?"

'Up against the wall,' Man-Mountain Officer instructs.

Complying in silence, the Officers commence a body

search while asking them where they are going, where have they been and other stupid pointless stupid questions.

'We've got to go,' an Officer yells from the passenger seat of the Special Patrol Group tactical response vehicle, commonly known as a "SPS Wagon". 'Suspected assault near the market.'

Man-Mountain Officer looks at Devon. 'Looks like it's your lucky day-yah,' he winks before walking back toward the van, maintaining his death glare at both of them.

'What a touch,' Paul whispers, climbing back in.

'Babylon all over the place, man, they wanna get out and catch some real crooks,' Devon mutters.

Paul nods solemnly in agreement.

Wheels spinning furiously, they disappear along Coldharbour Lane toward Brixton town centre.

# Episode 3.
# "Community"

Saturday, 17 January, 7:45pm
The Community Centre
Brixton, London

An unmistakable hum from a large group kids can be heard in the distance, cheering and jumping around to what sounds like *"can you feel it"* by the The Jackson Five. 'This way toss-pot,' he giggles, tiptoeing in and out of the headstones.

'You sure it's this way?' Ashley queries, hoping it isn't so they can turn back.

'Settle yah-whining and follow me yeah,' Marlon tutts, leaping across a grave, being careful not to stand on a zombie. 'This better be worth it.'

'Mate, it will, trust me yeah,' Ashley smiles before leaping over a headstone. 'Heard some decent birds are coming down, from the convent school.'

'God fearing goodie-girls?' Marlon tuts.

'Nah, dirty as fuck naughty ones.'

'Best not be shitting me, man.'

'Have some faith yeah, come on.'

Making their way through the graveyard then across Loughborough Park, they approach the Community Centre. A yellow brick single story building with a flat roof, perfectly square apart from the glass pyramid atrium in the centre.

Every night apart from Saturdays, a small kitchen around the back of the building dishes out hot soup for the local homeless, squatters and hard-up from the boarded-up houses on Angel Town, Railton Road and the Somerleyton Estate. However, on Saturday night it sells lemonade and crisps to the local kids, while outside the wanna-be rude-boys and pickney youth share cans of lager. Friday night is the "Unity Disco," co-organised by Reverend Johnson from the Baptist Church running services in the centre on Saturday and Sunday mornings, and Father O'Donnell from the local Catholic Church a few hundred yards along Shakespeare Road. Attracting kids from all over Brixton and the wider south London area, the simple sound system consisting of twin turntables and a set of four speakers isn't up to much. The lighting system is quite simply crap, with a single set of disco traffic lights and a spotlight with three coloured discs spinning in front. As for the music selection, it's a poor show all round, with mostly inoffensive pop tunes, with the odd Specials track thrown in.

Done with weaving in and out of the headstones and graves, they crunch their way up the gravel path toward the Centre. As they approach, an increasingly loud chorus of kids chanting *"just another brick in the wall"* echoes around them. Looking at each other, they nod broad, spliff induced smiles. His mind full of the sweet goodness of the weed, Marlon imagines entering a film-set where he's the star, the main man, the one they've all come to see. Yeah man, he's a cool dude, a mother fucking bad-man, a line-man, a genuine rude-boy. Adding more than the usual bounce to his walk, he dips his left shoulder every other stride. Scanning the group of kids hanging around outside the front doors he smiles a broad smile, relieved Junior isn't there.

Ashley, on the other hand, has his eyes trained on the right-hand corner of the building and three fit girls in complete drunken state. The girl-in-the-middle is bent double being violently sick while the girl-on-the-left holds her friends hair out of the stream of yellow bile. He giggles as the girl-on-the-right covers her mouth just before projectile vomiting into the same small pile left by the girl in the middle. Jokes, man.

'No Junior then,' Marlon says, happily.

'Can't see why we just don't sort him out,' Ashley says without taking his eyes off the massive mound of sick forming at the feet of the vomiting girls.

'We?'

'Alright, you, can't see why *you* don't sort him out.'

'If only it was that simple Ash.'

Junior is the leader of the Peckham-Boys gang, a set of dirty scum-ridden dickheads based a couple of miles east of Brixton on the notorious North Peckham Estate. Every now and again they wander into Brixton looking for trouble, just as they did last Saturday night.

'Their time will come, soon come,' Marlon boasts, secretly hoping their time doesn't come soon. With the swelling around his eye just about subsided, he doesn't fancy getting another black-eye, or, even worse, stabbed or cut.

Pushing their way through the kids leaving the Centre to consume more cheap lager or to get off with each other, or to be sick, they enter the disco. *"Call me, call me any time,"* by Blondie rings around the half empty hall as the flashing disco lights chase long silhouettes across the walls.

'Where are these fit catholic birds at then?' Marlon teases.

'Still early mate, give it time.'

'Hold on, hold on,' Marlon mutters, spotting someone weaving their way toward them at speed. 'What the fuck.'

A small, skinny kid wearing a slightly-too-small red and black chequered shirt, faded jeans with a ripped-hole on the left knee and scuffed red monkey-boots approaches.

'Alright Ash,' Kingy grins, keenly. 'Watcha Marlon.'

'Looking sharp my man,' Ashley teases.

'Sharp as a knife rude boy,' Marlon joins in, gently tugging at Kingys shirt. 'Out on the pull tonight?'

'You know how it is, gotta make an impression int-cha,' Kingy grins, a smile stretching across his acne ridden face.

'So anyway, I'll see you bum-boys later, yeah,' Ashley yells, loud enough for half the room to hear before making his way across to the other side of the hall towards a group of giggling girls.

Marlon takes the opportunity to head in the opposite direction to the far corner where his cousin Delroy is holding court along with a few other mean-looking rude-boys, 'Hold up Marl,' Kingy follows.

Spotting Marlon, Delroy reaches out a hand. 'Easy-nah, Dee,' Marlon smiles, slapping his hand.

'Respeck Marlon, safe man, safe,' Delroy nods. 'Brought your puppy-dog with you then,' he glares at Kingy.

'He alright man, lef-him be yeah,' Marlon tuts. 'Anyway, wha-gwan?'

'Yaw-nah, every-ting cool man, got a lickle business to attend to later though, you know what I mean?' Delroy fancies himself as a rude-boy businessman and big-time drug dealer, even though he only sells the odd spliff here and there to friends and friends of friends.

'And the man who can, easy-nah Gladstone,' Marlon high-fives Gladstone, Delroys best mate and right hand man.

Ever so gently and tenderly, Gladstone feels Marlons eye. 'Swelling's gone down, good, good,' he nods sagely.

'Alright Doctor Gladstone, easy with the batty-boy business yeah,' Marlon pulls away giggling as Kingy over exaggerates his elaborate laugh, patting Marlon on the back as he does.

Saturday, 17 January, 10:56pm
Wooden Bench, outside the Community Centre
Brixton, London

With the disco winding down, the music selection slows and the mellow sounds of Earth, Wind and Fire echo through the steadily emptying Centre. Well out of sight from prying eyes the group, apart from Ashley who hasn't been seen for forty-five minutes or so, sit on the moss-stained rotting wooden bench overlooking the park, and in the distance the graveyard. Joints are skinned-up and passed around while Kingy shares a quarter bottle of white rum he stole earlier from the mini-mart on Electric Avenue. They chat for ages about everything and nothing, including…

Girls, who they would like to get off with. Football, and who's best, Viv Anderson or Kevin Keegan. Kingy, and whether he buys his clothes at Oxfam. Girls, who they fancy and would freely admit they fancy. Beasts, and x-amount of sus-stops. Gladstone, and whether he is the best fighter at school. Girls, who they have got off with. Marlon, and if he can have Junior in a straight fight. Junior, and what a pussy-hole he is… and how ugly he is… and how much he and is Momma must stink of fish, (enough jokes man). Girls, who they'll definitely bone given half the chance. The Peckham Boys, and what idiot fools they really are. Ashley, and whether he's a queer, (consensus is, he is). Girls, who will suck them off for sure. Delroy, and whether he is a rude-boy or just a fool, and, Babylon, and how racist they actually are.

Then…

In the distance, a shadowy silhouette approaches.

Junior?

The Peckham Boys?

Skinheads?

Babylon?

'What the fuck!' Delroy whispers, steadying himself.

'Easy-nah man, easy, be cool yeah,' Marlon asserts.

The approaching shadow quickly morphs into Ashley, who recites tales of his carnal adventures with the several girls he got talking to earlier. Pausing, they hear the sound of gravel crushing beneath tyres.

'Beastman-dem come,' Delroy whispers, seeing the reflective stripes of the Jam-Jar glowing in the darkness.

Marlon throws the dog end of a spliff into the bushes while Kingy downs the last of the rum before launching the empty bottle into the park. Straightening out their jackets, they prepare for the inevitable sus-stop.

'Relax man, don't let them break our hearts-nah,' Marlon suggests, trying to keep the others calm.

The Jam-Jar comes to a rest and three Officers get out, the first in uniform, the other two in plain clothes. The uniformed Officer heads toward the Centre before disappearing through the entrance while the plain clothed Officers approach the group.

'Evening chaps, alright?' an older looking Beast with grey greased-back hair and a long brown trench coat smiles.

They share shrugs and head shakes, apart from Kingy. 'Thank you, Cunt-stable, we've had a brilliant night,' he jokes, looking around for approval.

'Don't get smart with us, right,' the old grey Beast snaps, grabbing Kingy by the shoulder and leading him away toward the trees.

The other Officer, younger with a brown leather jacket proceeds to throw questions toward the group: 'Been drinking lads… had a little smoke maybe… who's been dealing all the drugs?'

The group shrug in silence.

'Okay, not very talkative, let's get this over with then boys,' the Beast suggests, ushering Gladstone and Delroy away in the opposite direction to where Kingy was taken. 'You two, wait here,' he points at Marlon and Ashley.

The uniformed Officer, a huge man with an angry face and a dick-van-dyke cockney accent approaches from the Centre, with Reverend Johnson in tow. 'We've had reports of drug dealing here tonight-yah, you know anything about that?' he says, staring suspiciously at Marlon.

'Boys, if you know anything, you must tell dah-man,' the Reverend adds with an angry tone. 'Dis be a good place, the Lords place, we don't need no trouble around here.'

'We've been here since eight o'clock and haven't seen anything, we only come here for the music, and the girls, here, smell.' Ashley says, holding his hands out.

Marlon giggles.

'Never mind that-yah,' the uniformed Officer frowns,

turning toward Marlon. 'What about you, what have you got to say about all this?'

'All this what? Jesus-christ, there's been no dealing around here man,' Marlon replies.

'Don't be taking the Lords name,' the Reverend tuts.

'The Reverend here puts a lot of effort in for you lot to enjoy yourselves-yah,' the Officer shakes his head. 'But all you lot do is take liberties, mugging old folk, dealing your drugs, smashing windows and all that. Give you an inch…'

'Muggings and drugs?' Marlon protests. 'There's no muggers or drug dealers here,' he pauses, before tilting his head, pushing his chin forward ever so slightly before continuing. 'Cunt-stable.'

In a single movement, the Officer grabs him by the scruff of his neck while pushing his wrist up his back.

'You, my son, are well and truly nicked-yah,' he shouts.

'What for?' Ashley yells.

'Shut it you,' the Officer growls, bending Marlon double, pushing his arm further behind his back.

'Officer please, what's going on?' the Reverend pats down the air, trying to calm the situation.

'Threatening behaviour,' he says, leading Marlon away.

'There is no need for this,' the Reverend pleads.

'Too late-yah, way too late, he's nicked.'

Bent over the bonnet of the Jam-Jar, the Officer uses his other hand to reach in through the window. Grabbing the black telephone handset, he calls for back up.

Five minutes later…

A Police Transit van arrives and Marlon is promptly bundled into the back, along with the two plain clothed Officers. With that, the uniformed Officer climbs back into the Jam-Jar telling the group to 'piss off home,' before reversing back down the gravel drive.

Saturday, 17 January, 11:22pm
Custody Suite
Brixton Police Station, London

Sitting on the long wooden bench, the ultra-bright lights above his head burn into his eyes as a weird stench of urine and bleach irritates his nostrils. Sitting to his left is a bad-man who he recognises from the Frontline as Chewbacca, a massive man with a huge sway of dreadlocks turning a gingery-grey toward the ends, bound by a red, gold and green sweatband. In a bad way, he's half asleep mumbling something about Police brutality. Even with his head tilting forward, Marlon can make out a dark red crusty gash above his left eye and a stream of dried blood running down the side of his temple. Shit man, he thinks, if they've mash-up Chewy, then they're going to string me up for sure.

To the other side sits an old drunken tramp, Irish by the sound of it, happily fighting an imaginary wasp buzzing around his head singing 'ye-bastard,' and 'I'll get-che'. In the background he can hear yells from the cells, "fuck da Babylon" and "release, Beastman, release." Scanning around, he's surprised how busy and noisy the custody suite is with lots of Officers coming and going, dropping off forms and generally being busy. In front of the screwed-to-the-wall wooden bench he's sitting on stands a high counter with a seriously overweight Beast behind. Looks like his job is to book suspects in, assign them to specific cells, then, sometime after that, get them back out of the cells when it's their turn to be questioned or, as he suspects, their turn for a beating or a bumming.

Then…

Eyes scanning right toward the door to the car park, he spots another prisoner entering known as "Ready-Brek". In the year above him at school, he gained his unusual nickname due to the fact that he's permanently stoned, so much so that he seems to glow all the time, just like the boy on the tasty breakfast cereal advert. As well as a complete weed-head, he's infamous as an untrustworthy thief.

Spotting Marlon, his face lifts. 'Fancy seeing you here.'

'What?'

'It's me yeah, what you doing here?'

'Not on holiday, am I?' Marlon says, raising a disbelieving single eyebrow.

'Eh?'

'I got nicked, yeah.'

'Ahh-right, me too!' Ready-Brek nods with a grin.

'Fucking hell, how much longer?' Marlon asks, flicking his chin toward the Beast behind the counter, not wanting to spend any more time with Ready-Brek than necessary.

Looking up, Behind-the-Counter Beast stares at Marlon for a few seconds before returning to whatever was reading without saying a word.

'So, what you in for?' Ready-Brek whispers eagerly.

'What?'

'What d'you do, where'd they catch-yah?'

'Threatening behaviour, so the Beastman reckon,' Marlon says, raising his voice. 'What about you?' He can't bring himself to call him by his nickname.

'Parking meter.'

'Eh?'

'Crack them babies open, easy money yeah.'

'You robbed a parking meter?'

'Full of cash, aint-they,' Ready Brek says, moving closer to the edge of the bench.

'A parking meter?'

'Yeah!'

'How'd you rob that then?'

'Ahh, that'd be telling.'

Marlon shrugs, he's not that interested anyway, robbing a parking meter sounds like madness.

Hearing the door to the car park go again he looks over Ready-Breks shoulder and sees a flash of red and black and the back of a small skinny ugly kid going through a set of double swing doors into the main part of the building.

'You see that?' Marlon says, standing, straining his neck to gain a better view.

'Sit... down,' Behind-the-Counter Beast commands.

'See what?' Ready-Brek's head darts from side to side.
'Who they just brought in, you see that?'
'What, what-what?'
'That was Kingy yeah, here, in the Station,' his words tail-off as he replays what he's just seen.
'What you on about?'
'You know Kingy, the little mug who follows me around everywhere,' Marlon says, impatiently.
'The trampy one?'
'Yeah.'
'The Oxfam-second-hand-clothes-spotty little kid one?'
'Yeah man.'
'The stinky, glue-sniffing muggy little mug?'
'Yes, that one,' Marlons head buzzes. 'Oi, oi, boss-man, where's dat other kid gone?'
'What other kid?' Behind-the-Counter Beast says slowly, still not looking up.
'That kid they just brought in, what's through there, where's he gone, why aint he in here with us?'
Behind-the-Counter Beast looks up without moving his head. 'What's through there my son is the land of mind-your-own-business.'
Kingy, arrested as well?
What the fuck for?
And why aint he in here, with us?
Tired, drunk and definitely more than a bit stoned, he decides it can't have been Kingy and he's seeing things. As Ready-Brek is led away to be questioned Marlon leans his head back against the wall and closes his eyes. It'll all make sense in the morning, he tells himself.

# Episode 4.
# "Yard-Man"

Saturday, 17 January, 1:52pm
Bedsit 3, 34 Booth Road
Hendon, London

Eyes open, he lays still for a few seconds before letting out a loud sigh. Fingers locking together he pushes out his palms and stretches, before swinging his legs around and standing. Gazing out of the window at the overcast sky and rolling clouds, he glances down toward the back yard and the puddles forming as the rain pitter-patters off the flagstones. Turning, he looks around the bedsit, sighs and shakes his head. This is as far removed from the family home in Berkshire as one can get. He seldom looks back to his upbringing fondly, but today, for some reason, he can't help but yearn for the lush green countryside rather than the sub-urban greyness outside his window. His single bed stretches along the far wall underneath a long narrow window while parallel to this stands a symbolic dining table with solitary chair. To the right, a cooker, sink and small worktop with an opaque glass sliding door cupboard above.

Oh well, such is life, he sighs.

Deciding against using the communal shared bathroom, he heads to the sink, twists the hot tap and proceeds to wash his face before smothering shaving cream over his cheeks, chin and neck. Flinching, he feels a sharp tug and, through the glass cupboard door, sees a stain of red seeping through the creamy whiteness. Damn, he tuts to himself, spending longer than necessary swirling his razor through the water, staring into the miniature vortex he's created. His thoughts are scrambled, so much so he can't think of anything in particular, only the growing tension in his stomach and the knot becoming tighter and tighter.

In the final few weeks before graduation, all cadets are required to undertake "work experience" consisting of three shifts per week. He's very grateful for his posting to "West End Central", which, by all accounts, is far more interesting than Donnies posting to the North-West Division and much safer than Andrews posting to Lambeth Division and Brixton Police Station. Today, before his nightshift, he's been called to New Scotland Yard for what Sergeant Smith, his tutor and mentor at Hendon, refers to as a "performance review" with Deputy Commissioner Jenkins. Both he and the Sergeant agree the request for such a review is most uncommon, however, he is the stand-out cadet of his intake and, according to the Sergeant, the stand-out cadet for all of the nine years he's been the Lead Instructor. Ever since he learned of the review, he's tried to keep his mind active by focusing on more mundane matters. However, the more mundane the task, the more he dwells on the review, questioning why such a meeting is necessary and how it might play out. As ever, his ponderings and reflections have become all encompassing.

Continuing his preparations, he stares at the handsome and extremely smart Officer staring back through the glass. His mind drifts to when he was a young boy playing cops and robbers, Mother as the criminal mastermind, him as the Chief of Police and all-round super-hero. He'll give chase through to the woods beyond the boundary for hours until, eventually, he captures her. Leading her by the wrist back to the Station, doubling up as the summerhouse at the bottom of the flower garden, he'll interrogate her before giving her a conditional discharge, after a stern talking to of course.

'Happy days' he sighs.

Final check.

Hair neat, tie tight, collar straightened.

Good.

Taking a step back to admire the whole ensemble, his six-foot frame doesn't quite fit into the full length mirror. He looks good though, feels good too. Look the part, feel the part, he tells himself. Pivoting his hips while moving his shoulders, he nods his approval and smiles. Smoothing his hair with the palm of his hand, he picks a couple of rogue hairs from his shoulder. Chuckling to himself, he shakes his head, he absolutely loathes his own vanity.

'Right then John, all set, let's go,' he says out loud.

As the rain subsides and clouds lighten, carved open by late afternoon winter sun, he decides to take the short and surprisingly enjoyable walk to Colindale Tube Station. On the way, he exchanges nods and smiles with a few young mothers carrying shopping home and a couple of older ladies who seem pleased to see a young man looking so smart. Turning the corner onto Colindale Avenue, at the entrance to the tube station, up ahead he sees a pair of pensioner war veterans, both in red velvet blazers with rows of medals and dark purple berets, collecting donations. Popping some loose change into their makeshift bucket, they salute him and a tangible sense of pride washes over him. Utterly humbling, he feels totally unworthy and has so much respect for what they went through, and sacrifices they must made.

Standing at the edge of the platform, the headlights of the tube-train appear through the darkness. The sound of clattering wheels grinding against the aging tracks grates through him while his nostrils fill with the musty smell of the super-heated brake blocks bringing the train to a halt. Doors sliding open, instinctively he scans the carriage, once a copper, always a copper, he thinks with a smile. Not much to worry about though, several old folk and some kids at the far end hanging off the handrails. He finds a seat opposite a young couple staring into each other's eyes, seemingly oblivious to the world around them. He watches as the young chap teases his girlfriend by walking his fingers up her leg toward her inner thigh until she playfully slaps his hand.

Ah, young love, he smiles.

Life is good.

Saturday, 17 January, 3:10pm
New Scotland Yard
Westminster, London

Exiting Saint James's tube station, he stops abruptly. Stretching high into the darkening grey sky behind the Victorian town houses he sees the beautiful, everlasting spires of Westminster Abbey. Taking a moment to embrace the architecture, he heads right toward the staff entrance of the Yard. An intimidating concrete nineteen sixties office block, maybe twenty or twenty-five floors tall, New Scotland Yard is located less than a quarter mile from the Houses of Parliament. He literally hates the juxtaposition between the Yards harsh, modern, almost brutalist exterior and its historic Westminster surroundings and wonders what on earth the local planning department were thinking when they approved the design.

After signing the visitors book and receiving his guest pass, approaching the lift he gently presses the "up" button and watches the dimly lit floor indicator move agonisingly slowly. Eventually entering the lift, catching himself in the mirror he smooths his hair for a final time. Lift ascending, he feels the knot in his stomach tighten floor by floor. Doors juttering open, following the sequential door numbering along the long corridor, he finds room eleven-zero-four.

Stomach-knot excruciatingly tight, he swallows hard.

Deep breath.

Knock, knock-knock, knock.

'Come,' a high-pitched female sings.

Door opening, he faces a good-looking blonde with bright red lipstick wearing a rather revealing red dress sitting behind a state-of-the-art electric typewriter. 'Cadet Cummings?' she asks, not looking up nor breaking her typing rhythm.

Clearing his drying-up-by-the-second throat, he struggles to speak. 'Erm, er-hum yes, I'm here to see…'

'Take a seat,' she cuts in. 'You'll be called when it's time.'

Time for what?

Sitting down, he takes in the monochrome surroundings. The walls are adorned with black and white photos of older looking officers and gentleman shaking hands with an array of dignitaries.

'Ah, Cummings, good,' a bellowing voice hums. "Come.'

Turning his head, he sees the tail end of who he presumes is Deputy Commissioner Jenkins disappearing through the doorway to the left of still-typing secretary. Breathing deeply, he tries to control his racing heart rate before standing and stepping through the doorway.

In stark contrast to the 1960s exterior and the bland outer office, this office resembles a turn of the century gentlemans club, with dark wood panel walls surrounding a large oak desk inlayed with heavily worn green leather, drying out and cracking with age. The room's dimly lit with several low-voltage wall lights and an ornate brass desk lamp with a green glass shade.

Facing Jenkins, he's somewhat taken aback with the sheer scale of the man. For some reason, he imagined him as a keen strategist, slightly built with perhaps thin rimmed reading glasses whereas, the reality couldn't be further from the truth. Well over six feet tall and easily eighteen stone with slicked-back silver-grey hair which, he muses, has probably been the same shape since he bought his first tub of Brylcreem decades before. His forehead is a criss-cross river-bed of lines and folds and his eyebrows are overgrown and in need of a good trim, as too are his ears and nostrils. He detests nasal hair, always has, maybe something to do with his grandpa and the unbelievable volume of hair protruding from not only his over-sized nose, but also his jug-like cauliflower ears too.

Sitting down, Jenkins leans back, clasping his hands behind his head. 'Thanks for popping in on a Saturday,' he says, staring deep. 'Please, take a seat.'

'Erm, thank you, Sir.'

The stomach knot is excruciatingly tight now.

Nodding slowly, Jenkins smiles. 'Any idea why you've been called here today?'

He finds himself surprised by Jenkins broad cockney accent, he presumed only those enjoying an Ox-Bridge education rose to the higher levels of the Met. 'Er-hum,' he struggles to clear his throat. 'Informal discussions with cadets, ascertaining how training is progressing?' he replies, knowing full well this isn't why he's here.

'Good answer, text-book,' Jenkins smiles, rubbing the end of his bulbous nose. 'I'd expect nothing less my boy.'

John smiles, surprisingly pleased with the praise.

'When you pass-out, any idea what you'd like to do?'

What sort of question is that?

He must think quickly.

'I have a choice, Sir?' John learnt the best way to deflect a tricky question is with a question.

'You have potential,' Jenkins nods, his eyes narrowing.

Only too aware of what everyone perceives as his potential, he's been told that his entire life, sometimes as an honest reflection of his life chances, other times, as a platitude to soften negative feedback. 'Thank you Sir, I'm, erm, happy my efforts have been noted,' he says as a cloak of suspicion wraps around his shoulders.

'Old Smithy keeps me informed, so, any idea?' Jenkins seems impatient.

'I haven't really thought about it, Sir, just focusing on the training if I'm honest,' he lies, he has of course thought deeply about many different and various scenarios.

Jenkins looks disinterested.

'However, if pushed Sir, I'd perhaps enjoy a role in an investigatory Division?'

'C.I.D, not really you, is it John?' left eye squinting, Jenkins top lip curls slightly as John struggles to hide his disappointment.

Placing both hands onto the desk, fingers spread far apart, Jenkins leans forward. 'Armstrong wants a new way. Old-school-hard-line policing isn't working, and we don't have the time nor resource to deal with broken windows or comforting little old ladies.'

'No, Sir,' he replies, now thoroughly intrigued. Jenkins is in the middle of performing a perfect sales pitch, especially referencing Commissioner Armstrong, head of the entire Metropolitan Police. However, he's is struggling to work out what exactly is being sold.

'Intelligence led policing,' Jenkins nods, looking deep into him. 'We must address the root causes of crime, not just the after-effects. I know you know what I'm talking about, what did you call it, "antecedent variables producing to non-compliant behaviour…" that's about right, yes?'

That isn't "about right", that is exactly right. Jenkins has just recited the title of the dissertation John completed in his final year at Cambridge, for which he's very proud to receive a first-class degree.

'I know you believe in this approach, John. I must say though, your university stuff is a tough read, interesting for sure, but hard going for the likes of me.'

'Erm, thank you, Sir.' Diligently authoring his twenty-five-thousand-word dissertation, he never considered for one moment it would have made its out of his tutors office, let alone be read by the higher echelons at the Yard.

'How about an Inspector position?' Jenkins interrupts.

'Inspector, Sir?' John couldn't quite make out what he said, it sounded suspiciously like he said "Inspector". A recently graduated Constable being promoted effectively three ranks is unheard of.

'Unconventional yes, I get it, but we need change, radical

change. Coppers like you can make a difference.'

Mind racing, ideas dart in all directions.

Is this real or, in fact, a huge wind-up, part of an elaborate initiation process? Did somehow Andrew and Donnie sort this out? Is Smithy in on it, are they all back at Hendon bent double laughing at Johns expense. Is the chap in front of him really Jenkins or one of Andrews old muckers putting on a show while the real Jenkins is improving his handicap on his local golf course. However, if this is indeed the real Jenkins, has he really read his dissertation?

Rising from his seat Jenkins winces, feeling his lower back before stretching his increasingly stiff lumber region. 'Right,' he offers John his right hand. 'See you in a couple of weeks.'

Turning, gently opening the door, he notes the blonde behind the typewriter still typing, and a young chap waiting in the same spot he had occupied a matter of minutes ago, presumably waiting to receive a similar briefing. A vaguely familiar looking guy in civilian clothes with round brown rimmed glasses and wispy fair hair, he smiles as he stands, looking around him toward Jenkins.

Along the corridor, into the lift, John breathes deeply as he looks at the ceiling while descending to the entrance lobby. Exiting, he turns back to face the Yard.

Has what just happened in there, really happened?

He needs to clear his head.

Turning left, crossing Parliament Square he passes the Houses of Parliament with Big Ben on the right. Memories of his childhood flood through his mind, the summertime walks with his Mother touring around London, taking in the sights and learning about the history of England.

He smiles.

Happy, simple times.

Saturday, 17 January, 4:34pm
River Thames
London

Sun setting, the biting January air stings his ears. Finding a bench mid-way along the Victoria Embankment in front of the Ministry of Defence Building opposite County Hall, he folds his arms around his torso and watches the Thames roll slowly by. Closing his eyes, he replays his time with Jenkins over and over. His mind drifts with romantic notions of a simple life, perhaps after a long and distinguished career he can retire somewhere warm, near the sea. He loves the sea.

After god knows how long, the coldness of the bench seeps through his overcoat, bringing him back to reality. No matter how hard he thinks, he can't quite make sense of it all. Was this an elaborate wind up and simply locker-room banter or, is Jenkins actually for real. If it is a wind up, this would surely be a world-record, Hollywood movie-esque wind up, wind up of the century. However, if Jenkins is for real, does he really believe in a new way or is he going through the motions in order to satisfy some young upstart with highfaluting ambitions? Perhaps this is a new Government policy, the new administration have been in power now for nearly eighteen months, maybe this is the next big thing? Maybe the Met is indeed in dire need of radical change, and the only viable way is to take brand new recruits and promote them into senior positions. Or, is Jenkins an old-school traditionalist who scoffs at this new-age hippy thinking, and the notion of over-promoting graduates is merely a way of ensuring failure and maintenance of the status-quo.

Quite the conundrum, and, rather annoyingly, he's enjoying the intellectual stimulus it brings. What intrigues him most, however, is the notion of why him, why has he been identified for such a posting? For sure, he's acutely aware of his academic prowess, his intellectual superiority and his physical capabilities. Equally, he's conscious of his natural leadership qualities and ability to see reason under pressure, but, surely, he is only one among many equals. So, why him?

With time to pass, he strolls the mile or so along the

Thames toward Embankment and Charing Cross Police Station. Several cordial nods and smiles with passers-by and tourists later, he enters the staff entrance at the rear of the building. After freshening up, he positions himself in the canteen and reads the Times newspaper cover to cover before attending the pre-shift roll call. Sitting toward the front of the briefing room, he and his colleagues are made aware of significant incidents occurring during the day. Opening his pocketbook, he jots down a few noteworthy details including a few new pubs opening, several more homeless reported at Centre-Point and a faulty burglar alarm at an adult bookstore in Soho. He sighs a comforting sigh, all in all, apart from the odd tourist mugging or punch-up between token Punk-rockers at Piccadilly Circus, the nightshift's usually pretty tame and relatively uneventful.

# Episode 5.
# "Wild West"

Saturday, 17 January, 8:40pm
Corner of Brixton Road and Atlantic Road
Brixton, London

Torrential rain shimmers through the dark sky, glistening like tiny shards of silver against the dark cloud-filled sky.

'Look at that fool,' Devon sighs, nodding toward the six-foot-six, seventeen-stone brick-shithouse standing under the "Welcome to Brixton" sign straddling the railway bridge across Brixton Road.

Gently pressing the brake pedal, Paul pulls in just passed the bridge before giving a couple of toots on the horn. Looking through the rear-view mirror he shakes his head. Even after all these years, the sight of Super screwing up his face while pulling his light-brown Crombie coat across his broad chest sends a shiver down his spine.

'Fookin' soaked,' Super spits, flinging the back-door open. 'Star, you did dat on purpose-yeah.'

'Did what?'

'Making me jog in the rasclat wet,' he grunts, struggling to drag his huge feet into the unfeasibly small back seats.

'Just get in nah-man and stop moaning,' Devon smiles.

Grinning, Paul flicks the stereo on. *"That's-where-I-get-my-reward"* blares out followed by a barrage of echoing horns and up-tempo, nonstop snares.

Super screws-up his face even further.

'What's wrong now rude-boy, don't you like Teardrop Explodes?' Paul teases.

'T'cha, roots and culture, strictly dub style-star, not dis top-of-the-pops bullshit,' Super spits, shaking his head.

Paul laughs as Devon passes Super, or Winston as only his Momma calls him, the remains of a tidy five-skin spliff.

'Just listen to some tunes and get mellow yeah,' Devon suggests with a smile.

Sucking deeply, Super holds it in for several seconds before releasing a plume of thick white smoke. 'You'd be whining too if you were wet through like me-star. Four quid to get this dry-cleaned-man, four fookin' quid.'

'Cleaned? Yeah right,' Paul teases, pressing the accelerator.

'Of course cleaned, duppy-boy-lemon, and dry-cleaned at dat, anyhow, how comes you late, quick bumming session around the corner before you come fetch me?'

'You wish,' Paul giggles. 'In your wet-dreams big boy.'

'Nah man, sus-stop by SPG,' Devon groans, gazing aimlessly through the window at nothing in particular.

'Fookin' Beasts,' Super spits. 'Hear me now-star, dey mess with me much longer, dey-gonna feel my fookin' steel-yeah.'

'You gonna cut a Beastman now?' Paul goads.

'Stripe them, den hack their bom-ba-clat heads clean off.'

'Behead them?' Devon joins in. 'Why not go the whole hog and plant a bomb in the Station, have done with it?'

'Take the piss if you want-star, but I'm telling you rude-boy, their fookin' time soon come,' Super smiles to himself, chewing on his train of thought while playing out the slow-motion, live-action sequences. Yeah man, him unfeasibly defying the laws of gravity laying some serious Bruce Lee moves on the Beastman while slicing his beloved machete through the air.

'Anyway, up West yeah?' Devon breaks the silence before beckoning for the spliff to be returned.

'West, again,' Super spits. He hates it up West.

'There's a new club opening tonight, near Charing Cross,

like that one in Covent Garden,' Paul adds.

'T'cha, "The Bunker", the batty-man place?' Super kisses his teeth. 'Nah-man-nah, we need roots-star, roots!'

'Calmness,' Devon hovers his hand mid-air.

'Just suck on your spliff and get mellow yeah,' Paul suggests, pressing the clutch and putting the car into gear.

'Tcha, eye-an-eye never be calm, not in this shit-tip of a motor, with lemon bwai-der.'

Silence surrounds them, before they all burst out laughing. Floodlights of the Oval cricket ground blaze through dark sky as the car turns into Stockwell Road, heading for the West End.

Ten minutes later…

They pass Big Ben and the Houses of Parliament, a minute after that, Trafalgar Square comes into view.

Saturday, 17 January, 9:10pm
Soho
London

'So, star, where de-poonani at?' Super looks left then right.

'Hold it down big boy, easy yeah, let's just get a drink, eh?' Paul says, leading the way along Greek Street onto Dean Street and the heart of Soho. Approaching a small bar, the mellow grooves of Earth Wind and Fire emanate from the half-open door. 'This place looks pretty cool.'

Through the thin doorway, Devon quickly scans the bar. Blacked out windows and dimly lit other than the ultraviolet lights dotted around. Yeah man, he nods his approval with a massive grin.

At the bar, Paul orders three dark rums while they chat about the week's trials and tribulations…

Devon, about how crap work is. He hates the dirt and the muck and the stigma of working in a scrapyard, but, at least he's earning some steady money and his boss, Nev, is okay, he supposes.

Paul, about the unbelievably attractive secretaries whom

he'd like to sleep with at his father's commodity trading firm based in the City. Over the past few years he's been serving a short and pointless apprenticeship as everyone knows he'll be on the board within five years, and, once daddy pops his clogs, eventually inherit everything.

And finally, Super, about doing absolutely nothing all week other than collecting his unemployment-cheque for which he blames the foolish Government and dickhead politicians in grey suits.

Several rums later, all three are nodding along to *"can you feel the force,"* by the Real Thing. In the meantime, the bar has filled up with a few wanna-be rude-boys, overly fashion-conscious plebs wearing too much make-up, plus a few fine-looking women. Knocking back his rum, Paul waves a ten-pound note at the barman. At around six feet tall with sandy-coloured short cropped hair and dimpled cheeks, his boyish face makes him look younger than his twenty-five years and, as a result, he's often asked for identification. No problem tonight though as the barman promptly pours three more delicious dark rums.

Super finds a small table at the other side of the empty dancefloor. As Paul walks back with three short tumblers, each a quarter filled with rich, dark rum, he spots a group of well turned out ladies sitting at the corner of the bar. One a blonde super-star-stunner, one pretty cute looking brunette and one a big girl with enormous breasts falling out of her one-size-too-small-boob-tube.

'Oi-oi, aw-right girls,' Paul smiles, throwing a cheeky wink.

The blonde, with what looks like a tall vodka and orange takes a sip through her straw then waves back, before turning to her friends as they all giggle.

'Blimey, she's well fit,' Paul sighs as he sits down.

'Ged-in-dere rude-boy,' Super leans forward. 'I'll have de other brown-haired girl and Devon, star, you've got the fatty-bom-batty,' he nods toward the larger girl dressed in a short black, sequined dress with ribbons in her hair.

'Slow down big-boy,' Paul laughs.

'What, nah-man-nah, you've no chance with her,' Devon adds, noting the brunette. 'Out of your league breddah.'

'T'cha, course I got a chance-star, what's not to like?' Super looks himself up and down before standing to perform a three-sixty twirl.

After another round of dark rum and a quick visit outside to share a spliff, they position themselves along the bar from the girls. Three more rums ordered, Paul turns to the blonde and leans in. 'So sweetheart, where're you from?' he says, struggling to be heard.

'Greenwich,' she smiles.

'Greenwich, nice.'

'It's alright, yeah.'

'So, what's your name?'

'Sammie.'

'Sammie, what a beautiful name.'

'Yeah?'

'Yeah.' Paul doesn't break her stare. 'Who you with?'

'Chantelle and Shirley,' she says, nodding.

'Nice, nice. Greenwich eh, south side yeah?'

'Geography your strong point then?' she smiles.

'Eh?'

'What about you, where you from?'

'Brixton.'

'Brixton, you'll all be drug dealers then?'

'Nah, business-men,' Paul laughs. 'Strictly business-yeah.'

'Oh yeah?' she smiles, prodding the ice with her straw.

'Yeah, that's right?' Paul moves closer.

'Well, I suppose that's okay then,' she smiles.

After ten minutes of chatting, flirting and another round of drinks, Paul suggests the girls accompany them to the new club in Charing Cross, "Paradise," where he'll arrange for them to be on the guest list.

Saturday, 17 January, 10:50pm
Charing Cross Rail Station
London

Walking through the back streets of Soho, the stark coldness of the bright lights coming from the train station serve as a harsh reminder of their reality. Attracting suspicious looks from a group of British Transport Police and Ticket Inspectors congregating in the concourse, they instinctively up their pace.

'Look pon dem fools der,' Super growls through gritting teeth. 'We done fook all yet dey still eye-balling us. Eye-an-eye should take the steel to dem pussyclats.'

'Bit aggressive,' Sammie whispers to Paul.

'Ignore him, he's always like that,' Paul says, tightening his hold around her waist.

Making their way through the back of the station, the group exit on the left down some steps onto Villiers Street. In the distance, they see the entrance to Embankment Tube Station with a fruit and veg stall packed up ready for the morning. With a muffled sound and vibrations from bass-boxes rumbling below their feet, Paul rubs his hands together in expectation of a good night. Turning right, they head underneath the Station into a small, dark arcade with stairs leading upward at the other end. Midway along, a small group of well-dressed lads and cute girls stand in line in front of an arched heavy wooden door. A bit like a fashion parade, they're dressed in unisex combinations of frilly shirts and sharp suits, big hair and dark eye makeup. Almost a punk-rocker vibe but somehow softer, more stylish and much more avantgarde.

'Dis better not be no batty-man dance,' Super grunts, using his deepest voice.

'Scared you'll be felt-up big man?' Devon teases, pinching his backside. Paul follows in with a gentle stroke of his leg.

'What-the… fook-arf batty man!'

'Come nah-Super, your donkey-dick will be a prize asset to these guys,' Paul teases.

'Nah-man-nah, mans snake is purely for the ladies yeah, no man-on-man business around here-star, no way,' Super announces, pulling the collar of his Crombie up.

Making his way to the front of the queue, Paul exchanges a few quick words with the two body-builder-no-neck-bald-headed bouncers on the door. Both wearing standard issue long black overcoats, black scarves and black leather gloves, they study their clipboards. After some deliberation, they push the door open and Paul waves for the rest of the group to follow. Down a flight of stairs and past a weird looking cloakroom attendant who, nonchalantly, nods them through where they are engulfed by heavy synthesizers phasing across a four-four disco beat with breathy *"we fade away"* vocals reverbing on top. Strobe lights provide intermittent freeze frames of the gyrating inhabitants occupying the dancefloor, silhouetting against the ornately plush surroundings. Ultraviolet lamps adorn the back and side walls as well as behind a small bar to the right. The centre of the room has an obligatory dancefloor with multi-coloured floor tiles pulsing in time with the four-to-the-floor drum rhythm.

'Hate dis fookin' shit already-star,' Super grunts, making his way to the bar, disgust and disappointment straining through his voice.

Devon shakes his head, he loves Super like a brother, but his constant negative vibes are frustrating. Smiling, he watches Paul move into the dancefloor along with the three girls, pirouetting with his arms stretching out stroking each of their cheeks with the back of his hand.

Meanwhile…

Super argues with the young guy behind the bar that Bacardi, although technically rum, isn't actually real rum, and a place like this should get some proper dark rum. After five minutes of heated debate, he orders three straight Bacardi's with ice, and three Pina-Coladas for the girls, whatever the fuck they are. Nodding his head in time with the beating thud of the futuristic disco sounds, he tries getting into the groove, but the breathy, *"ahh-haaa, we fade to grey"* vocals and synthesisers are a far cry from his beloved dub reggae.

'Easy-nah Super,' Devon says, joining him at the bar. 'The

disco ting bubbling yeah.'

'Suppose so… jus-look at him over there though,' Super motions to the dancefloor and Paul. 'Look at the state of him, it's embarrassing you know.'

Appearing to glide across the dancefloor, Paul effortlessly rotates from woman to woman, occasionally man to man, throwing in the odd avantgarde twirl as he does.

'He's got to be a batty,' Super shakes his head in disgust, before downing his Bacardi.

Several drinks later, Paul returns with all three girls in tow, his arm wrapping around Sammies waist, the other around Chantelles shoulder. Sammie, tall, blonde and slim with shapely breasts, accentuated by her dayglow-pink strappy top is indeed a stunner. Her cheeks, covered with stencilled blusher to create the impression of angled cheekbones, along with way too much dark eye makeup finishes the look. She looks even better than she did earlier, whereas the other two girls look worse for wear.

'Watcha-ladies,' Devon smiles, quickly followed up with an 'easy babes' from a grinning Super, his teeth glowing yellow under the black-light lamps behind the bar.

More drinks later, Paul and Sammie disappear into the darkness of the dancefloor while Super props Chantelle up at the bar, which takes some doing as she phases in and out of drunken consciousness. Not unattractive, she's a big girl with frizzy afro hair and red, yellow and white ribbons weaving through. Super can't take his eyes off her large breasts heaving in and out of her sparkly blue boob-tube, practically dribbling at the thought of unleashing them and flicking her erect nipples with his tongue.

Meanwhile…

Devon leads Shirley by the hand onto the dancefloor. Grooving in front of each other hand in hand, eyes locked, they share a series of short kisses. Shorter than Devon, she's pretty with round cheeks, a small button nose and cute dimples either side of her pouting mouth. Staring into her as they dance, her blue eyes sparkle in sync with the glitter ball above their heads. 'Fancy coming outside,' he says, leaning in, making sure he pushes his torso against her breasts.

'Why?' she smiles, playfully.

'Why?'

'Yeah, why?'

'Err, I think you know why.'

'Nah, I'm okay here thanks,' she smiles, spinning around.

'Alright then,' he shrugs, not wanting to appear too keen, secretly enjoying her playing hard to get.

She spins around again, her back facing his front.

The throbbing mass on the dancefloor simultaneously erupt as the deejay spins a punk sounding tune with a catchy hook, something like, *"un-plug the juke-box and do us all a favour…"* Shirley stretches her arms around her back, reaching for, and eventually grabbing Devon close.

Reciprocating, Devon moves his hands from Shirleys flat, tight stomach toward her plentiful breasts. She responds by driving further into his pelvis. Head spinning with the rum and the weed and the super-cute girl, the music takes hold. He's loving the vibe and loving the moment.

Meanwhile…

Super is bored, beyond bored, in fact, he's seriously upset. Both his mates look odds-on for some sexing, while he's lumbered with a big-breasted drunken, and now, fully comatose bitch. Shifting Chantelles considerable weight from his shoulder to the wall behind he stands, stretches and loosens his shoulder before yelling toward the young guy behind the bar, asking where the toilets are. The bartender stares at him for what seems an age before tilting his head to the right and nonchalantly pointing in the direction of the far corner.

Sunday 18 January, 12:09am
Toilet, Paradise Club
Charing Cross, London

Decked out just like the club, black walls with plush red

velvet panels and white marble fittings, these toilets are something else. Standing in the doorway he scans around. 'Star… dis gaff is better dan my fookin-flat,' he whispers. Approaching the urinal, widening his stance, he unzips and lets out a long and drawn out 'ahh' as he tilts his head back, staring into the ceiling.

Shit.

Peripheral vision, he spots something.

What the..?

'I can make that feel sooooo-muuuuuch better my-darling.'

Swinging around, he's confronted by a man with a girls face, or a girl with a mans body. Whatever it is, it stares at him with eyes wide and an even wider smile. Lightening quick, he grabs him or her around the throat. 'Fookin-dutty-rasclat,' he seethes.

The girl/boy freezes, fear filling his or her eyes.

The electronic assault from the dancefloor outside fades into silence as his internal sound system clicks on with the soothing sounds of Gregory Isaacs. That's more like it he thinks, yeah man, roots and culture. The haunting guitar riffs of "Wailing Rudie" echo around his head. Yesh-my-star, now we feeling it Super-star, now we feeling it. Gripping his or her throat harder, he continues to urinate, covering the girl/boy before slowly pushing himself back into his trousers, all while maintaining eye contact. Then smash, a savage head-butt cracks into the bridge of his or her nose. Screaming, he/she struggles to break free as blood pumps out. 'Now you gonna learn some fookin-manners yeah,' he screams before unleashing a barrage of lightning punches.

'No, no, please, no, I'm sorry, I'm sorry,' he or she pleads, collapsing to the floor then rolling into the foetal position.

Grabbing his or hers long, back-combed hair, Super aims a knee per word into his or her face, 'dutty… blood… clat… arse… rider.' Feeling the vibe, the night is turning out to be alright after all, he thinks to himself. Completing the onslaught, he looks at the lifeless body curled up on the floor, floating in a shallow pool of urine and blood. The adrenalin rushes through every blood vessel in his body, and he feels alive. The raw essence of life itself flows through him and, with that, his hand wanders to his breast pocket and his steel. Reaching in, he touches the handle and feels it vibrate. Yeah man, that'll teach it good and proper. The steel begins humming, singing almost, serenading him in angelic tones, "Suuuuuper." Stroking its handle, he knows he can fuck this pussyclat up big time, if he wants to. He has the power, the will and the strength, he is the magnificent and amazing Super-man from Brixton, an unstoppable mother fucker of hate. But, all things being equal, tonight's not the night for cutting, nah-man, tonight is for weed and rum, for friends and living life large. Yeah man, tonight is for fucking and hopefully sucking, ideally both.

Instinctively he looks around for witnesses and catches his reflection in the mirror. 'Eye-an-eye a bad-man,' he says out loud with a smile. 'A bom-ba-clat rude-boy if ever der is one.' Straightening his coat, he looks at his knuckles before back into his reflection, and then toward his victim. Tilting his head, he looks for a different angle to observe his prey. 'The wetting can wait man, don't need no tribulation tonight,' he sighs, almost apologising. 'You've had a fookin' touch,' he whispers before snorting a huge ball of saliva and spitting onto its head.

Opening the door to re-enter the club, he's immediately surrounded by a minimalist mini-moog synthesizer and a posh guy signing about cars. Returning to the bar, Paul's sitting next to Sammie, his usually neat hair dishevelled as he bobs along to the vocoder sounds etching the vocals, *"in the year twenty-five, twenty-five"*. Turning to Sammie, she smiles coyly with faded lipstick smudging across her face.

'How's it going big-boy?' Paul slurs, swinging his arm around Supers shoulders.

'T'cha, dis gal-inna-coma,' he scowls, frowning at Chantelle. 'But, least dis place got nice toilets,' he chuckles.

'Ohhkay… where's Dev?' Paul shakes his head.

'Look-der,' Super nods toward the dancefloor, strobing

between pure darkness and multiple flashes of super-white brightness. Squinting, they can make out the unmistakable silhouette of Devon in a clinch with Shirley.

'Awww,' Sammie smiles.

'Sammie reckons there's an after-hours party at some place down Deptford way, fancy it?' Paul suggests.

'T'cha!' Super flings his arms in the air, 'Deptford's shit!' Stopping himself, he looks around the bar and then the dancefloor. 'But still, Deptford's better than dis dutty-piece of shit place.'

Twenty minutes later…

Leading the way, Devon realises his flimsy Gabicci top is no match for the harsh winter weather as the cold night air bites hard into his chest. Holding Shirley tight, she reciprocates, placing her arm around his waist and pulling him closer.

'Eye-eye,' Paul says, spotting a single Police car parked at the end of the arcade on Villiers Street. Two Officers get out, the first a young tall guy with fair hair, the second older, shorter with a large bulbous, pock-marked nose.

'Evening all,' the older Officer says as they approach.

'Lovely night for it, eh?' Paul chirps.

Both Officers smile without breaking their stride.

'What da fuck, no sus-stop?' Super whispers, amazed.

'This aint the Frontline man,' Devon says, not looking back. 'Just keep walking yeah.'

# Episode 6.
# "I See Three"

Saturday, 17 January, 9:10pm
Charing Cross Police Station
Agar Street, London

'Not much on tonight then, easy shift eh?'

'Erm, I guess so Derek, no.'

'It's Rich, Rich Tea… okay?'

'But, Derek is in fact your name,' John smiles, stating the obvious. Although he detests using childish nicknames, he does however enjoy playfully teasing Derek or "Rich Tea" as he likes to be known.

'Look, everyone calls me Rich, Rich Tea.'

John observed most Officers seem to prefer nicknames, probably, he concludes, a mechanism to separate work from home, the professional versus the personal, thereby making the transition back to civilian life post-shift easier, or, a subconscious anchor back to simpler times when they were children. 'Let's just get on with it, shall we?' he sighs, straightening his tie and giving himself the once over before heading to the stairs.

Even though work experience is at times tedious and a necessary evil, he's thankful for his assignment to the West End Division, and not a godforsaken Station in one of the poverty-stricken boroughs in the East End or the crime ridden no-go areas of South London where Andrew is assigned. Andrew will often recount life in Lambeth, his shifts filled with street robberies, drug dealing and prostitution, all of which make him feel very grateful for his relatively easy assignment.

'You okay driving?' Rich Tea yells, his voice echoing around the half empty underground car park while launching the keys to Victor Five. Catching the keys, John unlocks the door and climbs in. Adjusting the seat and mirrors, as per procedure, he checks the mileage. Victor Five is a battered once-white-now-grey 1973 Rover 3500, with a thick red and yellow stripe along the side and a large dark blue spinning lamp on the roof. Once a good-looking car with a long-curved bonnet and sleek headlights, nowadays, with more than a hundred thousand miles on the clock, it looks more than its age.

Each night shift typically involves driving around Londons landmarks picking up late night brawlers, ladies of the night and low-life bag snatchers. The monotony is interrupted, when on shift with Rich Tea in any case, with as many rest breaks as possible. Dereks penchant for dunking ultra-dry biscuits into strong sweat tea earned him his nickname many years ago.

'You know what John?'

'No, I don't know what,' John replies, opening his pocket book and recording the mileage.

'We ought to sort you out with a nickname, you know.'

'I already have one Derek, it's John.'

'Oh, come on, you know what I mean.'

'Erm, no thanks, I'm fine with John.'

'No, no really, we should.'

'Oh god.'

'Yeah, a nickname will sort you right out, a sort of rights of passage I reckon,' Rich Tea ponders, looking sideways at John through narrowing eyes. 'Hmm, what should it be?' he continues, theatrically stroking on one of his many chins.

'Ohkay, what do you suppose then?' John decides to indulge him, might help pass the time and be a useful insight into what Derek really thinks of him.

'Let's see then, obviously a posho… public school?'

'Yes Derek, you know that already.'

'Good-looking lad too…'

Waiting eagerly, John is surprised how interested he is.

Derek grins and nods, seemingly very pleased-with-himself. 'Oh, I've got it.'

'Right, okay, let's have it then.'

'Posh-Plonker?'

Surprise quickly turning to resigned disappointment, he knows he always expects too much. 'Yes Derek, very original, bound to catch on that one!' Shaking his head, he twists the ignition key and the engine splutters into life with plumes of thick blue-grey smoke choking out of the twin exhausts.

Victor Five pulls slowly up the ramp, and, upon exiting turns left, heading along the Strand toward Trafalgar Square. No matter how many times he sees the magnificence of Nelsons Column, he never fails to feel a wave of pride and awe of the achievement. The landmarks remind him of when he was a young boy and the many fieldtrips Mother organised…

When Father departed, his mother gave up teaching to home educate her only child. In their rural Berkshire community, this was most unusual as the majority of parents elected to send their children to boarding school or employ full time nannies. Even though she was seen as a bit of an oddity and, in certain circles, ostracised, she was adamant her son would have a grounded upbringing. Rather than traditional lessons, she would arrange day trips to London, the west country or the south coast, calling them "active learning experiences." Aged nine, John found these extremely exciting, train journeys, picnic lunches and falling asleep in Mothers lap the way back home. They'd visit landmarks such as Saint Pauls Cathedral in the city of London, Stonehenge in Wiltshire or the Roman baths in Bath, as well as to West End theatres to see shows and operas. He mostly enjoyed the long walks through the City of London out toward the East End and Petticoat Lane where they would eat Bangladeshi food and chat with stall mongers at the many markets on the way…

Wonderful times, he thinks. Shaking his head, the echoes of yesterday quickly dissipate.

'Look at the state of that,' Rich Tea tuts, pointing to the far side of the Square. In between the fountains, they spot a group of teenagers falling about, arguing with one another. John knows exactly what's happening, youngsters from the suburbs doing the weekly drunken night-time sightseeing tour of the West End. A common sight most weekends.

'We ought to stop,' John suggests.

'Nah, let them knock each other out.'

'Sorry?' John raises his eyebrows.

'Oh John, you've got to lighten up, take a joke.'

'Youngsters trying to kill each other is hardly a laughing matter, Derek.' John never jokes about work.

'Come on then,' Rich Tea sighs. 'Let's sort them out.'

Ten minutes later…

After rousing what appears to be the victim and dealing with various uncontrolled alcohol induced emotional outbursts, the group are eventually moved on.

Back in Victor Five, they proceed north along Piccadilly toward the statute of Eros and the massive lights of the advertisement sign high above Piccadilly Circus.

'Fancy a thrill John, Soho?' Rich Tea suggests, shuffling in his seat while winding his window down.

Seedy and dirty and sordid, along with Rich Tea, John enjoys cruising around Soho, indeed, he finds it highly exhilarating. Indicating left, they turn into Dean Street and Victor Five slows down to a crawl. John continues to scan the environment, as per his training, seeking out wrongdoing while Derek peruses the many and varied sex shops and scantily clad girls in doorways looking for business. He'll usually receive a cheery wave or, if he's lucky, a kiss blown in his direction.

'Stop John, Stop.'

Instinctively, and rather dramatically, John slams the breaks, even though they are travelling at less than ten miles per hour. Derek points to the other side of the crossroads toward Soho Square and two punk-rockers. They both sport skin-tight bleached-mottled jeans rolled halfway-up along with twenty-two-hole Doc Martin boots, elaborate eight to ten-inch Mohican haircuts with anarchistic "A" logos painted on the backs of their black leather jackets. Oblivious to the Police car suddenly stopping, they're in the midst of roughing up what looks to be a middle-aged man who's pinned against the railings as they pound into him. John knows Punks are more often than not intoxicated on amphetamines or industrial solvent fumes and therefore usually up for a fight. He must act fast. Jumping out, he grabs his truncheon from behind his seat. 'You two, stop,' he yells.

Spinning around, fists frozen in mid-air, the Punks take a second or two to comprehend what's happening. The one on the left, slightly shorter of the two, turns and sprints off. John points after him, indicating for Derek to give chase. The other turns back to his victim, lands a couple more blows before bolting in the other direction.

John starts running.

Through the narrow alleyways he avoids the voyeuristic tourists, teenagers looking for thrills and middle-aged men stocking up on blue movies. Making up ground, the brightly lit shop fronts blur into a non-descript multi-coloured wallpaper. Kicking out, he catches the trailing heel of the Punk who tumbles forward. Hovering in mid-air for what seems like an age, he eventually slams into the pavement and skids along the floor. Cracking his head against the window of a "private" shop with blacked out windows and rainbow-coloured streamers over the doorway, he comes to an abrupt halt. Staring at John through dazed and confused eyes, blood seeps from a gash in the middle of his forehead. Then, he kicks out while trying to scramble to his feet.

'Police!' John shouts, turning sideways, raising his truncheon high above his head. 'I'm warning you.'

The Punk, now on his feet, launches himself forward. John strikes diagonally down, connecting with the outside of the Punks left thigh. Another blow diagonally up to the back of the right leg and the Punk is back on the floor, curling into the foetal position. Landing a knee into his stomach, John grabs a wrist while reaching for his handcuffs.

Marching the Punk back to Victor Five, the local shop owners cheer and clap him on his way and, as they do, his heart swells with pride. This is what Policing is all about, doing good in the community, earning respect, Policing with consent and advocacy. Arriving back at the crime scene, John spots Rich Tea leaning against Victor Five sipping tea from a polystyrene cup. 'Bravo John, excellent work,' he smiles, raising his cup, toasting Johns fine work.

'So, where is he then?' John looks around.

'Who?'

'The other assailant, Derek!'

'Bad news I'm afraid, he got away,' Derek shrugs. 'Fast runners the Punks.'

'And, the victim?'

'Yeah, more bad news, when I got back, he'd gone too.'

The handcuffed Punk chuckles to himself.

'Honestly Derek,' John shakes his head.

Thirty-five minutes later…

Having locked up the seventeen-year-old, who, it turns out hails from the scenic commuter village of Epsom, rather than an East End ghetto estate, they exit the custody suite. With no previous convictions, the youngster will be let out in the morning with a conditional discharge. After yet another quick tea-break, they head back to Victor Five. Pulling out of the car park the antiquated radio crackles into life with double beeps. 'Victor Five, receiving,' Derek replies. Diligently, he notes the particulars of the incident and are quickly on their way. 'Night club underneath Charing Cross Station apparently, do you know it?'

'Can't say that I do, not really my scene,' John lies, he has of course heard of this nightclub and it's loose association with the ever-popular Bunker Club in Covent Garden. He's been there a few times since commencing his training at Hendon and, on his last visit just a few weeks ago, was given a hand-written invitation to the opening night, which is tonight. Usually playing new-wave and disco, about a year ago, The Bunker started playing a new type of interesting electronic music, accompanied by a whole new fashion look. Back-combed hair, heavy makeup, frilly collars and cuffs are the norm, as too Elizabethan pirate and Japanese concubine outfits, anything goes at the Shelter, as long as it's avant-garde and fabulous.

Sunday 18 January, 12:24am
Paradise Club
Charing Cross, London

Gliding shark-like along the Strand, John manoeuvres Victor Five left into Villiers Street, bringing the vehicle to halt opposite the entrance to a small arcade running underneath the train Station.

Cocking his ear, Derek can hear the muffled sound of what the kids nowadays call music coming from within. 'Right John, this is more you than me, you take the lead with this one,' he suggests.

'My scene, erm, I don't think so Derek.'

'Shouldn't be too much of a problem, probably a couple of dandies having handbags over a lipstick.'

'Derek, please,' John tuts. Climbing out then turning toward the arcade, he spots a group of six early to mid-twenty something's approaching. Coppers-instinct in over-drive, he scans them…

Three females, all scantily clad, all very intoxicated. No immediate threat.

More interestingly, the three men.

The first, Identity Code Three, very tall sporting a neat

Crombie-coat, muscular, angry, refuses to make eye contact. Potential suspect.

The second, another IC3, smaller than the first at approximately six feet, slender and toned, wearing only a T-Shirt and smiling a lot, most likely feeling the effects of drink and or drugs. Potential suspect.

The third, IC1, young, piercing blue eyes and a good suit, over-confident, arrogant, maybe hiding something. Potential suspect.

He'll be sure to make copious notes as soon as possible for evidential sake, just in case. For now, he'll proceed with caution and flank the group to the left while Derek passes to the right. As they pass, the IC1 male says something to Derek, but he can't quite make out what.

Derek shakes his head, 'nah, leave them,' he mouths.

Feeling the floor beneath pulsate, John hears the dull rumble from inside. Noting the Officers approaching, the two bouncers pull the doors open and as the dull rumble gains definition, the hairs on the back of his neck stand on end. Although he hasn't been to one of these clubs in uniform before, he suspects those inside will love the high drama of real-life Police in full regalia, shiny buttons, bells and whistles and all that cliché nonsense. Ultraviolet lights illuminate the stairs leading down to what looks to be the cloak room. A huge man dressed as a girl with full make-up and ribbon woven dreadlocks sits through an unglazed window. 'Hello, my dears,' the attendant says, grinning through a bored expression. John is transfixed by his deep cockney accent and the juxtaposition between this and his attempt at creating a deeply feminine look. 'Head straight through, constable handsome,' he smiles, pointing down a corridor to his right while looking totally disinterested the other way.

Sunday 18 January, 12:21am
Back Office
Paradise Club, London

Heading down the long dark corridor toward the door at the end, slightly ajar with light from the other side chiselling into the darkness, John takes a deep breath, knocks and enters. Elaborate Japanese fans hang from the red painted walls with a dark-brown leather sofa running along the left-hand side. Two young guys, perhaps twins, sit either end with, based on the state of him, the victim in the middle. With his frilly white shirt covered with dark red blood and his head tilting back, he sits motionless pinching the bridge of his nose. A large dark wooden table dominates the centre of the room with two chairs in front. Behind sits a sweaty slightly overweight chap leaning forward, his hands clasping together, chin resting on his nicotine-stained fingertips. After a dramatic pause, he slams his hands down onto the desk. 'Ah-bout time,' he yells incredulously with a heavy dose of sarcasm tearing through his broad Welsh accent.

'Sir, we made our way here as quickly as possible.'

'I bet you fewcking have, it's ow-har fewcking op-ning night-see, and we don't need this, not tonight,' he whispers, pointing at the wiry broken-nosed victim.

'Erm, okay, I understand.' Johns training suggests avoiding getting into an emotional discussion, instead, he'll focus on facts and evidence. 'May I take some details please?' he smiles, flipping his pocket-book open.

The chap behind the desk, the club manager John presumes, motions toward the chairs in front of the desk.

'Go ah-head Shew-lock-Holmes, take a seat.'

John looks toward Derek, who appears pre-occupied with the two guys sitting on the sofa either side of the victim. Cropped fair hair, white vests and blue jeans they have the physique of body builders or Olympic standard athletes.

The Manager nods. 'Take some de-tails, right,' he whispers, looking down at his desk. 'Right there are all the details you fewcking need,' he yells, slamming his hands down while standing up. 'Look at him, he's had sev-ven bells of shit kicked out of him… and his nose bro-ken too!'

John detests swearing, nearly as much as over-dramatic emotional outbursts, and, right now, both are flooding out of this guy like the sweat from his forehead. It dawns on him the potential suspects he saw on his way in may have something to do with it. 'Sir, this isn't helping,' he raises his voice slightly while dropping down a tone. The ability to use voice control was part of the initial phases of training at Hendon.

Sitting back down the Manager fumbles a cigarette into his mouth, sparks his Zippo lighter and sucks in sharply. 'It's oh-kay though, it's fine, see… we know who they are.' Wiping beads of sweat from his forehead, he strokes his mid length, blonde-highlighted hair back across his head. 'That's bloody right Sher-lock,' he continues. 'Friends of a guest they-are, friends, for fewks-sake.'

'Great,' Derek interjects, peeling back the first few pages of his pocketbook before licking the nib of his ball-point pen, suspecting an early tea-break might be on the cards.

'Paul Richardson,' the Manager says, slowly. 'That's the bast-ards name… you got that Shew-lock?'

Derek scribbles the name and notes some additional details including names and dates of birth of both the Manager and the victim, addresses too and details of the vested pair of body builders, ex-army apparently, personal bodyguards for Steve, the sweaty Welsh Manager.

John turns to the victim. 'Hello Sir, can you tell me what happened,' his tone is caring and genuine.

'You habbing a laugh?' the victim gurgles.

The two body-builder twins stifle their giggles.

'Erm, sorry?' John struggles to understand.

'Loob at me, just loob at me,' the victim says, tears welling. 'My nose hab been broben, habbn't it, all bendt anb bloody and broben!!!'

'Stop snivelling and get on with it, we haven't got alnight-see,' Steve the Manager yells in disgust.

John looks sternly at him before reaching to the victim. 'It's okay,' he says, tapping him gently on the knee. 'It'll be fine, now, what actually happened?'

Theatrically, still holding his nose, the Victim explains…

'Well, I went in-bo the loo to, you know, hab a wee and I'm mind-bing my own bub-ness when I ged heab butted and beaben up, then kick'b on the floor. He cobbered me in wee too, dirty dinking wee from a bib barstab.'

'He urinated on you?' John queries.

'Big you say,' Derek adds, looking deep into his pocketbook so not to laugh.

'Yeb, pee'd all over me,' the victim breaks down into tears.

The body-builder twins both turn away, covering their chuckling mouths.

'And yesh, he wab massive, a beast ob a man.'

John nods, definitely the IC3 he saw earlier.

Stepping around the table toward the victim, Steve the Manager manically sucks on his cigarette, blowing smoke into his face. 'Cut the dram-ah my dear, and tell Shew-lock here what actually happened,' he whispers close to his ears.

'Okay,' John points at the Steve the Manager. 'Sit down and be quiet, and you,' he looks toward the victim. 'Less of the drama, and start at the beginning.'

Deciphering the victims statement, John nods while continuing to make notes. 'Description?' he asks, without looking up.

'Oh bib… huge.'

'Can you be a little more precise?'

'Tall, bery tall, taller than you… but nob as handsome.'

John feels his cheeks blush. 'How much taller?'

'Oh, maybe seben foot?'

'Seven foot?' Derek mocks.

'Sir, seven foot is extremely tall,' John probes.

A trickle of blood appears just under the victims nose.

'Yeb, seben foot with a long brown coab,' he whines, pinching his nose and tilting his head back again.

John has heard enough, he concludes it was definitely the angry looking IC3 he saw earlier. Thanking the victim, he promised to be back in touch.

‘I say, Sher-lock,” the Manager yells as John reaches for the door.

John looks back over his shoulder and sees Steve the Manager standing in between the body-builder twins.

‘If you don’t get them… we will.’

# Episode 7.
# “Blues & Twos”

Sunday 18 January, 12:50am
Tower Bridge
London

‘Fuck me.’

‘Bit forward aint-cha,’ she giggles.

‘What, nah, fuck me she’s fast, I mean,’ Paul splutters as he struggles to keep up with Shirleys white VW Golf.

‘Staaarrrr,’ Super shakes his head. ‘Man can’t even keep up with a girl, shame man, shame.’

‘Just concentrate on keeping your bird awake, mate,’ Paul winks through the rear-view mirror, pressing the accelerator harder while Sammie gently caresses his leg, staring at his ever-growing excitement.

‘Where you from again?’ she smiles.

‘Brixton, why?’ Even her voice is sexy, he thinks.

‘Brixton, really Paul, you-ah from Brixton are-yah?’ Super interjects, hoping to expose his mates web of lies, resulting in him receiving zero sex.

‘Alright then, he’s from Brixton, I’m from just down the road from there,’ Paul admits.

‘Down the road, nah-man-nah, try Dulwich darling, in daddies mansion.’

‘A mansion, really?’ Sammie quizzes, her soft caresses turning into frenetic rubbing. ‘And, what is it you do again?’

‘Work in the City, just an office job.’
‘Stockbroker, yesh-Paul?’
‘Nah, man-nah. Corporate finance, boring really.’
‘And what about you,’ Sammie says over her shoulder.
‘Me, me-ah work pon da frontline-star.’
‘The frontline,’ Sammie giggles. ‘Like in the Army?’
‘Yeah man, kind of, I suppose,’ Super continues, ‘Grafting all hours, choring for a living, scraping a crust yeah, not sitting on my lardy arse all day playing with a calculator or whatever the fook it is you do-star.’
Paul shakes his head.
‘So anyway, a mansion eh?’ Sammie smiles, eagerly running her hand over Pauls balls through his tightening trousers.
‘T’cha,’ Supers tuts.
His poor attempt at sabotaging Pauls potential sexing has backfired and now he feels even more sorry for himself. He’s trapped in a shitty car with a drunken fatty fast asleep beside him, with no prospect of any sex, not even a blowjob. All this is made miles worse because Paul’s in the front with a super-star-stunner rubbing his cock, while Devons tucked up cosy in the VW in front with the pretty one. Nudging Chantelles head from his shoulder, his face screws up. Tonight can’t get any worse.
‘What-am Super?’ Paul says, in a mock accent through the rear-view mirror. ‘What’s the matter big-boy?’
‘T’cha, just keep driving duppy-bwai.’
‘Come on mate, why you screwing?’
‘Look-star, fookin’ leave it yeah.’
‘Didn’t you like the club?’ Sammie asks.
‘The club’s shit, ram full of batty-man.’ He can hear the voice inside his head again whispering to him, “the fookin’ bitch don’t even know you, yet she’s chatting like that.”
‘Batty?’ she queries.
‘You know, sausage jockey, arse bandit,’ Paul giggles.
‘Ah, okay, that’s what you call the queers then?’
‘Listen, eye-an-eye can’t be done with none of that shit,’ Supers growls, his voice deeper, louder and more deliberate.

'Adam and Eve-star, not Adam and Steve.'

'Alright, just asking,' Sammie tuts.

Super smiles. 'Dat's why de queen in dere get mash up, yesh-star, he or she aint gunna fook around with no-one no more,' his words tail off into a chuckle.

Paul shudders as a wave of panic rush through him. He's on the guest list, they know his name. His eyes dart into the rear-view mirror. 'You did someone, at the club?'

'Yesh-star, I sure did,' Super smiles, his wide grin has a sinister edge to it. 'Gave it a beating-yesh.'

Paul breathes a sigh of relief. All he needs is the Police on his case for a stabbing or attempted murder or something.

Stopping her rubbing, Sammie suddenly feels weird and awkward as the realisation sweeps through her that she's in a car with two men she doesn't know. Even if one is cute, the other is clearly a queer-bashing psychopath.

Crossing the Thames, they enter South London and she's relieved to see the road signs for Deptford, and not Brixton where she'll be gang raped, tortured and then killed.

Meanwhile…

As they reach the apex of the Bricklayers Arms fly-over, Devon sees the mile or so of pubs, clubs and fast-food takeaways that is the Old Kent Road. All tastes are catered for down there, gangster gin palaces, under-age drinking bars, staunch Millwall supporting pubs and skinhead fighting dens masquerading as pubs. Yep, anything and everything is available on the Old Kent Road.

'What you doing, don't stop,' he urges as Shirley slows down approaching a set of traffic lights changing from amber to red. He knows not to linger around these parts. Foot down, through the lights, they progress east and Devons head starts to spin. The rum, the goodness of the weed, the gorgeous girl and the cold fresh air from the wound down window is taking its toll. Enjoying the drive, he leans back against the headrest and sucks gently on his joint. Looking at Shirley, he smiles a content and happy smile. For once, life is good.

Sunday 18 January, 1:02am
New Cross Gate Tube Station
London

Easing off the accelerator, Shirley tentatively presses the break as she spots an array of blue flashing lights ahead.

'Just be cool yeah,' Devon says reassuringly.

Having never been stopped by the Police, she finds herself gripping the steering wheel tighter than ever before. Drink driving with a big guy smoking drugs in the passenger seat is sure to lead to her being arrested and packed off to prison. Slowing down, she sees a fire engine and two Police cars blocking the road.

'What the fuck?' Devon sighs, he don't need no sus-stop by the Beasts, especially when he's on for what he hopes is a serious session of hardcore sex. Thinking quickly, he opens the glovebox. Shit, empty. 'Fuck,' he shouts, realising the bag of weed is in Pauls car, under the passenger seat. Leaning out of the window, he looks back toward the Dolomite in the distance. Miming, he exaggerates a massive draw on an imaginary giant spliff.

Sammie belly laughs at the unfeasible sight in front of her while Paul, spotting the blue lights further ahead, gets the message. Slowing down while reaching across Sammie he feels under the seat.

'Oh-hello, steady on,' she smiles.

'Easy!' Super yells as Paul pulls out the large bag of weed.

'Easy-nah-star, easy,' Super pleads.

Ignoring him, Paul flings the stash through Sammies open window into the dark London sky followed by the Supers echoing yell, 'staaaarrrrrr…'

Chantelle awakes from her drunken slumber. 'What, what, what?' she pants, reaching out in all directions.

'Hush-baby, easy-nah, easy,' Super smiles, grabbing her arms. Spirits lifted, a smile spreads across his face as sex may well be on the cards after all. Reaching into the inside pocket of his coat, he pulls out his steel. Won't be needing that now, don't need no Beastman lifting me for it neither he thinks, sliding it down the gap between the back of the back seat while giving it a gentle stroke. Hush-nah baby he whispers, daddy soon come.

Meanwhile…

A lone Officer stands in front of the Police cars spread across the road, each with their blue lights spinning. He points directly at Shirley, motioning for her to pull in adjacent to a row of three storey town houses. Approaching, the Officer taps the window. 'Evening Miss, PC Dalby,' he smiles, poking his head through as Shirley winds it down.

'Hiya.' Shirley says, turning her head toward Devon, struggling to contain the onset of unintended giggles.

'May I ask where you are heading to at this late hour?'

'What's the problem?' Devon asks, leaning across Shirley.

'Going to the blues party?'

'Blues, nah-man, we don't know nothing about no Blues, we're off to Cheeks nightclub, in Deptford,' Devon lies.

'Right, okay, and where have you come from tonight?'

'Up West man, what's the problem?' Devon knows not to be specific about times or dates or locations or where he's from. Any mention of Brixton is sure to end up with a beating or an intimate finger-up-the-arse body search.

'Up West eh, one of those fancy nightclubs?'

'Yeah man,' Devon nods with a broad grin. He can see the Beast thinking "cheeky bastard".

'Okay, out the car please.' The Officer makes his way round to Devons side, calling over to three other Beasts.

The search, like every other, sees Devon with hands against a wall and legs wide apart, then, a not so gentle feel-up from the overly eager Officers.

One of the Officers, the smallest of the three and quite overweight with striking ginger hair pats him down. 'You stink,' he whispers.

'What's that Red?' Devon responds, having heard every put down before.

'I think, you stink, you disgusting dirty bastard.'

‘Ah, you mean the fanny juice,’ Devon motions with his head toward the car. He’s fully aware of the Police tactics, stimulate and provoke a response and all that, therefore, whenever he can, he’ll wind them up instead.

‘Apart from your bee-ow, I smell gain-jah, bet you’ve been smoking dope, dealing it too I’d expect?’

‘Nah-man-nah, eye-an-eye a natural brother-seen, can’t stand weed, plays havoc with my head, gives me a limp cock too if you know what I mean.’

‘Shut your mouth son, or you’ll end up down Carter Street with a good hiding,’ the Ginger Officer spits, kicking at the inside of Devons left foot, making him wobble to the side.

Carter Street, fuck that, Devon thinks. Carter Street is a fearsome Station in Walworth, near East Street Market, not far from the Elephant and Castle, is renowned for bent coppers, the regular fitting up of suspects and multiple beating of anyone unlucky enough to find themselves there, worse if you’re from Brixton.

With that, the Ginger Officer turns his attention to the car, who, along with PC Dalby who together execute a thorough search, convinced they’ll find drugs or an offensive weapon or, ideally, both. Search unsuccessful, the Ginger Officer and PC Dalby head toward Pauls car which has pulled up behind.

Climbing back in, Devon tips Paul a sly wink. Not waiting for Pauls stash to be discovered and be guilty by association, he tells Shirley to drive on. Manoeuvring past the Jam-Jars, she nods toward the fire engine and other blue lights. ‘What do you reckon happened?’

Devon stares for a few seconds. ‘God knows,’ he says, shaking his head. ‘Let’s just get out of here.’

Meanwhile…

Paul knows to stay in the car until they’ve finish with Devon. As Devon is searched by the Beast with ginger hair, the other others circle Shirleys car like sharks, looking it over and kicking the tyres. An Officer splits off and approaches, bending his head into Pauls window.

'Evening Officer?' Paul says, mimicking a posh accent.

'Evening, PC Dalby, heading to the blues party tonight?'

'Blues, err, no, we're off to Cheeks in Deptford actually.' Paul lies. Cheeks is a well-known after-hours night club and, although a dive, is far more respectable than an all-night "blues" house party.

PC Dalby eye-balls Sammie, now sprawling across the front seat and Super in the back with Chantelle who, much to Supers disgust, is now back fast asleep with her face glued against the window.

'Come on, let's get it over with,' PC Dalby nods at Paul. 'You too big boy, out you come.'

'T'cha, what the fook-star,' Super growls, flinging the back-door open. 'I fookin' hate New Cross.'

'Steady with the door,' Paul tuts.

'T'cha, piece of shit anyway.'

'Just get out the car you two,' PC Dalby interrupts as Ginger approaches.

Super already has his hands against the wall waiting for his search when Paul stops and turns to PC Dalby. 'Is all this really necessary?'

Ginger pushes him toward the wall Super is holding up. 'Never mind the chit-chat, just get over there.'

'This is wholly uncalled for,' Paul winks toward Super. 'You haven't even told us why we've been stopped, or what cause you might have to initiate a body-search.'

Spinning him around, Ginger grabs Paul by the throat.

'Lef-him-nah-star, pick on someone ya-own size,' Super turns, only to be stopped by PC Dalby.

Ignoring the suspect, Ginger pushes Paul further against the wall. 'Yes, it is necessary,' he whispers, his two-day old ginger stubble hovering inches away from Pauls face. 'We have reasonable suspicion that you or your comrades may have recently commitment a crime, or indeed be on your way to commit such an offense, that'll do you, shit-for-brains?'

'Fookin' out of order,' Super mutters. 'Can't test man one

on one, two on one even, so dey pick on duppy bwai lemon.' Ear cocked, his Wailing Rudie soundtrack plays faintly in the background. *"To live a righteous life to him seems poor…"* Nah-man, not here he thinks, focusing on the wall, focusing hard. But, with Paul arguing in the background and the blue lights bouncing off the surrounding buildings, he can't help it, the voices start whispering… *"gwan bad boy Super, hack these motherfuckers to bits,"* they say. Then, the ghetto blaster in his head clicks on and the volume dial twists. All of a sudden, he's surrounded by Wailing Rudie, the lyrics whirl-winding around him. *"Lef pon the street, like a raging storm."* Yesh-my-star, Beastman going to get wet-up and dead-up big time. Death and destruction cometh.

Suddenly…

He feels a sharp pain tugging around his groin. Rudie vanishes and a dark silence fills his mind as he's jerked back to the reality. 'T'cha, easy with me snake, man,' he says.

Ginger, seemingly finished with Paul, is running his hand up and down Supers upper leg while asking him his name, age and address. Heartrate slowing, he breathes easy. He's not sure what scares him the most, the thought of the beating he'll get from the Beasts if he kicks off, or, the thought of what he's capable of doing when Rudie and the voices start. 'So, what's happen anyway?' he says, looking toward the army of blue lights.

'There's been a fire, at one of your blues parties.'

'Our blues party, what foolishness you on about, we only just got here.'

Ginger administers a swift punch to his kidneys.

'Officer, this is unacceptable, your red-headed colleague is completely out of order,' Paul says, over pronouncing every word, staring deep into PC Dalby. 'You have no right to attack my friend, this is nothing short of Police brutality and I'll be complaining to the chief constable in the morning.'

'Call it reasonable cause, now, shut the fuck up,' PC Dalby says, running his hands inside Pauls jacket.

'Reasonable cause my arse,' Pauls tuts.

Finding nothing, PC Dalby turns to the car. Leaning casually into the window, he explains to Sammie about the fire. Several suspected deceased, including some kids. As soon as he mentions fire, her nostrils flare with the pungent smell of burning embers.

Suspected dead, kids too? She wants kids someday.

Two minutes, two body searches and a quick shake down of the car later, they're on their way with an official notice instructing Paul to produce his driving license, tax and insurance documents at a Police Station within seven days.

Sunday 18 January, 1:32am
Cheeks Nightclub
Deptford, London

After a quick detour through Lewisham and the arse-end of South East London, Paul eventually finds his way to Deptford. Parking just down the road from Cheeks nightclub, opposite a furniture shop. Paul, Super and the two girls walk in silence toward the club and the small crowd waiting outside, including Devon and Shirley.

'Club shut-up early, man, you lot okay?' Devon nods.

'Yesh-star, safe-man, safe, you hear about the Blues?' Super says, checking out the other rude-boys mingling in and around the crowd.

'Babylon must have it wrong,' Devon shakes his head.

'Something about kids being killed?' Sammie snuffles.

'Whatever happen, it's pure and utter badness-star, serious shit,' Super scowls. 'Fookin' hate dese-sides man, we got to get back to the frontline yah-naw.'

'Hush-nah man, I'll find out,' Devon says, heading toward a face he vaguely recognises, quickly trying to remember his name, "Hammerhead" or something, from Peckham maybe.

'Easy-nah line-man,' Hammerhead, or whatever his name growls. Clearly, he knows Devon. 'Long way from Brixton.'

'Chirpsing a local gal, then back home for sure,' Devon says, nodding toward the others.

Hammerhead looks over Devons shoulder. 'Yesh-my-breddah, dat some sweet pussy you got there dred.'

'True-say man, anyhow, wha-gwan with the Blues?'

'Line-man, let me tell you, it's dark breddah, dark. Lickle pickney yout has his sixteenth birthday party at his grandmas yard, den petrol bomb get hurl true da window.'

'What?'

'Yeah-man, hear me now, the whole place burn-down dred, enough pickney get trap and dead-up. Me tell you line-man, Babylon and Fronter in cahoots wid-each other, scheming and ting.'

Devon shakes his head.

'Tings serious round these parts yeah, tings not controlled like on Coldharbour and Railton.' Hammerhead is on a roll, and his patois increasing word by word. 'Bloodclat Babylon all over da-place dred wit' sus-stop and ting, an-den da the Fronters, man, dey marching pon the high street with the union jack and tarring and feathering and ting. Ya-nah-line-man, man can't get no peace round dese parts.'

Devon nods, acknowledging and agreeing with how bad it must be, but not really listening. Eventually, they agree to keep in touch, each knowing full well they probably won't.

Returning to the others, as Devon recounts what Hammerhead said the stark confirmation turns the vibe sour. With Cheeks closed, they agree to drive the short distance to Greenwich, and Shirleys flat.

Sunday 18 January, 1:49am
17 Hamilton House, Peabody Estate
Greenwich, London

With the Cutty Sark tall ship in dry dock on the right, and the river Thames straight ahead, they turn left into the Peabody Estate. The low-rise estate consists of six blocks surrounding a central grassy area with rows of parked cars along each side. The group quietly clamber up the graffiti stained walls of the central stairwell, then along the open walkway to flat seventeen. Fumbling through her clutch bag, Shirley eventually locates the keys and, after two attempts, finds the right one and opens the door.

'Come-on girl,' Super sighs, crossing his legs as his bladder is about to burst. Normally he'd wash the walls down in the stairwell, but, with girls in tow and fit birds at that, he's on his best behaviour. Through the door, Devon follows Shirley, who has her arm around Chantelle, through to the living room while Super heads straight to the toilet. Shirley deposits her comatose friend in the armchair before disappearing into the kitchen.

Meanwhile…

Out on the walkway, Sammie leans against the wall to the right of the front door with Paul pressing onto her. Lips joining, they share a slow, passionate kiss.

'Who's for tea then?' Shirley yells, filling the kettle.

'Got any rum, stout maybe?' Super shouts from the toilet.

'It's tea or tea I'm afraid.'

Falling into the sofa, Devon looks across at Chantelle, now snoring loudly, with a line of saliva forming to the left of her half open mouth. A nice flat, comfortable and sort of familiar too. He imagines Shirley cooking dinner for him while he watches their young son playing with Lego in front of the television. Shit man, he must be more buzzing than he realises. His mind wanders, eventually finding its way back to the fire in New Cross. Could the Police really be involved? Fronters maybe, but not Babylon, surely. Harassing youths, sus-stopping and the occasional beating now and again, yeah, that's bad enough, but arson, maybe murder? He shakes his head, nah-man, that's pure madness.

Shirley walks through with a tray of cups, a pot of tea and half a packet of custard cream biscuits. Super follows, tutting as he nods toward Chantelle. Sex out of the question, he turns his attention to the stereo in the corner standing on a fake wooden stand with a stack of seven-inch singles resting against it. Flicking through he stops. 'Phil Collins, in de air 'pon night, shit girl, you need educating,' he smiles.

Sitting next to Devon, she passes him a cup of tea while he stretches an arm around her shoulder.

'Educating, really, bet you can't even spell it,' she jokes.

Devon laughs, squeezing her shoulder. He likes a girl who can give as good as she gets.

Turning the stereo on, Super tunes the dial to "Love-2-Love", his favourite pirate radio station, playing nothing but roots and culture. 'Anyway, of course I can spell it, eye-tee,' he beams. 'Get it?'

Devon shakes his head. 'You make Marlon look brainy.'

'Who's that?' Shirley smiles.

'His pickney little brother,' Super answers. 'Fifteen going on thirty, and better looking than monster munch dere.'

Devon mocks surprise and hurt, pointing at his face then his heart. 'A good kid, thinks he's a man already though.'

'Can't imagine you as a big brother,' Shirley smiles. 'Anyway, why do they call you "Super"?'

'Long story-star,' Super nods.

'T'cha, don't go there babes, we'll be here all night,' Devon squeezes her shoulder as they all laugh.

# Episode 8.
# "Woods and Trees"

Sunday 18 January, 8:55am
47 Saltoun Road
Brixton, London

'Why can't I just stay at home?'

'You coming wid us bwai,' Momma scowls, pulling on her full length dark green coat. 'Especially, after lass-night.'

'Momma, please,' Marlon whines, punching his arm through the sleeve on his hand-me-down leather jacket.

'Mister Marlon Walters,' Pops interrupts. 'Hush yourself now boy, if I go, you go, ya-understand?' Pops says, tipping him a wink as Marlon struggles to contain a giggle.

Having arrived home only a couple of hours earlier from a night in the West End followed by a detour around New Cross and then on to Shirleys flat in Greenwich, Devon watches on in silence. He's too old for all this and definitely too tired, but, Sunday in Brixton belongs to the Mommas who get dressed up in their Sunday-bests and lead the family to Church. Momma is wearing her colourful floral dress with matching hat, while Pops looks smart in a three-quarter length tailored coat and pork-pie hat.

With the weather surprisingly mild for the time of year, the short walk along Shakespeare Road to the Church accompanied by the smell of sizzling bacon wafting through the air and the echoing sounds of Bob Marley and the

Wailers in the distance is sheer delight. As well as Marlons late-night entertainment spot, where only a few hours ago he found himself arrested and taken to the custody suite of Brixton Police Station, the Church is based in the community centre. Marlon glances toward the Roman Catholic Church at the other side of the graveyard. Both buildings can't be any more different. While the Romans pray for forgiveness on bent knee in a cold and sterile mausoleum, the Walters family, along with other predominately Caribbean families, will sing their hearts out giving praise to the Lord with guitars and drums plus the choir keeping the vibe lively and warm.

Walking through the open doors, the family are greeted with an unsettlingly sombre atmosphere, with rumours rippling through the congregation about a group of youngsters being killed last night. Scanning around, Devon sees shocked frowns and sad tears rolling down horrified faces. Feeling it too, he replays images from last night, the array of blue strobing lights, the fire engines, the musty smell of fire in the air, the sus-stopping Beasts and the rumours about the National Front. Closing his eyes, he sees Shirleys kind and beautiful face smiling back at him, he hasn't felt this way about any girl and a long time, if ever, come to think of it.

Meanwhile…

Mommas hug each other as others cry uncontrollably while kids share gossip about Beasts or Fronters being to blame, before bigging themselves up with their "if they come around here, they'll get mash up" claims. Marlon nods along, knowing these kids are full of crap, and will do jack shit if it ever came to it. After a few minutes, Reverend Johnson calls everyone together to begin his sermon…

'Praise the lord. Thank you all for gathering here today, I have grave and sad news to bring you. I must report a great loss our community, indeed, our society, Lord God, we have all suffered greatly overnight. No doubt many of you will have heard about it on the radio or seen it on the television, some of you may have heard about it from friend or neighbour. I can confirm there has indeed been a tragic event where, at a celebratory birthday party, a group of youngsters sadly passed through the light, praise be to the Lord. Some of these youngsters are still bravely battling for life in hospital…"

Communal gasps echo through the Church, followed by cries of, "oh Lord" and "Lord have mercy."

'Lord above stand our witness,' the Reverend continues. 'While we as a society struggle coming to terms with one another and to embrace our differences, I have been assured by the authorities that the fire is nothing more than a terrible accident, and any talk about the authorities or anyone else somehow being involved is completely wrong. Lord god, as a single, united community, we must come together and stay strong at this saddest hour…"

The Reverend then proceeds with his normal service, and, after what seems like an age, the drums crash as the traditional last song always sung begins, *"all things bright and beautiful."* After that the congregation make their way outside where everyone shakes hands, smiles politely and consoles each other about the sad loss of life.

Looking around, Marlon senses something isn't right. It's late morning and Shakespeare Road is deserted, with no sign of the usual hustle and bustle or stream of nose to tail traffic. In the distance, he spots an old brown Ford Cortina approaching. Fucking hell, plain clothes Beasts, he can spot them a mile off. Heart pumping, he counts five people inside. What a liberty, on a Sunday and after last night too. Then, panic surges through him as he sees a passenger leaning out of the back window. Short-cropped hair, sporting a green bomber jacket, his arm stretches out and his middle finger salutes the sky. 'Fuck off back to where ya-from,' he shouts as the wheels screech as the car speeds away. God damn, that's no plain clothed unit, nah, that's the mother fucking National Front.

The congregation collectively gasp.

Throwing a punch in the direction of the car, Marlon bolts from the crowd as some of the momma's cow away, shielding their eyes. Reaching out with her left arm, Momma yanks him back while slapping him around the head with her right. Now isn't the time for that, especially in front of the Reverend, nor the congregation. After much headshaking and tutting, the Walters family set off for home. Marlon smiles, watching Momma march out in front. Yeah, she's proud as punch, defiant and strong, but, he knows, even if she doesn't show it, deep down inside the news of the fire and the shouting from the passing car will have upset her.

A couple of hours later…

Finishing his lunch, Marlon downs his sarsaparilla and puts his glass and plate into the sink before making his way out to the hallway and grabbing his coat.

'Bwai, where yah-ago?'

'Out Momma, back later yeah.'

'After last night?' Devon teases.

'You not allow-out today.' Momma says, sternly.

'I'm leaving school in six months, you can't keep me in.'

'Bwai, my house, my rules.'

Smiling, Devon shakes his head judgementally.

'Let the boy go Momma,' Pops says, in his always-calm-and-mellow voice. 'He practically a man now.'

Kissing her teeth, Momma nods toward the door.

Sunday, 18 January, 4:15pm
Corner of Saltoun Road and Effra Road
Brixton, London

'You're out then, didn't know if you'd come.'

'Of course I'm out, Babylon can't hold me,' Marlon gives Ashley a not-so-soft mock punch to the arm.

'Oi, steady with the garments,' Ashley says, straightening out his black nylon Adidas tracksuit top, the one with bright yellow stripes along the arms.

'Call them garms, more like Oxfam rejects.'

'Nah-mate-nah, none of that.'

'You just a bin-raider, in fact, you know what, I think I threw them out last month.'

'Eh?' Ashley puts on a hurt look. 'These, my man, are quality merchandise, and brand fucking new too.'

'Bloodclat C&A more like.'

Looking at each other, smiles crack across their faces.

'Come on, we can do this all night,' Ashley nods.

'True-say, true, let's cut through the park yeah?'

Setting off, Marlon tells him about his night in the Police Station and seeing Ready Brek. He doesn't mention seeing Kingy, nah, he wants to be one-hundred percent sure before he tells anyone. He goes on to tell him about the fire at New Cross, Devon getting sus-stopped and the Fronters he saw at the Church earlier in the day.

'Mugs,' Ashley tuts, disgusted. He never realised there was such a thing as racism until aged eleven and his first few weeks at secondary school. Once there, he saw how the black and white kids kept to their own, and of the white kids, the Irish and Italians kept to their own too. That is, apart from him and Marlon, who've been best friends since primary school. Nowadays, with the growing influence of the National Front, he's more aware than ever of racists and how they treat kids like him.

Jumping over the meter-high metal railings into the park they hear shouting. 'You two, stay right there.'

'What the fuck,' they say simultaneously.

Two men jog toward them. The first, big and muscular wearing a blue bomber jacket looks angry as fuck while the second is fat, much older and wearing a dirty donkey jacket.

'Fuck this,' Marlon says, looking back over the fence. Just then, a blue Morris Marina screeches next to the curb, blocking any potential exit route.

Trapped.

An even older guy with greased back grey hair and a long brown coat climbs out before making his way over.

'Fucking hell man,' Marlon tuts.

Frozen to the spot, Ashley panics, he's heard about the National Front targeting kids like him.

'Stay right where you are,' the big angry younger looking guy shouts with a deep, gravelly voice. 'Don't fucking move,' he grunts, grabbing Marlons shoulder.

Forced against the railings, Marlon feels his bodyweight shifting to the other side. Bracing himself for an unhappy meeting between head and pavement, his tumble is stopped by the big angry guy pressing onto him while twisting his arm further up his back, tell-tale signs of a sus-stop. Marlon quickly realises these guys aren't Fronters at all, most definitely Babylon.

'Lef dem alone Beast,' an old lady dog walker shouts from across the street, over the top of the blue Marina. 'Lef dem be, Babylon, dey only pickney, not done nutton.'

From deep within the park a couple of kids on bikes ride over, circling around them.

'We're just walking,' Ashley whines as the fat older man leads him away toward the trees. With so many witnesses about, he hopes he won't be beaten too bad.

Still sprawled over the fence, Marlon looks up at the old grey man approaching from the beat-up wreck of a car.

'Stop and search me old mucker,' Old Grey sighs, brandishing a warrant card in front of his face. He sees the blur of a silver coat of arms on the left and a Metropolitan Police sign on the other.

'Heading into town, bit of mugging, touch of drug dealing maybe?' Big Angry spits, his tone a disturbing mix of sarcasm and threat.

'T'cha,' Marlon kisses his teeth, glancing over to Ashley and sees the Fat Man taking down his name and the usual particulars. 'What's this about, why you-ah sus-stop me?' he asks Old Grey.

Like lightening, Big Angry lands a body-blow into his kidneys.

Bent double, Marlon gasps for air.

The dog-walking old lady across the street yells hysterically while her dog yaps loudly. 'Babylon, Babylon,' she screams. 'They only kids man, lef dem be.'

'Watch your manners, boy,' Big Angry snarls before being pushed aside by the Old Grey who takes hold of Marlon across the fence, straightening up his jacket and brushing off imaginary lint from the shoulders. 'We're clamping down on you lot with your muggings and your drugs,' he whispers. 'Now, be a good lad, get yourself together and piss off.'

Sunday, 18 January, 4:24pm
Kids Playground
Brockwell Park, Brixton, London

'You alright mate?' Ashley smiles, noticing the strained look on his face and tears in his eyes.

'Yeah man, fuck the Beasts.' Winded, he still fronts up.

'We've got to complain or something.'

'What?'

'All they did is question me, but you get a punch, it's not right you know, not right at all.'

Marlon stops. 'Too right it's not right.'

'So, let's go to the station, complain yeah.'

'Are you mad, complain where Ashley, to who, they don't give a shit man, they all in this together?' he spits, shaking his head in an "are-you-stupid" kind of way.

Further into the park, looking back Marlon sees Big Angry waving, before blowing him a kiss.

'Absolute tosser,' Ashely tuts. 'He's alright picking on us, let's see how he'd fair against likes of Devon or Super.'

'True say man, true,' Marlon agrees. 'Super would fuck him up, the fat fucking wanker.'

Approaching the playground, the Beasts disappear into the dusky background and they spot Delroy and Gladstone sitting on top of the climbing frame sharing a spliff. With all the shops closing early, Sunday evening are mad-boring.

'Wha-gwan,' Delroy shouts as they approach. 'Dutty Babylon gone shank-yah-yeah?'

'Last night, and now dis?' Gladstone kisses his teeth.

'Anyways, you got out quick yeah, they charge you already?' Delroy asks.

'Man, inna-cuffs for half the night, den inna-cell with a stinking tramp,' Marlon says. 'Reach home dis morning and Momma take a belt to my arse.' Pulling his coat up and jeans down, he reveals several belt-strap bruises.

'Enough of the batty-business,' Delroy suggests, turning away from the sight of Marlons bare arse-cheek.

'You like that, eh?' Marlon smiles playfully.

'Bloodclat queers,' Gladstone shakes his head before quickly changing the subject. 'So, Ashley, listen man, you want some draw, we holding a quarter weight here, serious shit man, no twigs nor branches no nuttin.'

'Nah-it's cool yeah, we're sorted,' Ashley says, having earlier helped Marlon liberate several joints worth from Devons stash on top of the wardrobe.

'This aint no dried-up banana skin-shit, this is real draw, the best leaf from the best plants-yesh,' Delroy adds.

'Ha-hah, your Mommas cooking herbs more like,' Marlon laughs, slapping Ashleys shoulder.

During the next twenty minutes, several spliffs are built, ignited and smoked as the group fall about laughing, generally taking the piss out of each other. Then, as a cloak of night-time darkness creeps across the park, a small figure appears in the distance.

'Who dah fuck is dis?' Gladstone squints, only able to make out it was a skinny kid with a faded denim jacket.

'Tucker fucking Jenkins or someone,' Ashley giggles, before they all recognise Kingy jogging toward them.

'Rasclat rat-boy cometh,' Delroy says, rubbing his hands together in anticipation.

'Don't be bullying him man,' Marlon mixes a question with a statement.

'What?' Delroy shrugs.

'Alright Kingy, what you been up to?' Marlon says, patting him on the back while really thinking what were you up to at the station last night, helping Her Majesty's constabulary with their enquiries perhaps?

'Ducking and diving, you know how it goes,' Kingy grins.

'Safe man, safe.' Marlon looks deep into his eyes, hoping to read his mind and find out what he's up to.

'Got a bag on me if anyone fancies a sniff?' Kingy suggests. With red rings around the eyes and severe acne around the mouth, Kingy is most definitely partial to a spot of glue sniffing.

'Glue, oh come on,' Ashley shakes his head.

'Dat shit's for Fronters,' Gladstone sighs.

'True-say Gladstone, bags are for penniless skins Kingy-mate.' Marlon tuts. He hates glue.

'Glue, skins, Fronters, what the fuck,' Delroy adds, jumping down and putting his face into Kingys.

Marlon readies himself, he's not about to let Kingy take a beating, not until he knows for sure if it was him he saw in the station last night and what he was doing there.

'Why the fuck you gluing?' Delroy whispers into his ear. 'You with the National Front or what?'

Kingy steps back. 'What… what… course not.'

Not particularly tall nor muscular, Delroys deep-frowning forehead gives him a much older, meaner look. His eyes seem to slope inward toward his wide nose, accentuating his permanently angry look.

'Delroy, I, I…I… come on, you know me…'

'Dee, come on mate,' Ashley suggests.

'Are you a fucking Fronter or what?' Delroy snarls grabbing him by the throat. 'And don't give me no eye-eye-eye bullshit, you think I'm a thick Irish mick?'

Kingys face morphs into a scribble of fear.

'Lef him be Dee,' Marlon pleads.

'Nah-man-nah, I ask him a simple fucking question, but rat boy stutters,' Delroys head pushes deep into Kingys.

'Dee,' Kingy cracks a nervous smile. 'You know me.'

'Why you smiling?' Delroy pushes his head even deeper as frustration tears through his voice. 'I'm not smiling.'

Kingys smile drops as tears well.

Silence spreads across the playground.

Tension fills the air.

'Ha, a fucking Fronter,' Delroy yells, releasing his pray. 'Kingy, a bom-ba-clat Fronter, as if.'

Marlon stares at Delroy.

'What?' he protests, arms out stretched. 'I aint hurt him,' he says re-mounting the climbing frame, and taking a freshly built joint from Gladstone. Igniting it, he takes a long deep draw. 'Hear me now rat-boy, if I really did think you were a Fronter,' he blows thick white smoke directly up into the sky. 'I'll not ask you no questions, nah-man, I'll stripe your rasclat ugly face.'

'Two times,' Gladstone adds with a nod.

Straightening his jacket, Kingy turns to Marlon. 'So anyway, I'm gonna get off yeah.' Eyes full of sadness, he looks awkward and embarrassed.

'Don't go man, ignore him,' Marlon says. Whatever the reason he was at the station last night, he still feels for him.

'Nah, really mate, I'm off.'

'Kingy-mate,' Ashley pulls at his arm.

'See-yah laters,' Kingy turns and walks away, shoulders hunching as his head dips low.

Marlon watches him disappear into the darkness before turning to Delroy. 'Why you got be like that Dee?'

'Listen,' Delroy snaps. 'He's nothing to us, fuck him.'

'Nah-nah-nah, you're out of order, well out of order,' Marlons eyes narrow.

'Calm down rude-boy,' Delroy smiles.

'I told you to leave it, yeah.'

'You told me?'

'Yeah, I told you.'

'When did you start telling me anything?'

'I'm fucking telling you now,' Marlon edges forward.

'Come on chaps, leave it eh,' Ashley suggests.

'Leave them be Ash,' Gladstone asserts, he loves a tear-up. 'They both men of the world.'

'Look at yourself,' Delroy says, jumping down from the climbing frame to face Marlon. 'We gonna fight over a fucking rat-boy-piece-of-shit?'

In a flash Marlon swings, slapping Delroy on the side of the head with his open hand, the clapping sound bouncing off the nearby trees.

With that, Delroy lunges forward with a jab.

Avoiding the blow, Marlon shuffles back.

Ashley runs in as Gladstone jumps down from the climbing frame, both holding Delroy back.

'Dickhead,' Delroy shouts. 'Fucking with your own blood because of that mother-fucker-fronter-rat-boy?'

Standing southpaw, Marlon stares. 'I told you.'

'He a mug, a Fronter, a fucking wrong-un,' Delroy yells.

Images of last night in the Police Station bombardes Marlons thoughts. What was Kingy doing there, is he a grass or maybe he's there for something to do with social services, his mum's a slag, his sisters on the game and his old man fucked off years back, I've known him since primary school.

'Well?' Delroy yells, shrugging Ashley and Gladstone off.

'T'cha, I'm off home,' Marlon shakes his head before turning to set off walking.

'Marlon, come on, don't go,' Ashley calls after him.

'We'll see you tomorrow,' Delroy shouts. 'When you've come to your rarted senses.'

# Episode 9.
# "Old Nick"

Sunday, 18 January, 2:00pm
Brixton Police Station
Brixton, London

With ceramic tiles floor to ceiling, a lack of adequate heating and ultra-bright strip lights above, the sparse locker room in the basement has a cold and sterile atmosphere. Even so, a dozen or so half-dressed coppers are mid-way through shedding their civilian skin, preparing to become the despised authority, otherwise known locally, much to the hilarity of the Officers, as either "Beasts" or "Babylon" or the "mother of all prostitutes". Buttons fastened, shoes polished and neckties done up, an un-nerving cocktail of anticipation mixed with anxiousness fills the room.

'Barst-ard-fuck-king-shit-cunt,' Andrew grunts, violence reverberating around the locker room. His angry words synchronising with his pounding fists, creating a deep dent in the two-foot tall steel door.

'There're easier ways to get a couple of weeks on the sick you know,' a passing colleague whispers.

Fuck off, cunt, Andrew thinks to himself. Don't you dare speak to me like that you slag.

A huge man, Sergeant Lacy stands in the doorway to the locker room legs astride with hands on hips, filling the gap where the door once was. Surveying the room, he clears his throat. 'Right you lot,' he yells, breaking the hum of the dozen or so blokes getting changed. 'Collins, Jones, Higgston, you lot are in plain clothes tonight, report to the C.I.D. office in five minutes, the rest of you, get a move on.' Waiting a couple of seconds to ensure his instructions are understood, he turns to climb the stairs back toward the custody suite.

Plain clothes he smiles well, that's just terrific. He hasn't worked a shift in plain clothes during his entire work experience posting at Brixton. At last, this is it, your chance to shine Andrew me-old-son, he tells himself. Having left school with a single 'O' level in woodwork, he's determined to make a real go of it as a copper. A "proper job" his proud-as-punch dad calls it. Although he'll never admit it, he feels the weighty expectations of his family on his broad shoulders, but, the way he sees it, it's extra motivation not to fail. In any case, he has to think of himself, any job is better than his old man giving his teenage self no end of grief for "lazing about" and "not getting out there" or "earning a crust". From as young as he can remember, success means discipline and discipline means pain, punishment and fear, especially fear, he knows a lot about fear. Nowadays, as a man, he understands why his dad did what he did way back when, of course he does. The way he sees it, the older generation didn't know any better, with their lack of education and reliance on brawn, rather than brains. That's how it was back then, not like today in the enlightened eighties, where we talk things through, understand the motivations for our actions and all that crap. If and when he has a kid, he'll teach him right from wrong without the need for his fists or belts or metal chains from the second-hand motorbike his old man won playing cards during a drunken night down the boozer.

So anyway, tonight, in plain clothes, he'll make a statement and finally prove his worth, make his family proud. Normally, cadets on work experience are assigned to a senior officer and sent on patrol to one of the many sink estates, where they'll be showered with, at best, urine, or at worst glass bottles from the inter-connecting walkways hanging between the high-rise blocks.

Feeling happier by the second in the knowledge he doesn't have to face the ordeal of patrol, at least for tonight, he ceases his assault on the impregnable locker. No need for the uniform tonight, nah, he'll keep his jeans and white tennis trainers on. Pulling on his blue bomber jacket, he realises he feels way more at home in his civvies than the starchy-straight formal uniform. He decides right there and then to aim for a career in C.I.D, this is the life for him.

Quickly followed by Collins and Higgston, he bounces upstairs heading to the C.I.D office. Outside, he stops abruptly and thinks about knocking. Polite and professional, good first impression and all that, but, on the other hand, the hardcore detectives inside might take the piss at the new boy knocking like a fairy and he'll never hear the end of it. Yeah, they'll cook up some kind of bullshit nickname for him like "fairy-boy" or "gentle" or "andy-fucking-pandy".

'What you fannying around with?' Higgston barges him out of the way, heading for a desk at the far-right hand side.

Edging in, Andrew perches on the edge of Higgstons desk. Glancing around, he can't believe his eyes, the office is covered with half open files, several cups of what looks to be unfinished mouldy coffee and a typewriter which is nearly as old as Higgston, which is fucking old, he chuckles to himself. All in all, the C.I.D. department are dirty filthy bastards he nods to himself, no wonder their detection rate is the lowest in the entire Met Police, at a lowly seven-percent. The walls are covered with white-boards, cork-boards and pinned up A3 sheets of paper, each dotted around in between the dirty never been cleaned windows. The boards are filled with vaguely familiar names from the South London underworld and a few mugshots of complete wrong-uns. He counts nine other Detectives, some busy reading files, a few chat between themselves while a couple sit quietly enjoying a cigarette. Nose twitching, the office stinks of sweat and stale cigarette smoke as well as, intriguingly, old fashioned real ale, the smell of C.I.D. he smiles to himself. The hustle and bustle of the room tapers off as Andrew looks around to see a middle-aged uniformed Officer standing near the door. 'Right then ladies,' he growls in a broad Northern Irish accent. 'Let's get this party started shall we.'

Detective Chief Inspector McCrudden, tall and slender with greying hair and a lined face has an awe about him, something Andrew can't quite put his finger on, other than that he's immediately impressed. The locker-room rumours about him suddenly make perfect sense… apparently, back in the sixties, he was part of the B-Specials based in Londonderry, infamous for interrogating catholic suspects with the aid of copper wire, bowls of water and car batteries.

'I see we have re-enforcements tonight,' McCrudden says, looking first at Collins, then at Andrew. 'Welcome fellas, welcome. Higgy's back too, nice holiday wee-fella?'

Higgston spent the last two weeks on a surveillance rotation watching a house suspected to be a drug-den.

'Good hunting, I hear' McCrudden nods. 'Yer-man-there nailed a few dirty bastards so he did.'

'Yeah great, locked in the back of a freezing cold van, pissing into an empty cola-bottle watching slags and skagg-heads all day and night.' Higgston tuts, gaining a few laughs from colleagues.

'Sounds like your kind of thing, right up your street sure-enough,' McCrudden nods, reasserting his authority. 'Right then, tonight we keep the pressure on, especially after the business in New Cross.' He steps further into the room, closing the door nonchalantly behind him with his heel.

Now, that is fucking cool, Andrew smiles to himself.

McCruddens voice lowers to a near whisper. 'Orders from Divisional Headquarters, we stop and search any and all bastards out there, make our presence felt.' McCrudden points in the direction of Andrew. 'Sierra One for you fellas,' he lobs the keys toward Collins.

The room ripples with a few coughs and giggles.

Although often deployed for C.I.D. duties, Collins never wanted to take the Detective Inspector exams so remained a P.C. Having worked at Brixton Station since the early sixties, mainly as patrol-plod, nowadays he tries to keep out of trouble until he eventually retires later on in the year. Due to his long service, he automatically gains a level of respect allowing him to keep his head down with light driving duties. 'Right then, let's get going shall we,' Collins smiles before winking at Andrew. 'Our chariot waits.'

Andrew leads the way out through the custody suite into the rear car park, quickly followed by Higgy and Collins. 'Fucking-aida,' he says, struck dumb, unable to move. Eyes locked, open mouthed, he stares in awe of Sierra One, a beaten-up navy blue 1973 Morris Marina. With what he suspects is a broken rear suspension, it has a decidedly lopsided look, like an old man struggling with a dodgy back. Adding to the geriatric look, the bumper clings on to the front wings with nothing more than crispy-brittle rust. 'That is not a real Police car-yah,' Andrew thinks out loud. Commonly known as "shit-one", Sierra One, (or Squad Car Number One to give it it's formal name), is the oldest car in the pool and, with a modest 1.7 litre engine, is notoriously unreliable and painfully slow. 'That's a fucking death-trap,' he shakes his head.

'Here's hoping,' Collins says, climbing in hoping a minor non life-threatening injury will lead to early retirement.

'We're on foot then,' Higgston says, patting Andrew on the back. 'Meet you on the Frontline Collins, other side of the park.'

Andrew hates the Frontline, nearly as much as the Loughborough Estate. The area known to locals and Police as the "Frontline" is the square mile around the Railton Road area. The streets and alleyways are narrow with thin footpaths flanked by mostly derelict three or four story terraced town houses with steps leading up to first floor front doors. The area is increasingly used by the local council to house a transient population of homeless and immigrants, subsequently, it's become a magnet for low-life scum seeking to take advantage of those unfortunate enough to reside there. Crime is rife, so rife, at times it verges on out of control with drug dealing, prostitution, mugging and robbery a daily occurrence amongst the illegal drinking and gambling dens, squats and all-night blues parties. Everything and anything goes down on the Frontline, apart from the Police, that is. Although not officially tolerated, the level of crime is so widespread the Police simply don't have the resources available to arrest everyone, or to deal with the unrest this might cause. As long as the criminals keep themselves to themselves, the authorities won't rock the boat too much. Some rank and file coppers refer to it in whispers as a "no go" area, while others refuse point blank to pass through, let alone deal with any incidents. These types don't last long in Brixton.

'Other side of Brockwell Park, corner of Dulwich Road and Hurst Street,' Collins confirms.

Andrew looks sideways. 'Who made you the boss?'

'I've been at this since before you were even born-lad,' Collins says, using the most patronising of patronising tones. 'Plus, me old china, I'm the one with the keys.'

'Like I give a shit, that motor is a fucking death trap, we're better off on foot,' Andrew says, zipping up his jacket while following Higgy out of the car park. Turning right onto Brixton Hill they head South toward the Railway Station.

Sixty seconds later…

Sierra One trundles passed with a toot-toot as Collins leans out of the window, waving Queen-Mother style.

'Wanker.'

'Ignore him,' Higgston suggests. 'Just on the wind up.'

'Yeah, true, anyway, what do-yah know Higgy?' Andrew asks, attempting conversation to pass the time.

'Not much pal, what about you, what do you know?' Higgy replies, intending to make Andrew work for any information.

'Me, I don't know jack shit, I'm just on work experience.'

'You're doing alright Andy, you'll be just fine.'

'Really, cheers mate, so anyway, what about this push on stop and search?' Andrew probes.

'Crazy times, we've got to retake control I suppose, stop this place going up in flames.' Higgy pans his arm across the horizon, surveying Brixton in all its glory. 'You know, when I first came here it was a lot different…'

Picking up the pace, Andrew senses a reminiscence of granddad-esque proportions.

'Oh yes, very different,' Higgy nods. 'Look around you Andy, no respect, the place is full of him-e-grants and sh-lags who couldn't care less about the place, drug dealers, whores, skinheads…'

'Yah-yah, I know what you mean Higgy.'

'Scum, pure and utter scum,' Higgy continues. 'This place has turned into the arsehole of the world.'

'Too right,' Andrew agrees, Higgston has that much right.

'We're here to protect everyone right, black, white, young and old, so why the attitude, why the chip on the shoulder, answer me that one then?' Before Andrew can reply, he continues without pausing for breath. 'This new generation thinks the world owes them a living.'

'Spot on.' Andrew goads, this is amusing and will pass the time nicely.

'I'll tell you what Andy, lazy, that's what they are, lazy, and hun-grateful,' Higgys words trail off…

Continuing their walk, they pass under the railway bridge occasionally looking in the shop windows while avoiding eye contact with the locals they pass by.

Sunday, 18 January, 4:20pm
Brockwell Park
Brixton, London

Continuing in silence for a couple of minutes, Andrews mind wanders to his graduation from Hendon and becoming a real, proper full-time copper. He remembers his wishful thinking on his first day at Hendon, about what it is to be a copper and in particular C.I.D. but, with all this boring walking and talking crap, his appetite is waning. He assumed, wrongly it seems, C.I.D. involves painstakingly deep under-cover investigations, disrupting organised crime or looking into robberies or murders or rapes, definitely not walking for miles listening to an old fool reminiscing about the so called "good old days". 'Cut through the park-yah?' he suggests, thinking the change of scenery might liven things up.

'Good idea,' Higgston smiles. 'Collins should be waiting at the other end,'

A sparse open space with a couple of trees flanking the boundary with a playground near the middle, the park is well known as an under-age drinking area for teenagers. More recently, skinheads and "rude-boys" would congregate to consume solvents and marijuana. In the distance, Andrew spots some kids on bikes racing around with a couple playing on the climbing frame.

'What do you reckon Higgy, Section 4?'

'Sus-stop?'

'Yah, why not?'

'Suspected Persons, the Vagrancy Act?' Higgston tuts. 'They're about ten years old Andy, get a grip.'

Embarrassed by his eagerness, Andrew feels his face flush pink. Passing the swings, he eyes two shifty looking teenagers crossing the road toward the park.

'Here we go, now we're talking,' Higgston nods in their direction. 'This is more like it.'

Both teenagers jump the railings into the park.

'Oi, stay there,' Andrews voice bounces off the trees.

Both teenagers freeze. The first, a good-looking lad just under six feet tall with a bit of an afro and the beginnings of a bum fluff hanging on his top lip looks particularly shifty. Eyes darting around, he's no doubt looking for a way to run, a sure sign of guilt Andrew thinks.

'Easy does it Jonesy,' Higgy calmly suggests, noting

Andrews excitement. 'Stay where you are, Police.'

'Don't fucking move,' Andrew growls, jogging over and grabbing the suspect, pushing him back toward the railings. He can see Sierra One approaching along Dulwich Road, slowing down then stopping near the curb while in the background a woman is shouting obscenities. Ignore the slag, he says to himself grabbing the youth's right arm, spinning him to his left while pushing his wrist further around his back. Forcing him forward toward the railings, the suspect resists a little, which is great, Andrew thinks.

Meanwhile, Higgy has hold of the other lad, a skinny streak of piss, and leads him away in the opposite direction.

Pushing the suspect onto the fence, Andrew pins him down. No way on earth this guy is getting away, no fucking way, he tells himself.

From the other side of the railings, Collins lumbers out of Sierra One and approaches, brandishing his warrant card.

The suspect continues to struggle and resist, a sure sign of guilt, definitely up to something, must be hiding something, drugs, a weapon maybe Andrew presumes? His heart rate jumps, yeah, this is it. By now a small crowd's formed, mostly kids on bikes but the local women is still shouting from across the street. Her yells jar his nerves. Why don't she just shut the fuck up and fuck the fuck off. 'Heading into town-yah, do some robbing, drug dealing?' Andrew suggests, observing his reaction.

The suspect kisses his teeth.

How dare he, I'm the fucking Police, Andrew screams inside his head. Mug me off, make a fucking mug of me, the fucking little prick.

How fucking dare he.

'I aint done nothing,' the suspect moans, lifting his head toward Collins.

Now the little shit's ignoring me, Andrew grunts to himself. Ignore me, mug me off? I'm the fucking Police.

The fucking little bastard.

WHACK.

Andrew lands a peach of a punch into the suspects kidneys. Bending double, he struggles for air.

Good, the cunt.

Releasing him, Andrew steps back to admire his handywork hoping the suspect will retaliate, but he doesn't. What a punch though, yeah, still got it, never fucking lost it, never forgot those boxing sessions as a young kid…

Sitting there supping light ale and smoking Old Holbern roll-ups his dad and his uncle Tommy watch the impromptu sparring session blow-by-blow. Twelve-year-old Andrew and his older teenage cousin Kenneth, both wearing antique four-ounce Lonsdale bag-gloves knock seven bells out of each other. Every time Kenneth lands a blow, Andrews dad shouts for him to "man-up" and "take it like a man", while his Uncle Tommy cheers and claps his sons pinpoint accuracy. Stinging left jab and a heavy right cross later, Andrew is on his backside seeing stars while Kenneth does the Ali-shuffle in front of him. "Get up you pansy" his dad spits, so, tears in his eyes, Andrew rolls over onto his side and pushes himself up. Wiping his nose, he nods toward Kenneth. Hands up, let's go again…

Blinking hard, Andrew looks to Collins expecting a round of applause or something. Instead, he receives a stern, dismissive glare and feels his smile drop. Looking daggers at him, Collins reaches over the railings and pulls Andrew away from the suspect. He tells both lads to watch their manners and be on their way, and to keep out of trouble. Higgy lets the skinny kid go and they watch them make their way further into the park toward the playground come under-age-drinking-den.

'What on earth are you doing,' Collins frowns, pulling him further away. 'That's completely out of order, totally not on Andy, not on at all.'

Engulfed with a confusing mix of rage and guilt, Andrew feels the veins in his neck throbbing. He bites the inside of his bottom lip.

'Under no circumstances do we ever attack suspects,'

Collins explains. 'Especially and ab-so-lutley never, ever, in broad daylight. NEVER.'

Dipping his head, Andrew stares at the ground, tasting the sour-iron taste of blood in his mouth.

'With multiple witnesses too,' Collins tuts. 'What do they teach you up at Hendon?' His words are serious and stern.

'Sorry Guv,' Andrew blurts, struggling for words while his head tilts even further downward.

Ashamed, he feels like a little kid again, half expecting the leather belt treatment from his old man for being stupid, not standing up for himself, not being a man and not hitting Kenneth back.

'You owe me, right, owe me big time,' Collins shakes his head. 'Best you stay with me in Sierra One for the rest of the shift I reckon. You too Higgy.'

Throughout the remainder of the shift, including several more stop and searches, Andrew is restricted to the passenger seat. Replaying what happened over and over, he can't stop thinking about it and finds himself melancholic, questioning why he even wants to be a copper in the first place. He knows he's ruined any chance of getting into C.I.D, at least for the foreseeable future.

Later, at the Station, Collins will check whether a complaint has been made and, if so, will scribble down some notes in his notebook to cover himself. If there's no complaint, he'll forget about it, apart from Andrew owing him one, good coppers never forget a favour. Either way though, first thing Monday morning he'll call Smithy at Hendon to tell him about Andrew and his temper. In the meantime, he'll continue to count the days and hours until his retirement.

# Episode 10.
# "Estate"

Thursday 12 February, 8:52am
Saint Saviours Secondary School
Herne Hill, London

'Have you heard, have you heard?'
'What'am-man, calmness yeah.'
'I saw him.'
'Who?'
'This morning, I'm telling you, I saw him…'
'Who?' Marlon screws, growing impatient.
'The fucking wanker.'
'Who man, who!'
'The man like Yellowman.'
'Yellowman?' Marlon looks sideways, concern scribbling a path across his frowning forehead. 'You okay?'
'Yeah, nothing to worry about,' Ashley lies, he's not about to tell his best mate what really happened. 'Anyhow, Yellowman reckons Junior's coming down here on Friday after school, for a straightener.'
'A straightener?'
'Yeah, reckons you're gonna get mash-up.'
'T'cha, he can't test me,' Marlon says, puffing out his chest having no choice but to big himself up. 'Man on man he knows I'll smash him up.'
Ashley smiles, taking courage from his friends confidence,

unlike when he saw Yellowman earlier on in the day…

After his breakfast of porridge and fresh orange juice, Ashley sits on the top deck of the bus heading north from Dulwich to Saint Saviours Secondary School in Hearne Hill. Occupying his usual position at the back, left of the spiral stairs leading up from the open platform, he watches the world go by as they trundle along. The warmth of the bus makes the windows mist, so he wipes away the fresh condensation with his sleeve. Gazing at nothing in particular, his eyes suddenly zoom into focus. Oh no, it can't be? Panic shivers through him as the bus slows to a stop. He counts the footsteps slowly coming up the stairs to the opening bars of Jeff Waynes War of the Worlds his Dad made him listen to only a few weeks ago …

*"Dum-dum-dummmmm… da-da-dah, da-da-dah."*

Then, he sees him.

Yellowman.

He stares into Yellowmans bloodshot and yellowy at the edge eyes. What the fuck is he doing over here, this far from Peckham and this early in the morning, Ashley thinks. With his father from the States or the Caribbean or Mexico or somewhere and his mother the Far East, Yellowman looks decidedly odd. Infamous for his use of so-called martial arts including self-taught kicks perfected by watching hours of Bruce Lee movies and, Yellowman more often than not uses any type of weaponry he can lay his hands on. Stomach churning, Ashley feels the soles of his feet tingle as the haunting voice of Richard Burton narrates his life…

*"Early in the nineteen-eighties, little did he believe he was being watched, studied, observed through a microscope like a small insignificant creature…"*

'Watcha, Yella,' he says, hoping a friendly, direct approach is better than sliding down his seat and trying to hide.

'Ah, Ash-lee-da-fairy-boy,' Yellowman says, almost singing a warped nursery rhyme, slowly and deliberately, aggression ripping through his voice.

Sitting sideways on in the seat in front, Yellowman slides

his right arm over the back and strokes Ashleys leg. Staring in silence, he watches Ashley squirm. 'So, batty-man,' he eventually breaks the silence before scanning the top deck, sparsely filled with only a couple of school kids and a middle-aged bloke. 'Me-nah see your ugly face from time.'

'Been busy, yeah.' This is nice and civil, a bit of small-talky chit-chat is fine, nothing to worry about Ashley thinks.

'So anyways, how's your bum-chum boy-friend, recovering from his bruising? He took some licks yah-naw,' Yellowman chuckles, over exaggerating his patois.

How do I answer that, he thinks. This close, Yellowman seems even weirder than usual, more fucked up and definitely more crazy. Short afro, almost pubic hair with a ginger shimmer, he has slitty eyes and thin lips with a light skin tone with speckled freckles across his distinct roman looking nose. With his front-teeth off-centre, broken with sharp with angled edges, he has a look of a piranha or shark or something.

'Yo, I'm fucking chatting to you, bwai,' Yellowman grunts, seemingly in no mood for daydreaming. 'So?' he prompts, raising his voice.

'So, what?'

'Your bloodclat girlfriend?'

'Marlon?'

'Yes Marlon, you fucking pussyclat'

'He's okay I suppose, some bumps and grazes.'

'Took his beating like a little girl yah-naw.'

Yellowman, Junior and half a dozen youths from the North Peckham Estate waited outside the Community Centre late on a Friday night a few weeks ago and jumped Marlon, kicking the shit out of him. Ashley and the others rushed out of the hall and, a short gang fight later, the Peckham lot ran off leaving Marlon with a bloody nose and a huge black eye, not to mention cracked ribs and a massive bruise down his right leg where they took turns laying into him.

'I'm sure you all gave him a real pasting.'

SMASH.

Swinging his right hand toward his face, Yellowman lands a slapping backhand. Head bouncing off the window, he hears the slap just before feeling the stinging pain. Stars spin before his brain catches up with his nervous system.

'Don't tess-me tinker-fucking-bell, or I'll wet yah-rasclat face,' Yellowman growls, leaning forward while pulling his coat open to reveal a leather-bound handle. 'Dis-a ten-inch chiv yah-naw, it'll gash in your fucking batty-clat.' Grabbing his face between his thumb and index finger, Yellowman squeezes his mouth open like a dead fish, before moving his head closer. Feeling the warmth of his breath, Ashley can smell the unmistakable smell of stale weed. 'Here me now yah-dutty-batty-bwai, tell yah girlfriend we'll be down on Friday night watching dah-man like Junior sort out shit for brains out once and for all,' his words are slow and deliberate and menacing.

Ashley feels dizzy. *"Da-da-dah, d-da-dah,"* War of the Worlds stabs spin around him as he struggles to breath. His vision forms a long dark tunnel toward Yellowmans face which zooms and spirals away from him.

'Oi, you listening to me batty-bwai?'

Eyes welling-up, at the total mercy of this over-baring crazy, he can't summon the words so just nods slowly.

Releasing him, Yellowman softly strokes his cheek. 'Now then, you be a good lickle daisy and tell Walters, yeah.' Standing, Yellowman maintains his stare before disappearing down the stairs.

Squeezes his eyes together, Ashley shakes his head…

The bus fades into the distance and he's transported back to the here and now and School. 'True-say Marlon, the idiot fool can't touch you mate, you'll smash him up.'

'T'cha, of course I will, he's a fucking fool thinking he can come round here and take me on one on one,' Marlon scowls, gaining confidence from his friends belief. Deep down inside though, he feels quite the opposite.

Thursday, 12 February, 9:42pm
North Peckham Estate
Peckham, London

With around sixty, eight story blocks linked together with criss-crossing elevated walkways, the North Peckham Estate houses twenty thousand or so inhabitants. A sprawling labyrinth of urine filled stairwells and crumbling graffiti-covered concrete walkways, the estate is notorious for low life scum, skinheads, anarchists and heroin addicts. Millwall-racist-fuck-you-up country around here, Marlon thinks, extending his stride while dipping his head so that he won't be spotted. Nervous and on edge, the vibe around here is off-key with a collage of reggae, ska and punk sounds emanating from behind the dirty net curtain windows, adding to the weirdness. Progressing deeper into the estate, the Wurlitzer organ sounds from "Skinhead Moonstomp" echo around the concrete walls and babies can be heard crying through open windows while young kids whistle in code to each other from different sides of the estate. Feeling the freezing night biting into his chest, he zips his leather bomber jacket and pulls his woollen hat down to cover the top of his tingling ears.

Passing under the high-level walkways, in and out of the car parks outside each high rise, eventually he finds Saint Helena House. A carbon copy of the other blocks, the only difference is the four feet high lettering above the double doorway to the lift lobby. The doorway to the lift lobby is fire-damaged and a single door hangs on by the hinges, with a gap where the other door once stood. Staring through to dimly lit graffiti covered walls and smashed out windows, he shakes his head, this shithole makes Brixton look decidedly posh, well, at least not that bad anyway. It's dark, with only one of the two plastic covered strip-lights working, sparking on and off intermittently, plus, the place stinks of vintage piss. In between the aged layers of graffiti, he can make out a giant 'A' with a circle around sprayed in black on the dented lift door. Looking around, he nods to himself, yeah, definitely a place Junior, his evil and very ugly nemesis, would live.

Back outside, he looks around for a tool. Although confident he can handle Junior in a fist fight, he's strong and a good fighter, and, more than likely will have a tool himself. Scavenging around the back of the block, he finds a sturdy stick, maybe three feet long. He gives the air in front of him a few whacks hooligan style before weighing it up. Nah, this won't do, too light, too fragile. Around to the front of the block he pulls open the freezing cold steel doors leading to the bin room where tall metal bins collect communal rubbish falling from the waste-chutes above. Looking around, he spots an old bit of pipe with a bolted t-joint at the end. Grabbing it, a cold shiver runs down his spine as the gravity of what he's about to do weighs on his mind. Slapping it into his hand a couple of times, he swings it through the air back and forth. Feels good, weightier, harder, colder, meaner, angrier, scarier.

Perfect.

Back to the lobby.

A few swings above his head and the single semi-working light smashes, showering splitters of glass around his feet. With that, darkness fills the room while a dim glow from the streetlights outside warms the edges of the doorway. He places the pipe in the darkest corner, just in case. 'Right then', he says out loud walking back outside. 'Where the fuck can he be?' No way Junior will be at home this time of night, nah, he'll be out juggling with his wanker mates or checking out some dirty Peckham slags. So, where would a dickhead like him be, he asks himself. Yeah, that's it, the off-licence, getting pissed on cheap lager.

Heading back out of the estate the way he came, he makes his way to the Commercial Road and a row of shops. Suddenly, he sees the silhouette of a group of youths standing at the entrance to the estate. No fucking way, he whispers, diving behind a rusted-to-fuck Transit Van. He recognises the porkpie hat of Stevie Gentle, Juniors right-hand man and, given his tendency for hardcore violence, the living embodiment of irony. Scanning left, he sees the ugly as fuck profile of Yellowman acting out a series of crap kicks and punches, no doubt sharing tall stories of his most recent victory or what he hopes to do to us on Friday, the fucking fool. Edging his head further around the front wing, he spots him, no mistake, it's him, the motherfucker named Junior. Damn, all of them together is bad news, no way he can take on all three.

Crouching his way back to the lobby, he dodges in between the parked cars and waits at the corner of Saint Helena House. Positioning himself between the corner of the block and the bushes out back, just outside the glare of the streetlight above, he waits, and waits, and fucking waits. What the fuck are they talking about he wonders, probably planning my demise, the idiots. Suddenly, he's aware of a presence behind him. Shit. Swinging around he's faced with a collage of leather jackets, crap hair styles, safety pins. God damn punks, two of them, arm in arm and quite obviously pissed-up-drunk weaving their way toward the lobby. The stupid fucks don't even notice the six-foot-tall rude-boy standing suspiciously in the shadows right in front of them.

Entering the lobby, the taller one, presumably male, bangs the lift button several times before sharing a kiss with the smaller, presumably female. Seemingly lost in the lingering kiss, the man-punk unzips the skin-tight jeans of the girl-punk and slides his hand inside. Not in the fucking lift lobby you dirty bastards, he says to himself. A couple of seconds and a few moans and groans later, the lift doors grind open and, still entwined, the couple enter.

Then…

SMASH.

Head crunching into concrete, he and Saint Helena House become one and red-hot pain sears through his neck and into his shoulder. Crazy-mad confused thoughts rip through his mind, the fucking Punks, how could I have been so stupid! A boot explodes into his back, kicking the wind out of his lungs. Gasping for air, he tumbles to the floor before rolling, and looking up at his attacker.

Junior.

Face screwed-up, pure hate laser-beams from his eyes direct into Marlons brain. Jumping through the air, he lands the heel of his red snake-skin slip-ons into Marlons groin. Knees toward stomach, he hears himself groan.

'Round my gates, try and trick me?' Junior yells, spit flying from his ugly mouth.

Get-up-Marlon-get-up-nah-man, face this fucking cunt he says to himself, before kicking out wildly catching Juniors knee, forcing him to stumble back. Using the wall and his right shoulder, he gets up on one knee but, before he can stand, Junior steams back in, landing a strong right hook to his rib cage followed by a left hook into the side of his head. Left arm out, he hooks Juniors leg in an attempt to pull him over. Junior responds by landing a series of strong punches into his lower back. Reaching out for something, anything, he finds Juniors groin. Squeezing hard, his forearm aches with the tightness of his grip as Junior groans deeply. 'You like that yeah,' he yells, yanking harder.

Junior stumbles back, holding his balls, his skinny frame bent-over in the foetal position.

Marlon gets to his feet. Yeah man, I'm up, he says to himself, now we can have it. He feels a cold wetness flow down the back of his neck, must have been cut by the dirty-snake of a cheap shot from behind. 'Let's have it then,' he says slowly, squaring up like an old-time bare-knuckle pugilist. 'Me and you Junior, one on one.'

'You cant test me,' Junior whispers. 'You just a fookin' ugly bitch.'

'Like your Momma then, dickhead.'

'Come-nah,' Junior screams, standing upright, charging forward throwing windmill punches.

Moving quickly, Marlon dodges to the left, shuffles his feet before connecting with a strong left hook counter.

Momentum and the lightning quick punch forces Junior to stumble forward toward the lobby. Hitting the step, he tumbles to the ground.

'Yeah man, there's plenty more of that,' Marlon smiles, bouncing on his toes Apollo Creed style.

Junior gets to a knee, then stands up slowly. 'I fuckin' tripped,' he says, forehead down.

Pouncing forward, Marlon flashes a left jab then right cross and, both stumbling, Junior kicks out a long leg connecting with Marlons groin before he lands on his back just inside the lobby.

Falling to his knees, Marlon cradles his swelling balls. Squeezing his eyes together to block out the pain, adrenalin surges and his heart rate jumps.

BOOM.

Back to his feet, Junior aims a kick into the side of his head. A lightning bolt strikes as Big-Ben ding-dongs inside his skull. Knees crumpling, he rolls onto the cold wet floor. World spinning, he tries to move, but can't.

'You nuttin but a dutty-wretch,' Junior seethes, accentuating every word as he kneels-down, grabbing his throat.

Panic surging, this isn't going to plan, not by a long shot. He's made a big mistake, a fucking huge one and now the Peckham-pussy-hole is on top, literally.

Straddling him, Junior lands a head-butt into his face and the back of his head bounces off the tiled floor. Eyes rolling, he wants to sleep, forget and float off to safer times...

Yeah man, he's back at home, warm and tucked up in bed, Momma calling him from the foot of the stairs, telling him to get up as breakfast is ready.

Helpless, he knows he's drifting into unconsciousness.

'Should have sorted you out when all this first started,' Junior whispers. 'T'cha-look at yah-nah... I thought you were better dan-dis,' he seethes, pushing his forehead further into Marlons face, forcing the back of his head deeper into the cold urine-stained concrete floor.

'Please,' Marlon whispers, struggling for breath.

Junior laughs. 'Please, you idiot-joker, dis is the end, Marl-on from Brixt-on.'

Eyes narrowing, his surroundings fade into darkness as Juniors face zooms away, further down a long dark tunnel. He's got to do something, anything. Lifting his head from the floor he knows he has to resist and somehow fight back. He pushes his forehead against Juniors. Mouth open, he bites hard, then even harder. Trying to pull away, Junior lets out a deep, painful scream. Biting hard, Marlon feels his jaw muscles spasm as thick, warm blood rushes into his mouth. Biting even harder, he hears a crunch as his teeth meet and Juniors screams reach a prehistoric un-godly crescendo.

Pushing Junior off, he spits out whatever's in his mouth before rolling to his knees. On all fours his hands scramble toward the corner, and he finds what he's looking for. 'The end for me?' he yells above Juniors screams as his eyes adjust to the darkness. Dark thoughts filling his mind, he feels dirty, sinister and evil. A shiver runs down his spine as he morphs into a cold, calculating death-bringer, an orphan-maker, a fucking bad-man killer. 'Nah-man-nah, this is the end for you son, you're fucking dead dred.' Marlons words are slow, lazy and drawn out.

As Juniors screams turn into wails, groans and eventually whimpers, Marlon stands over him. Raising the pipe above his head executioner style…

He pauses.

Life will never be the same.

But, fuck it.

This pussy has it coming.

SMASH.

Connecting with Juniors skull, an unforgettable choral chime rings out throughout the lobby, eventually reverberating into silence. The room's still and dark now, and Marlon is frozen to the spot. As an icy frost descends, he can see his breath hanging in the air and hear his own heartbeat. Shivering, head pounding, he feels tired, dizzy and confused. What now? He can finish him off right here right now, put him out of his misery and end this entire saga with one more strike. Nobody knows he's here, who would know? He could do it, kill the motherfucker right now, end it once and for all.

Breathing in, he looks out of the lobby and spots his woollen hat on the floor near the concrete wall.

Thoughts dart to Momma, and then Pops.

Devon too.

Kill him?

Become a killer?

All he wanted was a straightener, sort the problems out once and for all. He don't want any of this, never even wanted a rumble in the first place to be honest.

He stares at the lifeless body on the cold lobby floor, all still and silent. Shit. Panic surges, maybe he's already dead, maybe I'm already a stone-cold killer. Turning, he heads out of the lobby, grabs his hat and starts running. Turning left toward the car park, he launches the pipe into the bushes in the distance. Sprinting full pelt now, he hears screams and shouts echoing through the estate. Fuck, the body's been found, Babylon soon come. He can see it now…

Police manhunt…

Posters with his photofit picture…

Rewards for information received…

Momma crying…

Interviewed on the evening news…

Such a good, god fearing boy…

Attend church every week without fail…

Studying for is exams at school…

A good student, popular too…

Please son, give yah-sef up nah…

But, maybe it's Junior who's screaming.

Maybe he's not dead afterall…

Maybe he's on his feet, screaming, screaming mad…

Maybe he's chasing right behind…

Maybe he's found the pipe…

Maybe I'm going to get done…
Maybe he'll kill me…
Yeah man, that's it.
He won't stop, like what I did…
He won't pause to think, like what I did…
He won't flinch, like what I did…
He won't see reason, like what I did…
Nah, he'll kill me for sure…

Stopping abruptly, he gingerly feels the gash on his head. A stream of sweat and blood runs down his face, merging with his tears. No screams now, no Junior chasing. Tripping out, his mind's confused with a thousand random thoughts. Fucking hell, supposing Junior is actually dead though? Maybe I should go back, he might be laid out bleeding, near to death or something? I could save him, save me, but, he might actually be dead though. Yeah, returning to the scene of the crime is dangerous…

Might get me arrested…
Sent down for life…
Double life, never get out life…
Fucked in the showers by racist skinheads life…
Bed-sheet round neck suicide life…
Razor blade up the forearm life…
Fuck.

Sprinting now, faster and faster.

The shadows of the estate quickly evaporate into the stark street-light-reality of Commercial Road. He's suddenly aware of himself, an urban youth running at pace around the wrong side of Peckham with blood smeared across his head. He slows down to a jog, then a walk. Wiping his face with his sleeve he pulls his hat on to cover the gash, and heads for the taxi office mid-way down the row of shops next to the off-license.

'Can I get a taxi please?'

Studying the horoscopes in the newspaper, the overweight middle-aged women with greasy brown hair doesn't look up. 'Where to?' she grunts.

'Brixton, how long?'

'Nah, don't do Brixton mate.'

'Just wanna get home,' his voice trembles.

Looking up, she peers through the perspex security screen. 'Look mate, we-don't-do-Brixton,' she stresses every word, just in case he doesn't understand English.

Marlons face falls as more tears track down his face.

'Best we can do is Stockwell, abart ten minutes.'

Looking back through the door toward the estate in the distance, it's dark and black and bleak, just like him. Fuck it, Stockwell will do, I'll walk from there. He turns back and nods. 'Stockwell, yeah thanks.'

Twenty five minutes later…

The clapped-out Ford Cortina passes the Oval Cricket Ground. Head pounding, he looks around in all directions, anywhere to avoid eye contact with the driver. The old overweight fat guy stares at him through the rear-view mirror. 'Bit of trouble tonight then son?' he asks.

Holding back the tears, he nods. He's not about to tell him he's just killed someone, nah, the Police will be round to Mommas quick-time.

Thoughts racing, maybe he can do a runner, leave Brixton and go to his aunties in Tottenham, maybe his cousin in Birmingham, abroad even. What would he do though, no cash, no qualifications or any idea about anywhere other than Brixton.

Besides, he can't run forever.

It's only a matter of time.

# Episode 11.
# "Yard-Man"

Friday 13 February, 7:10am
47 Saltoun Road,
Brixton, London

Knock, knock.
No answer.
Knock, knock-knock, knock.
'Devon, ged-up-nah. Marlon, yah-awake-bwai?'
No answer.
Bang, bang, bang.
'Hey-hey-hey idle-pickney, ged-up-nah.'

Momma is the morning alarm clock. Up an hour before everyone else, she prepares the usual full English breakfast for Pops before he leaves at five-thirty then, around seven, she'll try and rouse the boys before getting their breakfasts too. After that, she'll clean the house top to bottom, paying special attention to the guest room at the front of the house, the one nobody is allowed to enter, unless guests are present. After that, she'll make her way to the hospital to start her shift at ten a.m, getting back home at about seven-thirty in the evening.

'Marlon, get yah-uniform on and don't forget yah-tie.'

Every morning the same, a soft, gentle knock to begin with, then multiple knocks and calls, each getting louder and heavier. On the odd occasion when they refuse to get up promptly, the over-sleeping offender will receive a swift clap around the head.

'We up,' Marlon yells, pulling the pillow over his head.

Flinging back the yellow, blue and pink striped cotton sheet and itchy chocolate-brown blankets, Devon swings his legs out, stands and stretches toward the high ceiling. 'Ged-up nah-man,' he sighs, kicking Marlons bed on the way out to the landing, and then the toilet. 'Otherwise-she be up here quick time.'

'T'cha, I'm up man, I'm up,' Marlon yawns, annoyed.

A minute later, Devon returns, stopping at the mirror on the wardrobe door to admire his highly developed chest and six-pack. Smiling, he nods to himself.

Sitting up, Marlon pulls his sheets up around him.

Catching a glimpse of his little brothers bruised body through the mirror Devon swings around, eyes zoning in on the dark red scab on his head. 'What der fucks dat?'

'What?'

'The blood on your pillow for a start,' Devon tuts. 'Not to mention the gash and bumps and ting.'

'Nuttin-man, leave it.'

'Listen, dey no ruck-in-the-park bumps,' Devon whispers, moving his head to get a better look. Rumbles are one thing, part and parcel of growing up, but heavy-duty damage such as this is something far more concerning.

Marlon pulls his pillow around and looks at the large, red stain in the centre before gently touching the bloodied scab on his head. His whole-body aches as images of what happened last night flood through his mind.

'So?' Devon perches on the edge of his bed.

'So-nothing, man, just a rumble.'

'A rumble?'

'A pussy-hole from Peckham, everything's cool.' Although he appreciates his brothers concern, he's not ready to tell him what really happened.

'You got to be careful yeah, Babylon looking to test us now more than ever… we don't need no troubles around here.' Devon looks deep into his eyes. 'You understand?'

'T'cha, don't break me-heart-nah,' Marlon looks away.

'Right, get that cleaned up and put your pillowcase in the wash before Momma catches sight.'

Feeling a warm glow rising, Marlon nods.

'Listen,' Devon continues. 'If you can't deal with this you tell me yeah, dem Peckham fools can't be trusted. Me and Super will sort it out, you understand what I'm saying?'

Fifteen minutes later…

At the kitchen table, after a lengthy inquisition from Momma about where the cuts and bruises came from, Devon swigs the remains of his cup of tea as Marlon mops up the remaining beans in tomato sauce with a final slice of toast. They both kiss Momma goodbye before heading through the front door.

Outside, their breath hangs in the cold South London air. With the darkness of the night giving way to the brightness of the early morning late winter sun, wispy fog skews the sight of the shops at the end of the Road. Turning left, then left again, they walk along Atlantic Road before Marlon stops at the bus stop for his ride to Saint Saviours School. 'Laters Dev," he shouts.

'Remember what I said yeah,' Devon yells, continuing towards Coldharbour Lane and the scrap yard.

Friday 13 February, 8:02am
The Scrap Yard, Coldharbour Lane
Brixton, London

Located between a row of town houses on the left and a shops on the right and backing on to railway arches, the entrance is through two metal fences painted blue, with coils of barbed wire around the top. Resembling a high security compound, in reality, it houses nothing more than near-worthless half rotten scrapped cars and a man-made mountain of part worn tyres. A pathway the width of a large car has been chiselled through the oil and mud-covered ground, from the entrance gates to the Portakabin at the far side on the left.

Devon has a love-hate relationship with the scrap yard. He hates the oil, muck and especially the wide-boy cockney clientele who nearly always refer to him as "boy". His boss though, Neville, from Birmingham or Debry or somewhere up North, is okay, plus, it's steady work and the pay's sort of okay, and, working here is better than being a professional full time rude-boy-juggler on the Frontline. Nearly all his friends, like Super, have never worked since leaving school. Super argues he doesn't need to work in a shit job for shit money with shit people doing shit things, instead, he'll take his chances on the Frontline.

Getting close, Devon notices the fifteen-foot-high iron gates are already open. They're never open at eight in the morning, nah, Devon usually has to open up and get the kettle on and tea brewing before Neville rolls in some time after. Through the gates then across the yard, he spots Neville covered head to toe in oil with his head deep under the bonnet of an old Rover. His overalls are tied around his bulging waist and hairy arse-crack is hanging out. 'Ey-up, lovely morning eh?' Neville shouts in his normal overly jolly way. 'Put kettle on me-duck.'

Devon sees Neville is a mad puzzle. Covered in shit all day every day, in a shitty mud-hole in shitty Brixton, yet, he's always so full of life and jovial, apparently happy with his lot.

'Come on lado,' Neville shouts. 'Look lively eh, I'm going boz-eyed here, me mouths as dry as a nuns fanny.'

Shaking his head, Devon enters the porta-cabin-come-office containing a desk, couple of flea-bitten chairs, a small sink, fridge and kettle and a Calor-Gas heater that's always on full blast, even in summer. Filling the kettle, he flicks the switch before warming his hands near the heater. Smiling, his mind wanders as thoughts drift to Shirley. Things are good with her, she makes him smile and the sex is good, great actually and life, for once, is sweet.

'Ew-eck', nice cup of tea to start the day, eh?' Neville

chuckles as his dips through the door, furiously rubbing his hands together. 'Looking forward to the weekend, Dev?'

'Eh?'

'You know, out on the town, chasing the skirt?'

Devon just stares.

'You know, fah-ney.'

'What?'

'Snatch, clute, gash, you know… birds, tarts, treacles, fanny, skirt… you know, how do you say it, pun-ting?'

'Pun-ting? You're a funny guy Nev,' he smiles, appreciating Nevilles attempt at connecting with him. 'So anyway, what we got on today?'

'Got another Rover coming in soon enough, that'll need stripping down and once that's done, make a start on them tyres over yonder.'

Good, Devon thinks, being busy makes the time go faster. He can't wait to knock off and go see Shirley.

Just after ten o'clock, as Neville predicted, the Rover arrives driven by a fat middle aged guy who, as soon as he parks up, looks daggers at Devon.

'Easy-nah man,' Devon shouts in an over-elaborate mock accent, just to wind him up.

Giving him a sideways look, the fat guy makes his way to the cabin mouthing what looks like to be "fucking bastard." Expecting something like that, Devon smiles.

Five minutes later…

Shadowed by the fatty, Neville comes out pointing at the Rover. 'Devon me-duck, make a start on that while I drop Eddie home will you?'

Grinning, Devon gives him a sarcastic double thumbs up and broad false grin.

Neville waves back before climbing into his eleven-year-old, dent ridden Jaguar. The suspension creaks before the large engine chokes to life with a plume of dark grey smoke coughing from the double twin exhausts. Wheels spinning, mud and oil is launched into the air as they speed off.

Devon knows he's unlikely to see Neville again until mid-afternoon, when he'll come back half-pissed after a liquid lunch in a local pub with the fat racist. Not to worry, it's cool, he has the run of the place, just as he likes it. He'll make a start on the Rover, taking the wheels off then the doors, have lunch, then embark on the engine.

Couple of hours later…

'Easy-nah dutty-man,' Super nods, tip-toeing passed Devon through the puddles of oily mud toward the cabin. Devon follows and they huddle around the heater.

'Dutty-man?'

'Yeah man, you fookin' covered head to toe in shit.'

'Listen, I'm grafting a living, you unlike you, yah-front-line-rude-boy-lay-about-bombaclat-idiot-fool.'

'Jokes-star, jokes. Cold today though, fucking freezing dred,' Super rubs his hands together over the heater.

'True-say, can't even feel my feet yah-naw,' Devon agrees, stamping his feet

'Goodness, yeah?'

'Of course,' Devon nods. 'Skin up nah-man.'

Pulling out five Rizzla Super nods to the sink. 'Do the honours-star, stick the kettle on then.'

That's all I ever do, Devon thinks, flicking the kettle on, make tea for fucking fools.

Two minutes later…

Warming their hands around mugs of tea, they share the five-skin joint.

'Listen-star, I forgot.'

'Forgot what?'

'Me got something for you yah-naw,' Super nods.

'Wha-gwan rudie.'

'Just a lickle something, to show my appreciation, I know you gonna-like it.'

'For me,' Devon smiles. 'You shouldn't have.'

'My little treat bro,' Super smiles back. 'It's my pleasure.'

'I like the sound of that bread-bin, what is it then?'

'You really wanna-see it?'

'Yesh-star, if it's what I think it is, bring it on yeah.'

'Alright sexy, me gonna give you it good yeah.'

'You such a tease Super, just give it me big-time.'

Reaching into his jacket, Super pulls out a paper bag containing three spicy meat patties with a yellow crust. Opening the bag and sniffing inside with a smile, he reaches in and gives one to Devon.

'T'cha,' Devon scowls. 'A patty, that's it, man, there's me thinking about your donkey dick.'

'Ha-ha, funny rude-boy, you'd be lucky.'

They both laugh before biting into their patties.

'So anyway, wha-gwan rude-boy?' Super quizzes.

'Thinking about Shirley earlier, and the fire too,' Devon says, chewing slowly on the tough but tasty pastry.

'Yesh-star, those girls are fine,' Super nods slowly. 'I hear Babylon pay the Fronters to petrol bomb the party.'

'Is that what you hear, shit man.'

'Erm-hummm,' Super nods, taking another bite.

'The world's getting dark, enough sus-stops and beatings and ting, even Marlon got bust-up last night.'

'Marlon, he okay?' Super's tone is serious, he sees Marlon as the baby brother he never had.

'Gash on his head and some bumps, says he mash up a Peckham idiot fool even worse-doh.'

'Peckham?' Super sits forward. 'Enough tribulation down dem parts yah-naw, dey got little time for us 'line-man.'

'True say, true,' Devon agrees with a vacant tone. 'We got to watch dat shit before it gets out of hand for real.'

Then.

Bring, Bring.

What the fuck?

Devon looks at Super, who shrugs. They both look around trying to locate the source of this weird sound.

Bring, Bring.

Their eyes lock onto the fridge and the several volumes of the Yellow-Pages on top. On top of these, a dirty cream telephone with the handset sitting horizontally across the top with a ring of numbers below.

Bring, Bring.

'What the fuck?' Super quizzes.

Devon tentatively picks up the receiver. 'Hello… err, Coldharbour Scrap Yard,' he says, using his most polite accent while shrugging his shoulders toward Super, who's falling back in his chair laughing. Listening to the one-sided conversation, he prepares another five-skin.

'In three years, that's the first time I ever answer that,' Devon places the receiver down. 'Didn't know it worked.'

'Coldharbour Scrap Yard? You a secretary now-star,' Super goads. 'Hmm-yesh, damn sexy too, dutty-as fuck I imagine.'

'Stop staring at my arse, batty-man.'

'Star, you call that an arse?' Super stands up and twists his body so that he can see his behind. 'Now, this is an arse.'

'You even know what you're saying brother?'

'What?' Super smiles, shrugging his shoulders.

'Idiot-fool,' Devon shakes his head. 'Anyhow, it's Paul yeah, asking if we're up for a party at a wine bar tonight, meet some of his work mates and some high-class girls.'

'How he get dis number?'

'Fuck knows, him clever-doh,' Devon nods.

'High class action, I'm der already,' Super says, presenting a perfectly built five-skin to the heavens.

An hour or so later…

As expected, after an extended lunch, Neville returns, even more cheerful than normal, swaying from side to side. Often, after an afternoon in the pub he'll become overly friendly, telling Devon about how much he likes working with him, and that he doesn't have many friends.

'Ah, Whin-stone me-ol-mucker,' Neville sings, reaching out to embrace.

'Nev, mate, how's it going,' Super says, extending his hand for a shake, rather than a hug.

'Super's just going, aren't you?' Devon interjects.

'Nah-man-nah. I'll just hang out here, that okay Nev?'

'Of course it is Whin-stone, stay as long as you like,' Neville beams.

'Nah, he's off now,' Devon asserts. 'Aren't you rudie.'
'Ah, that's my boy Devon, such a professional.'
'Professional?' Super looks sideways.
'Yes professional, nah fuck-arf dickhead, I'll see you later yeah,' Devon smiles.

Friday, 13 February, 6:12pm
London Underground Station
Brixton, London

Bowling along, they look like two male models heading down the catwalk at a high-class fashion show…
On our right, we have the devilishly handsome Devon looking sharp in a dark blue suit, tight trousers and a crisp white shirt with his top two buttons buttoned. Rather than a tie, he opts for the obligatory thick gold chain hanging around the outside of his shirt. Finishing his look, he's rocking a glistening set of dark red crocodile skin slip-on shoes.
To our left, the rugged Superman-Super from South London. Today he's sporting a looser fitting brown suit with an electric blue silk shirt. Rather daringly, he elects to unbutton it down to mid-chest, showing off his manly muscles, oh, he's so brave and strong, if you've got them, flaunt them darling! Completing the ensemble, a light brown velvet stingy-brim trilby with a dark brown band…
'Look at you, prancing around like a fairy,' Devon smiles.
'Me, look at you with the Miss World swagger.'
After a five second debate about getting a ticket versus the potential for being stopped by Babylon for fare-evasion, Devon hands a pound note to the bored looking middle-aged guy sitting through the ticket office window. At this time of day tube-trains going into London are empty ghost trains, whereas those coming out to the suburbs are jam packed with commuters, pick pockets and the odd tramp trying to keep warm. Devon counts the six stations to Oxford Circus where they'll change to the Central Line. 'Be

about forty minutes I reckon,' he sighs.

'T'cha, can't wait for tonight-star, all those prim and proper city-girls wanting a dutty ghetto-sexing,' Super nods, allowing himself to break into a cunning smile.

Fifteen minutes later…

The train slows along the platform as it enters Oxford Circus station. 'This is us,' Devon nods.

'Beasts,' Super whispers, spotting three uniformed Officers mid-way down the platform.

Too late to turn back, sure sign of guilt, so Devon slows down to buy some time. 'I'm clean man, you carrying?'

'Smoked it earlier-star,' Super smiles, adding a little more bounce to his sway. 'We cool yeah.'

'What about your steel?'

'Cool-nah-star, me baby safely tucked up at home.'

Spotting the two super-cool catwalk models, the Officers spread shoulder to shoulder across the platform. 'Evening fellas,' the middle Officer smiles, stepping further into the platform.

'Evening Constable,' Devon nods, moving passed.

'Where're you off to tonight fellas?' the middle Officer says, placing his hand into Devons chest.

Both absolutely clean, no herbs and no steel, there's no reason to be stopped, Super is vexed. 'Star, we fookin' law abiding yeah,' he frowns. 'Off to meet our colleague in the City for some wine and women-yesh.'

'Colleague?' Devon looks sideways.

'Mugging you mean…' the Officer to the left raises his nose toward the two-stereotypical pimp-looking blokes, giving them the visual once over.

'Fook-arf mugging…'

'Don't break our hearts now,' Devon interjects, instinctively moving to the wall putting his hands up at head height. 'Get this over with so we can be on our way.'

The Officers look at each other, confused. They had hoped to administer a thorough goading leading to an arrest for breach of the peace or some other made up charge.

‘Nobody said anything about a search, feeling guilty?’

‘Just get on with it, Beast,’ Super says, following Devons lead and placing his palms on the cold tiled wall.

Quick frisk and details taken, they’re told to be on their way, so follow the signs to the Central Line.

‘You got to calm it down, man,’ Devon says, putting his arm around Supers shoulder. ‘You giving them grief all the time and bigging it up is no good you know.’

‘What?’ Super shrugs his arm off.

‘Listen, all you do is make them plant some shit on you or something,’ Devon continues. ‘Best case you in chains, worst case you getting a beating then in chains same-way.’

‘What you on about-star, fuck dem cunts,’ Super shrugs him off before marching ahead.

Friday, 13 February, 7:10pm
Florentines Wine Bar
Ludgate Hill, City of London

Exiting the station, they head through a large communal square with St Pauls Cathedral on their left and tall building flanking the right. They walk for a few minutes through the narrow City of London lanes, dodging the city-workers, who, in turn, dodge them and avoid eye contact. Very quickly they realise they’re completely lost, so Devon stops a street vendor selling late editions of the Evening Standard and asks directions.

Five minutes later…

‘Fookin’ hell-star, it’s rammed, some tidy birds though,’ Super says, peaking through the window.

Sitting at the far side of the bar, Paul spots them and waves them in. He’s sitting in the middle of two attractive girls, a blonde and brunette, along with a couple of city-slicker guys.

‘Dev, Winston, you’ve made it,’ he greets them, struggling to be heard over the dulcet tones of Sister Sledge. ‘What do you want to drink guys?’

Super squints. 'Winston?'

Devon looks sideways. 'Guys?'

Paul smiles, shrugs and throws them a wink.

'Red Stripe, or dark rum,' Super smiles.

'Nah-nah, mate, no beer in here, it's wine yeah,' Paul blushes. 'I'll get you a Chardonnay.' Turning to the bar, he waves a ten-pound note toward the bartender.

'Shardon-what?' Devon shrugs.

'Sharon-who?' Super plays along with a grin.

A couple of bottles of "sharon-aid" later…

The wine proves to be both tasty and potent. Super sits next to Andrea, the tidy blonde, and is busy twirling her curly hair around his fingers while telling her how pretty she is. Devon, with brunette Debbie to his left and two city slickers to the right struggles to make conversation and is thoroughly bored. All he can think about is Shirley and what's she up to right now, he wishes he was there with her, rather than in this shit-hole with these fools.

The city slicker guys, Kenneth and Geoff are "Account Managers" and are living up to their stereotypes. Loud, brash and full of themselves, both with gelled back hair, white shirts and coloured braces, and Kenneth has his initials on the double cuffs just above the cufflink. According to Geoff, him and Kenneth are trainee stock-brokers who, in a year or so, will make it onto the floor of the London Stock Exchange. When there, they will earn three times their current twenty thousand a year salary and up to ten times that in bonuses, clearing what Kenneth says is an easy half-a-mill, per year. Both of them are all over Devon, asking him question upon question about Brixton and living on the Frontline. Instinctively fearful of plain clothes Babylon, he's wary of giving too much away, however, in this feel-good-drunken state, he's happy to oblige with tales of woe, heroics and urban fables.

Much later…

The group continue quaffing more and more bottles of wine / sharon-aide while exchanging more stories, tall tales and jokes and more and more flirting. Kenneth, or Kenny as he likes to be known, doesn't seem as pissed as the others and looks to be taking charge. 'Right then, who fancies going on somewhere?' he says, standing with a wide stance, furiously rubbing his hands together. 'Devon, you up for it?'

Drunk, tired and missing Shirley, the wine has taken its toll. Devon shakes his head while his head spins.

Paul steps in, this is his party and they are his friends. 'Kenny, mate, Dev's got a big deal going down tomorrow so we better get off yeah.'

'Nah-nah-nah-nah, fucking hell, the night's young,' Kenny buzzes with excitement and a broad grin.

'Business first, you know that,' Paul gives him a wink.

'You're right,' Kenny agrees. 'Business first, all about the business yeah. What is it then, dodgy cars, puff, what?'

'Mate, come on, no need to go into details yeah.'

'Oh come on you tosser, spill the beans.'

Although drunk, Devon sees Paul struggling. 'Where's Geoff gone, and where's big-boy-Super?' he says, draping himself over Pauls shoulder while looking around the quickly emptying bar.

'Geoffs fucked off early, the light-weight,' Kenny tuts.

'Don't know where Super is, in the toilet knobbing Andrea I think,' Paul suggests, miming an exaggerated sex thrust.

Waiting outside for Super to do his thing, Kenny places himself between Paul and Devon with his arms around each shoulder. 'What a fucking blinding night, eh?'

Hailing from Canning Town in the East End, Kenny started working at Richardson International Investments about two years ago as a messenger-come-office junior. Working his way up, six months ago he gained promotion, and, although his new job title is Account Manager, he still runs clearing tickets from the floor of the stock exchange to various brokerage firms in around the City. Upwardly mobile, nowadays, he lives close by in the Barbican, an upper-class mixed-use complex built in the heart of the City of London. 'Listen,' he says, leaning in and lowering his voice. 'About this bit of business you got tomorrow…'

'What?' Devon doesn't have a clue what he's on about.

'What is it, china-white, columbian, snow?'

'Lishen man, me-nah deal with no cocaine, eye-an-eye a natural breddah-seen, shtrictly herb and ting,' Devon slurs, taking Kennys arm off his shoulder.

Eyebrows raising, Kenny looks theatrically left, then right. 'It's alright, I get it,' he winks. 'Nod-nod, wink-wink, a mate of a mate can sort me out if the price is right, right?'

'Anything's possible,' Paul says, regretting it straight away.

'Yesss, of course it is,' Kenny grins, turning and hailing a passing black cab. Grabbing Debbie by the wrist, he leads her through the back door, slapping her arse as she gets in. 'We'll sort everything out next week,' he yells, slamming the door shut.

Devon and Paul stand in silence as they watch the taxi disappear into the now deserted City of London streets before spinning back toward the bar.

'Where the fuck has Super got to?'

# Episode 12.
# "Ladies & Gentlemen"

Saturday 21 February, 8:55am
Hilton Hotel,
North Circular Road, London

A first from Cambridge and months at Police college have led to this single point in time, passing-out day. Having booked himself and Mother into a local hotel just off the North Circular Road, today, he feels increasingly tense, anxious and completely on edge. Waking before the alarm, (as he normally does), he decides a jog around grounds of the hotel including several laps of the lake might calm the nerves somewhat. After that, he'll meet Mother for a light breakfast, return to his room and dress in full ceremonial uniform, collect Mother at reception and share a taxi to meet the team at a local pub before heading to the Police Training Centre.

Thinking, thinking, always thinking.

His minds in overdrive.

Pulling on his sky-blue Adidas t-shirt, he feels a wave of panic shudder through him as he considers the prospect that Jenkins might actually follow through on what he said at the Yard a couple of weeks ago. The knot inside his stomach tightens, he hates feeling like this. Adding to his anxiety, very soon he'll be seeing Mother for the first time in nearly a year. Acid rises and his mouth waters. Breathing deeply, he closes his eyes and pulls on his dark blue Nike sneakers, colour coordinated to match his t-shirt. Even though its cold outside, he anticipates getting sweaty and still wants to look good. Damn this vanity, he says to himself.

His jog includes multiple rotations of five-minute jogging at roughly ten miles per hour, then a minute or as long as he can manage sprinting at full pace, typically fourteen miles per hour. The exhaustion and pulsing waves of adrenaline mixed with dopamine, plus the quite wonderful backdrop of the lake gives him time to put both Jenkins and Mother into perspective.

After a refreshing shower, he re-irons his already ironed uniform and hangs it back up, using his cloths brush to clean away the final few microscopic bits of lint and fluff. Slipping on a clean sweatshirt and jog-pants, he makes his way to the dining room to meet Mother, he'll change into his formal ceremonial wear afterward. Dated and tired, the hotel is surprisingly busy for a weekend. Entering the dining room, he scans the forty or so tables, each cloaked in nearly white tablecloths, uniformly set with four places including knives, forks and wine glasses, who drinks wine at breakfast, he muses with a smile. He spots Mother sitting at a table adjacent to patio doors overlooking the pleasant gardens. What on earth was I thinking, he says to himself, that's who drinks wine with breakfast!

'Yoo-hoo, John… my love,' she sings, waving him over.

Meeting him halfway, she stretches her arms out.

'Ah, my handsome son,' she cradles his face in her hands.

'Thanks for coming Mother, have you checked in?'

'Not yet, don't worry about that though, let's eat.'

John orders eggs benedict while she orders smoked salmon. He gazes into her while she pours tea. She's aged, her smile seems forced and somewhat melancholic while her once sparkling eyes have clouded a little. Regret pangs through him.

After some uncomfortable small talk, the food arrives. Johns dish turns out to be nothing more than over-done egg on toast with some form of gloopy sauce on top while Mothers salmon smells too fishy to be fresh and her "home-made" brown bread is dry and a tad stale.

'John, my love,' she says.

'Mother,' he interrupts. 'Please let's not rehash old ground, hey?' He can't tolerate an overly deep conversation today, especially not before the ceremony, and in any case, he hates sentimentality at the best of times.

'I really need you to know.'

'Please, Mother.'

'I never wanted us to fall out, not like that.'

'Not like that?' emotion cracks through his voice as he deliberately and carefully places his knife and fork down.

'John, please.'

'Not… like… that,' he whispers, exaggerating every word.

'John.'

'Best part of a year, and that's all you can muster. This, Mother dear, is typical.' Grabbing the napkin, he dabs the edge of his mouth.

'You're still my son.'

He stares blankly into her.

'Okay, I admit, I made a mistake, an…' she struggles to think of the words. 'An error of judgement.'

'Error… of… judgement?'

'I'm only human my love.'

'Well, I am too, that's exactly the point, Mother.'

'I'm so sorry,' she sobs. 'I've missed you, missed us.'

He takes her shaking hand. 'Listen, you're here now, that's all that counts,' he says, wiping her running mascara from her blushing cheeks.

Neither of them speak.

Brushing her hair over her faintly lined forehead, forcing a smile, she continues sobbing. 'I do love you,' she mouths, tears streaming.

Standing, John holds her hand. 'Come, let's get you checked in, we have to leave in thirty-five minutes.'

Saturday, 21 February, 12:36pm
Dog and Duck Public House
Hendon, London

Cheap perfume and cigarette smoke wafts through the air as mothers, wives and girlfriends along with children watch the soon to be commissioned Metropolitan Police Officers consume pint after pint and engage in increasingly boisterous locker-room banter. Looking around in wonder, Mother smiles, she loves new experiences and meeting new and interesting people. John, on the other hand, feels uncomfortable in any social situation, let alone a pub full of semi-intoxicated soon-to-be Police Officers.

'Hoy, John-boy, over here big-man,' Donnie shouts along the bar, tieless, sleeves rolled up and cigarette butt stuck to his top lip with sweat oozing from his forehead.

John sighs a disappointed sigh before leading Mother over to meet the team.

'Didne-know you wuh-bringing yah-sister,' Donnie grins. Taking Mothers hand, he places a sloppy kiss on her cheek.

'Ohh-kay.' John pulls her away. 'This is Max, that's Roger and right here is, erm, Andrew.'

'Alright darling,' Andrew pulls her close before catching Johns glare. 'Er-hum, very nice to meet you missus Cummings.'

'It's Miss, actually,' Mother blushes.

John orders a lager shandy for him and gin and tonic for Mother. 'Make that a double please, with a slice of lime rather than lemon my dear,' Mother yells after the barmaid.

Several drinks later, John is busy clock-watching, feeling the knot in his stomach tighten.

Ten minutes to go.

'Johnnnn,' Andrew slurs.

Oh, here we go, John thinks.

'I've got ta-tell yah-mate, sheriously, I hope you don't mind, but I got ta-tell you.'

Hesitating, John suspects he's about to receive a

declaration of admiration, fuelled by alcohol. He detests public acts of emotion.

'When we first met, I thought you were a shtuck up hooray-henry, a bit of a bender, if you know what I mean.'

Always wary of drunken behaviour, John wonders where this is going, especially with talk of hoorays and benders.

'I'm no queer or anything, nah, into birds yah, got nothing against the queers though, love-em really. Anyway, I've got to say, overall, at the end of the day… you're not that bad.'

Listening to Andrews homophobic words, John cringes, but, they are at least honest words and well intentioned, especially from an emotionally limited sort like Andrew. He would take "not that bad" as a massive compliment and attribute any homophobic references to a lack of education and ignorance. All the while, he can't help worrying about the amount of saliva being sprayed over his shoulder, and how long he spent ironing his jacket.

'I've learnt sho-much from ya-Gov,' Andrew continues, his vice like grip contracting around Johns neck. 'I'd have dropped out by now if it weren't for you. I owe you everything John, seriously yah.'

'Erm, feeling's mutual Andrew, I'm glad you're on the team,' John nods before receiving a massive bear hug, thankfully interrupted by the last orders bell, rung by a proud-as-punch Sergeant Smith. 'Now then you pack of horrible-gits,' he yells, struggling to be heard.

Slowly, the raucous hum subsides as more and more cadets become aware of the Sarge standing near the exit.

'Listen, before we leave, I want to say something,' the Sergeant clears his throat, pulling his neck through his two sizes too small shirt while pushing his chin in the air. 'You lot have made me so proud, you've made the Met proud and you've made your families proud.'

The entire pub reacts with cheers and claps.

'Most importantly, you've made yourselves proud,' Smithy continues as the pub reaches a crescendo. 'Shush, shush, listen, I'm being serious for a second,' he drops his tone an octave. 'When I first set eyes on you lot, I was, to be honest, absolutely gutted.'

The entire pub laughs in unison.

With a satisfying smile, Smithy soaks it up. 'Yep, I thought to myself, Smithy me' old son, it's going be a slog of a course, and you're not getting any younger.'

John glances toward Andrew, and then Donnie. Both look on, mesmerised, held by this seasoned performer.

'But, I'm pleased to say you've grown into real, proper coppers,' Smithy smiles, raising his half full pint glass. 'Here's to you, class of Eighty-One.'

Cheering erupts.

Wives kiss their husbands, husbands kiss their children and coppers hug each other.

'Right then, who fancies passing-out?' Smithy yells to the deafening sound of dozens of coppers cheering. 'What you waiting for then, chop-chop, let's get going.'

As the pub streams outside to the waiting fleet of taxis John becomes separated from Mother. Examining the doorway for her exit, she eventually emerges along with the stragglers. 'John, my darling, there you are,' she slurs, wrapping her arms around his neck, planting a kiss on his cheek. 'I'm so proud of you my son.'

Saturday, 21 February, 1:52pm
Metropolitan Police Training Establishment
Hendon, London

With pretty much the same facilities as when it first opened back in the 1930s, today, with the late winter sun shining brightly, Hendon looks great. The lawns have received their first cut of the year, the picket fences have had a fresh lick of paint and the parade ground has fresh white lining. The early morning chill in the air has dissipated, and, with the sun shining, it feels almost spring-like. Guided into the centre of the parade ground, the cadets line up in team formation, each of the twenty teams in three rows of four, headed by the team leader.

Seemingly right on cue, an immaculate jet-black 1961 Bentley S2 Continental glides toward the edge of the parade ground where Smithy is waiting. Commissioner Armstrong, head of the entire Metropolitan Police climbs out, followed by three other officials including Deputy Commissioner Jenkins. Smithy greets the visitors warmly and they share a few words before looking over toward the assembled cadets. With that, Armstrong leads the dignitaries toward the centre of the parade ground and the single microphone stand. Pausing, Commissioner Armstrong stares at the cadets before tapping gently on the silver microphone gleaming in the sunlight. In unison, the cadets stand to attention, showing no ill effect from the jubilant early session at the Dog and Duck.

'Ladies and gentlemen, guests and cadets,' Armstrong begins. 'Thank you all for attending today, this day of thanks and celebration. I'd like to welcome you all to Hendon, the world-renowned home of Police training.' Armstrong opens his arms wide with a grin to match. A seasoned performer, John concludes. 'Cadets, today is your last day here at Hendon, and your last day as cadets. After your most excellent efforts, studying, training and testing, you will leave this parade ground as fully-fledged Metropolitan Police Officers, upholders of the law of this country.' Pausing, he allows the solemn statement to wash over the entire parade ground. 'You have chosen to dedicate your lives to serving the people of this great city, and, this is to be admired and applauded.' He leads the audience in a round of applause as the cadets stand unmoved.

Scanning around, John struggles to contain the lump growing in his throat.

'Cadets,' Armstrong continues. 'You have all taken the oath and committed to serve our Queen and country in the office of constable, with fairness, integrity, diligence and impartiality, giving equal respect to all people. We, the Metropolitan Police, are role models for all Police Officers across the globe. Without us and those who've gone before, there would be no such thing as police officers and, as such, you will be granted positions of respect and trust. It is with the consent of the citizen we Police, we are here to serve.'

'You wanna take a trip to Brixton-man,' Andrew mutters under his breath in a mock accent. John tuts loudly while Donnie bites into his lip to stop himself laughing.

'Cadets, never forget why you are here and the reason you choose to serve. Never forget, no matter how hard your day, no matter how many criminals you lock up or how many old-aged pensioners you help across the road, you are the living embodiment of the law. Respect it, trust it and most importantly, live it. You, quite simply, are the law.' Armstrongs words echo around the otherwise silent parade ground as he steps back a couple of paces before turning to shake hands with Smithy.

After a short exchange, Smithy approaches the microphone. 'Righty, anyone for passing out?' With that, the parade ground erupts with cheers and claps.

Armstrong turns to the official on his left holding a briefcase horizontally. Opening it, Armstrong reaches in and collects a handful of medals, which, in a few seconds, he'll proudly present to the newly commissioned Officers. In the weeks leading up to today, the cadets have all been fully briefed on the itinerary for the day. After a short exchange of words with Armstrong, they'll receive their medals, then collect all personal items from the locker room before reporting to Governor Zarbelettos office to receive their postings. The team are then called up in alphabetical order where Armstrong hands over the medal with his left, offers a handshake with his right, before posing for a photo. The cadets return to their teams before the special commendations are presented. Unsurprisingly, John receives a special award for academic achievement, with the highest aggregate pass mark of the entire intake.

The new Police Officers are then instructed by Smithy, for the very last time, to "fall out" before they re-join their families. Before they do, John quickly gathers his team around him. 'Er-hum, listen guys, no long speeches, I just wanted to say, erm, it's been a pleasure working with you all. Truly, it's been a privilege. I wish you all good health and good luck in the future.'

'Here, here,' the team jeer in unison before giving John, and themselves, a hearty round of applause.

After hugs, kisses and handshakes, John heads to the locker room to collect his personal belonging, then to Zarbelettos office. After several frustrating time-checks on his watch, he's called in and is greeted by a small, over-weight, Italian-looking chap with a small pencil-straight moustache, round glasses and greying slicked back hair. Desk-bound since a car accident in the early Sixties, Zarbeletto is the chief administrator at Hendon. 'Ah, Cummings, come in, come-come-come,' he smiles. 'Excellent work this year young man, excellent-excellent-excellent, you should be very proud, very proud indeed.'

John shakes his hand while taking the sealed envelope containing his posting in the other. 'Big things for you me-lad, big-big-big things,' Zarbeletto nods.

Outside, the newly appointed Officers and their families mingle, sharing details of their postings. Most, it seems, are posted to local Stations and one or two to central functions at New Scotland Yard.

'SGP, fucking SPG,' Donnie yells, jumping around like a five-year-old on Christmas morning.

'Wow, the Special Patrol Group Donald, just your cup of tea,' John smiles, doubting the wisdom of the posting. 'And you, Andrew?'

'Fucking Brixton-yah, Brixton,' Andrews voice cracks, disappointment and frustration etching across his face.

'How about you big-man, Commissioners Office is it?' Donnie grins, mocking Johns ambition.

'Erm… haven't opened it yet.'

'Oh John, my love, shall I?' mother suggests with a smile.

Frowning at Mothers suggestion, he runs his finger under

the envelope flap and slips the cream card out. He stares for a few seconds then reads from it word for word. 'Inspector, Lambeth Division. Report to Colbalt Square, 0830 hours, Monday 21st February 1981.'

'Inspector?' Andrews face screws up with a mixture of puzzlement and disbelief.

'In-fucking-spector?' Donnie queries in a not-so-stage-whisper, snatching the letter. 'Aiy, Inspector sure enough, fuckin-hell, been greasing the right poles there so yer have.'

'Wow, well done John,' Andrew pats him on the back.

'You know what this means?' Donnie says, pleased with himself. 'Means you two pansies will be working together.'

John and Andrew look at each other, simultaneously realising Brixton is indeed within the Lambeth Division and they will, as Donnie suggests, be working together.

# Episode 13.
# "Live by the Sword"

Wednesday, 4 February, 6:01am
Ryecoates Meadow Lane,
Dulwich Village, London

Just two miles south of Brixton, Dulwich Village might as well have been a million miles away. No tower blocks, no graffiti, no burnt out cars, no rude boys and definitely no drugs. Instead, old fashioned thatched roofs, picture postcard cottages and white-washed picket fences surround the village green where cricket is played on lazy Sunday afternoons. Instead of sprawling council estates, large detached family homes dominate the horizon, housing high net worth families employing cleaners and nannies and gardeners. An idyllic oil painting parish church rests in between the village green and local pub where members of the croquet club share sandwiches, cups of tea and warm beer outside on sunny afternoons. With boutique stores stocking flowery dresses, fancy bakeries selling multi-tiered wedding cakes and delicatessens serving hard-to-find European cheeses, the local high street is the polar opposite of Brixton and its market stalls selling plantain, yams and sugar cane. Residents know the local bobby, George Arrowman, by name as he spends most of his time chit-chatting to local shop owners and passers-by about bygone times, as well as helping locate lost cats and dogs.

The Richardson family home Paul shares with his parents and younger brother backs onto an exclusive golf club, one of the most exclusive not only in London, but the entire south east of England. At the front of the property, the gated driveway leads to an imposing five-bedroom mock Tudor mansion with dark beams, cream rendering and leaded windows. On the driveway an array of motor vehicles, his mothers yellow TR7 sports car, his fathers Jaguar XJS "Supercat", the families dark green Range Rover, plus, conspicuously out of place, Pauls Triumph Dolomite.

The living embodiment of the modern capitalist society and "Thatchers Britain", his father acquired the Dolomite as a run-around in an attempt to teach his eldest son the "real" value of money. Being seen by his golf club friends and business associates as responsible and indeed magnanimous with his "new money" is a good thing, generating significant kudos. His choice of family home too is relatively modest. For sure, while it's magnificently expensive and in an exclusive area, he could easily afford a much larger house in Surrey or the Cotswolds or indeed anywhere in the world, other than maybe New York City, (where he could probably afford a spacious loft apartment in the Tribeca district of lower Manhattan). His choice of car too told much of his prudence, a ten-year-old Jaguar, even though he could afford a brand-new Porsche 911 Turbo or Ferrari 365 Berlinetta, or both. Lastly, his unconventional choice of education for his two children is most telling. The majority of his peers will send their children to private boarding schools in rural England such as Charterhouse, Notre Dame or Harrow, whereas both his children attended an inner-city comprehensive school to learn about "real-life."

A true rags-to-riches story, Pauls father, Charles grew up in Dartford on the south-easterly outskirts of London. Leaving school at fifteen with no qualifications, he had a pretty ordinary and uneventful life, working here and there in factories, building sites and anywhere that paid cash-in-hand. However, at twenty three, after a significant win on the horses, he bought his first house, a two-up two-down house in Woolwich for the princely sum of two-thousand pounds. Then, at twenty-six, he re-mortgaged the home he shared with his wife and children and, along with several associates, invested in a small mixed-use development in Catford, a rundown urban area of South East London. After acquiring the site, they renovated part of it and built the other half literally by hand, converting it into a small shopping complex and office space. Then, two years after completion, they sold their initial stakes for just over two-million pounds to a global real-estate firm.

A number short-term investments later, including the purchase of several scrap-metal businesses in south London, he opens his City based financial services business specialising in brown-belt land-bank real estate, corporate restructuring of failing companies, otherwise known as asset-stripping and, most recently, trading in copper and metals futures, as well as foreign currency. Nowadays, he spends his time playing golf and volunteering as a business coach for young entrepreneurs, allowing his millionaire management team to deliver a steady flow of high end returns into his bank account every month. Perhaps once a year he, as he puts it, "gets-his-hands-dirty" facilitating a complex series of finance deals, usually acquiring a failing FTSE 250 firms, then systematically liquidating the company assets, thereby maximising it's true value and banking a tidy profit. This is both the most profitable aspect of his portfolio and, from his personal perspective, the most gratifying.

Paul works in the firms London trading office, adjacent to St Pauls Cathedral. With his younger brother likely to become a professional sportsman, having signed apprentice forms with Crystal Palace Football Club, he will eventually progress to run the office and, over time, become Chief Executive of the entire company.

Up and dressed, he waits for his father to drop him off at West Dulwich train station for the thirty-minute journey into Blackfriars through, ironically, the Frontline via Loughborough Junction. Staring out of the train window, he'll often wonder what Devon and Super were up to before going through the motions of glancing through the Financial Times, all the while humming the latest dub reggae tunes in his head.

Most of the time, the journey is thankfully quick and uneventful, but, this particular morning, he's agitated and nervous. He's not looking forward to today one single bit. Over the last couple of weeks, ever since the drunken evening in the wine bar with Devon and Super, his co-worker Kenny has been giving him a hard time about getting hold of a large amount of cocaine. Over the past year or so, he's enjoyed a few lines after work or just before an important meeting to give him an edge, but, he isn't really into coke, let alone dealing it, nor Super and definitely not Devon, who both detest chemicals. However, Kenny just can't leave it, quite the opposite in fact, he's become increasingly insistent and aggressive.

The walk from Blackfriars Station to the office takes deliberately longer than usual. He does everything he can not to find his way to the reception desk, then the lift to the twelfth floor, then to the bank of four desks he shares with Spencer, Geoff and of course, Kenny.

Wednesday, 4 February, 8:42am
Richardson International Investments
Ludgate Hill, City of London

'Here he is, the fucking scarlet pimpernel.' Kenny yells, louder and more obnoxiously than usual. 'Where you been daisy, it's gone half eight?'

Paul ignores him.

'Oi, Daddies boy, where you been, we've been here grafting for hours, aint we boys?'

Paul ignores him while Spencer and Geoff nod and grin.

'Been down da frontline or something?'

'The train's late, just leave it yeah,' Paul tuts.

'Oh-hark-at-her,' Spencer and Geoff, sitting either side of Kenny sing in unison.

'Anyway,' Paul rubs his hands together hoping to change the subject. 'What we got on today?'

'Well, you, my friend, will be off to get hold of your Brixtonian brothers and get us some snow, then, after making your old man copious amounts of cash, we're off to snort our way to oblivion. Got that right boys?' Kenny cheers, triumphantly punching the air before taking a bow.

'Too right,' Spencer nods, quickly followed by Geoff agreeing, 'got that right Ken.'

'Not this again,' Paul shakes his head wearily. 'They're not interested Ken, no matter what the price.'

'Is that right my little flower? Well, let me tell yah-something,' Kenny stands up. 'I've just about had enough of you and your bullshit, so, if you haven't got good news for me by close of play today, I might well give daddy a call. Yeah, yeah, that's right petal, might just tell him what lovely company his boy's keeping, might let him know what a public relations disaster that might pose if it ever got out that his son's a cocaine addict and hangs around the Brixton frontline with a pair of queers.'

Paul stares at him for an age before shaking his head and turning on his screens. He's bluffing, he thinks, and a fucking homophobic racist mug too.

As lunchtime approaches, Piers, the office manager, a jet-black slicked-back hair, hooked nose and slightly olive skin character stands up and asks for everyone's attention. A ripple of silence flows throughout the office as he informs the thirty-strong team they have broken the months turnover target already, only a couple of days into the month. Cheers, claps and much joy follows. He goes on to say, as a sign of appreciation, they will celebrate their success with several bottles of bubbly over canopies at lunch time.

Paul doesn't give a shit about celebrating, or champagne or disgusting canopies for that matter, he has problems, real problems, Kenny shaped problems. The French-ponce will book it all to expenses anyway, it's not gift on his part, that much is for sure. In any case, Paul plans to deal with Kenny as soon as the coffee guzzling East End fuck-wit leaves his desk to take a regular as clockwork piss.

Forty agonising minutes later…

Eventually Kenny, the fat fuck, stands, stretches his long arms out and extends his broad chest. 'Right ladies, time to siphon the python,' he sighs as his pink and white striped shirt pulls out of his trousers revealing an over-hanging, hairy beer belly. Tucking his shirt back in, he fondles his balls before heading to the toilets.

"Now bwai, now's the time." Paul hears Devons voice inside his head. Legs like concrete, he stands and follows Kenny toward the toilets, his eyes zoning in on the back of his fat head. He can hear Super this time, goading him, "smash dis bloodclat fools head in man, you hearing me Paul? Paul… Paul? T'cha, fookin' idiot fool…"

Eyes closing, he shakes his head and Super disappears.

Got to think straight.

Using his foot, Kenny pushes the door open.

Five seconds later, Paul quietly follows.

Covered floor to ceiling with cream Italian marble, the toilet has three urinals hanging on the wall with three floor-to-ceiling cedar wood doors directly opposite, leading to cubicles. No sign of Kenny, must be taking a shit. That's appropriate, Paul muses with a nervous smile, a big shit taking a shit.

He gently pushes each door.

The first two edge open, unlocked.

He's in the third.

'Errr, get-out, you cunt,' Paul hears Kenny groan.

Splash.

Struggling not to laugh, Paul imagines the image of a red-faced-blood-vessel-popping Kenny forcing out a large turd.

Toilet flushing, the lock clicks and door opens.

Sucking in the energy around him like a weapons grade

electro-magnet, Paul feels the blood pulsing through his veins. This is it.

Flying toward the door with his knee high and foot outstretched he bursts through, knocking Kenny back onto the toilet with a groan. Momentum carrying him forward, he lands straddling Kennys girthy torso and starts punching. The small space renders knock-out punches impossible, but, he's on top and giving Kenny a pasting as both voices echo in his head… "gwan Paul, kick the shit out of him man,' Devon says. "Yesh-star, mash him up, fook his bom-baclat," Super spits.

What?

Fuck his what?

Never mind that, I'm on top and I'm fucking doing it, teaching him a proper lesson too, Paul encourages himself.

But, hang on.

Pain. Panic. Shit.

Searing pain enters his stomach.

What the fuck.

"Paul, what-da-rasclat?"

Balls… tears… tears and pain… balls… more pain!

In a flash, Kenny's bent over, looking down on Paul who's quickly disappearing in between the wall and the toilet basin. 'Fucking prick,' he seethes continuing to squeeze Pauls balls with his immense might. His eyebrows meet in the middle as his forehead sinks below his eye line while his top lip forms a v-shape across his stained yellow teeth. 'Fucking liberty, absolute fucking liberty, I'm gunna fuck you up you daddies-boy-cunt.'

Three lightning knees to the head later, Paul lays in the foetal position wrapping around the toilet, cradling his bleeding nose and his swollen testicles.

Resting back against the now locked cubicle door, Kenny stands legs astride, staring at his prey. 'Yah-stupid-cunt,' he whispers, his words are slow and deliberate. 'Think you can do me like that, like a fucking mug, do me a favour,' his words fade into a sadistic Ming-the-Merciless laugh.

With his head banging and his nuts the size of tennis balls, Paul's in pain, dejected and completely humiliated. He'll have to face the whole office in this state or worse, depending on how Kenny decides to deal with him. His old man will fire him for being an embarrassment and, even worse, Devon and Super, especially Super, will take the piss for ever and a day. He could live to be a billion years old and never live this down.

'Nah-then, listen up fairy-boy,' Kenny spits, his laugh switching to rip-your-heart-out seriousness. 'I'm not gonna say this again,' he continues. 'I'm getting more than a little fucked off with you and your mates stalling and taking the piss. I want the couple of ounces of coke you lot promised me and, for making me wait like a cunt, I want the name of your contact too.'

Name of our contact?

Kenny see's the suspicion on Pauls face. 'That's right knob-head, I want the name. Listen, I'm not interested in a couple of shitty ounces from you queer-lords, this is business yeah, it's all about the business. I can sort my own blow out down the road yeah, no problems, fuck me, the whole City's awash with it. Nah, I want the importer, I'm going wholesale yeah.'

'What on earth you on about Ken?'

'Shut the fuck up, cunt, you'll get yours soon enough. This is the deal, you and your bread-bins fetch a couple of ounces round to mine tomorrow at nine, along with the contact details, right. You do that and we're straight. If you don't though, I'm gonna-ring daddy and tell him everything, every-fucking-thing. Then, I'll call my mate who's a copper down there and give him the names of your bread-a-rins.'

He's blagging now, no way he's got a mate, let alone one who's a Beast.

'That's right shit-head,' Kenny grins. 'One call from me and he'll fuck your mates, your mates-mates, their families and the whole fucking tribe down there. Front doors kicked in, houses rumbled, shit planted on them, the works.'

Pausing, Kenny watches Pauls face weighing up whether this is all front.

'You aint got a clue who you're fucking with do-yah?' Kenny whispers, stepping forward. 'Now then daisy, I'm off for a well-deserved extended lunch, think I've earned it, don't you? Suggest you take the afternoon off, maybe take a trip down south, get things moving yeah.'

Unlocking the door, he sniffs up a massive ball of dark green phlegm and spits toward Paul, winks, then exits.

Wednesday, 4 February, 3:22pm
The Scrap Yard, Coldharbour Lane
Brixton, London

'What da-fook man?' Devon tuts, disappointed.

'What?' Paul shrugs.

'You let him gob on yah-head, man, that's disgusting yeah.'

'Makes me wanna-retch-star,' Super covers his mouth. 'Jus-gross man, gross.'

'Like I don't know?' Paul offers them both his palms.

'Listen, either way, dis rasclat deserves a wetting-star,' Super punches the side of the cabin.

'Nah, he's clever, we got to be cunning.' Paul nods, massaging his forehead with his thumb and index finger.

'What on earth are you chatting about?' Super grunts. 'He mashed you up-star, look at yah-fookin' nose t'rass.'

'True, but still handsome yeah.' Paul says, turning profile then stroking his swollen face.

'Plus,' Super continues. 'He threaten me and Devon, yet you're going on like it's nuttin, nah-man nah, him a dead man walking-star, a fookin dead man.'

'Paul's right,' Devon interjects. 'We got to sort this out good otherwise he's gonna be on our case forever.' Devon rubs his hands together, nodding slowly.

'Listen, it's simple-star, I say we drive up there, kick his door in and hack him to bits,' Super yells, standing up to demonstrate his moves.

'I got a better idea. If a-man live by the sword,' Devon nods. 'He fucking die by the sword.'

Thursday, 5 February, 7:34pm
Windsor Public House
Leeson Road, Brixton, London

The ten-minute walk to the Windsor is fraught. Fish-eyed by a Jam-Jar and then again by a SPG van full of Babylon, Devon's thankful he isn't sus-stopped. Carrying three hundred quid in cash will surely see him in chains and in a cell with a heap of Beastman jumping all over his head. Through the door, the pub is packed with all the usual folk, plus a few new faces. The comforting smell of stale beer mixed with the sweet aroma of freshly burnt herbs hangs heavy in the air. He spots Crissy in his usual seat in the far corner, flanked, as ever, by Claude and Snakehead.

'Easy now yout, love and peace,' Crissy nods respectfully as Claude gives him a soft punch on the arm. Snakehead continues to stare into space, oblivious to his surroundings.

'Wha-me provide fah-ya-breddah?' Crissy smiles, taking his glasses off, slowly and deliberately placing them in between the half drunken pints of Guinness.

'Something kind of different,' Devon nods cautiously, leaning into the middle of the table.

'Different?' Claude queries.

'Yeah man.'

'How so,' Crissy asks through narrow eyes.

'Wha-kind of different?' Snakehead follows up, suddenly hyper interested.

'You know, different.'

Crissy looks sideways. 'Wha-yah-a-mean?'

'It's a special request,' Devon says, checking around that nobody can hear.

'Me-nah what man needs,' Snakehead suggests, his voice deep and his patois broad. 'Him require arms, right?'

'Is it dred?' Claude probes, stunned and excited.

‘Arms?’ Crissy asks, his eyes narrowing.

‘Nah, man-don’t need no arms, I need Columbian.’

All three look at each other before bursting into laughter.

‘Look Dee,’ Crissy sits forward, inter-locking his fingers. ‘Eye-know you since you ah-lickle pickney-yesh, running errands fah-me an-ting. You recall-dat?’

‘True-say man, all day yeah,’ Devon says, remembering when he was eleven years old and the brown paper bags.

‘Yah-a-big-man-now-star, you steady-yeah, dealing yah-herb, juggling yah-ting,’ Crissy stares deep into his eyes. ‘Me respect the pass-yah-nah. Yah-muddah and eye-an-eye hail from-a-dah same yard, you know dat-star?’

Devon never knew that.

‘I see-er help at dah-church-yah-naw, when she a young-woman an eye-an-eye a pickney runnin-wit bare-foot and scraggy-tee. Yeah man, she look-pon me kindly yah-nah.’

Devon sees Crissy go a bit misty eyed.

‘So, nah, me nah-help man wid-no chemical,’ Crissy sits back in his seat while offering Devon his palms. ‘An don-nah-worry-nah-man, me nah-got no bombshell bout eye-an-eye being yah-real daddy no-nuttin.’ he chuckles.

‘Criss, I appreciate you looking out for me an all, but I got the cash with me right now. I aint sniffing it, aint even dealing it, just need it for a friend.’

‘A friend?’ Claude nods.

‘You got friend?’ Snakehead laughs.

‘Yeah, I got a friend, it’s complicated. You serving or not?’

‘Hear me-nah Devon,’ Crissy leans forward. ‘Eye-rung tings yeah, an-eye decide who I deal wid-an-what I deal, yah-understand? So listen, do-yah-sef and yah-Momma a favour, and stick wit-natural tings-yeah.’

‘Good advice, man,’ Claude adds, gulping his Guinness.

Standing up, Devon looks at each of them before navigating his way back outside. As the doors swing shut behind, he hears rumbling reggae tones bouncing around the surrounding streets as the cold chill of reality washes over him. He’s failed.

'Yo, pickney, hol-up-nah.'

Swinging around, he sees Snakehead in the doorway.

'If yah-wan what yah-say you wan, den call dis number in arf-hour yeah.' Snakehead forces a small bit of paper with a telephone number on into his hand, before disappearing back into the pub.

Thirty minutes later…

Ring-ring. Ring-ring.

'El-low.'

'Err, yeah, this is Devon.'

'Who?'

'Devon.'

'Devon?'

'Yeah, Devon.'

'Nah-mate,' the cockney voice croaks. 'No Devon round here mate.'

'No, no-no. I'm Devon.'

'Ahh-right. Devon yeah?

'Yeah.'

'Who do you know, Devon?'

'Erm, Snakehead pass me the number yeah.'

'Bring the cash, in an hour,' the cockney voice interrupts.

'Where?'

'ABC Taxi's, Southwark Park Road. Come on your own.'

Click.

'That's weird.' Devon places the phone back on its stand.

'It's cool, it's normal, that's how these things work right. You're the weird one,' Paul smiles.

'Listen, you both weird,' Super nods. 'And battyman too.'

Forty minutes later…

The drive north to Bermondsey takes an age. Turning onto Southwark Park Road they approach a row of shops with a Union-Jack-in-the-window pub on the corner called the "Lions Den." On the other side of the road sprawls a yellow brick estate consisting of several blocks of five or six floors with open balconies. A few kids sit on the kerb in front of the taxi shop, while others race around on BMX bikes.

'Fucking grim around here,' Paul sighs.

'Grim, more like utter shitness,' Super shakes his head.

'Pull up over there,' Devon points toward the chip shop, six or seven shops down from the taxi shop.

'National Front around dese parts-yah-naw,' Super grunts. He hates Bermondsey or "bandit country" as he calls it.

'Listen, this needs doing, hold tight yeah, back soon,' Devon opens the door and climbs out. Looking up and down the road he sets off toward the taxi office.

A couple of minutes later…

'The bird in there told me to wait out here.'

'Wait for what, you've got it, right?' Paul urges.

'She says wait out here.'

'You've paid her?' Super laughs.

'Fucking hell, you gave her three hundred big ones, my big ones, and she tells you to wait here,' Paul whispers, straining his neck as he struggles to get a clear look at the shop. 'Hope you got a receipt,'

'A receipt,' Super cracks a giggle. 'Jokes-star, jokes.'

A long five minutes later…

A scraggy teenager skids to a halt on a battered old push-bike. Looking in through Devons window, he gives each of them the once over before knocking. As Devon winds it down, he hands him a cigarette carton and speeds off.

They each stare at each other.

Reaching in Devon pulls out a plastic moneybag, half filled with white powder.

'What we waiting for?'

Pushing the gearstick into first, Paul presses the accelerator and wheels spin. 'Don't worry, we're out of this shit hole.'

Thursday, 5 February, 10:04pm
Lauderdale Heights
The Barbican, London

A concrete clad mixed use development built in a giant figure of eight design resting the shadow of the City of

London, the Barbican visually resembles the estates in Brixton, particularly Angel Town or the Loughborough Estate to give it is proper name. However, rather than the urine ridden lift lobbies, squats and drug dens of Angel Town, the Barbican houses refined wine bars, award winning restaurants and acclaimed theatres. It's home to highly rewarded and aspirational City of London stockbrokers, traders and financiers. Parking near Moorgate Tube Station, Paul consults the handily located map at the Silk Street entrance, and, after a magical mystery tour where Paul refuses to admit they're lost, even though they obviously are, they eventually locate Kennys block. Pressing the intercom, Paul looks around nervously.

No answer.

'Oh well, he's not in,' Paul shrugs.

'Of-course he's in, stop being a dick,' Super tuts, straining as he looks to the top of the block.

Lock clicking, Devon pulls the entrance door.

Ten seconds later, they're in the lift ascending to the eleventh floor. Turning left out of the lift, they find number forty-two. Paul raises his fist.

Bang, bang, bang.

'Who is it?' Kenny shouts from behind the door.

'It's us,' Paul sighs.

'Us who?' Kenny giggles.

'You know who, you're looking at us through the peep-hole, I can see your fat fucking eye,' Paul whispers loudly.

'Sorry, who is it… Avon calling?' Kenny sings.

'It's us-star, open the fook up,' Super growls.

Click-click-click, the door swings open and Kenny stands in the doorway, legs astride, hands on hips king-of-the-world style. In the background, they can hear a punk tune, something about "no few-ture, no few-ture." Staring into each of them, Kenny glances each way along the lobby. 'Abart fucking time, it's gone ten,' he says, making his way down the dimly lit hallway.

The threesome follow him through to a small living room

with a glass wall leading to a tiny balcony overlooking the communal square, tennis courts and the other blocks.

Pauls eyes zone-in on two girls lounging over beanbags, moulding around their sleek torsos. Heavy make-up, back-combed hair, safety pins and ripped t-shirts, obviously punks, but very tidy, he smiles.

Meanwhile…

Super fish-eyes the skinhead sitting on the sofa. A 1970s throw-back sporting a yellow Fred Perry t-shirt with red braces and mottled bleached jeans, he's sitting on the edge of the sofa leaning over the chessboard inlaid coffee table, burning a block of black resin into a few Rizla papers while sipping on a can of lager. Kenny stands in front of the television nodding along to punk tune. 'Glad you eventually came to your senses chaps.'

Devon nods.

Super continues to fish-eye the skinhead.

Paul, eyeing-up the girls, throws them a wink and a smile. They stare blankly back, no emotion, just boredom in their dead eyes. Probably lesbians anyway, he nods to himself.

'What's the matter fellas, not into the Pistols?' Kenny juts his chin toward the stereo near the balcony door.

'Nah-star, we-a roots and culture people,' Super says, maintaining his stare at the skinhead. 'We not into dis shit.'

'Winston, my man, it's a classic, a right-royal *British* classic.' Kenny adds, accentuating the word "British".

'Fuck the selection,' Devon looks into Kenny. 'This no social call, we not here for no cup of *English* fucking tea.'

Kenny nods. 'Yeah-yeah, quite right Devon, too fucking right my old son, strictly business. I knew I liked you, fucking love this guy.' Kenny holds his arms out, embracing the room as the two girls giggle.

Devon stands silent, continuing to stare into Kenny.

'So, anyway, let's get down to it. You got something for me daisy?' Kenny prompts, rubbing his large hands together.

Paul looks at Devon, shrugs his shoulders then reaches into his jacket. Feeling the bag, he flings in into the centre of coffee table. 'Two ounces, that'll be seven hundred.'

'Seven-tonne?' Kenny yells, looking at the skinhead, then back at Paul. 'This aint the Bank of fucking England?'

Paul doesn't flinch.

'Do I look like a street-walking-idiot-punter to you? I aint paying no fucking high street prices, it's wholesale, right.'

Super steps forward. 'Look-nah-star, the price is the price,' his tone adding to the tension. 'You want coke, we bring coke, so, take the damn-ting an-pass us dah money, den leave lemon-boy alone, right.'

The skinhead places his can of lager and his now fully built spliff onto the coffee table.

Realising the escalation, Kenny waves his arms down. 'Okay-okay, let's calm the fuck shall we, let's slow this shit way down.' He turns, looking through the window toward the City with the dome of Saint Pauls in the distance. 'Nobody's kicking off in here tonight, right, no fucking chance, life's too short yeah, besides… we got the beautiful Shaz and Trace over there eagerly awaiting a pounding, once you cunts fuck off.'

The girls giggle some more.

'Listen, it's seven Ken,' Paul says, calmly.

'Okay, I'm a reasonable guy, I'll give you five hundred when you give me your importer contact, and at five you're still making a tidy profit.'

'What-am Paul, what da-fuck, dis fool crazy,' Devon says, turning toward Paul.

'Ken, we can't do that,' Paul says, his palms up. 'You turning up asking for a carrier bag of white won't go down well at all. These are serious people.'

'It's aw-right petal, I get it, all I need's the name, I wont even mention you lot.'

'Why?' Super growls, stepping forward.

'Easy-nah Super, easy,' Devon nods. 'Here me-nah, you aint getting no name, tings-don't work that dat. You want a heavier load, dat's cool-yeah, but, you buy direct from us.'

Kenny points at Devon, searching for words. Tension

increasing with every passing millisecond. Face changing, his nose and eyes scrunch up while his eyebrows angle inward. 'Listen, cunt,' he seethes. 'I want that name, or fairy-boy is going over that fucking balcony.' His face boils red, veins bulge and biceps tense.

The girls scream in unison as the skinhead reaches behind the sofa to reveal a sawn-off shotgun before leaping to his feet while cocking it shut.

Turning side-on Super reaches inside his jacket and pulls out his two-foot long machete while Devon steps to his right and raises his fists into high guard position.

Paul freezes. Guns, knives and good-looking fellas going over the balcony is not part of the plan, not by a long way.

'Shut the fuck up, slags,' Kenny shouts before turning back to Devon. 'Nah-then, you Brixton bad boys, what's it gonna-be, a simple name, or world-war fucking three?'

'It's Windsor,' Paul blurts out, nervously patting the air in front of him. 'His name's Windsor, okay.'

'What the fuck Paul, shut your mouth,' Devon shouts, urgency etching through his voice.

Kenny looks over to the sworn-off skinhead who slowly lowers the barrels. 'Glad at least one of you can see sense, nah-then, where can I find this Windsor chap?'

'Cash first,' Paul puts his hand out.

Devon turns away in disgust.

'T'cha!' Super kisses his teeth. 'Why Paul, why?'

Kenny laughs out loud. 'Cheeky bastard, that's why I like you Richardson, you're a fucking geezer.' Reaching into his back pocket, he counts out five hundred in fifty-pound notes then, leaning over the coffee table, picks up the bag of white, replacing it with the cash. 'There you go, there's five and that's all you're fucking getting, right. Nah-then, where do I find this Windsor fella?'

Paul grabs the cash. 'Hangs out at the back of the fish and chip shop on Southwark Park Road, near ABC Taxis.'

'What-am, Paul?' Devon shakes his head.

'Bermondsey, you sure?'

Super turns away, wanting no part.

'Yes I'm sure. Now you've got it, leave me the fuck alone.'

'Alright darling, touchy-touchy,' Kenny whispers.

Paul motions to Super and Devon it's time to leave and follows them through the door.

Kenny follows. 'Paul?' he says, softly.

Paul turns.

SMASH!

Kenny launches his head into Pauls face. Landing flush on his nose, his head bangs off the doorframe.

Spinning around, Super jabs his blade over Pauls shoulder toward Kenny who, stepping back, pushes Paul into Super.

'Muggy cunts,' Kenny yells. 'Go on, fuck off back to banana-central or wherever the fuck you're from.'

The skinhead points the sawn-off into the hallway, over Kennys shoulder and cocks the trigger.

Pulling at Supers arm, Devon drags him out of the front door. Paul, moaning and groaning with blood seeping through his fingers stumbles out cradling his nose.

'Go on, fuck off slags,' Kenny yells after them.

'We out of here.' Devon pushes Super toward the stairwell while placing his arm around Pauls back. Jogging down a couple of flights they stop at the ninth floor to wait for the lift, they hear the front door slam shut.

Fifteen minutes later…

With Super at the wheel, the Dolomite heads south toward Tower Bridge. Paul sits in the back, head tilting back pinching the bridge of his nose with blood spread across his face and down his shirt. 'Dat-mudder-bucker-broke-de-dose,' he struggles to speak.

'Pull up here,' Devon points to a red telephone box a hundred yards from the Bridge.

A few minutes later…

He climbs back in, head in hands massaging his temples. 'It's done,' he whispers.

Six hours later…

Eyes open, an array of torches scorch ultra-bright light

into his pupils as three Heckler & Koch MP5 sub machine guns point toward his head. He's given instructions to get out of bed, then, slowly, lay face down on the floor. Special Branch, supported by Firearms Command, had covertly broken in through the balcony and recovered two guns along with ammunition. In addition, a sword and several small knives were collected along with a large amount of low quality, heavily cut cocaine. Later that day, Mr. Kenneth Arthur George McCoy is formally charged then remanded in custody awaiting a court appearance.

# Episode 14.
# "Monsters from the Swamp"

Friday, 27 March, 4:11pm
Metropolitan Police Divisional HQ
Lambeth, London

'Cummings?'

'Erm, Sir.'

'Come in, sit down,' Assistant Commissioner George Warren sighs, gesturing to the chair in front of his desk. In charge of the five Divisions south of the River Thames, Warren reports directly to Jenkins who in turn reports to Armstrong, Commissioner of the entire Metropolitan Police. One of fourteen operational Divisions across London, Lambeth consumes approximately twenty two percent of all Metropolitan Police resources while dealing with nearly thirty four percent of all the serious crime in London. Quite simply, the borough struggles to cope, like it always has. 'Please, make yourself comfortable.'

'Sir,' John nods, taking a seat.

'So, six weeks in, how's it going?'

Pausing, John wants to give a measured and accurate response. 'Well Sir, erm, thank you for asking,' he smiles. 'It's been an interesting start, encouraging I'd say.'

'John, let me share something with you, when you're asked by a senior officer "how's it going", don't offer platitudes. I'm asking because I want to know.'

'Ah, erm, very good Sir.' John hesitates, wondering how much to share. The borough has serious and deep-rooted problems, but surely Warrens knows all this already. 'I've erm, made some in-roads into community relations, making contract with a few church leaders, an anti-fascist political activist responsible for publishing several offensive pamphlets, an ex-convict who is running an after school and summer holiday play-scheme for the kids on the Loughborough Estate, and, I've just come from an interesting meetings with the council housing department.'

'Right, okay, and how's that going?'

'Early days Sir, the council can't do much about the quality of housing without proper funding from central Government, apparently.'

Supporting his chin with the tips of his fingers, Warren exhales wearily. For years he's tried, unsuccessfully, to do what John is attempting now. Given Johns background, he expected more progress. 'And the Church Leaders?'

'Yes Sir, they are good people, determined to make a difference. I've sat on a cross-faith panel with some Methodist Pastors and a couple of Reverends from the Diocese of Lambeth.'

'Excellent. Progress?'

'Best of intentions, but it's tough going I'm afraid Sir, although…' he hesitates for a moment wondering whether to make light of the situation. 'I did have a nice visit to Lambeth Palace though.'

'Right, I see… so, no real answers?' Warren sits back in his chair, seemingly not appreciating the light humour.

'Sir, may I be candid?' humour not working, John decides to be bold.

'Please, continue.'

'It's worse than I ever imagined, I've found the last month particularly challenging. I, erm-hum, can't pin down any single reason for the growth in the deviant behaviour.'

'Challenging? I appreciate that John.'

'I have formed a preliminary hypothesis though.'

'Okay,' Warren sits forward.

'Unfortunately, Sir, I take no pleasure in reporting we are in fact part of the problem.'

Warrens eyebrows arch as he nods. 'Explain.'

'The resentment the community feels is against all forms of authority, and is multi-directional. The Government for the lack of jobs, the Council for poor housing and us for our heavy-handed methods, and, I must say Sir, I've observed some heavy handedness myself. All this is underpinned and reinforced by chronic under-investment in education, housing and community-based activities.' John pauses, he hates letting his emotions get the better of him. 'We have an entire generation seemingly disaffected and angry.'

'Yes, I have had the pleasure of reading your dissertation, John,' Warrens chin disappears below his protruding bottom lip. 'However, crime is crime, the law must prevail.'

'Of course, Sir.'

'Otherwise, you know as well as I do, utter anarchy and complete chaos will descend, and the fabric of society will deteriorate.'

'Yes Sir, I agree, but to many, committing crime is purely a means to an end, it's not simply a choice anymore. Furthermore, I believe more often than not it's an act of disobedience more than any reward-based motivations.'

Warren returns to his finger on chin position. 'An interesting observation John. I'd like you to attend a briefing next Monday.'

'Briefing, Sir?'

'Jenkins is establishing a special group to tackle this head on, address the root-causes.'

'Sounds, erm, interesting,' John was indeed interested but didn't want to disclose how interested.

'Interesting… yes that's one way to view it. John, some advice, use your words carefully at the briefing.'

John looks deep into Warren.

What does he mean?

'I am genuinely concerned we may be reaching a point of

no return.' Warrens words are slow, solemn and grave.

Feeling the knot form in his stomach, John hates inevitable absolutes. Getting up, he shakes Warrens hand before leaving. Observing a senior Officer in such a resigned mood is troubling and disconcerting.

Monday, 30 March, 1:50pm
New Scotland Yard
Westminster, London

The last time he was here, which feels like an age ago, Jenkins had filled him with hope. Today though, he feels uneasy and troubled, with a sense of foreboding filling the pit of his stomach. He hasn't felt like this since last Easter when he spent time at the family home with Mother, resulting in nearly a year of not talking.

Deep breath.

Entering the large, oak panelled conference room he scans around, immediately recognising Commander Crow hovering near the tea urn. Responsible for the infamous Special Patrol Group, he's a tall, slender man around fifty years old with a mop of fair hair greying at the temples and odd looking silver framed almost feminine glasses veeing down toward the nose. Next to Crow is McCrudden, Head of CID for Lambeth Division who, apparently, transferred to the Met from Belfast a few years ago. Further around, he notes Jenkins huddled with Warren in the far corner and several civilians, presumably Home Department officials. John vaguely recognises one of the civilians but struggles to marry his face to a name. Gazing across the room, he quickly realises Jenkins has gathered together a quorum of the great-and-the-good of the Met. This is significant and he feels out of his depth like he doesn't belong here in a room full of senior officials. After a couple of excruciating minutes of small talk, nods and false smiles, Jenkins calls the meeting together and the attendees take their seats.

Then.

Commissioner David Armstrong, head of the entire Metropolitan Police breezes through the door to an audible gasp. John is surprised he has attended such a tactical meeting, and, more interestingly that he is in attendance on his own, without his menagerie of aides, advisors and assistants. More into politics than policing, the likes of Armstrong never usually involve themselves with operational issues and most definitely, never on their own. Taking his seat, Armstrong thanks everyone for attending before silently scanning the room catching the eye of every attendee. 'Gentleman,' he begins. 'We have one agenda item that we will, before we leave today, resolve once and for all.'

John subtly eyes the room, watching everyone eagerly waiting for Armstrong to continue.

'Brixton,' Armstrong nods solemnly.

Speechless, since passing-out from Hendon John observed hardly anyone referred to Brixton directly, instead they talk about the "social problems" of South London or the "community issues" in Lambeth. Brixton has become a dirty word nobody wants to be associated with.

'I assume we have all read and digested the papers issued last week,' Armstrong says, not looking up from his notes. John panics, he hasn't seen any papers and can't operate effectively without being fully prepared. 'The rise in crime across London, and in particular Brixton, is apparent to media commentators and the general public alike. Muggings, robbery, burglary, prostitution, assault, all fuelled by widespread drug consumption and subsequent dealing. The evening news and the papers are all over it, Whitelaw and the politicians too.' Pausing, he allows the audience to take in what his words. 'Our analysis suggests the exponential rise in street crime is in some way funding the drug trade which, of course, has a cumulative effect on more serious multi-national organised criminality, such money laundering and abuse of global financial markets.'

While impressed by Armstrong's articulation and poise, John questions the logic. Could a mugging in Brixton be linked directly to money laundering on Wall Street? At best a casual link, not causal, although he appreciates this subtlety and nuance may have been lost in translation.

'David, if I may,' the vaguely familiar civilian sitting nearly directly opposite John interjects, raising his hand in the air. John can't quite place him, but, his face is one to remember, a good-looking chap with tortoise-shell rimmed round glasses and wispy fair hair.

Armstrong gives an acknowledging nod.

'We have high quality intelligence suggesting several organised gangs are operating in the area,' the civilian says, seemingly reading from some notes. 'Some originating from the Caribbean with links to the east coast of America, others indigenous and some, of course, have far-right political and anti-establishment perspectives. While supported by no real hierarchical structure, the majority of these gangs are under the sphere of influence of a small number of protagonists.'

Tutting, John's face immediately flushes. This is highly reductive and over simplistic, an A-Level student could have worked it up in their lunch hour, he muses.

'We believe,' the civilian continues. 'The epicentre of what best can be classified as gangsterism, is concentrated around the Railton Road area, given its equidistant proximity to five inner-city housing estates, the A205 south circular road, two train lines and also the London Underground tube network.'

John becomes aware of several Officers shaking their heads at this assessment. He feels the same.

'Sorry to interject, whoever you are,' Jenkins steps in.

'Apologies, Giles Askwith-Parsons, security advisor from Thames House,' the civilian smiles, removing his glasses.

Thames House? Johns mind jumps into overdrive. Thames House, as in the headquarters for Military Intelligence? The knot in his stomach tightens even further.

'So, Giles,' Jenkins continues, his tone sarcastic, edging on patronising. 'A fifteen-year-old kid who robs a handbag for a drink, some new trainers and maybe a joint or two, is in fact doing this because he's part of some kind of crime superstructure, headed by some type of criminal overlord?'

Askwith-Parsons smiles, nodding nonchalantly.

Armstrong slams both hands down onto the large oval table. 'Peter, whether you accept the analysis or not, the youngster will rob the bag and buy drugs, both illegal acts, and the drugs will have been illegally imported from somewhere. Clearly, these issues are linked.'

John can't resist it, he has to say something. His heart pounds as his stomach churns. 'Erm, um, excuse me, may I interject?' He takes a deep breath. 'While there is an obvious link, it is surely nothing more than consequential consumerism.' Holding the room, confidence begins to flow and the knot in his stomach loosens somewhat. 'That is to say, what I mean is, erm, the yield from petty street crime will be spent somewhere. Given the lack of physical and social mobility, it stands to reason these gains will be spent within the geographic bounds of the perpetrator, on goods and services offered locally which are perceived as micro-sociably acceptable, such as drugs, prostitution or gambling. It is therefore difficult to accept the rationale of any highly organised economic structure, indeed, this may just be serendipitous or simple coincidence.'

The meeting falls silent.

He hopes he projected his thoughts articulately while not alienating the audience. The silence grows, and with it his anxiety. Maybe he's gone too far, addressed it too academically, too conceptual perhaps, maybe he's embarrassed himself.

Commander Crow clears his throat. 'David, if I… may,' his words are slow and deliberate, pitching up a semi-octave mid-sentence. John wrongly assumed Crow would be a fast-talking, adrenaline-fuelled vulture hell bent on aggression and the "force" aspect of policing. 'We can talk all day about the why's and where-for of crime, and use all manner of… university language,' Crow nods toward Giles, and then John. 'But we have good… honest… innocent citizens suffering at the hands of these, let's face it, criminals… I am absolutely-convinced stopping this street crime will slow down the demand for drugs… and as demand slows, supply will slow down too… in turn making our streets safer, which surely… is the… objective of the entire operation.'

John bites down on the inside of his lip.

'So, what do we do?' Armstrong huffs, seemingly frustrated with this pontificating.

Crow jumps back in. 'May I suggest a short term… deployment of SPG units… in and around the Railton Road area.' He smiles a simple smile. 'My units will respond decisively to every reported crime… no matter how small… or insignificant… providing a visible line of authority acting as… a real and present deterrent.'

The pitching up mid-sentence, pregnant pauses and lack of verbal punctuation grates on Johns nerves. He feels his face turning a deeper shade of red.

'Should an offence occur,' Crow continues. 'We will deal with it quickly and effectively… if there are no criminals on the streets… quite simply… there can be no crime.'

Crows proposal, although rudimental, did make sense at a superficial level John concedes, and, based on the approving nods and lack of disagreement, appears to be convincing all in attendance too.

'Commander Crow,' Warren steps in. 'You've obviously thought deeply about all of this, I do have a couple of questions if I may.'

Crow bows his head, welcoming questions.

'How much will all this cost? I'm guessing significant overtime for your guys?' Warrens question is heavily loaded with inuendo, and, John observes, presented with tongue firmly in cheek. 'Also, have you considered how this will be viewed by the local residents. The more resources we deploy, the more alienated the local community will feel, perhaps having the opposite reaction and actually fuelling crime.'

Impressed, John feels a surprising amount of pride.

'Yes… good questions… I understand I really do… if the problem was cited in one of my divisions… I'd probably feel the same,' looks like Crow intends to give as good as he gets. 'The deployment does… I'm afraid, come at a high price… fourteen units on patrol per shift… six Officers per unit… for an entire month.' Crow pauses, noting Warrens obvious shock. 'As for the effect our presence will have… I am certain we will regain control of the area… it is after all… no more than a square mile.'

John detests himself for feeling any sense of respect for Crows self-belief and conviction, but, it appears he's planned this out pretty well and delivered it with confidence and passion. In fact, the more John thinks about it, the more it appears extremely well planned, almost stage-managed. He concludes this has probably been on the agenda for some time now, and this meeting is more codification and confirmation than discussion and debate.

Armstrong looks to Warren. 'Brixton's your command.'

Breathing deeply, Warren looks to McCrudden who closes his eyes and nods. 'What we're doing right now isn't working and our resources are beyond stretched, I gather we blew the staff budget back in November due to sick-leave cover, and those who aren't sick are on the brink. We must do something.'

Armstrong looks toward one of the civilians sitting next to Giles Askwith-Parsons. 'Appetite from Downing Street for this type of deployment?'

The civilian put his pencil down. The room freezes in anticipation of his response.

'Thank you. Simon, from the PMs private office by the way. The proposal seems cost effective given the additional resources required to even maintain the status quo. Our analysis suggests the positive effects will be realised more quickly than other investment options. The PM is adamant we have to be seen to be taking positive, decisive action in line with manifesto commitments. We feel the general public will welcome this type of intervention,' he pauses as he scans the room. 'You'll need approval from Willie of course, and most probably Her too, before actual deployment. Also, I must point out public relations will need to be carefully managed.'

Shocked, John can't believe in less than fifteen minutes the proposal is about to be agreed. Knot tightening even further, he feels a sense of vertigo, like he's peeking over the edge of a cliff as hurricane force winds race around him.

'I would like to propose an alternative course of action,' Jenkins steps in. 'Admittedly, it's less well thought out than Crows, but I think worthy of consideration nonetheless.'

Yes, John thinks. At last!

Armstrong's eyebrows arch as he nods to continue.

'We must tackle the social issues as well as policing the situation, secure funding for housing repairs, the community centre needs revamping to engage the kids before they turn to crime.' As silence falls across the room, Jenkins senses this is a weak pitch. 'We need more bobbies on the beat too, actually talking to the locals, working with them, gaining their trust.'

Uneasiness growing, John glances around, noting nobody seems to be agreeing with Jenkins thoughts. This is disappointing, but he's pleased Jenkins is at least trying to add some balance.

Several agonising seconds later…

Armstrong breaks the silence.

'Okay, this is what we will do. Crow, Jenkins, you have forty-eight hours to firm up your proposals including deployment of SPG units as well as community focused activity. Giles, you will brief your people and Simon, you will brief the Downing Street press office while I engage the Home Secretary and the Prime Minister directly. We will meet again in a couple of days.' Standing, Armstrong smiles, nods and leaves.

Tuesday 31 March, 9:00am
Room Twelve Twenty-Two,
New Scotland Yard, Westminster, London

'Morning Guv,' Warren pulls out a chair.

Jenkins fixes his stare at Warren while John finds his seat too. 'No George, it's not a "good" morning,' Jenkins scowls. 'We are on the verge of declaring all-out war.'

John looks deep into Jenkins. His frowning forehead seems deeper than usual, his hair a little less well-kept and it's noticeable he hasn't shaved this morning. He looks older, burdened, worried. Warren doesn't seem his usual positive self either. The mood in the room feels serious and sombre, negative even. John detests negativity. 'Sir, erm, we still have an opportunity here.'

'We do?'

'Erm, we have a mandate from Armstrong, yes?'

'I applaud your optimism John, never lose that, ever,' Warrens words have a tone of inevitability.

'We must act Sir, anything has to be better than apathy.'

They spend the next forty minutes outlining a range of community related projects, each of them decent, robust and long term in nature. John feels a sense of pride building, this is exactly why in his final year at Cambridge he rejected the opportunity to enter the private sector into a well-paid, high prospect executive role in a public relations, advisory or accountancy firm.

Jenkins nods. 'Good work gentlemen. I'll see you both in an hour or so when we meet Crow,' he smiles, before getting up and sliding his large hands over his forehead and slicking back his hair.

Tuesday, 31 March, 8:43pm
Flat B, 22 Baylis Road
Lambeth, London

Walking home from the Yard, south across Westminster Bridge toward Waterloo, he glances across toward the homeless and destitute sleeping in cardboard boxes under the subway beneath the roundabout commonly known as Cardboard City. Waterloo at night isn't a place anyone wants to be, especially in full uniform. Head spinning, lightheaded and dizzy, he increases his stride. As a rising star within the Met, he usually feels a weight of expectation on his shoulders, but today, he feels the immaturity of his age and an acute awareness of his inexperience. Things are happening too quickly, without any real thought or insight into the long-term consequences. Reactionary strategy rarely succeeds, and typically causes more problems than it solves. There appears to be no coherent exit strategy or ongoing development plan, and that, John concludes, is concerning and disappointing in equal measure.

Stopping at the off-license at the end of his road, he hands over a ten-pound note in exchange for a bottle of single malt, purely to help him sleep, he reassures himself.

Two minutes later…

Front door closed and locked, resting back against it he looks to the ceiling. Closing his eyes, the enormity of what they planned today flows through him. Holding his breath, his face glows red. 'Arghhhh, John…' he yells.

Banging the bottle down onto the worktop next to the sink, he releases his grip from the neck as he slides his hand around the body, feeling both glass and label. Music, he says to himself, I need music. Stereo on, play button pressed, reels revolving… Joy Division, nice, just what I need. Love will tear us apart, he chuckles to himself, more like maniac coppers will tear us apart.

Bottle opening, glass poured, large one downed.

Teeth grinding, eyes squinting, burn subsiding.

Splash, another poured, another downed.

Burns less this time.

Undoing his tie, he breathes deeply. Shirt off, he twists the tap, hot water stinging as he splashes his face. He cuts a sorry sight, standing over the sink staring at the water spiralling around the plug hole. Refusing to look himself in the mirror, he feels a wave of guilt. He knows he's betraying his beliefs, going against what he stands for as a man, as a human being. He seriously considers phoning home to speak with Mother.

No, can't do that. Must not do that.

Another poured, another downed.

No burn this time.

Perfect.

Instead, he'll sooth himself to sleep with the final few gruelling chapters of "Karamazov Brothers" by Dostoevsky, plus a few more drams of single malt.

Head spinning, he plunges into his pillow, resolving tomorrow will be a new day.

Twenty-four hours later…

Commissioner David Armstrong, Head of the Metropolitan Police, signed the AP1 "Authorisation to Proceed" document that will be delivered via hand-messenger to Right Honourable William Whitelaw M.P. Home Secretary for "Red" Approval and then on to Downing Street and the Prime Minister for "Gold" Approval. The document contains detailed proposals relating to the mass deployment of Special Patrol Group resources incorporating an informant led, plain clothes operation aimed at tackling the wholesale drug market, along with a range of community-based initiatives.

Two days later…
2nd of April 1981

The Prime Minister, Margaret Thatcher eventually signs the order approving deployment of the operation code-name "Swamp 81." A decision that will change Brixton, and Britain forever.

# Episode 15.
# "Country Bumpkin"

Friday, 3 April, 3:34pm
Bus Stop outside Saint Saviours School
Herne Hill, London

'The Station, at five yeah, don't be late,' he yells, climbing into the dark green Range Rover. Ever since his encounter with Yellowman, he's been dropped off and picked up by his mum, which, no matter how much piss-taking this encourages from his so-called mates, is fine by him.

'Cool, cool, five yeah, five,' Marlon confirms, staring open-mouthed at Ashleys mum. For an old-bird, she's well fit, no doubt yearning for dirty as fuck sex with a young stallion like me, he greedily thinks to himself.

Meanwhile…

Delroy stands trance-like, thinking exactly the same thing, in fact, he's spent a lot of time pondering their sex sessions, given half the chance. Snapping himself out of his daydream, he sets off in the opposite direction toward the bus stop.

'Eh, where you a-go?' Marlon queries in a teasing tone.

'Business down the market yah-nah,' Delroy yells, deliberately loud enough for the fifty or so other kids hanging around to hear.

'Alright for five, yeah?'

'Yesh-mate, no worry-bout me, just make sure you're not late, know what I mean.'

'Cool man, laters then,' Marlon smiles, making his way past the line of kids toward the front of the queue.

The wait for the ride home after a boring day at School isn't long as, in the distance, he sees the bus setting off from the stop before. A minute later he climbs the twisting stairs and scans around for a seat. Even though he can shift any one of the up and coming youths sitting at the back, he decides against it. He knows one or two of them might, as he has, eventually graduate into full blow rudeness, probably crossing his path one day. The smart thing to do is not to make enemies of them, if he can help it.

'Oi, oi. Marlon, Marlon.'

Toward the front, he spots Kingy waving.

Shit.

'Down here mate, down here,' Kingy shouts excitedly.

'Watcha Kingy, long time no-see,' Marlon sighs, sitting beside him, taking a double-take. With cheek bones protruding more than usual and acne looking worse than ever, Kingy has a yellowish bruise around his left cheek and redness around his neck. With a large purple sore reaching up from his top lip to the bottom of his nose, it's obvious he's been glue-sniffing way too much. All in all, he looks a right state. Staring deep into him, Marlon wonders if it was him he saw in the Police Station, when he got arrested at the youth club. 'Not seen you in time mate, where you been lately, what you been up to?'

'Round and about, you know…' pausing, Kingy nods toward the scar on his head. 'Looks like you've had some troubles though.'

'This?' Marlon touches it gently. 'Nah-man, this is nothing, rumble with the Peckham fools, all sorted now.'

'It's true then, that was you?'

'What was me?'

'I hear Junior's still in hospital, had to have some hip bone grafted to his face or something.' Kingy smiles, holding his hand aloft, waiting for a high five.

'Nah-mate-nah,' Marlon shrugs, pulling his hand back

down. 'No need for any of that, just glad it's over.'
'The rozzers get hold of you then?'
'Eh?' Marlons eyes narrow with talk of the Police.
'Rumour is you nearly killed him.'
'What you on about?'
'Attempted murder, yeah?'
This sounds like informant talk, maybe he is a grass.
Silence sits uneasily between them.
'Murder?' Kingy adds. 'Ha-ha-ha, as if, I'm just kidding.'
'Funny, yeah good one,' Marlon forces a laugh. 'Just a straightener between me and him, man vee man, yeah.'
'Yeah,' Kingys eyes widen.
'Whatever the Peckham fool is, he's no grass, wouldn't blab his mouth to Babylon, wouldn't stoop so low.'
'True mate, true,' Kingy smiles.
'He knows what happens to grasses, right?'
Maintaining his smile, Kingy shrugs his shoulders.
Staring deeper into him, Marlon tries to read his mind. No reaction though, no sign of recognition, no panic, no "oh-shit-I've-been-rumbled" vibe. Maybe it's not true, maybe he's not a grass, maybe it's just coincidence or something, maybe I have it wrong, seeing something that wasn't there, he thinks.
'So anyway,' Kings chimes. 'I hear the Peckham lot are planning to go all Long-Good-Friday on you. Stevie Gentle an Yellowman and all that lot.'
'Yeah?'
'Yep.'
'Well, they aint bothered us since, have they?'
'Suppose not, just what I heard.'
'Listen, Peckham Boys, t'cha, I'll shit em,' Marlon kisses his teeth even though the thought of the crazy Yellowman unsettles him, scares him even. 'So, where you been, what you been up to, aint seen you for a while?'
'Nowhere really, hanging with McMahon and the Angel Town lot.'
'McMahon?'

'Yeah.'

'Angel Town?'

'Err, yeah.'

'T'cha, he's a Fronter and dat-place a shit-hole, what you doing hanging around with them lot?'

McMahon is a bleached-jean, twenty-hole Doc Martins, green bomber jacket wearing old-school anarchist as well as being a national fronter. He and Devon had a massive rumble years ago, with Devon coming out on top. Since then, he's kept a low profile, getting drunk, taking amphetamines and glue sniffing all the time. Apparently, he's living in a series of squats on the Angel Town estate and, rumour has it, a rude-boy got tarred and feathered by the Fronters in Lewisham, and McMahon was somehow involved.

'They're okay you know, just sit around listening to music, taking the piss and having a laugh.'

'And hating people like me?'

'Nah-Marlon-nah, they not into that, they hate racialism.'

'Snorting whizz and bagging glue?'

'You don't snort it mate,' Kingy laughs. 'You rub it around your gums, don't-cha.'

Fronters, speed, glue? This isn't the Kingy he grew-up with. All this second guessing about him being a grass is madness, he needs to know for sure.

This is it.

'Kingy, mate,' he whispers. 'Rumour has it you've been talking with Babylon.'

'What?' Kingy pulls away. 'Me, with the rozzers?'

'Tell me it's not true and I'm cool yeah.'

Kingy looks at him with tears in his eyes.

Marlons heart sinks.

'Been mates since we were little, and you think I'm a grass?' Kingy shakes his head. 'Where'd you hear all this pony, who's been talking shit?'

'Someone saw you at the Police Station, late one night.'

'Who, who's been talking crap?' Kingy looks angry.

'What does it matter who said what?'

'Listen, I aint been to no Police Station and haven't been chatting to any of them neither, no chance, what do you think I am?' Kingy frowns, standing up. 'Anyway, believe what you want, this is my stop yeah, I'm off.'

Marlons heart sinks even further, he knows this isn't his stop and now, more than ever, he knows for sure it was him at the station the night he was arrested.

Friday, 3 April, 3:57pm
Coldharbour Lane, near Saltoun Road
Brixton, London

Grabbing the handrail with his right hand and swinging out from the platform extending his left, he's flying like a bird or a plane or Superman. A big kid, playing on the back of the bus? Too right, fuck it, Marlon the super-hero!

As always, he ignores the shouts of the conductor and jumps off before the bus comes to a complete stop. Half jogging, half walking, he turns into his road where he's greeted by the echoing sounds of Aswad and *"Jah Children"* bouncing from house to house in the distance. The jangling high hats and reverb-driven vocals breathe a familiar goodness through him. Spotting a battered old blue Leyland Marina approaching with the passenger talking into a radio handset, he slows his pace. He sees the Beast in the passenger seat say something to the driver before leaning out of the window. Heart rate jumping, he doesn't want to look like he's hiding anything so keeps on walking without breaking his stride.

'Oi,' Passenger Beast yells as the car slows to a stop.

Marlon points at his chest gesturing "who me?"

'Yeah you, where you going?'

'Home,' Marlon says, motioning with his head toward his house before pointing at the crest on his blazers breast pocket, 'home from school, yeah.' There's something about Passenger Beast, he's somehow familiar.

'Where's home then?'
'Up there, number forty-seven.'
'What's happened to your head, spot of bother?'
Marlon touches his nearly healed scar. 'Nah, football.'
'Football?'
'Play for the school team, yeah.'
'You lot play football?'
'Never see Viv Anderson?'
'Yeah, I've seen him, he's no Trevor Brooking. Let's get this over with-yah, sus-stop my old son,' Passenger Beast yells in a broad cockney accent before climbing out and flashing a warrant card in front of his face. A massive lump of a man with huge biceps, he looks angry and pissed off. He points to the wall at the foot of the stairs leading to number fifteens front door. 'Over there-yah.'
Driver Beast takes his brown school bag with dirty yellow "Gola" lettering on the side and searches it, while Passenger Beast pats him down, turning his pockets out.
On the other side of the Road a tall, muscular Rasta struts slowly toward them. Marlon knows who he is, everyone knows who he is, it's Claude, full-time enforcer for Crissy, the main man on the Frontline. 'It's cool pickney, I clock every-ting,' he yells over.
Relaxing a little, Marlon knows he doesn't have anything on him he shouldn't have, and is less likely to get a beating with a witness present. 'So, why you happen-pon me then?' he questions Passenger Beast. 'Why I get a sus-stop?'
'Shut it,' Passenger Beast scowls. 'We got a job to do-yah.'
'Why-doh, why stop me?'
'Aw-right then, you appeared to be acting suspiciously when you noticed us-yah, therefore, we believe you might have recently committed, or be on your way to commit an offence.' His old-world-London accent has a Dick van-Dyke twang about it, sounds like the man from the "Charley says" public information adverts on the television.
'Acting suspicious, come on, I've just come from school.'
'Tell Babylon nutton-pickney,' Claude yells, closely

monitoring the situation.

Driver Beast, still searching his school bag turns to Claude. 'Move along, Sir.'

Passenger Beast comes in close, his mouth an inch or so from Marlons ear. 'I'm gonna-ask you a question-yah, and I suggest you tell me the fucking truth,' he whispers.

Marlon looks sideways.

'Think carefully about your answer, Marlon.'

'Eh?'

'It is Marlon-yah, Marlon Walters?'

Shit, he knows my name.

'Lies and deceit will get you into even more trouble, you understand what I'm saying-yah?'

God damn, he fucking knows my name.

'So, who's dealing all the smack around here?'

'Smack, what you on about?' Marlon raises his voice, giving Claude an early warning. 'I don't know nothing about no smack, rude-boy and bad-man control things around here. I'm just a boy.'

'We know all about you and your gang.'

'What?'

'And your brother Devon too.'

He knows Devon by name as well?

'Now, I'm going ask you again.'

Claude gently slopes off, questions about smack and dealers is something Crissy will definitely want to hear about, especially how Babylon asked for Devon by name.

Arrogance and bravado quickly fading, Marlon begins to panic, this is no run of the mill stop and search. How the fuck do they know his name, and Devons name too, and what's this about a gang? He never thought of his mates as a gang. 'Look man, I promise I don't know nothing about any smack or anything. Just set me on my way back home.'

Passenger Beast smiles while brushing him down, straightening out his school uniform. 'Okay Mister Walters, have it your way-yah. Go on, fuck off then.'

Marlon picks up his bag.

'We're watching you lot, tell your bread-a-rins their days are numbered,' Passenger Beast nods.

Marlon sets off walking, not looking back.

'We'll see you later then Marlon,' Passenger Beast yells loudly along the street.

Bastards, everyone will think I've helped them out, told them something or other, that I'm a snake in the grass. Springing up the eight steps leading to his front door, he pushes his key in and twists. Momma stands in the hallway, her face screwed up, chewing-a-wasp style. 'What'am boy, what yah-ado to fetch Police around, what me tell you about bringing trouble to this door?'

Flinging his bag down, he shows her his palms, shrugging his shoulders. 'T'cha, me nah-do nothing Momma. Beastman come at me as soon as I get off the bus and I aint even done a thing.'

'Listen bwai, don't chat like me-ah one of ya-pickney-yout' friends. An-listen to me, dey-nah Beasts, dey Policeman yah-ear.' Her forehead meets the bridge of her nose. 'Here me-nah-bwai, as sure as god look-pon us and I walk dis earth, you nah-bring no trouble to dis door. Me-nah work fingers to the bone for thirty-three years to have tribulation in our life, you understand?'

'Yes-Momma, thanks for caring,' he tuts, picking his bag up before heading upstairs, receiving a clip around the back of his head for good measure.

Flinging his bag onto his bed, he flicks the power switch on the JVC stereo and the cassette tape clicks into action. "Dub Station" flows with horns feeding-back through the echo chamber as the baseline rumbles. Jumping around, skanking in time with the high hats and snares, he yells out a loud, 'yeah-man!' Pulling his shirt over his head, he chucks it onto the landing for Momma to collect ready for tomorrows wash day. Pulling on his Adidas t-shirt, he replaces his grey school trousers with his Lois Jeans. Completing the look, he pulls on his tan and brown Adidas Samoa trainers. Looking in the mirror, he pats and pushes his mid length afro into shape. Then, squeezing a small spot on his cheek, he splashes on some of Devons Brut aftershave. The initial coldness quickly turns into a stinging pain. 'Holy shit,' he yells before heading to the bathroom.

Grabbing a few sheets of toilet paper, he returns to his bedroom. Yeah man, this will sort it out, just what I need to relieve some tension. Reaching on top of the oak panelled wardrobe he locates Devons personal stash. Holding a large amount of bush in his hands he tears off about a quarter-weight. What am I doing, he thinks, Babylon only just stop me not ten minutes ago. After a few seconds deliberation, he decides to fuck the Police and fuck Devon too, he'll beat my arse no matter how much I take, and proceeds to tear off another quarter-weight before wrapping it in the tissue. Stuffing the tissue into a ball of socks, he lobs them into his holdall along with a pair of pants, some bleached Jeans, a Fred Perry t-shirt inherited from Devon and his best electric-blue silk shirt.

Bag zipped up, leather jacket on, now, he's ready.

Poking around on the oak dressing table, pushing cassette tapes, Rizzla packets and half empty aftershave bottles out of the way he finds a half-torn beer mat Devon used for make-shift roaches. Tearing away the logo'd front, he reveals the buff cream card underneath before grabbing a small blue pen Devon must have taken from the local betting shop. Right, what to write?

*Oi Ugly!*
*Beasts stop me.*
*Ask for you by name, NAME !*
*Be careful man,*
*M*

Card and message deposited on Devons pillow, he descends the stairs two at a time before being halted at the bottom by a still angry Momma. 'Whoa, where you ah-go now bwai, and what's ina-dah bag, an why you not eating with us?' Momma pokes at his holdall through the barrage of questions.

'Staying at Ashleys,' he smiles. 'Told you last week, remember, when you were leaving for work?'

Mommas eyes suggest she's replaying last week's events in super-high speed, testing his assertion. 'Yes, yes-nah, that's right, that's right. I do remember.'

She doesn't remember.

Marlon smiles, kisses her on the cheek, throws his bag over his shoulder and heads through the front door.

Friday, 3 April, 4:59pm
Brixton Rail Station
London

Approaching the bridge with the "Welcome to Brixton" sign hanging above, he watches the bible-bashers wailing on about the world coming to an end and that Jesus is the one true saviour. Through the bustling crowds of shoppers and commuters, his eyes meet a skinny man in a black suit, white shirt and black tie. Looking like he's just attended a funeral or something, he's tall with almost grey skin and slicked-back black hair. An old man, maybe forty or fifty, holding a small square of cardboard with the words "IT'S COMING" scribbled in biro. His piercing blue eyes lock onto Marlons, like he recognises him from somewhere. He cant move, cant take his eyes off him, cant help but stare straight back. Their eyes are somehow locked together, like the Death-Star tractor-beam.

Then.

In a flash, the tall skinny man is gone, vanished.

What the fuck?

Then, over to the right, he spots Gladstone standing under the bridge in the shadows with two crates of twenty-four cans of Special Brew at his feet. Sporting a dark blue Parka jacket complete with furry hood and bright orange inner, he looks shady and every bit a potential rude-boy.

'Wha-gwan?' Marlon greets him.

'Easy-nah Marlon.'

'What's with all the doom-mongers, man?' Marlon scans around, trying to re-locate the tall skinny man.

'End of the world dred, it's coming yah-nah,' Gladstone chuckles. 'So, where's duppy-boy lemon?'

'He always late, soon come-doh. Where Delroy at?'

'Music Shack,' Gladstone motions over his shoulder into the market and the pre-eminent retailer of dub-plates and imported exclusives. 'Doing a little business, so he says.'

Five minutes and a few jokes about Delroy bigging himself up way too much later, Ashley bounces through the crowd. 'Watcha,' he beams.

'Assssh-leeee,' Gladstone high-fives him.

'Up for a wicked weekend then?' Ashley grins, pretend-punching Gladstones arm.

'Got the keys, all set?' Marlon queries.

'Yeah, yeah, all sorted, no problems,' Ashley nods.

'Easy-nah-man, easy,' Delroy sings, entering the circle of friends wearing a black donkey jacket with the high collars up around his ears, and a Sherlock Holmes hat perching on his head. Without stopping, he heads straight through the group toward the steps leading to the platforms. 'What the fuck are we bom-ba-clat waiting for?' he shouts. 'These country bumpkin gals won't fuck themselves.'

Friday, 3 April, 6:49pm
British Rail Intercity 125
Somewhere in England

Opposite Ashley, Marlon gazes out of the window as the setting sun casts long shadows as green fields trundle past, while the Gladstone and Delroy are busy chatting about how many girls they plan to get off with this weekend.

'How much longer Ash, this is dry, man.' Marlon sighs, boredom weaving through his words.

'Dunno, we usually come by car.' Ashley looks out toward

the dusky sky sitting above rolling countryside. 'Not long now I don't think.'

'You know what, I've never been on a train like this,' Marlon says, leaning in, lowering his tone. 'Never been out of London yah-nah.'

Ashley stares at him waiting for his usual broad grin to appear, for him to start laughing at his own joke. Marlon stares back through a blank expression. 'Serious, you've never been out of London?'

'Nope, never.'

'Fucking hell,' Ashely shakes his head, thinking about how different their lives actually are…

After another long hour, the train finally pulls into its last and final stop, Brighton Central. Grinding to a halt, the doors open and several pre-built spliffs are immediately ignited.

'Ah, smell da country air,' Delroy pronounces, breathing deeply before sucking on his five-skin.

'Looks like a shit-hole,' Gladstone tuts, looking around at the deserted Station. 'Jus-like that shit-tip train.'

Outside, Ashley hails a taxi and, within ten minutes, they pull up at the caravan site.

Friday, 3 April, 8:11pm
Hove Valley Caravan Park
Brighton

The group cut a dark silhouette against the disco lights shining brightly through the windows of the club-house. Crunching up the path, they hear the muffled sounds of Top of the Tops music distorting through what must have been a crappy sound system.

'This, this is it?' Delroy shakes his head at the sight of the small, shabby nineteen sixties single story block from where the light and sound emanates from.

'It's the fucking youth centre from back home,' Gladstone tuts. 'We've been on a magic roundabout train ride for hours man, and all it's done is taken us back to the Frontline.'

'True-say dred, true-say,' Delroy giggles.

'Which one is ours?' Marlon asks, scanning the fleet of practically identical luxury caravans spread-out across the five-acre site.

'Down there on the left,' Ashley whispers. 'But keep it down yeah, my old man don't know we're here. He knows everyone and they'll be on the blower to him pronto if they spot us.'

After a short walk, they stop at a huge caravan, significantly larger than the others with a wooden deck at the front and a table and a stack of chairs piled up to the side. In the middle of the deck, a set of long glass panelled doors, flanked by two windows either side.

Spinning around, Ashley raises his arms above his head. 'This, my brothers, is it.'

They all stand in silence.

'Rassssss-clat, dis place is bigger than Mommas flat on Somerleyton,' Delroy whispers, breaking the silence. 'Your family must be minted yeah.'

'T'cha, here me now,' Gladstone steps forward. 'We aint no fucking brothers, you understand?'

Ashley smiles, waiting for the punchline, but the group stand in silence watching Gladstones screwed up face.

'What, what's going on?' Ashley prompts.

'We aint brothers, so stop acting like we are.'

'Eh?' Ashley shakes his head. 'What you on about, Glad?'

'You heard me.'

'Lef-it nah-man,' Marlon says, patting the air in front of him, noting Gladstones serious tone.

'We aint his brothers though are we, him showing off all the time with his garms and money and ting,' Gladstone snarls, stepping forward.

'Come on Glad,' Ashley pleads. 'We've been mates from primary school.'

Marlon steps in between them both. 'We're all mates yeah, lets calm the fuck down.'

Gladstone hesitates, before turning to Ashley. 'Listen, we're not brothers and you're not like us, stop trying to be.'

Nobody says a word while Gladstone maintains his stare.

Marlon looks across to Gladstone, then to Delroy. A hundred different scenarios play through his mind as the silence pierces his eardrums.

'All-right-naw,' Delroy steps in. 'Enough been said and we all know where we stand now, don't we?'

'Yeah, but…'

'Yeah but nothing Ashley,' he smiles, putting his arm around his neck. 'We're here together, wherever the fuck here is, and we all mates yeah, so let's get this bom-ba-clat party started, yesh?'

Tension laughed away, they enter the caravan one by one, Ashley leading the way as Marlon closes the door behind them. Closing the door, he stares at Gladstone, wondering what the fuck was he on about and where did all that negative crap come from. The last thing he, or the group need is Gladstone putting everyone on a downer and ruining the vibe. They're supposed to be on holiday for fucks sake.

Anyway…

To the left, leather-bound benches reach across the entire side and back wall with a coffee table in the centre. Straight ahead is the toilet and shower room while on the right, three bedrooms, two singles and a large double. As Ashley has already dropped his bag onto the bed in the double bedroom, the others clamber to claim the remaining two bedrooms. Twenty minutes of arguing and several rounds of negotiation later, they sit around the coffee table having finally agreeing their sleeping arrangements.

'So, Ash,' Delroy says, sitting back sucking on his spliff. 'Your folks own this place then?'

'Err, yeah,' Ashley cringes. 'Bought it a few years ago, when prices were cheap.' The last thing he wants to do right now is talk about his folks money, not to mention their villa in La Cala de Mijas on the Costa del Sol his father is currently in the process of buying.

'Come down here a lot then?'

'Couple of weeks in summer, long weekend at Easter maybe, more often when me and my brother were little.'

Marlon looks up from building a five-skin. He doesn't want all this talk to annoy Gladstone. 'Listen, I wanna say something.'

Delroy and Gladstone look sideways at each other before back to Marlon.

'Listen up, I'm serious, we all up for a wicked weekend, yeah?' The others nod tentatively. 'So, I reckon we agree a pact between us, right here right now, all of us.'

'A pack?' Delroy queries, his eyebrows rising. 'Sounds like batty-man-business.'

'Nah-man, a pact. P.A.C.T.' Marlon spells it out.

'It means an agreement…' Gladstone cuts in.

'Err, yeah man,' Marlon nods sideways at Gladstone, who isn't known for his command of the English language. 'Whatever happens this weekend, it's between us right, no matter what. Boning birds, mashing up local youths or whatever, it stays here, just between us.' Marlon places his right hand in the centre of the table, Ashley follows, placing his hand on top. Delroy adds his hand and Gladstone slowly places the final hand.

'It stays here,' they yell together.

# Episode 16.
# "Rat Boy"

Wednesday, 1 April, 12:38pm
Locker Room
Brixton Police Station, London

'Andy.'

'Collins.'

'How's it going fella?'

'Good, thanks,' Andrew nods as the cogs of his mind clunk into gear. Why would Collins be in the locker room attempting small talk? 'Don't usually see you down here.'

'Listen, Andy, I need a favour, mate.'

Of course you do, and, I aint your mate, Andrew thinks to himself. Friendly chit-chat and bar room banter isn't Collins style. Play it cool Jonesy, he tells himself, play it cool.

Collins looks around before moving closer. 'Got this informant, been feeding him for ages.'

Andrew nods, conscious not to seem too eager.

'But, the little shits stalling on something, need to apply some pressure, if you catch my drift?' Collins nods.

'Pressure, yah?'

'Need an intimidating bastard to… well, you know… someone who isn't going to ask too many questions?'

Andrew heads to the end of the lockers, checking nobody's listening before returning. 'And I'm the intimidating bastard-yah?'

Andrew doesn't know Collins that well, so the fact he's asking him, a relative stranger, is a sure sign of desperation. This is okay though, Collins will owe him a favour. Very quickly after passing out from Hendon Andrew learned "favours" are powerful currency in the Met.

'So, you up for it big man?' Collins tone eager, too enthusiastic, he's most definitely desperate. This is good.

'Sure, fuck it,' Andrew nods. 'But, you owe me one, right.'

Shrugging his shoulders, Collins nods.

'Uniformed or plain clothed?'

Tongue in cheek, Collins stares into the floor then breathes deeply. 'Neither, this is a personal project.'

'Ahh-okay, I'll ask no questions then.'

'That's the spirit. I'll meet you at the Coach and Horses on Barrington Road, near the Loughborough, at closing time.'

'Alright, sweet, got to get home soon after though, Janice is giving me grief, reckons I'm having it off with some dirty barmaid or something.'

'Dirty barmaids?' Collins winks. 'You'd be lucky.'

Wednesday, 1 April, 10:58pm
Coach and Horses Public House
Barrington Road, Brixton, London

As the saloon doors open with a drawn-out ghost-story creak, he realises the dramatic entrance would have been more effective if the pub was full of punters to witness it. Mid-week and near closing time, only a few regulars are in and none of them look up from their solemn pints. The barman, a fat-faced stereotype points at the clock. 'Last orders already called pal.'

Looking around, Andrew sees a few old men sipping brown ales and a couple of youngsters playing the fruit machine. Approaching the bar, he flashes his warrant card. 'It's alright mate, just waiting for someone.'

'Oh, right, listen, I don't want no trouble in here, just about to lock up I am.'

'It's okay,' Andrew says, noticing the worried look on his fat face. 'Like I say-yah, I'm just waiting for someone.'

The barman grabs a glass and, without looking up from the pump, pours a pint and places next to Andrews elbow.

'Nah, you're alright,' Andrew shakes his head.

'On the house pal.'

Andrew tentatively smiles and takes a sip. He feels awkward and nervous, the combination of Collins, an old school wrong-un and thoroughly nasty piece of work, plus the Loughborough Estate is a recipe for certain disaster.

A few long minutes later…

Collins pushes his way through the swing doors. A short, overweight man in his trademark long brown trench coat, he has greasy grey hair and beady eyes, and, after a ten-hour shift, he looks even older than his sixty years.

Necking the remainder of his pint, Andrew nods toward the barman before following Collins outside. 'You're late,' Andrew points at his watch.

'Only by five.'

'Late is late, mate.'

'Relax big man, this little shit won't be a problem for us.'

'Don't like waiting like a pleb in a shithole pub-yah, especially around this fucking snake-pit.'

'Yeah, bit grim around here Andy, too right fella,' Collins smiles, spinning around scanning the scene before setting off toward the Loughborough. 'Anyway, let's get going.'

Andrew hates the Loughborough Estate or "Angel Town" as it's commonly known. A maze of high-rise tower blocks set out in regimentally symmetrical rows, each are elevated on grey concrete stilts with open walkways beneath connecting the blocks together. With around two thousand flats, over recent years it's become a cesspit of scum with squats, drug dens and whore houses popping up. Everything on the edge of society is drawn to Angel Town. Andrew was brought up on a similar estate in Canning Town, East London, but his estate, back in the seventies, was completely different to this utter shit hole. His estate was full of decent, hard-working families, good honest people and salt of the earth types, grateful for what they had, not like the scumbags around here who think the world owes them a living.

Arriving at Brixton Station as part of his work experience, he quickly learned the potted history of "Angel Town". Apparently, in the mid-sixties, the local council earmarked the whole area to be demolished in favour of an urban motorway through the centre of Brixton north toward the City of London. This would lead to massive investment in the area and a huge regeneration scheme for the whole South London area. Due to council red-tape, a change of political administration and huge local resistance, the plan ground to a halt. Throughout the long, drawn out planning process the local council refused to invest into the area or move new tenants in. As a result, the area rapidly fell into disrepair leading to an exodus of the locals who moved to less deprived areas of London or further afield to Kent, Surrey or the South Coast. This caused a huge problem as the council receive funding from central government based on the number of people housed, not the number of dwellings. Once the motorway plan was rejected, in order to secure more funding, the Council clambered to fill as many vacant properties as possible, offering flats to the homeless and then to those desperate enough to want a transfer from other parts of Great Britain and eventually the Commonwealth. As a result, the whole area was flooded with the vulnerable and disaffected, resentful undesirables which quickly turned it into an unofficial "no-go" area.

That was back then, this is now…

Andrew follows Collins along the main horse-shoe shaped road serving as the only way in and out of the estate. Approaching a gang of youths sitting on a low wall laughing and joking, he feels his heart rate increase. Scanning the group, he spots a couple drinking lager while others are smoking what smells suspiciously like cannabis resin. As soon as the gang spot the middle-aged white males approaching, obviously plain clothes Police, they stop fooling around and start eyeballing. Staring right back, Andrew knows any sign of doubt or fear will be seen as weakness. Passing, he maintains a steely glare over his shoulder, partly to keep the pressure on and partly to make sure they're not plotting to stab him in the back or lob a brick or two.

A couple of minutes later…

Collins stops at the entrance a high-rise block. Kicking the tyres of an old brown Ford Cortina, covered in rust with no tax disc he nods and smiles. 'This is their motor.'

Andrew looks up to the top of the tower block. "Their" implies more than one, fucking hell, how many, are they tooled up?

This escapade is quickly turning from bad to worse.

'Andy, listen, this toe-rag is nothing to worry about, nowt but a kid,' Collins suggests, noticing Andrews anxiety.

Yeah right, Andrew thinks, why need me then?

'But,' Collins continues. 'He's staying with a bit of a hard-nut, goes by the name of McMahon.'

Ah, that's the reason I'm here.

'A proper national-front-arsehole Andy, nasty piece of work, no match for you fella.'

Andrew smiles, an old-school skinhead, eh? Yeah, he feels a wave of adrenalin flow through him. Fucking hate skinheads, he says to himself.

'Say hello nicely,' Collins chuckles. 'Keep him busy while I'll sort my little problem out.'

'Let's just get it over with-yah,' Andrew says, pushing passed Collins. 'What number?'

Wednesday, 1 April, 11:06pm
No. 17, Kettle House
Loughborough Estate, Brixton, London

Peering through the window, shards of light from the hallway enter the kitchen beneath the closed door. He sees a table with two chairs and piles of plates, cups and general crap spread across the worktop and in the sink with a never been cleaned chard chip pan sitting on top of the disgustingly dirty cooker. Andrew nods, he always thought Angel Town was a shithole, and now, he knows it for sure.

Collins winks before knocking the front door in a friendly "knock, knock-knock, knock" way.

Silence.

No answer.

'They're definitely in,' Collins whispers.

He bangs hard. Three times.

'Fuck this, I'll open it,' Andrew steps forward.

'No, no-no wait,' Collins puts his arm. 'No need for drama just yet big lad.'

Removing one arm from his three-quarter length trench-coat, Collins rolls his sleeve up above his elbow and pushes his surprisingly slender forearm through the narrow letter box. Feeling around with his fingertips, he finds the handle and pushes it down.

Click.

The door opens.

Turning to Andrew, he mouths 'shush' before moving slowly along the hallway, past the kitchen, stopping outside the living room. Turning back, putting his finger to his lips, he mouths 'shush', again.

Shush? I fucking get it, Andrew thinks. Focusing on the door to the front room, he can hear the nursery rhyme-esque sounds of "Bankrobber" by The Clash coming from a cheap, tinny stereo inside. He likes The Clash, they're class.

Through the door, peeping his head into the living room, Collins stifles a chuckle.

'What?' Andrew whispers impatiently.

'The stupid fucks,' Collins giggles. 'They're fast asleep.'

Reaching inside his jacket Andrew feels for his truncheon then barges his way into the room. Eyes wide, he scans around. Grey council issue lino flooring and two dickheads asleep on a grey, heavily stained hessian sofa. To the left an up-turned milk crate with a red velvet cushion on top, used as a make-shift seat. In front of the sofa another milk crate with a sheet of plywood on top, posing as a coffee table. An over-filled ashtray, a couple of empty packets of cigarettes and three cans of lager sit on top of this. This place is disgusting, a complete shit hole. In the corner of the room is an old-fashioned wooden-boxed television and next to this, a paint-splattered transistor radio. Yep, it's a complete and utter shit-tip in here, how do these dogs live like this? His attention quickly focuses on the sofa and the two sleeping beauties. The first, mid to late twenties with a grade one skinhead, green bomber-jacket and faded skin-tight jeans, a cliché from a bygone era, obviously "McMahon". The second, snoring heavily, is younger, maybe late teens. A skinhead too with a black bomber jacket full of badges around the lapels. His face is covered in acne and, Andrew concludes he's a god-ugly mother-fucker. In between them both rests a crumpled-up carrier bag and beneath this on the floor, a nearly empty can of industrial adhesive with the lid half on half off.

'Fucking glue heads,' Andrew whispers before pointing his truncheon at the younger one. 'This one your snout?'

'Yeah, that's him,' Collins nods, using a pen to peer inside the cigarette boxes.

As he moves toward McMahon the Clash fades out as his own personal music fades in with the iconic snares of "Vienna" by Ultravox. In his element, he feels like he's playing the lead role in a movie and Vienna is the soundtrack.

*"Dum… t'ch, dum-dum-dum… t'ch-cha."*

Further forward, he grips his truncheon at each end and, in a flash, is forcing himself and the truncheon deep into McMahons throat.

*"This means nothing to me…"*

Andrews eyes widen, he feels alive.

McMahons eyes spring open, but he doesn't move, he's frozen with panic, unaware his brain is being starved of oxygen as the truncheon crushes his Adams-apple and windpipe. Looking deep into his glazed eyes, Andrew sees the outside edges narrow as his prey begins to struggle.

*"Dum, dum-dum-dum…"*

Gritting his teeth, he pushes his forehead into McMahons. 'Come on then,' he seethes pushing harder as the snares crash and echo.

*"Ahhhhhhh-Vienna… dumb-dud-dum… t'ch-cha."*

Looking on, Collins is impressed with Andrews aggression but ever so slightly concerned for McMahons health. 'Don't kill him fella,' he prompts.

Pushing for a few seconds more, McMahons eyes begin to roll back into his head. With that, Andrew releases him and he crumples sideways into the centre of the sofa, coughing and spluttering, cupping his damaged throat.

'Oi, shit-cunt,' Andrew prods him with the end of this truncheon. 'One wrong move and you're going over that fucking balcony.'

McMahon looks up.

Andrew recognises the fear in his eyes. 'That's right dickhead,' he continues. 'Fuck around, and tonight'll be your last, you understand-yah?'

McMahon nods slowly, tears in his eyes.

Collins kicks the outstretched legs of the still comatose younger one who murmurs something unintelligible about his mum and spaghetti on toast.

Chuckling, Collins kicks again, harder this time.

Opening his eyes, he looks at Collins, then Andrew then McMahon. Lightening quick, he jumps to his feet and bolts for the door. Reacting quickly, Collins aims a kick at his trailing leg. Tumbling, he hits the door shoulder first, landing on his back with a dramatic groan. Surprisingly agile for an old man, Collins is on him, knee landing on his stomach and hand around his neck. 'Easy now, easy, we just want to talk.'

Realising he's not necessarily in for a hiding and his chances of getting away are next to hopeless he stops struggling. 'Alright, alright,' he sighs as Collins releases him.

McMahon looks on, not moving a muscle as Collins leads the youngster into the kitchen.

Five seconds later…

'Take a seat Mister King, take the weight off, how've you been?' Collins asks, his tone sarcastic.

'Err, alright thanks.'

'Right, right, good,' Collins cut in. 'Glad to hear it.'

Kingy looks down into the table, knowing this is no social call. The small talk is unnerving.

'I'm trying to track down a very dangerous gang.'

'Yeah?' Kingy shrugs.

'Reckon you can point me in the right direction.'

'Not sure I can help you Mister Collins.'

'Oh, no-no-no, I disagree young man.'

'No, really, I don't know nothing.'

'Same terms as last time?'

'Twenty?' Kingy looks up, Oliver Twist asking for more.

'Yeah, okay, twenty then,' Collins counts out four five-pound notes before throwing them into the middle of the table. 'Right then, tell me about Paul Richardson.'

Kingy struggles not to show any sign of recognition. A thousand thoughts run through his buzzing mind.

'You know him, heard of him?'

'Not sure, rings a bell but…'

'Rings-a-bell bollocks, don't mess me around, boy.'

'Alright, I've heard of him, yeah,' Kingys voice cracks, he knows there's little point in trying to deny it.

'Good, good, that's the spirit. Now then, who are the two rude-boys he knocks about with?'

'Dunno, he hangs around with a load of different geezers.' Kingy lies, of course he knows them, everyone on the Frontline knows them, Marlons older brother, Devon, and the crazy motherfucker named Super.

'Listen,' Collins leans in, placing both hands on the table either side of the crumpled-up notes. 'I know you know them, so look lively and spill the beans.'

'Eh, what?'

'Names and addresses, or my mate next door'll be in here pronto to sort you out. His missus is at home clock watching so he's a bit on edge, if you catch my drift.'

Kingy looks back at the table, his mind working overtime. Can't drop Marlon in it, he's a pal. Maybe I can drop that cunt Delroy in it though, that'd teach him, the bullying bastard.

'So?' Collins stresses, his voice straining with impatience.

'Alright, alright,' Kingy decides against doing for Delroy in fear of the repercussions from both Delroy, and also Collins. 'Devon Walters and Winston something or other.'

'Something or other?'

'What?'

'Mind reader, am I?'

'Err-no, err-what?'

'Winston what, dickhead?'

'Don't know his name, everyone just calls him Super.'

Collins stares hard into Kingy. 'Super?'

'Yeah.'

'Sounds homosexual, a fairy?'

Smiling, Kingy struggles to contain a laugh. 'Not likely.'

'Okay, Devon and Winston, otherwise known as Super. Good, good. Addresses?'

'Look Guv, I don't know where they live, honest, around Somerleyton Estate or Railton Road I think.'

'You think? Think harder dickhead.'

'Fucking hell.'

Collins clips him around the head. 'Language, boy.'

'Alright-alright, one of them works down at the scrap yard around the corner from there, I think.' He's not about to send the Police around to Marlons house, nah, his mum always had time for him. When they were about ten or eleven while on the way to school, he'd knock for Marlon who was never ready on time. His momma would invite him in to wait and cook him an egg sandwich with tomato sauce because he needed "fattening up" as she'd say.

'Scrap yard you say, the oily shit-hole on Coldharbour?'
'Think so, can I go now?' Kingy reaches out for the cash.
Collins grabs his wrist. 'If you're messing me around, you know what'll be coming your way, don't you?'
Kingy nods slowly.
Collins lets go of his wrist and smiles. 'Right then,' he shouts through to the front room. 'We're off big guy, why don't you say goodbye to your new best mate.'
With that, Kingy hears the unmistakable sound of violence then a drawn-out moan before the big guy appears at the kitchen doorway, rubbing his knuckles.
'Right then,' Collins smiles. 'We're off now, be a good lad and don't do anything I wouldn't do.'

Friday, 3 April, 12:15pm
The Scrap Yard, Coldharbour Lane
Brixton, London

The long black Mercedes 300D comes to a smooth stop outside the taxi shop, just past the scrap yard.
'Right,' Steve-the-Manager sighs, looking over his shoulder at the twins spread across the back seats. 'Get in there, mess him around a bit and get the address of the big bah-stard.'
'Mess him up good my darlings,' adds the Wiry Queen sitting in the passenger seat.
The twins nod silently as the one on the left reaches into the footwell, producing a shotgun with a short black barrel and dark wood handle. Checking it's loaded, he locks it closed and flicks the safety off.
'What on earth… are you do-ing?' Steve-the-Manager whispers dramatically, placing his palms gently onto the barrel, lowering it behind the seat. 'We don't need any hass-al from the Flying-Squad, do we… just give him a beat-ing, get the address, then get back here as quick as you can.'
Meanwhile…
Neville, shuffling from his chair peers through the broken venetian blinds hanging aimlessly half-up-half-down across

the never been cleaned window. 'Looks like we've got customers,' he says cheerily, placing his cup of tea down on top of the Calor-gas heater. 'Don't worry ol-cock, I'll see to these two, yow finish your cuppa and keep warm.'

Sitting back, Devon smiles and sips his tea. This is the life, he thinks. A brummie twat from Birmingham or wherever the fuck, Neville's alright really, heart of gold, he smiles.

Pulling his overalls back over his shoulders as he walks, Neville approaches the two customers. With a welcoming smile he looks around them to clock what car they're driving, usually providing a good indication of how much he can charge or rip them off by. Spotting the tail end of a Merc' his smile stretches further across his face, great, he thinks, maybe we'll knock off early today. 'Morning chaps, what can I do for you?'

The Twin on the right smiles and nods, while the other unleashes a devastating blow to the left-hand side of Nevilles head. Eyes rolling, legs giving way, he crumples to the floor.

Staring at their felled prey, the twins exchange smiles before heading in silence toward the cabin.

Five seconds later…

Devon springs to his feet as the door crashes open, hinges and splinters of timber fly through the air.

In a flash, the Twins are inside.

Twin on the left stands six feet tall with short fair hair and an angled jawbone. With the physique of a body builder, he wears a black leather bomber jacket stretching over his highly developed chest. The Twin on the right is a carbon copy, other than a small scar above his right eye.

'What, what the fuck?' Devon yells, hands stretching out in front. Looking out into the yard he sees Neville collapsed in a lifeless heap. Oh shit!

'Devon?' the Right Twin probes, his voice soft and calm.

'Devon Walters?' queries the other, his voice also soft, almost feminine.

'Who?' Devon shrugs.

'You're in deep Devon,' Left Twin says, slowly.

'Messed with the wrong people,' adds Right Twin.

'And now,' Left Twin continues, reaching around his back to produce an eight-inch leather bound cosh. 'You're gonna pay the price.'

"Pay the price" do me a favour, Devon thinks, these two sound like extras from an old-time gangster movie. He stares at the cosh and the Twin stroking it slowly with a smile. Holy shit, queer skinheads. He can imagine the newspaper headlines, "Handsome Brixtonian man gang raped by batty-man skinheads."

Easing forward, maintaining their fighting stance the Twins pounce. Left Twin swings his cosh into Devons thigh while Right Twin aims a backhand toward his head.

Spinning one-eighty, landing face down on the floor, Devon yells as pain stings through him. Then, Right Twin lands a knee into his back as the other straddles his legs.

Still face down, Devon hears an un-zipping sound.

Shit, they are batty-man.

I'm fucked, literally!

Thankfully, his wrists are grabbed and tape wrapped around. Breathing a sigh of relief, he feels a weird sense of gratitude for not being violated.

Pulled to his feet, he's thrown into the chair where, only a matter of seconds ago, he sat peacefully drinking tea. He winces as his wrists crunch under his own weigh.

'Look man, I don't know what this is about…'

Left Twin smashes his cosh into his knees.

'Shut. Up.' Right Twin grunts.

'Where's your mate, Winston?' asks the other.

Super? What the fuck?

'Not seen him in ages,' Devon shakes his head.

Left Twin steps forward, raising his cosh while Right Twin speaks. 'Don't mess us around, Devon.'

'We'll off you and that fat fuck outside,' Left Twin adds. 'Cave both your skulls in then torch this place, all they'll find is your charred remains.'

His heart races. 'Listen man, I don't know shit, he lives at St Matthews Estate, near Acre Lane in a squat or something. I've not seen him in weeks.' He knows he's just fucked his boyhood best friend, but, it'll buy him some time, allow him to warn him, maybe get re-enforcements.

'Really?' Left Twin smiles sarcastically.

'He wasn't here yesterday, all afternoon, leaving at about three-thirty?' Right Twins adds.

Fucking hell, they've been watching us.

'Listen, he comes around here now and again, I don't keep a diary,' Devon tuts.

'Now and again?'

'Diary?'

'We'll just wait around then, might be our lucky day,' Right Twin says, perching on the worktop as the other leans against the wall. Both, Devon notes, well out of sight from the outside.

'If he's not here by two o'clock, you're getting buried, then we're off round to your old dears house,' Right Twin says, looking through Devon like he's not there.

'We'll torch her gaff, it'll be gone,' adds Left Twin.

Momma and Marlon, Pops too? Unable to face his destiny he looks away, feeling a cold shiver running down his spine as a been-here-before déjà-vu feeling washes over him drowning him in this living nightmare.

Friday, 3 April, 12:26pm
Black Mercedes 300D, outside the Scrapyard
Coldharbour Lane, Brixton, London

'Something's up, I just know it,' the Wiry Queen fidgets.

'Shush, qui-et,' Steve-the-Manager spits, his Welsh accent increasing in strength, annoyed with the queens need for constant reassurance.

'How can I possibly be quiet, something has definitely gone wrong, where are those two dear boys, oh, I'm so worried, I can't tell you.'

'Will you shut the fuck up and be patient?'

The Wiry Queen stares out of the window, tears in his eyes. 'No need to be so aggressive, I'm just saying.'

They continue to sit in silence and wait.

Until.

'Oh-oh, hold on.'

'What now?'

'No-no-no, please no, there he is, the brute,' the Wiry Queen urges, pointing at the oversized guy approaching, herbal cigarette in one hand, brown paper bag in the other.

'Don't point, you more-on.'

Passing by the black Mercedes, Super gives it a sideways glance, nice motor, he thinks. As he turns into the scrapyard, he spots Neville slumped on the floor. Slowing his pace, he drops the bag containing three delicious spiced-meat patties. Standing over Neville, staring at the lifeless body, his hand instinctively gravitates toward his inside breast pocket and his trusty blade.

Shit.

Looking to the sky, he can see it in his minds eye resting under his bed, all shiny and silver, reassuringly cold and calculating. He needs to feel its weight, feel comforted by its power. With the increasing number of sus-stops, and, on the shit advice of Devon, he'd left it at home.

Today of all days.

What a day…

Naked, vulnerable, at risk, he crouches down to touch Nevilles face with the back of his hand. Still warm, recently felled. Eyes darting, he quickly zones in on the cabin.

Door wide open.

Off its hinges.

Fuck.

Ninja-like, he quickly makes his way to the large mountain of worn tyres to the right of the cabin. Through the gap between door and broken frame he sees two pairs of feet. The first pair, oil-blackened steel toe caps with the dirty-grey steel protruding through the worn leather, Devons boots.

He doesn't recognise the other pair of slightly oiled white sneakers. Edging deftly around the tyre-mountain toward the cabin, he spots a rusty chain about three feet long, each link about four inches. Picking it up softly, being careful not to jangle it, he doubles it over and feels it for weight. Yeah man, nice, not quite "me-baby", but it'll do. Standing at the edge of the cabin he listens for signs of life… murmurings, but nothing conclusive. Heart racing, he smiles to himself as he flicks the switch on his mind-ghetto blaster. The opening bars of Wailing Rudie kicks in…

*"To live a righteous life seems poor…"*

Yeah man.

*"To my defence… strict badness in him I might defend."*

Blood coursing through his veins, fire sparks in his mind and electricity pops all around as dark clouds form above.

Deep breath, yeah man.

I'm alive.

Diving into the cabin time slows down…

In a single super-slow-motion-split-second he sees everything, eyes sucking the situation deep into his brain…

Devon taped up and in a bad way…

Tasty-looking skinhead…

In a fighting stance… ready to go…

The needle scratches across Rudie…

Silence fills his mind…

In a flash, chain swinging windmill style, he connects with the skinheads head who timbers like a felled tree.

Yeah man, Super-man to the rescue!

He looks at Devon, expecting a grateful smile but instead he sees fear and horror. Devon isn't even looking at him, but over his shoulder.

Danger.

Too late.

Searing pain rips across his head as he hears a cracking sound. He feels himself falling backward out of the cabin door. I've been hit, man down, Super-man down!

Bloodclat kryptonite-star.

A second skinhead.

Fuck.

Time speeds up as a whirlwind of violence surrounds him as they tumble through the doorway and the Right Twin continues to tear into him.

Forcing himself out of his chair, Devon steps passes the Left Twin who, writhing around on the floor, is clasping the side of his head with blood seeping through his fingers. Reaching the doorway, he can see Right Twin on top of Super, pounding into his head. Super's fighting back though, moving from side to side trying to dodge the blows while at the same time aiming punches up toward the Twins face. In the distance, he sees Neville, lifeless body in a heap.

What the fucks happening?

Wrists taped behind his back impeding his movement, Devon jumps the few steps leading from the cabin and runs toward the grappling pair. Without stopping, he hurls his boot into the head of the Twin, connecting with a dull thud.

Flying over the top, Devon lands maybe four feet away and pain slices through his shoulder. Lifting his head, he sees the Twin on his back, side by side with Super.

Super rolls over onto his side, placing his hand on top of the felled twins chest. 'You alright Dee?' he shouts over.

'Yeah man, you?' Devon sighs.

'Star, me head mash-up, but I'm okay.'

'What's the score with him?'

Leaning over Super puts his ear to the Twins mouth. 'Just sleeping yeah, what dah-fook happen-star, and what about Nev, Nev dead?' Super asks, mounting the Twin.

Looking across to Neville, Devon sees his over-sized stomach pushing in and out. 'Nah man, Nev not dead, still breathing, the fat fuck.'

Left Twin staggers into the doorway of the cabin still holding his face, blood oozing through his fingers, steadying himself while taking in the scene. 'Get off my brother,' he yells, his voice bouncing around the yard.

Looking up toward the cabin, Super searches around the

mud with his hand and locates the chain. Maintaining eye contact with the Twin in the cabin, he stands up with the other Twin between his legs and smashes the chain downward.

'Noooo,' Left Twin screams from the cabin.

'Here me nah-star,' Super yells. 'You got sixty seconds to clear dis place or you and him gonna get fooked up.'

The Left Twin, blood dripping down the side of his head and neck tentatively steps out of the cabin and approaches his brother, not taking his eyes off Super who backs away accordingly. Crouching down, he shakes his brother awake, then helps him get to his feet.

'This aint over,' Left Twin groans.

Arms over each others shoulders, the Twins stagger out of the yard toward the Mercedes. The near side rear door opens and they both fall in. With that, the car reverses into the yard and a fat guy leans out of the drivers window. 'Fuck-king cunts, you'll get yours,' he shouts as the back window edges open and the barrels of a shotgun edge out. With an orange flash, the gun fires, filling the air with a loud pop-cracking sound.

'Blooooodclaaaat,' Devon yells as he and Super dive sideways away from each other. Another pop-crack and the car speeds off, wheels spinning and white smoke bellowing from the exhaust.

Friday, 3 April, 6:01pm
Staff Canteen
Brixton Police Station, London

Legs astride at the front of the room, Commander Crows demeanour demands respect. Glancing around, he eyeballs the thirty or so Officers sitting on chairs, resting on tables and standing around at the back of the canteen. 'Gentlemen,' he clears his throat. 'Today we begin… to clean up our streets and… give Brixton back to its residents.'

Looking around the room with its peeling paintwork and flickering lights, John observes Crow holding the room, and inspiring the men. Even so, Crows pregnant pauses mid-sentence and his exponential increase in the use of clichés throughout the past week is testing his nerves, plus, with Crow giving such a rousing speech, he finds himself chewing the inside of his lip. However, what annoys and worries him in equal measure is the aggressive reaction Crows words evoke within the rank and file.

Thankfully, Crows briefing doesn't last long.

Assigned to "Operations Command", John will track the movement of each of the SPG groups deployed and receive street level information from plain clothes units and other sources. He'll then assess the validity of said information and, if appropriate, pass it on to the closest SPG group, uniformed patrols, CID, the Flying Squad or Special Ops, headed by Giles Askwith-Parsons, the civilian from the briefing John recently attended. This is all part of a massive operation where, during the next twelve hours, Brixton will be flooded with Officers from across the entire Met and other adjacent forces such as the Kent, Thames Valley and also the Middlesex Constabulary. The objective of the operation is to crack down on all types of crime, including petty offences that previously would have been ignored, as well as making multiple arrests which will, quite literally, clean up the streets. A Portakabin has been shipped into the car park of Brixton Police Station as a temporary holding area if, as they expect, the custody suite becomes overcrowded.

Seen to be fuelling the demand for drugs, the first big offensive of the night involves clearing the squatters from Leeson and Mayall Roads. Planned like a military operation, the local council have been serving eviction notices over the past two days, and, any squatters refusing to move on will be arrested. Council maintenance workers will then move in to board-up and secure the houses once cleared. Crow will act as "Field Commander", out on the street personally leading three patrols to Leeson Road, blocking it off at each end before serving final eviction notices. He'll then, in his own words, arrest the "squatter-scum" for breaching the peace or whatever offense he can make stick.

Although begrudgingly respecting Crow for not being a behind-the-desk leader, John holds major reservations about the operation, especially choosing to deploy on Friday evening which, in his opinion, is deliberately provocative. Crow convinced the Operations Committee that creating maximum awareness will ensure deviants take notice and alter their behaviour, thereby reducing the need for arrest. Although there is a level of rudimental logic in this, John believes it's an overtly high, and ultimately unacceptable risk to take. Instead, he advocates a community-based approach, suggesting this will be less disruptive to citizens, less resource intensive for the Met and ultimately more effective in the longer term. He believes, as stated in his university dissertation, communities function more cohesively when they self-Police, create their own social-norms, and build trust horizontally across the community and vertically within the various governmental support structures, such as the Council and Police.

Leaving the canteen, through the custody suite, then down the stairs to the locker room, John hears "the Jam" or some other contemporary pop-group blaring out of a tinny transistor radio. He often considers the role music plays in preparing the Officers for their shifts, some type of emotional conditioning or motivational factor he concludes. Upon entering, he's greeted by a mass of Officers changing from their civilian clothes into their outdoor wear, each going through their own personal per-shift ritual, some polishing their boots, some pretend wrestling with their buddies while others sit quietly contemplating their destiny. Dodging his way through the Officers, he makes his way toward the big guy in the corner.

With three colleagues surrounding him, Andrew is holding court, boasting about how he'll deal with any 'dirty-cunts' who dare to play up tonight. The other Officers, on seeing John approach, make their excuses and fade into the scenery. John realised very quickly he's seen as a "boss", and the rank and file will apparently do everything they can to avoid contact with him.

'Evening Inspector,' Andrew sings, a grin spreading across his freshly shaved face as he holds out his hand.

'Andrew, erm, long time no see.'

Shaking hands, they share a moment, not speaking, just looking into each other. Andrew looks weathered, hardened and much older than before, the couple of months since passing-out from Hendon seems to have taken its toll. John, on the other hand, is well groomed, neat and tidy, every inch the young hot-shot rapidly rising through the ranks.

'Looking good boss, sharp.'

'Really?' Johns face flushes. 'One tries, anyway, look at, um, you, all pumped up and…'

'Gym every day,' Andrew cuts in, tensing his pectorals and at the same time his fifty-pence shaped trapezius muscles.

'Erm, ready for tonight?' John asks, already knowing the answer, coppers like Andrew live for this type of operation.

'About time we got on the front foot.'

Quite right, yes, we have to do something,' John lies. He doesn't want to dampen any enthusiasm or, for that matter, share his own misgivings.

'This'll sort it out, once and for all,' Andrew nods. 'Better than bulldozing the place-yah?'

Patting Andrews shoulder, John smiles before wishing him good luck and promising to keep in touch. Ascending the stairs back to Warrens office which, for the next week or so, will double-up as "Operations Command", he can't help but dwell on Andrews flippant comment. Maybe clearing the place, re-housing the inhabitants and starting afresh is actually an idea of utter genius. However, John reflects, the costs, practicalities and admission of failure would mean this radical, yet beautifully simple idea will never be seriously considered.

# Episode 17.
# "Double Zero"

Saturday 4 April, 9:05am
Caravan Thirty-Two,
Hove Valley Caravan Park, Brighton

It's carnage.

A nuclear bomb has been detonated.

Littered with the dog-ends of five-skin spliffs, empty cigarette packets and crushed beer cans, the caravan looks like a derelict old pub rather than a luxury holiday home. If his parents saw this place, he'd be in double-deep, no pocket money forever trouble, grounded until he's eighteen trouble.

Ashley pulls the blind up and tunes the radio to the only Station with a decent reception. An Adam and the Ants song is playing with driving drums and something about *"we are the family"*.

Marlon steps back in through the metal framed door from the campsite shop with a loaf of bread, three packs of bacon and a bottle of milk. 'Right, who's for breakfast?' he asks, attempting to turn on the two-ring stove.

'Look at Marlon-da-momma, gwan-make us breakfast and ting,' Gladstone laughs.

'Makes a change from chewing on the noses of Peckham pussyclat fools,' Delroy adds, with a cheeky grin.

'T'cha', don't be talking about dat shit here and now man,' Marlon shakes his head, continuing to mess with the stove.

'Yah-naw, I see Kingy on the bus the other day.'

'Pussy-hole,' Delroy kisses his teeth.

'He say Yellowman and Stevie Gee are hunting me like hit-men or something,' Marlon continues. 'So man got enough troubles yeah, don't wanna think about that shit for a lickle while yet.'

'Fuck-dem idiot fools, man,' Gladstone says sternly, pushing his fist into his hand.

'Mate, we're miles away from London, just relax,' Ashley urges in a caring tone. 'We're on holiday, yeah.'

They all smile and nod in complete agreement.

Bacon sandwiches and cups of tea follow, while spliffs are assembled to the uplifting sounds of *"can you feel it"* by the Jackson Five beating out of the radio. Marlon stands at the open door, surveying the grounds of the campsite. Breathing deeply, the salty-seaside air catches the back of his throat. Tastes good, helps him feel refreshed, new, excited. Turning back inside, he clears his throat. 'Here me now rude-boys of Brixton,' he says in his broadest patios. 'We're gonna rip dis town up, yeah, sip some beers, smoke some draw and check out some of these country girls.'

'Yeah man!' the group yell in unison, high fives, cheers and smiles follow.

Good times, happy times.

After a serious amount of time getting ready, Ashley eventually ushers the group outside where they make their way to the clubhouse and the small mini-mart shop.

A few minutes later…

'Taxi reckons twenty-five minutes.'

'What?' Gladstone tuts. 'Why Ashley, why?'

'Twenty-five, shit man,' Marlon adds.

Delroy shakes his head. 'Shit man, that is time man, time.'

'What the fuck we gonna-do?' Gladstone shrugs.

'Calm down guys, it's not like an hour or something, we can probably walk it in twenty,' Ashley smiles.

'Walk?' Delroy queries. 'We on holiday man, we not trekking twenty fucking minutes through the countryside, me garms'll get sweaty and shit.'

'True say, you do sweat a whole heap of sweat, man,' Marlon teases.

'Yeah-yeah-yeah, it's true, you are a stinky mother-fucker,' Gladstone joins in, wafting the air.

'Fook-arf pussy-holes,' Delroy spits, he hates being teased.

'How about a kick around?' Ashley suggests, walking back toward the shop. Thirty seconds later he emerges with a football and they quickly split into teams, Marlon and Ashley versus Gladstone and Delroy.

Setting up a make-shift goal between a waste bin and the car park gate, its rush-keeper, attack versus defence. Ashley proves his class with a few skilful dribbles, artfully avoiding the attempted hacks by Gladstone and scoring a couple of back-healed goals. The world cup final comes to an end when they see the Toyota mini-cab approaching slowly down the dirt-track from the main road.

Saturday 4 April, 11:32am
Grand Parade, Opposite Brighton Pier
Brighton

Pulling up outside the entrance to the pier, Gladstone is first to climb out. Spinning full circle, he surveys the bustling town and, to the right, spots a group of Mods congregating around several elaborately decorated Vespa scooters. Scanning to the left, he sees a crowd of Punks outside a pub facing the sea-front staring over at the Mods.

'Where now Ash?' Marlon drapes his arm over his shoulder.

'Arcades, the beach, the pier, whatever?'

'That thing there, where's the fucking sand gone?' Delroy laughs, pointing toward the pebble beach.

'Fuck the beach, let's bring a little Brixton to dis town man,' Marlon suggests. 'Let's sit on the pier, smoke some weed and get the measure of the place.'

Ten minutes and several spliffs later the group stand

around a bench at the middle of the pier. 'Look at the sea,' Gladstone sucks deeply on his freshly ignited spliff. 'It never stops, never ceases, it's constant.'

'Been reading poetry?' Delroy looks sideways toward Gladstone who, smiling back, gives him the middle finger.

'Easy-nah, we're being screwed over yonder,' Marlon nods suspiciously toward a middle-aged man standing a hundred yards or so down the pier, smiling and nodding.

The Smiling Stranger, late twenties with short hair, long green coat, light blue jeans and black ankle boots realises the group have spotted him and begins walking toward them.

'The man brave or stupid,' Delroy sighs, standing up.

'If him test, he gonna get mash up and dumped into the fookin-sea, the idiot,' Gladstone adds, steadying himself.

Not wanting any trouble as he might have to come back here at a later date with his family, Ashley looks toward Marlon for help. Marlon understands. 'Gladstone,' he says. 'Easy-nah rude boy, we're on holiday yeah.'

'Hey fellas,' Smiling Stranger says, with a friendly smile and posh accent. 'Not from round here, are you?'

'What's it to you?' Delroy says, slowly exhaling thick white smoke and squaring up.

'It's okay boys, I'm cool yeah, cool, not with the Police or anything like that,' the Smiling Stranger raises his palms surrender style. 'Quite the contrary, actually.'

The group stare deep into him, each sharing a collective thought, wondering what the fuck is he on about?

Chuckling, the Smiling Stranger looks left then right before moving closer. 'Look,' he says. 'I've got acid, if you're interested. I'm on the level, no need to worry.'

'Let's get this right,' Gladstone quizzes. 'You, a middle-aged man, is offering to sell us, a group of youths, drugs?'

'Sounds like Babylon business to me,' Delroy adds.

'Entrapment, I believe,' Gladstone nods, as the others look sideways at him.

'Babylon? The Police? Middle-aged?'

Delroy nods.

'Hmm, Babylon? Okay-yes-yes, Mesopotamia… Zionistic enslavery… yes, I get it, I like it actually. Anyway, listen guys, nobody gives a damn about drugs around here, just look around you my friends,' the Smiling Stranger spins around three-sixty with his arms wide. 'The Police, or, as you say, the Babylon, are only interested in is stopping the Mods and Rockers from fighting. Bad for local business and tourism you see, the local economy and all that.'

The group look at each other without saying a word.

'Listen chaps, I can see you're busy, so I'll get to the point. Normally, these baby's are two pounds each, but I'll do one for each of you for a fiver,' he holds out a small strip of grey blotting paper, perforated into small squares each with a black and white Indian symbol in the middle.

'Nah-man, we-a herbal people-yeah,' Delroy says, closely studying the strip. 'We're not into no chemicals, right.'

'Ah, okay, not to worry, I get it. I've some special resin you might be interested in then, from Turkey I believe.'

'Resin, nah-man,' Delroy sighs.

'Turkey-what?' Gladstone squints.

'I call it "double zero" and it'll blow your minds.' Hand in pocket, the Smiling Stranger presents a small black block of resin, coated in a white powder, wrapped in cellophane.

The group gaze at it trance like.

'What's the white shit?' Marlon asks.

'Ah-ha-that, my friends, would be telling, wouldn't it, and where is the fun in that? I'll do this for a fiver too.'

'I'm in,' Ashley nods eagerly, 'I'll sort the cash.'

'Yeah, me too,' Gladstone says, still studying the block.

'What about you?' Delroy nods toward Marlon.

'Not into resin, man…' Marlon shakes his head. 'But we have our pact, so if we all in, then fuck it, I'm in too.'

Ashley counts out five pounds.

Gladstone continues to study the block, sniffing it too.

'Well done chaps, you have quite exquisite taste, if I may say so. Listen, I'll be around here all day so, if you have any problems, or you'd like a second helping, come back and see me, okay?' the Smiling Stranger smiles, then heads back toward the entrance to the Pier.

They all study the small black block.

'Hmm, that's yo-yay yah-naw, definitely yo-yay,' Delroy says, grabbing it and putting it to his nose.

'Nah-man, skagg, we all skagg-heads now,' Gladstone says, triumphantly.

'Let's just skin up, man,' Marlon says, taking control of the block, setting off toward the far end of the pier. Finding an unoccupied bench facing out to Sea, a couple of minutes later two spliffs are fired up.

'If this shit sends me mad, I'm coming back to smash that weirdo to bits,' Gladstone pronounces, taking a long and deep tote on the spliff before coughing up white balls of smoke. 'Bloodclat, dat shit is harsh, man.'

Sharing the spliffs, they talk about how shit Brighton is and what they intend to do if, or when, they get with any local girls. Shortly after, they make their way back along the Pier, through the arcade and out toward the town centre. Less than a hundred yards from the Pier they spot two Beasts on foot patrol.

'Shit, Babylon, be cool yeah, be cool,' Gladstone panics.

Marlon looks at Gladstone, who's now tiptoeing like a cat on a hot tin roof, before bursting out laughing, quickly followed by Delroy. A few feet ahead Ashley stalks along like he's just landed on the moon, anti-gravity style.

'Serious, get rid of the stash, get rid,' Gladstone whispers through an uncontrollable smile.

Marlon and Delroy fall about laughing.

'Morning chaps,' one of the Officers sings as they approach, his cheery tone matching his smiling face.

'Lovely morning, eh?' Marlon replies, holding-in the giggles as Delroy bends double with laughter.

Without breaking their stride, one of the Officer waves toward the group while the other Officer yells, 'take it easy boys, it's a long day.'

Marlon stares as the Police continue past the Pier. Can't

believe it, he thinks, here they are, a group of urban youths obviously off their heads yet the Police don't stop them, let alone call for back-up or initiate a stop and search.

Brighton is different.

Or, London is different.

He can't decide.

Still stalking anti-gravity style, Ashley studies his feet. They're somehow lighter than he knows they actually are, and, thinking about it, the pavement has an unreal, bouncy-soft feeling to it. He begins humming, *"walking on the moon,"* by the Police.

'Ashley, you okay?' Marlons words zoom through the air phasing in and out of reality as the blur of shops, Mods, Punks and holidaying families whirl all around him. 'This shit's trippy, man.'

'Giant steps are what we take…' Ashley sings, his arms stretched out either side.

Marlon catches his vibe and finishes the line off, 'walking on da' moon.'

They both burst out laughing.

'This resin is crazy, you feeling it?' Delroy yells, jumping on both Ashley and Marlons backs, fixing a hand and a leg on each. 'Onward bredrin', onward,' he orders to his newly formed human chariot, who promptly obey and set off.

Saturday, 4 April, 12:57pm
Catch of the Day Restaurant
Western Road, Brighton

Making their way into the town centre Marlon checks his watch, one o'clock, fuck, where's the time gone? 'You know what the time is?'

'Course I do,' Ashley sniggers. 'Munch-time.'

'Chips,' Delroy yells, pushing his way through the door. 'Bring me hot chips brothers.'

With a blue and white naval theme, the restaurant has seating on the right for about thirty people and a counter on the left. In the centre is an eight-seat miniature ship for kids to play in with tables and chairs dotted around the edges.

Behind the counter, according to Ashley, are two reasonably fit girls, both mid-twenties with long blond ponytails poking out the back of blue and white sailor hats. In between them, a big fat cook with bright red rosy cheeks. Along with his way-too-small sailors hat, he has a long white coat dotted with brown and yellow stains. 'Hey fellas, what can I getch-yah?' he bellows in an unmistakable cockney accent. The volume and firmness of his voice brings the group to attention. 'So, what'll be chaps?'

'Four fish and chips please squire,' Marlon orders.

'Nah, big-fat battered sausage for me guv,' Delroy shouts over as the others all burst out laughing.

Big Fat Cook nods slowly as a smile stretches from chubby cheek to chubby cheek. 'You fellas from London-then, sarf-sides by the sound of it?'

'Rude-boys from Brixton,' Delroy yells, forcing himself into the kids ship.

'Oi, don't break that boys,' Big Fat Cook yells, pointing.

Marlon bursts out laughing.

Big Fat Cook stares at the group before nodding his head. 'Awright, I getch-yah, battered sausage is it?' he beams with arching eyebrows and a generous smile. 'Come-here son,' he beckons Marlon toward him.

Raising his chin Different Strokes "what's-up-boss" style Marlon approaches. Waving him even closer, Big Fat Cook moves quickly, grabbing him around the neck with his thumb squeezing his adams apple.

Shit.

Marlon tries to pull away but can't, panic surges.

Pinned to the counter, he tries turning his head toward the others to signal he's in trouble, but just can't do it. Is this really happening or is he tripping on the weird resin shit?

'Listen-shit-cunt and listen-good,' Big Fat Cook whispers venomously. 'I'll fucking serve-you lot, take your-money no worries, but there'll be no fucking-trouble in here, awright.'

Frozen, Marlon blinks an acknowledgement.

'You and your muggy cunt mates fuck-around in my shop,' Big Fat Cook continues. 'You'll find your head in the fucking-fryer, and your scrawny body minced into fucking-fish-cakes. That ab-so-lutely fucking clear, boy?'

Marlon feels his knees tremble, he can't work out the odd mixture of super-hard-bastard east-end-meat-head and country-bumpkin-fat-as-fuck-fish-shop-wanker. Either way, it's clear this particular Big Fat Cook is a serious psychopath, not to be messed with.

'You hearing-me, boy?' Big Fat Cook stares into his eyes.

Struggling for air, tunnel vision forming, he forces a slow nod. As he does, Big Fat Cook immediately releases him.

'Okay boys, three fish-n-chips, and one battered-sausage with chips? Tell you what, I'll chuck in a couple of pickled eggs too, on the house eh,' he yells.

Shaking, Marlon reaches into his pocket, pulls out a bundle of notes and fumbles out seven pounds, placing it gently on the counter. Feeling his neck, he turns to the mini-ship, expecting his mates to be pointing at him and laughing. Instead, he sees Delroy captaining his crew who are sailing with imaginary paddles, humming the "Hawaii-Five-O" theme tune, completely oblivious to his ordeal. Approaching the ship, he takes a seat toward the back and sits quietly looking at the floor, re-living what has just happened.

After fish, chips, battered sausages, bottles of Rola-Cola, free pickled eggs plus another short mission in the ship, they set off for an afternoon of fun and adventure.

Saturday, 4 April, 6:16pm
Caravan Thirty-Two
Hove Valley Caravan Park, Brighton

As the group recount tales from earlier in the day, Marlon relives what happened with the Big Fat Cook in the chip shop. As sympathetic as ever, the group provide a full thirty minutes of piss taking with yells of "battered-Marl-on" and "fat-cunt-and-chips-please." Afterward, Ashley makes dinner, consisting of a heap of freshly cut chips and ten fried eggs, washed down with several cups of tea. With the pop tunes from Radio-1 providing the soundtrack they get ready for a big night out with "Geno" by Dexys Midnight Runners has the caravan chanting in unison, 'oh-ho-ho Gene-oh!'

Around eight o'clock…

Dressed in their best Gabicci tops, silk shirts and Fred Perry t-shirts, they walk along the dimly lit path to the club house. Entering the small hall, they're met with audible gasps and stares from the regular clientele. Nonetheless, Geoff the barman greets them warmly, serving them four pints of flat-as-fuck cheap lager. Finding a circular table at the edge of the empty dancefloor, they sit listening to the previous years chart hits spun not so skilfully by deejay Andy, who, during the day, also works behind the counter at the camp-site mini-mart shop.

'T'cha, dis place is dry man, pure shit-ness,' Gladstone shakes his head in disgust. 'Let's skip this place and get a taxi back into town.'

'Reckon we stay here,' Ashley suggests, worried the gang will encounter, find and or make trouble in town. 'The beer is cheap and we've no worries about being served.'

Gladstone stares at Ashley, how dare he disagree with his most excellent suggestion.

'Yeah man, I hear the town is full of batty-man at night anyway,' Marlon adds, noting Gladstones screwed up face while doing everything possible not to cross paths with the Big Fat Cook ever again.

Gladstone continues to stare into Ashley before, several agonising moments later, his face turns into a beaming smile. 'Easy-nah-man, dis place not too bad, yeah. Who's up for some more beers?'

Ashley smiles as a collective sigh of relief washes over the group. 'No worries mate, I'll get them in then,' he says, heading for the bar, returning a couple of minutes later with four more pints on a circular metal tray. At the same time,

Gladstone weaves his way over to deejay Andy, to request some "roots and culture." The best he can do though, turns out, is a few Specials and Madness tunes.

Sitting back, Marlon sips his drink and scans the room. He counts maybe thirty or so middle-aged people plus a few younger teenagers all sitting around small tables as a couple of little kids take turns sprinting across the dancefloor then skidding on their knees. Smiling, he remembers doing the exact same thing when he was around their age at the many dances, christenings and weddings Momma dragged him along to. Back to the here and now, he spots two decent looking girls maybe a similar age or just a bit younger sitting with their parents. 'Del, Delroy,' he says. 'Dem girls giving us the eye yeah, what do-yah think?'

'What, where?' Delroy queries, quickly locating them. 'Yeah, not bad, not bad, look like daddies girls though, and he's got a look of a Fronter.'

Nodding, Marlon mulls over ways of somehow getting to talk to them.

'Spliff time,' Gladstone announces out of nowhere, standing up. 'Let's go outside,'

'Easy mate, let's be discreet… maybe take it in turns?' Ashley squeezes his knee before quickly releasing.

The group decide Gladstone and Delroy will go outside first, then Marlon and Ashley will take a turn.

'Ash,' Marlon whispers moving around the leatherette seating to get closer as Delroy and Gladstone disappear through the door. 'Dem girls over yonder?'

'Yeah-yeah, I know them,' Ashley nods slowly through narrow eyes.

'You know them?'

'Yeah,' Ashley giggles.

'Know them as in "know-them" or you just know them?'

'Know them as in I know them,' Ashley over-pronounces each word, with his eyes wide. 'Anyway, which one you interested in?'

'Fuck it, either, both even,' Marlon can't decide. 'Who

gives a fuck, as long as they fucking, right?'

'Too right mate, but, their old man is a bit of a dick though, they're the apple of his eye if you know what I mean,' Ashley nods. 'I'll see what I can do though.'

Enhanced by the goodness of the weed, Gladstone and Delroy come back in, the cue for the Marlon and Ashley to step outside for some mother-earth goodness too.

Several hours, pints and spliffs later…

The gang head back to the caravan, minus the "daddies-girls" who, as suspected, wouldn't leave the gaze of their over-bearing father. Spotting a small kids bike resting next to a caravan, Gladstones eyes light up. Surprisingly ninja-like, he deftly tip-toes over and places his large frame on the tiny seat before peddling furiously down the path with his knees up near his ears. Showing off, he alternates between riding with no hands and pulling short wheelies before picking up some speed. The group fall around laughing while slapping each other backs.

Then.

Silence descends.

A cloak of seriousness surrounds them.

In slow motion, he approaches a sharp right-hand bend.

Shit.

'He'll never make it,' Marlon whispers, wiping away tears of laughter.

'Oh god,' Ashley cringes.

'He's fucked man,' Delroy bounces on the balls of his feet in anticipation. 'Fucked.'

As anticipated, he turns the handlebars but momentum carries him forward.

Whack!

The sound bounces across the campsite as he collides with the caravan in front.

'Fuck-ing-hell,' Delroy shouts excitedly.

Gladstone rolls around on the floor, giggling. The bike though, is seriously damaged with the front wheel bent, spokes pointing everywhere and the handlebars twisted.

'What have you done,' Ashley whispers while Gladstone, in the foetal position, gasps for air due to uncontrollable laughter. Turning away Ashley studies the caravan for damage. Fortunately unoccupied, miraculously it's unscathed with literally no sign of any damage at all. He takes what remains of the bike back to its natural home, hoping the damage won't be noticed until they are well on their way back home to London.

Helping Gladstone to his feet, they make their way back to the caravan. Once inside, the radio is turned up loud, multiple joints built and Marlon shuffles the pack ready for a game of cards as they laugh the night away.

# Episode 18.
# “Welcome to Brixton”

Sunday, 5 April, 8:04pm
Rail Station, Atlantic Road
Brixton.

After changing trains at Victoria, the local train to Brixton labours slowly across the river Thames passing Battersea Power Station on the right. Weaving their way through South London, they eventually spot the runway-straight streetlights of Brixton Hill. Closer, they see flashing blue lights racing toward Brockwell Park. Grabbing their bags, slamming the train doors shut, they head wearily down the steps from the platform into the ticket hall. Instinctively, their pace slows as they spot three uniformed Officers standing between the ticket gate and the exit.

Noting the group, the Officers look at each other before spreading shoulder to shoulder across the ticket barrier. ‘Hello chaps, welcome to Brixton,’ the smallest of the three Officers grunts, a midget man with a snout shaped nose.

The other two Officers stand silent, scanning the gang for troublemakers and potential weapons.

‘Okay fuck-wits, sus-stop,’ Midget Officer growls, motioning to the far wall.

‘T’cha,’ Delroy spits, dropping his bag to face the wall, both hands head high.

Knowing the drill, Marlon and Ashley follow suit.

'Nah-man-nah,' Gladstone shakes his head. 'Not being searched tonight, we just got off the train, you got no reason for stopping us.'

The Officers stare at the mouthy teenager, his fists clenched and eyes wide. Around five feet eight, bladed short hair with an unusually high hair line for a kid of sixteen, he's stocky with a muscular neck. His chubby cheeks and a dimpled chin gives him a baby-faced look, completely at odds with his otherwise middleweight boxer exterior.

'We're on here chaps,' Midget Officer smiles, rubbing his knuckles lovingly.

Gladstone moves his right foot back, readying himself.

'What's he doing?' Ashley whispers nervously.

'Standing up,' Marlon says.

'What… why, why now?'

'It kicks-off we're in yeah,' Marlon nods. 'Three of them, four of us.'

'What, nah-mate-nah… what the fuck's happening?'

'Fuck the Beasts,' Delroy whispers.

'Stay cool yeah,' Ashley urges, panic flowing.

'Easy-nah rude-boy, settle-man,' Delroy shouts, his voice echoing in the ticket hall. 'We got you bro.'

Gladstones eyes lock onto the Officers.

Midget Officer steps forward, while the Officer on the left uses his radio to call for back-up.

'Don't let this get out of hand lad,' the Officer on the right says, patting the air down. 'Quick search and you'll be on your way.'

Gladstone doesn't move.

'Think this through,' the Officer on the left adds. 'Couple of SPG wagons are on the way, they'll be here in a couple of minutes.'

'Done fuck-all,' Gladstone growls, teeth clenched, stressing each word. 'Don't deserve no sus-stop.'

The tension is palpable.

The darkness of the ticket hall fills with blue lights from the arriving SPG wagons. 'Thirty seconds till the meat-heads get in here,' Midget Officer smiles, eyes wide.

Steadying himself, Gladstone raises his fists, staring directly into Midget Officers eyes. 'Fuck-you, Beast!'

As the arriving SPG Officers fill the ticket hall, Marlon, Delroy and Ashley are escorted outside.

Gladstone stands firm.

Outside, as they line up to be searched, they hear Gladstone yelling 'COME-NAH, BEAST.'

Then.

The unmistakable sound of violence.

After no more than ten seconds, a struggling Gladstone appears feet first in mid-air, an Officer on each limb and one clasping his head. He's followed by two more Officers plus Midget Officer nursing a bloody nose.

Turning away, Marlon looks along the deserted street. Something isn't right, where are all the usual bible bashers and doom mongers, they'd make perfect witnesses.

'Babylon get me,' Gladstone screams. 'Police brutality!'

In an awful state, his left eye is closed over and a trickle of blood runs down the side of his head.

'Fuck,' Marlon yells, fighting the instinct to run.

'The idiot-fool, why make a stand, why now?' Delroy turns away, covering his eyes.

'Done some damage,' Ashley nods toward Midget Officer holding his face, blood streaming between his fingers.

'Damage?' Marlons forehead wrinkles as his eyes close. 'He's gonna get the shit kicked out of him dred.'

They watch open mouthed as Gladstone is hurled into the back of the SGP wagon. As the doors slam shut, it begins to rock from side to side and they hear the muffled sounds of a struggle and Gladstone wailing.

Marlon, tears welling, places his hands over his ears.

Meanwhile, Ashley protests to an Officer with a flat-cap and stripes on his forearms, suggesting this is isn't right and that Gladstone just a boy.

'Don't worry man, we tell yah-momma where you at,' Delroy shouts toward the wagon.

Eventually, the van stops rocking and the engine turns over. Dark grey smoke plunges from the exhaust and the van disappears into the horizon.

With no wailing god-squad-do-gooders or rude-boys hanging around outside the Station, the entire neighbourhood feels deserted and eerily silent. The normal collage of dub reggae tunes hanging in the air is noticeably vacant. 'Somethings not right,' Marlon shakes his head.

'True-say man, where is everyone?' Delroy agrees.

'Let's get back to mine quick-time,' Marlon suggests.

'My old man was expecting me back ages ago, he'll be waiting for me,' Ashley nods.

'Yeah-man, eye-an-eye got to see Devon for some herb-yeah,' Delroy nods as they set off along Atlantic Road toward Marlons house.

After a hundred yards or so they spot a Jam-Jar in the distance, slowing as it approaches.

'Fuck-ing-hell,' Marlon tuts, slowing his pace.

'Twice, in what, ten minutes?' Ashley adds, wiping some tears away. He feels physically sick witnessing what just happened with poor Gladstone. Even worse is the prospect of his Dad, who's due to pick him up from Marlons house, might see him being sus-stopped.

'First Gladstone, now us?' Delroy grunts.

'Just be cool, don't mess with them,' Marlon says, in low, meaningful tones. 'Enough tribulation already.'

The Jam-Jar squeals as it stops abruptly.

'Fellas, hold up,' a cockney sounding Officer sitting in the passenger seat yells.

'We just been stopped down at the train station,' Delroy shouts, stepping closer. 'Me spar's already in chains receiving enough licks and ting,' his voice cracks with emotion.

'We not here to give you a beating, alright.'

'Nah?'

'Naw,' the Cockney Officer smiles. 'Anyway, you lot know Marlon?'

'Who?'

'Marlon, Marlon Walters?'

The words float across the pavement in slow motion as Marlons veins fill with adrenalin. Mind spinning, he feels dizzy, like he's drifting into a dream-world state. A million thoughts bounce across his brain…

Marlon Walters…

Asked for by name…

Wanted by the Police…

Attempted murder…

Of an ugly Peckham mother fucker…

Hunted down and jailed…

Grassed on by his mate…

Police informer…

Forensic evidence…

Crown court…

Fronter judge and jury…

Guilty, before a words been said…

Sent down for life…

Momma crying…

Bum-raped in his cell…

Abused…

Ashamed and embarrassed…

Couldn't cope…

Took a long bath…

With a razor blade…

And bottle of gin…

Buried six-feet under…

Momma, heart-broken…

Dies five months later…

That's the sorry story of poor, sad and fragile…

Marlon Walters…

Every part of his body screams run, run, run, don't stop running. Where too though, what would he do?

He steps back slightly, behind Delroy.

'Who?' Ashley queries, shrugging his shoulders in a don't-know-what-your-talking-about kind of way.

'About your age-yah, lives around here,' Cockney Officer

smiles, hanging further out of the window, his enormous bicep pushing against the door frame. 'Wondered if you know might him?'

'Marlon, Marlon Walters?' Delroy ponders, shaking his head. 'Nope, don't ring no bells with me boss.'

'What's he done anyway?' Ashley nods.

Cockney Officer stares at him. 'He's not in any trouble or anything like that, you know him then?'

The radio cracks into life, "Charlie-Ten, receiving over."

'Wrap it up Andy,' the driver says, revving the engine.

'Listen, if you do see him, be good lads and tell him to pop down to the Station,' Cockney Officer says as the Jam-Jar sets off, picking up speed as it turns onto Brixton Hill.

Sunday, 5 April, 8:56pm
47 Saltoun Road
Brixton, London

Turning the corner, they spot a good looking black Jaguar XJS sitting with its engine idling, just along from Marlons house. Approaching, they feel the rumbling from the massive exhausts.

It sounds good.

'Dat is one sweet motor,' Delroy nods circling the car, gently running his hand along the wing then across the warm bonnet.

The driver, an overweight middle-aged guy, gestures for him move away while mouthing "get lost".

Ignoring him, Delroy strokes the miniature silver cat perching at the end of the bonnet. 'Gonna get me one of these when I control tings, you know what I mean?'

'T'cha!' Marlon kisses his teeth dismissively.

'Of course you will,' Ashley follows up, shaking his head.

'Alright fellas,' the overweight middle-aged driver chirps, dipping his head through the now open window.

'Laters,' Ashley nods, opening the passenger door.

'Tomorrow yeah,' Marlon waves.

Engine roaring, the wheels spin and they're quickly gone.

Two minutes later…

Inside, after a short chat with Auntie, Delroy follows Marlon upstairs. Pushing the bedroom door open they're greeted by Devon laying on his bed, one arm above his head the other resting on his chest with the remains of a spliff in between his fingers. 'Come nah-girls,' he says, waving away the cloud of think white smoke above his cadaver.

Smiling, Marlon looks toward the stereo in the corner, nodding to the *"when I was a yout"* vocals of Pablo Gad. With the baseline and detuned piano keys pulsing through his core, he feels relaxed, relieved they've made it home. A short time after that, three spliffs are ignited before they tell Devon all about the weekend, the resin procured from the Smiling Stranger on the pier, the psychopathic Big Fat Cook and then what happened to Gladstone and Midget Officer.

'Tell him about you being hunted,' Delroy prompts before blowing an angel-ring above his head.

'Jus-after Gladstone get mash-up, Babylon pull up in a Jam-Jar and ask if we know Marlon Walters.'

'By name?' Devon shits up. 'After they ask for me too?'

'What?' Marlon shakes his head.

'I got your note, yeah,' Devon nods. 'Listen, we got to hold it down, keep a low profile till whatever this is blows over. Babylon been rife since we got shot at the other day.'

'What?' Marlon misheard, sounded like "got shot at."

'Shot?' Delroy whispers, leaning forward. 'With a gun?'

'Easy-nah-man,' Devon laughs. 'Long story, but a team of batty-man get mash-up by Super down at the scrap yard, and their crew fire off a few shots.'

'Shot, with a gun-yah-naw,' Delroy smiles sitting at the foot of Devons bed, seemingly proud of the achievement.

'You okay?' Marlon asks, he always thought of his brother as indestructible but, being shot at is serious business.

'Yeah man, of course, but we got to hold it down,' Devon urges. 'You lot need calm it down too yeah.'

Monday 6 April, 8:55am
Saint Saviours Secondary School,
Herne Hill, London

Walking through the entrance, Delroy spots Marlon standing in his usual spot near the foot of the stairs. 'Easy rude-boy, wha-gwan?' he nods. 'Any sign of Gladstone?'

'Nah-man, nothing,' Delroy replies. 'His Momma came around to mine last night though, ranting and raving.'

'Serious?'

'She go crazy-mad, clap me around the face yah-naw,' Delroy over exaggerates the windmill motion of her hand slapping his face.

'Clap yah-face?' Marlon cries with laughter.

'Listen, she quick for a big woman, yah-naw.'

They both giggle, but the laughter quickly fades as Gladstones plight comes back into focus.

Heads twisting in unison, they hear a familiar voice from the top of the stairs.

'Marlon, Marlon!' leaping over the handrail kung-fu-style Kingy jumps the final flight. 'Heard about Gladstone, what a shitter,' he says excitedly.

'Bom-ba-clat, rat-boy,' Delroy spits, his eyes lighting up.

A young puppy showing visible subservience to a more aggressive dog, Kingy cowers away.

'Yeah, tragic,' Marlon says, shaking his head, ignoring Delroy and moving the conversation on.

'So anyway, you hear about Junior?' Kingy smiles, appreciating Marlons help.

'What?' Delroy swings around. 'What about Junior?'

'What do you know Kingy?' Marlon prompts.

'Out of hospital now, I hear he wants to leave things as they are, move on, let the past be the past.'

Marlon can't help a smile edging out.

This is great news.

Things are looking up.

'But,' Kingy continues. 'Everyone reckons Yellowman has

gone all Darth Vadar or something, walking around with a blade-come-light-sabre saying he's gonna wet you up.'

Marlons stomach churns.

These guys are nothing but persistent!

The school bell rings for first assembly.

'And?' Delroy probes impatiently, setting off toward the main hall. 'What else rat boy, spill the fucking beans?'

'Him and a whole heap of North Peckham are coming down here Friday night, settle it once and for all.'

Once and for all?

Marlon doesn't like the sound of that.

Sounds serious.

Sounds dangerous.

Sounds final.

# Episode 19.
# "Rise & Shine"

Thursday, 9 April, 8:30pm
47 Saltoun Road
Brixton, London

Bang. Bang. Bang.

The door swings open.

Dressed in a blue tabard from her shift at the hospital, Momma stands in the doorway. 'What-am-bwai, why hammer down me door?' she scowls.

'Ah, Mrs Walters, looking well today my love,' Super smiles, trying his best to be charming.

'My love? T'cha, don't mess with me-nah Winston,' she says, chewing a wasp. 'He in his room.'

Creeping up the stairs, tiptoeing across the landing, he hears the squelching horns licking through an echo chamber. Yeah man, he thinks, "Burning Spear."

'Bow!' he yells, slamming the door open.

'What?' Devon sits upright. 'Why you sneaking around?'

'Murderation out there-star, madness-yesh.'

'But still, no need for no SAS kick me door in business.'

'Serious man, Babylon everywhere. Taken me a full half hour to reach here yaw-nah, enough back-street stalking and looking over me-shoulder,' Super continues. 'See what the bad-boy-line-man bring us-star, with der drugs, muggings and inner-city depravation, throughout the nation!'

'True-say man, true, the youth of today don't know dey born, dred,' Devon plays along.

'Then, there's pickney Marlon and his bum-chums, drinking, smoking and getting into fights, what's the world coming to?'

'The truth brother,' Devon loves it. 'The truth!'

'Biting off noses and ting, dey bring all dis strife and tribulation on us. T'cha, all fookin' week Babylon have been out in force.'

'Testify man, hallelujah,' Devon giggles.

'He speaks the truth-yeah, the truth!' Paul, until now laying silent across Marlons bed, chips in. 'Took me a while to reach here too, I was just saying that they blocking roads, stopping cars and shit.'

'Star,' Super kisses his teeth. 'How we gonna get to the Windsor, see Crissy, we need stock, man.'

'Got to ponder on this,' Devon strokes his beard. 'We got to hold it down with the neighbourhood going all Belfast-check-point-Charlie and shit.'

'That's just what it's like,' Paul agrees. 'We're being locked down, locked the fuck down.'

'What the fook you chatting about, we,' Super screws with a squinting eye. 'You can go home tonight to your old mans mansion in Dulwich.'

Easing himself up the bed, Paul leans against the wooden headboard. 'Can I help any of that, shall I just give it back?'

'What?' Supers isn't used to Paul biting back.

'Would it be different if I was crusty living on Leesons Road in a squat?' Paul adds.

'Settle down ladies,' Devon shakes his head.

'It aint about where you live, it's what you feeling yeah.' Paul looks to Devon for acknowledgement.

'Alright, exactly what are you feeling-star?' Super prompts.

'Pussyclats, you both need to be thinking on our problems yeah, not this tit-for-tat feeling dis or dat bullshit,' Devon looks at both of them. 'Belfast or not, we got customers who need serving and money to be making.' Swinging his legs around, he stands and reaches on top of his wardrobe. Feeling around, he pulls down an elastic-band bound bundle of ten-pound notes. Counting out two hundred, he straightens out each note before folding in two and shoving into his back pocket. 'Right, I'm off to see Crissy. You two stay here, smoke some weed and try not to bum each other.'

'Be careful,' Paul shouts after him.

'Be careful?' Super teases. 'Star, you got to at least swing both ways, if not a full-on arse-rider.'

'Well, if I am of the gentleman persuasion,' Paul turns his head. 'You better watch out, big boy'

Both wait for the other to move first.

Like in a Clint Eastwood spaghetti-western, the tension is unbearable. As always, Super cracks first, belching out a huge belly-laugh, quickly followed by Paul.

They both fall about laughing.

Front door slamming, Devon leaps the steps leading to the street. Turning onto Railton Road, he sees two young guys with white trainers, short crew-cut hair and both clean-shaven standing on the corner, whispering to each other. Obviously plain clothes Babylon.

Super has it right, the place is locked down.

Heading south, he notices the louder than usual dub reggae and ska tunes bouncing between the buildings. The Frontline is lively no matter what night of the week but tonight, it seems far more busy than usual. Along with more Babylon, he sees a lot more youth hanging around, some blatantly smoking weed while others drinking from cans of Special Brew. Quickening his pace, he counts eight rude-boys hanging around outside Petersons Pool Hall, eye-balling the passing cars. He knows one of them as Chewbacca, who waves over. 'Easy-nah rude-bwai,' he yells, beating his chest one handed King Kong style.

Without stopping, Devon nods and puts his head down.

This amount of blatant rude-boy behaviour, openly smoking weed, drinking beer and shouting patois across street isn't his style, nah-man, a sure-fire way of getting sus-stopped, fitted up and locked away.

Fuck that.

Tonight, he'll keep his head down for sure, see Crissy, get his stock then go straight home or might even head up West out of this madness. Just before turning onto Leeson Road, he spots a Jam-Jar parked on the corner. Doors wide open, three Beasts look to be mid-way through sus-stopping two youths. Spotting him, they pause what they're doing and stare. Head down, he carries on walking nice and easy, not too obvious. He knows what they're thinking though…

Handsome guy…

Strolling along the Frontline…

Pocket-full of serious cash…

Suspected drug dealer…

Sus-stopped…

Money taxed…

Fitted up…

Mashed up and then…

Locked up.

Nah, he tells himself, not tonight, no way. Approaching the Windsor, he sees two SPG vans outside. Damn. Can't turn back, that'll look suspicious and the Jam-Jar Beasts will stop him for sure. He'll have to keep walking and check the Windsor as he gets closer. If things are cool, he'll enter or, if not, he'll drift by trying his best to be invisible.

Getting closer, passing the SPG vans he sees a battered blue Marina parked further down the road with two plain clothed Officers sitting inside. Way too hot around here he thinks, plan B it is. Passing the Windsor, the doors are wedged open and he counts eight, maybe ten Beasts inside searching the domino playing regulars.

He looks toward Crissys normal table.

Empty.

Friday, 10 April, 7:24pm
47 Saltoun Road
Brixton, London

'So, the centre?'

'It's Friday night, what else is there to do?'

'Err, Brighton?' Ashley smiles.

'Ha-fucking-ha, what do we normally do?'

'Okay, the Centre it is then,' Ashley concedes.

With sirens in the distance, they decide to take the short-cut through the graveyard.

'They're looking for you, you know,' Ashley teases.

'Who, Babylon?'

'Yeah, that's them speeding down Atlantic Road with their blues-and-twos, searching for the famous Brixton-nose-biter, Mister Marlon Walters.'

'Well, they haven't found me, have they?'

'Seriously, mate.'

'You worry too much, relax-yeah,' Marlon hops over a headstone. 'All this lock-down madness can't be down to me, anyway, everything's cool yeah, Peckham never showed up at school, did they?'

'Still, this is crazy.'

'Listen, we just heading to the disco, going to smoke some weed and drink some beer,' Marlon bounces on the balls of his feet, imitating Muhammad Ali. 'No problems man, everything's cool.'

Approaching the Community Centre, the sounds of "Lip-up Fatty" float across the graveyard as they spot Delroy standing near the doorway. 'Easy-nah rude-boy, why aren't you inside?' Marlon smiles.

Delroy looks sombre and serious, worried almost.

'What's up?' Marlon asks, his smile fading.

'Peckham, dem come,' Delroy says, slowly.

'Yeah right,' Ashley giggles.

'True-say, man,' Delroy sighs. 'I bump into Stevie Gentle earlier, down the market. Full of shit, he reckons they all coming down tonight at half-eight to sort it out, once and for all. Reckons Junior is coming too, down at the underground station.'

'Stevie Gee is a wanker,' Ashley spits.

Feeling a tingle in his spine, Marlons stomach does a double backflip. He normally feels this way before a rumble but tonight, in front of his mates, he can't show any sign of fear. 'Well, if they come to test, we'll have to deal with them,' he nods. 'This is our yard yeah, we got to stand tall.'

'Yeah?' Delroy queries, a doubting tone in his voice.

'Yeah,' Ashley nods in agreement.

'We've got about an hour so let's get down there pronto,' Marlon suggests, unconvincingly.

'We got anyone in there?' Ashley nods toward the disco.

'Nah, nobody, just kids,' Delroy shakes his head.

'Fuck it, it's just us then,' Marlon claps his hands.

'What about Devon and Super?' Delroy suggests. 'Big Claude or even dat Snakehead madness?'

'Listen, fuck them queers,' Marlon spits, his aggressive and angry. 'They're out tonight anyway, it's just us and whoever we can rope in on the way.'

'Yes brother, that's the spirit,' Delroy says, gaining confidence as he puts his arm around Marlons shoulder.

Gathering around the bench near the edge of the car park, they build several joints before setting off toward Brixton town centre and the train station.

Ten minutes later…

Marlons head spins as the creamy whiteness of the herb takes effect. In addition, the thought of sorting all this out once and for all fills him with a weird sense peace, he can literally feel the weight lifting from his shoulders. Continuing toward Coldharbour Lane and the tube station, a SPG van followed by a couple of Jam-Jars flies by, sirens blaring and bells whistling.

'Something's going down for sure,' Ashley suggests.

'Yeah man,' Delroy adds. 'I hear the Fronters are planning a march or something,'

'Nah-nah,' Ashley interjects. 'Heard on the news last night the Police and the Government are cracking down on street crime, muggings and shit.'

Stopping, Marlon glares at Ashley. 'What you doing watching the fucking news?'

'What? I'm not allowed to watch TV now?'

'Will you fools focus?' Delroy pushes them both on. 'We got heads to mash, you know what I mean?'

Then…

'Ditch the spliff, ditch the spliff,' Marlon whispers urgently, nodding toward the SPG van pulling onto the pavement in front of them. A split second later, three half-smoked spliffs and a few spliffs worth of weed wrapped in tissue paper are ditched over the adjacent garden wall. At the same time, a Jam-Jar approaches from behind, pulling up against the curb. Twenty seconds later, they are lined up against the wall and searched then separated and questioned.

A shout comes from the SGP van and the Officers rush back before speeding off, sirens echoing into the distance.

'What the fuck?' Marlon shrugs.

Delroy rubs Marlons head before moving on, 'they just fucking with our heads rube-boy.'

'I'm telling you, something's wrong,' Ashley nods, following Delroy.

Eventually turning onto Electric Avenue, they head for the underground station, their pace slowing when they see the unusually large amount of people milling around underneath the bridge. The normal hustle and bustle of the market seems louder, the crazies are still outside the entrance yelling of Judgement Day, while rude-boys hang around eyeballing anyone unlucky enough to make eye contact. With the air smelling of sweet-weed and the bubbling baseline of "King Tubby" thumping from the sound system of the Record Shack, there's an almost party atmosphere.

'Look at dis place?' Marlon shakes his head.

'Yeah man, like Carnival or something,' Delroy beams, spinning around with his arms open.

'So, what now?' Ashley nervously looks around. Thoughts of the Peckham Boys, the darkness of the night and the weird atmosphere makes him feel threatened and on edge.

'Let's wait over here,' Marlon dodges between the stationery traffic as he heads toward a spot at the other side of the road, just under the bridge. With the Crown pub to their left and the market over the road on their right, they stand facing the entrance to the ticket hall. 'Stay sharp, we'll spot them before they spot us.'

'Gwan Marlon, man like Churchill planning it all out,' Delroy grins, smoothing his hand across Marlons head.

'Leave Junior to me yeah, you two make sure none of those other Peckham idiots get in the way,' Marlon continues. 'I've got to finish this shit, once and for all.'

The waiting is excruciating.

The noise of the hustle and bustle fades into the background as Marlon drifts a little, his thoughts turning to what happened on that dark, cold, bleak night in Peckham. Juices flowing into his mouth, he feels sick as images of Junior in the lift lobby, lying on the stone-cold floor deadly still flash through his mind. Maybe he should have finished it all there and then, no witnesses, nothing. The idea that he could have killed him that night, and probably got away with it too, sends a shiver down is spine. What scares him most though, what frightens him to his core is the notion of what he might be capable of, who he might become. Everyone has a demon, he reckons, a dark side and all that. He's secretly always known, deep down inside, that his demon is a fucking crazy-mad monster. It's a well-hidden monster, but still, it's there waiting, biding its time until it's unleashed and set free to cause chaos. Equally as scary, and probably more disturbing is that the more he thinks about killing, the more mortal he feels. Thoughts turn to Momma, Pops and Devon. Sadness fills him. He thinks about his life, and his life to come, learning to drive, getting a girlfriend, falling in love and having a baby…

This feels like the end, not the beginning.

Tears well in his eyes.

He wants all this to be over, once and for all.

He needs peace.

Twenty long minutes later…

Adrenaline surging, his eyes narrow. 'Yellowman,' he says, calmly. Feet tingling, feeling dizzy, he's five-hundred feet up, looking over the edge of a tower block.

Delroy and Paul spin around to see Yellowman standing in the middle of the ticket hall surrounded by six or seven others. Behind him, they see Juniors unforgettable face moving in and out of the crowd. His nose doesn't look right, flat, two dimensional and skewed across his face, the centre covered with a large dark-red scar.

Then.

Marlons eyes are drawn to the right of the ticket hall, just under the bridge. A weird looking old man is screwing him. Looks familiar, like he's seen him before somewhere, shit, it's the Skinny Man from before, when they were on their way to Brighton. He can feel the Skinny Mans stare penetrate his mind, reading his darkest thoughts, monstering thoughts, thoughts of killing and being a killer. The Skinny Man raises his left hand and slowly points directly toward Marlon. With his other hand, he holds up a torn bit of brown cardboard, maybe twelve inches square. Etched onto this, in scribbled blue biro pen, is the words, "THE END IS NIGH".

The end?

Marlon can't help but stare back, no matter how much he wants to, he can't break his gaze.

He has a bad feeling.

Heart beating out of his chest, he wants to run.

He has to run, but…

Fuck it, this needs to be done.

He needs peace.

'Let's have it!' Delroy roars.

And, with that, the Skinny Man is gone.

In and out of the static cars spread nose to tail across the road, they move as one with Marlon leading the way.

Reaching the edge of the ticket hall, Marlon leaps into the air, his right foot drilling into Yellowman's stomach who falls backward into the crowd behind. Screams follow as pandemonium breaks out with citizens running for cover as kicks and punches are thrown in all directions. Scanning around, Marlon spots Junior sharking his way through the crowd which seems to part as he progresses, as if he's surrounded by a force-field of serenity and calmness.

To his left, Delroy swings a peach of left hook toward Stevie Gentles head. Knuckles crunch, head shakes, knees judder and he tumbles to the floor. Delroy follows in with several kicks to the head. 'Fucking pussy,' he shouts, disappointed, he expected more of a fight from the supposed hard-man from Peckham.

Meanwhile…

Just inside the entrance, Marlon has Junior pinned against the wall. Looking left he sees Yellowman getting back to his feet, he knows he doesn't have long. Gripping Juniors throat with his left, he aims punches to his head with his right. Screaming with every blow, Junior tries ducking out of the way but Marlon is strong and way too fast.

Yellowman moves through the crowd slowly as the action spins around him. His face contorting with anger, his brow is way below his eye-line as his jaggered teeth nash together. Marlon can't believe his eyes. Yellowmans nose morphs into an ugly snout while the whites of his eyes tinge blood-red. The edges of his forehead bulge and eventually rip open as huge horns push through.

Shit.

With that, the ticket hall is plunged into near darkness and an eerie red mist surrounds them. Growling as his face distorts even more, reaching into his jacket Yellowman pulls out a sliver of steel which shimmers and glows red. 'Yeahhhhhhhh!!!!!' he sings, his chorus of demonic voices phasing in and out of reality.

Panicking, Marlon releases Junior and the red mist evaporates and the ticket hall lights flick back on.

A knife.

He's got a fucking knife.

Screams of 'Marlon! Run!' surround him.
As.
Yellowman lunges.
Blade aiming toward Marlons heart.
And then…

Time…

Slows…

Down…

Screams echo and time-stretches into the blurring background as silence fills the ticket hall. Eventually, time slows to a standstill, fists and feet hover unfeasibly anti-gravity-style in mid-air as angry faces stand frozen in time.
Something terrible has happened.
Marlon!!!
He can feel his heart slowing.
Beat after beat.
Breath after breath.
Thoughts rush through his mind…
Devon…
Pops…
Ashley…
Delroy…
Junior…
Momma…
He can see himself holding a small baby…
His new-born son…
In glorious technicolour…
He sees a beautiful girl with golden hair…
Gleaming white teeth and a gorgeous smile…
Her hand moves toward her mouth…
She smiles and blows him a kiss…
Violins surround him and his heart swells…
Then.

The scene dissolves into black and white and the girl fades away into oblivion…

He's now in a graveyard…

Surrounded by hundreds of mourners…

All dressed in black…

Some with veils…

Others covering their faces…

He can hear sobbing…

And whispering and wailing…

Can't quite make out what they're saying…

Turning slowly, he spots an open grave…

A coffin lowered…

Stepping forward…

He squints at the headstone…

Marlon Walters…

Rest in Peace…

Eyes squeezing together…

Hands onto his ears…

No, please…

Feet tingling…

The ground sways like he's on a ship…

Stranded in one hundred feet waves…

It's the ship in the chip shop, in Brighton…

Yeah, that's it.

It's Brighton, not a graveyard at all…

He feels light-headed, dizzy, sick…

"HE'S BEEN STABBED!!!"

The words echo through the ticket hall, out to the street then back into the centre of Marlons mind.

'He's been stabbed,' a female voice shrieks. 'Stabbed!'

Then.

Reality hits him like a bolt of lightning.

STABBED?

Time speeds back up.

The wailing sounds of sirens quickly replace the silent stillness as everyone darts in all directions, fear filling their screams.

'Babylon dem come.'

He looks back to Yellowman who now looks like an eight-year-old boy, naïve and small and scared. Dropping the blade, he turns and runs back down the stairs toward the platforms. Marlon spins one-eighty and runs out of the ticket hall then left. Junior follows, chasing him left onto Electric Avenue, then into the indoor market.

Meanwhile…

Ashley, scuffling with a tall, lanky Peckham fool who can't fight to save his life and looks shit scared, spots Marlon run off. With that, he breaks free, calls the Peckham fool a "cunt" and exits the station, sprinting in the other direction toward Brixton Hill.

Looking over, Delroy sees Marlon and Junior exit, and then Ashley. After several more kicks to Stevie Gentles head, he stuffs his bloodied right fist into his pocket before walking slowly after them. Casually, he heads into the market, hoping to merge innocently into the background.

Then, in the market…

Traders are busy clearing their stalls away while mommas sift through the remains of the days trading, looking for cheap produce and perhaps a bargain or two.

Marlon, running full pace now, is followed by a wave of shocked gasps and screams.

"He's been stabbed."

"Lord God!"

"Get help."

He can feel someone close behind giving chase. Glancing over his shoulder he see's Junior.

Shit, this guy is relentless.

Then.

SLAM!

Melons, yams and plantain fly into the air as he tumbles head-first over a stall. Junior collides into his back and they hit the floor together.

Back to his feet, Marlon runs his hands all over his chest.

Blood. Fuck.

Probing his chest, he can't believe it. 'I'm okay,' he whispers before looking over to Junior who's rolling around on the floor forcing out deep, unrecognisable groans.

'Help me, please.'

Yellowman missed.

Stabbed Junior instead.

The fucking idiot.

Within seconds they're surrounded by a large crowd of shoppers and market traders.

Police approach, blowing whistles, 'halt… don't move… you're under arrest…' they yell.

Two Officers grab Junior, one on each arm. The Officer on the right pulls at his coat to see the extent of the stabbing while Junior crumples in pain. With that, the market explodes with noise as shoppers and traders shout for the Officer to let the boy go.

Hearing more sirens outside, Marlon locks onto more and more Police helmets moving through the sea of market stalls like a shiver of sharks. 'Run Junior, run.'

Struggling to his feet, Junior breaks free and staggers outside. Several rude-boys hanging out around the shops opposite wave him over. Staggering across the road, he's surrounded by rude-boys, pickneys and by-passers who sit him down. Weak and delirious, his head tilts before his body slouches over on his side.

The following ten minutes see the Police Officers come under attack by a growing crowd of youths, angry at the news that the Police have stabbed a local boy.

# Episode 20.
# “Paradise Lost”

Saturday 11 April 4:50am
Brixton Police Station,
London

‘WHERE. ARE. THEY.’

Eyes springing open, the slumbering custody Sergeant wakes with a start. ‘Jenkins, err-hum, Sir,’ he spurts instinctively.

‘Well?’

‘Sorry, Jenkins, Sir, ah, fourth floor,’ he stutters, straightening his tie and tucking his shirt in. As Deputy Commissioner, second in command of the entire Metropolitan Police, Jenkins instils the fear of god into the rank and file. This morning, with a bright red face, lined forehead and narrow eyes, Jenkins looks seriously upset.

‘Over there, Sir,’ the custody Sergeant points toward the double doors leading to the stairs.

Stepping onto the fourth-floor, he looks each way along the corridor. No sign of life. ‘Warren, Crow, where are you?’ he yells, so loud his booming voice shakes the dusty pictures hanging on the wall.

Warren appears from a conference room at the end of the corridor. ‘In here, Sir…’

Jenkins enters with pace and urgency. The room’s pack full with the Operation Swamp team. ‘Look at the state of it in here, clear this place up and let's get started.'

The dozen or so Officers spring into action and the drawn-all-over maps, half drunken cups of tea and over-flowing cigarette trays are cleared from the long oval desk.

'Let's get to it, what on earth happened?' Jenkins glares into Crows eyes. 'And why wasn't I made aware last night?'

The room falls silent as the Officers look toward each other, then simultaneously toward Crow.

'Crow? Somebody? Anybody?' Jenkins demands.

John has never seen Jenkins this angry, he notes his cockney accent is much stronger under stress.

Removing his glasses, Crow pushes his chin forward through his shirt as his cheeks flush.

Noticing his discomfort, Warren begins to explain…

Upward of a hundred local youths attacked five-foot patrolling Officers and three SPG patrols, resulting in sixteen Officers injured and eleven locals arrested. The teenager with stab wounds remains in hospital, seriously injured, but stable.

'This is what you meant by retaking the streets?' Jenkins looks daggers into Crow, his face turning a deeper shade of red while his nose turns purple.

'Sir, you and I know the deployment was… approved by Armstrong and of course… Downing Street,' Crow asserts, showing no emotion.

Jenkins stands. 'With good men injured, and a young boy stabbed, don't you dare,' he growls.

While fascinated by the exchange, John is extremely uncomfortable with this amount of raw emotion. Rarely does it ever produce logically efficient solutions.

Crow pokes his neck further through his collar, wriggling his chin in the air. 'The boy's stable… he'll be okay.'

Johns eyes widen, astounded Crows attempts to defend his position, and, in the process, taking on Jenkins.

Jenkins, incredulous, stares deep into Crow and the room fills with the excruciating sound of silence.

'Err-hum,' John can't take it, he has to break the silence.

'Gentlemen, we are all-erm, tired and fatigued. May I suggest we focus on plans for today, and review what happened last night at a later date?' Johns initial nervousness upon joining Lambeth Division has quickly been replaced by an assertive, non-emotional and proactive posture.

Jenkins turns to John. 'You're right, we've started this, we owe it to everyone to see it through,' he says, taking a deep breath. 'Armstrong has instructed us to increase the presence today.'

Increase the presence? John can't believe what he's hearing. Clearly this is not the right strategy, fire on fire will do nothing to put the fire out.

Crows face, on the other hand, beams, his strategy seemingly vilified.

Warrens shakes his head. 'Sorry, increase the presence, did you say increase?'

'Yes George, increase, we cannot be seen to be backing down,' Jenkins shrugs. 'The fear is a tactical withdrawal will be seen as a retreat, which will be viewed as an admission of culpability and political failure, and breed even more unrest with the populous.'

John feels the knot in the pit of his stomach tighten. Continue the Swamp deployment, in light of last nights escalation, simply doesn't to make sense.

'If I may,' Crow clears his throat. 'My team and I have prepared a series of plans… in response to a… range of scenarios.'

Closing his eyes, John shakes his head.

Here we go again.

Crow provides a detailed account of his plans, including the arterial routes that will be blocked and where entrance and exit to what he refers to as "the target zone" will be restricted. The "target zone", or the radial half mile around the junction of Atlantic and Railton Roads will be flooded with Officers who'll take control of every street corner while thirty-seven suspect premises on Leesons and Mayall Roads will be subject to intrusive searches. At the same time, any suspicious pedestrians or vehicles will be stopped and searched. Multiple arrests will be executed for even the pettiest of crime or misdemeanour.

Fingers pressing into his temples, John can't believe what he's hearing. This is way beyond a simple increased presence, this is a take-over, an occupation, a coup d'état.

With little choice in the matter, Jenkins and the Operations Team offer minimal resistance. They agree to reconvene at nine-hundred hours when Jenkins returns from his early morning briefing with Commissioner Armstrong at New Scotland Yard. In the meantime, John will meet the community leaders in an attempt to use his influence and manage expectations.

Saturday 11 April, 8:22am
47 Saltoun Road
Brixton, London

'You awake?'

'Nah-man, go back to sleep,' Marlon whispers.

'Will you batty-boys settle down nah-man, some of us trying to get some kip yeah,' Delroy yawns across from Devons bed.

'Top and tailing don't make us benders,' Ashley protests.

'T'cha, as if, he's no way pretty enough,' Marlon teases.

'So anyway, wonder what happened to Junior?' Ashley pulls the blankets up around his chest, in turn pulling them off Marlon to reveal his yellow and brown Y-fronts.

'For fuck sake Ash, give me some threads,' Marlon urges, pulling the blanket back while pushing Ashleys feet to the other side of the bed. 'I'm not even thinking about him and the idiot-fool Yellow-fucking-man.'

'He might be dead-up yah-naw,' Delroy sits up.

'Where did all the rude-boys come from?' Ashley pushes Marlons feet to the other side. 'And fighting with the Police, mate, that can't be good.'

'They got what they deserve yeah,' Delroy spits, reaching

for the Rizzla. 'Same way as that Peckham piece of shit.'

'We should ring the hospital or something, maybe ask at the Police Station?' Ashley suggests.

'Nah-man-nah, Peckham aint bringing us no more problem.' Marlon smiles, rolling out of bed then heading for the toilet. 'Reckon we're in the clear.'

'True-say,' Delroy yells after him. 'It's Babylon we've got to watch for now though, they'll be tooled up today, just see.' He nods, stroking the fluffy beginnings of the moustache he's cultivating.

'What you on about, later on?'

'Later, as in not earlier or now, Ash-Lee. When we rise against the Beastman yeah, this is a revolution, yah-hear.'

'Last night will have made it even worse,' Ashley suggests. 'There'll be the army and shit out there today.'

Toilet flushed, Marlon comes back in. 'Army plus Babylon, Jesus Christ, der-gonna to be enough tribulation tonight. Reckon we get down there early, mix things up, make some money,' he smiles, seemingly refreshed and re-energised.

'Yeah man,' Delroy smiles. 'Marlon the man is back!'

Ashley sighs, looking to the heavens.

'Anyways,' Delroy raises his nose to the air. 'Is that bacon I smell?' He isn't wrong, Momma is busy cooking Bacon with fried eggs and sausages.

'You smell jack-shit,' Marlon dismisses, not wanting to share his breakfast. 'Anyway, Devon will be home soon, you better get out of his sheets and chip, yeah.'

Saturday 11 April. 10:15am
17 Hamilton House, Peabody Estate
Greenwich, London

Bang.

Bang-bang-bang-bang-bang-bang-bang-bang-bang…

Oh-ah-oh-oh-oh-ah-ah-ah.

Super pulls the pillow over his ears as the headboard bangs against the paper-thin wall. The last thing he wants is to listen to Devon engaging in some energetic early morning sex, especially after last night, where Chantelle, yet again, collapsed into a drunken pool of her own vomit.

The pounding continues, quicker and louder until Devon, much to the hilarity of Super, lets out a caveman groan followed by a high pitched, drawn out "ahh" from Shirley.

Looking across to the back of Chantelle who's snoring heavily, he realises sex isn't on the cards so swings out of bed. Pulling on last night's clothes, wide bottomed beige Farrah trousers and blue silk shirt, he grabs his three-quarter Crombie coat. Passing the living-room he sees Paul asleep on the sofa with stunning Sammie wrapped in his arms. Slamming the front door shut deliberately hard, he chuckles to himself knowing that he'll have woken everyone up.

Along the walkway then down the stairs, he heads east out of the estate parallel to the Thames, toward the aged rigging of the Cutty Sark ship in dry dock. Across the Thames he can make out the run-down-redundant warehouses in the East End and hears echoes from years past of dock workers unloading unusual spices and exotic silks from the orient. Breathing deeply, the crisp morning air tingles his lungs as the morning sun feels warm on his face.

He feels good.

Yeah man, he's had a good night last night at the wine bar in Soho before heading to the surprisingly trouble-free Albany Empire in Deptford for an after-hours soul and funk dance. Replaying last night in his mind, he decides he's actually enjoyed himself for a change and, apart from a lack of sex, life's actually good.

His thoughts turn to Chantelle, yeah, a piss-head for sure and always drunk, but, although a bit heavy with a wide batty, she isn't bad looking. Yeah man, he might give it a go with her, try go steady. Devon's going steady with Shirley and is doing okay, in fact, he's loved up and loving it.

Damn, life is actually pretty good, for real.

Dipping his head, he enters the newsagents. After a quick chat with the nice old fella behind the counter, he slides the packet of ten Silk Cut into his inside pocket. With that, he feels the handle of his steel. Damn, forgot about that, thought I left it in the back of Pauls car. Not to worry, no problem, I'll drop it off when I get back.

Securing the Daily Mirror under his arm, he turns to leave when the Nice Old Fella behind the counter clears his throat. 'Terrible business eh, terrible,' he shakes his head.

Stopping, Super looks sideways.

What the fooks he on about, the crazy old fool… what's terrible, my steel, how'd he know about that, maybe he's seen it… shit… he'll be on the phone to Babylon as soon as I leave, grassing me up, giving them a detailed description, getting me arrested and jailed… maybe the Nice Old Fella is an informant, bet he's seen all sort in here, heard all sorts of gossip and tittle-tattle, the dirty snake-in-the-grass-motherfucker… yeah, probably an informant planted here by Babylon, on the lookout for bad-boys, or more specifically, on the look-out for me… I fookin' knew it, they've been watching my movements, tracking my whereabouts from time… the devious little shit, he's definitely spotted my steel, the nosey old bastard, into all my business and getting me locked up, just when life is good… the bloodclat pussyhole, he don't even know me.

The opening bars of Wailing Rudie echo in the distance.

Oh no, he shakes his head.

Not now.

But.

Rudie is Wailing.

That can mean only one thing…

'NO!' he shouts to himself.

Stepping back, the Nice Old Fella stares at him, fear scribbled across his face, dread filling his eyes.

Rudie is Wailing.

*"When music play, he dance and sing."*

Gwan bad boy Super, he says to himself. Rob the old bastard and wet his rasclat face.

*"Claims at him… he aint got no friends."*

He can hear himself signing out loud.

Blocking out reality, he closes his eyes…

Slowly, reaching into his coat, his fingers wrap around the base. It feels good, comforting, reassuring. He pulls out his baby with a *schvrm* of a lightsaber and the steel shimmers as adrenaline pulses through him.

He feels alive.

Yesh-star, now we feeling it.

Come-nah man!

Raising the steel above his head he pauses, savouring the moment. Staring deep into his victims eyes, he slashes the blade diagonally down across the Nice Old Fella's face. A clean strike, a clinical performance by the doctor of doom, the bushido of Brixton, the Sith of South London. The Nice Old Fella stares blankly at him, void of emotion, before deep red blood seeps slowly from the cut running from the top of his hairline down through his nose and across his lower cheek. Then, mouth opening, he screams an ungodly scream as the left-hand side of his face begins to slide from his skull revealing the dark red skeleton beneath.

Rudie is Wailing.

*"A strict badness him defend."*

No.

NO!

Shaking his head, he squeezes his eyes tighter together.

Don't be thinking like that you head-case, he tells himself as Rudie echoes into silence. Opening his eyes, he sees the Nice Old Fella standing in front, smiling. 'You okay, son?' he asks, kindness in his voice.

No cuts, no blood, no skeletons, no terror.

'Yeah man, safe,' he says, turning and exiting the shop. Got to control the paranoia or I'll go mad, he says to himself. And now hallucinations, what the fuck? He scares himself sometimes, when the red-mist descends and his anger takes hold, when he's surrounded by craziness.

Head down, he sets off back to Shirleys flat. Although an estate, just like those back at Brixton, it seems different around here, somehow calmer, more mellow. Climbing the stairs, he heads along the balcony before letting himself in. Paul's up and in the kitchen making a pot of tea. 'Morning big boy,' he says, with a zing. 'Tea?'

'Yesh-star, cool, cool' Super smiles, flinging the newspaper onto the table before heading for the toilet.

Leaning over, Paul spins the paper around. 'What-the-fuck,' he whispers. 'Oi-oi,' he shouts. 'Get the fuck in here.'

Super dives back, heart pounding, eyes wide, Wailing Rudie selected, needle ready to drop.

Devon quickly follows, draped Roman-Emperor-style in a pink and blue cotton sheet.

'Youths Rampage Through Brixton,' Paul reads out loud.

They stand staring at the black and white picture of youths surrounding a SPG van. Bricks hover mid-air as bad-boys stand freeze-frame giving the Police the finger while others seemingly yell and point. Facing them, Babylon stand in a line, truncheons drawn with anger on their faces.

'Bloooood-claaaaat!' Devon sings.

Super stands open mouthed with his eyes bulging. 'The patty-shop, on Atlantic Road,' he whispers, noting his favourite lunchtime eating emporium in the background.

Shirley darts into the kitchen. 'What, what is it?'

Grabbing the paper, Devon reads out the report of an un-named teenager in hospital with stab wounds, and the subsequent disturbance. 'Got to get back, check on Marlon,' he says staring at Shirley, who nods in agreement.

Saturday, 11 April, 3:10pm
Atlantic Road
Brixton, London

'There Paul, there,' Devon points. 'Pull over, man.'

Paul manoeuvres the Dolomite, pulling up next to a crowd of youths. Marlon stands tall in the middle, with Delroy to his right and Ashley to his left.

'Marlon, Marl-on,' Devon yells, climbing out.

Looking over his shoulder, their eyes meet. 'Easy-nah-Dee, hear about last night?'

'Yeah man, saw it in the paper, you alright?' he pulls at Marlons shoulder, checking he's okay. 'What the fuck happened, where you been?'

Sitting on the bonnet, Marlon recounts the rumble with the Peckham Boys, Junior getting stabbed and the subsequent fight with Babylon.

'T'cha,' Devon tuts. 'We all gonna suffer because of this.'

Marlons face falls, he expected Devon to be proud.

'And what about you?' Paul calls to Ashley. 'Does the old man know you where you were last night?'

'Course not,' Ashley makes a don't-be-stupid face.

'Don't give it the big-un Ash, or I'll sort you out.'

'Yeah right, course you will.'

'Listen to your big brother, yah-idiot-fool,' Super growls as Ashley steps back.

'So anyway, you rude-boys standing firm with us tonight?' Delroy suggests, already tired of Paul and Ashley dancing around with each other.

'Stand firm-star? Listen to dah-pickney,' Super laughs.

'Pickney?' Delroy steps forward. 'So, where you at last night then?'

Leaning in, Super screws up his face. 'Here me nah-star, us men were fookin pussy, right.' Even though his tone is angry and aggressive, he secretly likes Delroy and his bravado, he reminds him of his younger self.

Stepping back a little, Delroy realises his mistake. 'Easy-nah-Super, easy,' he says, showing him his palms.

'Hold up, won't be a minute.' Devon cuts in, spotting Crissy across the road. Bouncing over, they exchange a few words before shaking hands and Devon jogs back. 'Crissy reckons the Beasts stabbed that kid last night,'

'What, nah-man,' Marlon squints, shaking his head. 'I was right there, it was his own that did it.'

'Reckons Babylon coming down tonight to clear this place out, army with bulldozers and ting.'

The others pause in silence.

'What about our weed-star?' Super nods impatiently. They've been without stock for nearly a week.

'No problem,' Devon smiles. 'Got to head to his yard in twenty minutes.'

'Right then,' Paul says, making his way around to the drivers side of the car. 'Ashley, you get off home yeah.'

'Marlon, you too,' Devon adds, opening the passenger door. 'Delroy, you better get off as well, Auntie be fretting.'

'Fuck that,' Delroy says, pointing at his feet. 'We're standing firm, right here. If Babylon think they can test us they better get ready for some serious licks.'

'Listen to the brave little solider,' Super says with a broad smile, ducking his head as he falls into the back seat.

'Just get home before dark,' Paul points at Ashley, opening the drivers door and climbing in.

Turning the key, the engine pops into life.

Wheels spinning, they set off.

Saturday, 11 April, 3:37pm
Flat 4, Gabriel House, Loughborough Estate
Brixton, London

Knock-knock.

Silence.

'He's not in, let's go yeah,' Paul suggests, looking either way along the corridor. He hates Angel Town, full of skagg-heads, frontline bad-boys, dirty whores and scrawny pimps.

'Star, knock again,' Super says impatiently. 'He's in.'

Knock, knock-knock, knock.

Still no answer.

'Come on, we'll pop back later, eh.'

'Stop being a dick, Paul, he's in, man, I'm telling you,' Super puts his ear to the door, listening for signs of life.

Bang, BANG!

Devon used the side of his fist.

'Hush-nah-man,' Super whispers, hearing footsteps.

'Who dat?' a voice yells from behind the door.
Super looks at Paul, who looks at Devon.
'It's me man, open up,' Devon whispers.
Silence.
The threesome look at each other.
More silence.
'T'cha, knock again,' Super suggests.
BANG. BANG.
'Who der?' the voice asks, his voice deep and patois broad.
'It's me man, Crissy say pass by,' Devon kisses his teeth.
'Me? Who me?'
'Fucking hell, it's Devon, open up nah-man,' he whispers loudly looking at Super, then at Paul, who both giggle and stifle a laugh.
Super bangs the door again. 'We aint got all day-star.'
'T'cha, who dere?' the voice yells, louder.
'It's Devon yeah, I'm looking for Crissy.'
With raised voices, Paul looks over the balcony to check they haven't been heard.
'Who?' the voice quizzes.
'Devon!'
'Devon?'
Silence.
'Devon not here,' the voice continues.
'Fookin-hell-star,' Super yells at the top of his voice. 'Is Crissy in or not?'
After three clicks the door swings open. Devon recognises the guy behind as Snakehead, from the Windsor Pub. He stands in the doorway with massive fifty pence shaped shoulders poking through his stringy white vest and a massive joint sticking out the side of his mouth. Pulling on the joint, he exhales a large plume of thick smoke which hangs around his shoulders like a fluffy white cloak. Pausing, he looks at each of them, one by one. 'Easy-nah rude-boys,' he smiles with a broad grin.
'Yesh-my-star,' Super nods.
With that, Snakehead explodes into a range of karate

chops and kicks aimed toward an invisible man just a yard in front of him. Holding his final Bruce-Lee stance for a few seconds he smiles, 'so, enter… dah-dragon,' he says, before heading through to the front room. The others look at each other in amazement before following through the hallway.

Well-furnished and surprisingly tidy, a dark wood coffee table rests in the middle of the room, surrounded by a plush dark green three-piece suite sofa across the back and side walls. The large television in the far corner is flanked by a couple of wooden bass boxes, both four feet tall, each housing what looks to be a pair of eighteen-inch bass bins and horn tweeters.

Crissy sits in the middle of a three-seater sofa with Claude next to him while Snakehead plonks himself in the chair in front of the television. 'What-um bredrin, tek-ah seat,' Crissy smiles, opening his arms wide.

Devon sits on the other chair and Super on a wooden stool next to the balcony door. Scanning the room, Paul uncomfortably sits next to Crissy. Noting his awkwardness, Crissy places his hand on his knee. 'Easy-nah-duppy,' he nods. 'You a guess-ina-me-yard, relax-nah man.'

'So, Winston,' Claude nods. 'Big night tonight, eh?'

'Yesh-star,' Super agrees, ignoring the use of his first name, which he hates. 'Already enough youth pon-da line, Babylon all over too da-place too.'

'Our time has come,' Crissy nods sagely, his eyes closing in a meditative state. 'We be oppressed fah-time-pon-time.' Instinctively, he knows he has everyone's attention. 'Sus-stop an-ting, beatings of line-man, even dah-pickney-der who get jook lass-night. We have to rise man, rise.'

Face blushing, Pauls eyes dart around the room, avoiding eye contact at all costs.

'Nah-worries brother,' Crissy looks deep into him and squeezes his knee. 'Dis-nah no racialist business, yah-hear, dis-ah rich-an-poor class war ting. Inheritance, aristocracy and power, the upper-class minority control da-working-class majority, it's a power ting, right.' Pausing for couple of seconds, re-igniting his joint, he takes a deep draw, holds it for a couple of seconds before exhaling through his nose. 'Jee-suz Snakehead-man, dis herb is power, man, me-ah feel-all political and radical and ting,' he chuckles.

Listening to Crissy, Devon wonders what life he could have had if he wasn't on the frontline. His wisdom and views of the world, combined with the slow and deliberate way he talks suggest he could have been a lawyer or doctor or stand up businessman or something.

'Nuff-rumpus wit-dah-der herb yah-naw,' Snakehead mutters, not talking his eyes of the television.

'So, anyway, can we get some weight Crissy?' Devon doesn't want to dwell for too long in a known drug-dealers flat, but, at the same time, doesn't want to disrespect his mentor by changing the subject too soon. He wants to get his stock then get out of there quick-time, so now isn't the time for a history lesson or a philosophical debate.

'Yesh-my yout, strictly business, cool... wha-me provide fah-yaw?' Crissy smiles.

'We'll take six weight, in quarters. yeah?'

'Make dat ten-star,' Super adds.

Crissy looks toward Snakehead. 'Fetch da goodness man.'

Snakehead, in a trance, sits oblivious to the request as he sucks on the largest spliff Devon has ever seen, a twenty-five skin or something.

'Snakehead, yo, Snakehead,' Crissy yells, his voice deeper and louder. 'Get dah-bloodclat goodness man!'

Jolting out of his trance, Snakehead moves from slouching to bolt upright in a single, lightning quick move. 'Alright-dred, easy-nah, what's da problem?' he sings making his way out of the living room. He returns twenty seconds later with a large carrier bag full of weed. Reaching under the sofa Claude pulls out an old antique wooden box and lifts out a large set of brass scales. Weighing out an ounce at a time, he roughly tears each into half, and half again before stuffing into small plastic Natwest Bank money bags, then pushing all these into a plain white carrier bag. Money exchanged and handshakes shared, they all agree to hook up later on down at the Pool Hall on Railton Road.

Saturday, 11 April, 4:45pm
Triple AAA Taxi Office, Railton Road
Brixton, London

'Watch out, you idiot.'
'What you say?'
'You'll spill it.'
'Eh?'
'Get it all over,' Paul says, looking through the rear-view mirror at Super devouring a spicy meat patty then swigging ginger beer from a small brown bottle. Sitting in a parked car on Railton Road, with a wholesale weight of weed in the glove box and hordes of Police swarming around, Paul feels conspicuous and on edge.
'Right,' Devon interjects. 'Finish munching, then drop this off yeah.' Leaning over the back of the seat, he hands Super four money bags, each containing a quarter-weight. Stuffing it inside his jacket, Super clambers out. Pushing his pelvis forward, he stretches his back and looks either way along the road before stepping into the taxi office.
A couple of minutes later…
Paul is drawn to a slim guy with cropped hair and a green bomber jacket standing to the right of the doorway, his back against the shop window. Vaguely familiar, Paul can't quite place his face. 'There's enough fronters around here tonight Dee, it's madness.'
'Stop being a pussy,' Devon tuts. 'Listen, we just gonna sell some draw, bank some cash and get out of dis shit-hole quick time. I'm not into no rebellion business, fuck that nah, we'll go see the girls tonight over in Greenwich, controlled over dem parts man.'
'Sounds like a plan to me,' Paul smiles.
Emerging from the doorway Super gives Paul a wink and a thumbs-up before stuffing a roll of cash into his left sock.

On spotting Super, the slim guy with a green bomber jacket swivels to face the doorway then nods to another guy who approaches from the other side with a black leather jacket stretched over a muscular frame with a look of a meathead about him. They grab Super an arm each.

'Where the fuck did they come from?' Devon looks all around then through the wing-mirror.

'Plain clothes,' Paul rattles the gearstick, ready to set off.

'Hush-naw, easy,' Devon whispers, slowly sliding down in his seat, pushing the remainder of the weed underneath.

Pauls hand hovers over the ignition key.

'Jus-be cool, yeah,' Devon urges. 'They aint gonna find jack-shit on him, probably don't even know he's with us. We're just gonna leave the weed here, glide away and come back for it later when Babylon a-dust.' Opening the door, Devon climbs out and casually strolls to the other side of the Road, then waves Paul over. With that, Paul gets out, gingerly closes the door and locks it. Looking over the roof toward Devon on the pavement opposite, he smiles. Fucking hell, we are actually pulling this off, he thinks, heart pounding against his rib cage.

Meanwhile...

As the Officers lead the suspect away toward the parked-up SGP van fifty yards down the road. Still grabbing the suspects right arm, PC Jones is drawn to the car parked just a few feet away, and a skinny guy gesturing toward a queer looking fella across the road.

Something's not right.

Coppers instinct.

Then it clicks.

Two big bastards and a queer skinny guy. It's fucking them, it must be them, Kenny wasn't bullshitting after all.

His cousin, Kenneth, faces an eight to ten stretch after being arrested in possession of cocaine and several firearms. These three bastards fitted him up, got him arrested and put away on remand. It must be them he tells himself. 'Stay there,' he growls, reaching out and grabbing Pauls shoulder.

'We'll be searching that too.'

'Andy, never mind him, we've got what we came for,' the Slim Officer yells over, dragging the suspect toward the SPG van by his left.

Paul freezes.

Fuck.

'Why you stop me Beast, why you stop me?' Super shouts, kicking up a stink, giving Paul a chance to get away.

A couple of taxi drivers come out and a few youths from along the road stroll down to watch. Within seconds, Super has an audience of maybe a dozen.

'Gut feel,' Andrew yells, releasing Super and heading toward Paul.

'Make it quick Andy, bit choppy out here,' the Slim Officer growls, gripping the suspects arm tighter.

Satisfied his colleague has control, Andrew turns his attention to the queer looking skinny guy and the car. Giving it a once over, he kicks the tyres and checks the tax disk.

The crowd, by now a couple of dozen strong, begin shouting and getting rowdy, "fawk-off Beast-man" and "retreat" they yell. Super pushes against the Slim Officer, who bounces against the side of the car.

With that, Andrew instinctively pulls his truncheon from the side of his trousers and re-focuses on the suspect rather than the queer looking skinny guy. Raising his truncheon, he yells at the crowd to get back while reaching into his jacket for his radio, calling for urgent support. Adrenalin flowing, he feels like a teenager again on the terraces of West Ham on a Saturday afternoon. 'Come here,' he seethes, grabbing the suspects wrist and clipping on a handcuff. This fucking snake isn't getting away, he says to himself.

'Fook-awf Beast,' Super yells.

'You're nicked son,' Andrew laughs, tugging the suspect closer, inches from his face.

Super smiles as the noise of the crowd fades and Wailing Rudie begins to echo, *"him can't go wail in jail."*

Nicked? Nah-star-nah, not me dred, no bloodclat way!

Rudie's wailing and everything's cool.

Leaning back, Super swings his head forward, landing a head-butt directly into the Officers face.

CRACK.

'Andy!' the Slim Officer yells.

The crowd falls silent as the bone-crunching sound bounces along Railton Road, blood and mucus spurting everywhere. With that, an arriving SPG van mounts the curb and the backdoors explode open. Half a dozen Officers jump out and move quickly toward the mass of rowdiness.

The crowd erupts.

Screams fill the air, kicks and punches follow.

Blood still pumping, Andrew wipes his sleeve across his broken nose, smearing a dark red line across his cheek. A decent head-butt, yeah, pretty tasty, he smiles to himself. Electricity sparks through his entire body as he tastes deliciously sour, iron-laced blood. Light-headed, he feels drunk, euphoric almost, totally up for it, he can hear his old man and his uncle shouting, urging him on…

Twelve years old, he's back in his boxing club where he and Kenny are knocking seven bells out of each other. The blurring sound of the fighting crowd and his uncle Tommy yelling fades out and he can hear echoes of Ultravox…

*"Ahhhhhhh Viennaaaaah, dumb-dudum, t'ch-cha!"*

A golden ray of sunshine beams down from heaven, warming his face. He feels beautiful and gorgeous, untouchable and invincible. 'You've got to do better than that, boy,' he shouts, yanking the handcuffed suspect back toward him. With a grunt of aggression, he lands a peach of a right hook on the side of the suspects head. 'Fucking hard bastard, eh?' he screams. Yanking the suspect backward, his fist drives down onto the back of the suspects head. 'Yeah,' he shouts, his lips splitting over his blood-stained teeth. He can see his old man jumping up and down, hugging his Uncle, celebrating the knockout punch, punch of the century they yell.

Landing on his knees, the suspect refuses to go down.

Andrew follows up with a crunching kick, followed by other Officers joining in. Multiple blows follow before six Officers, including Andrew, pick the suspect up and launch him into the back of the SPG van. Then, the van begins swaying from side to side.

The jeering crowd, a hundred strong now, knowing a serious beating is taking place, respond by kicking and rocking the van. Some try prizing the back doors open while others punch the windscreen.

Saturday, 11 April, 5:10pm
Operations Command
4th Floor, Brixton Police Station, London

'Mid-twenties male in custody, being treated by the doctor. He'll, erm, be charged as soon as he's well enough with possession, resisting arrest, assaulting a Police Officer and affray. We have an Officer with a broken nose, currently receiving first aid. I gather he'll be fine.'

'Cut to the chase Cummings, I asked you for a status update, not a roll-call from the custody suite,' Jenkins yells.

'Erm, very good Sir. We have control of the target area and the crowd has, erm, pretty much dispersed. We have withdrawn to standing points A through to E.' John uses a long cane to point to the large map pinned to the wall indicating the location where SPG groups have gathered. 'Intelligence suggests, erm, the main agitators are frequenting three locations, namely several squats on Leeson road, the Windsor Public House and erm, the Pool Hall on Railton Road.'

'We cleared those squats…less than a week ago,' Crow seethes, his eyes narrowing.

'What a surprise,' Warren steps in. 'The homeless have found their way back into empty houses.'

'Homeless… hardened criminals I'd suggest,' Crow counters with a scowl.

'Erm, we intend to deploy several teams to carry out

snatch operations at each of the three locations,' John says assertively, ignoring Crow. 'We hope to, erm, arrest the key individuals thereby supressing the situation.'

'Okay, talk to me about containment, should the snatch-ops go not to plan?' Jenkins asks.

'Good question… very good,' Crow interjects, taking the long cane from John. 'If I may…'

Knowing Crow has no intention of stopping, John sits down as Crow stands up.

'We have a significant presence at the five standing points,' Crow begins. 'We'll draw resources inward… creating a controlled perimeter to… restrict movement within the more… heavily populated shopping precinct as well as… the target area… we have upward of six-hundred officers deployed… with another thousand or so on stand-by from neighbouring forces.'

'Very well Crow,' Jenkins sighs, linking his arms behind his head, looking toward Warren. 'Community leaders?'

'Where to start, they are very concerned about the heavy-handed nature of the operation,' Warren takes his glasses off to rub his forehead.

'God damn it… Warren,' Crow slams his left hand down onto the table. 'Of course they will say that… they will say anything to deflect attention away from… deviant behaviour.'

'Okay, let's all calm down shall we,' Jenkins interjects. 'John, go see the leaders, see what they can offer. I'll brief Armstrong and we'll meet again in a few hours.'

Saturday, 11 April, 5:32pm
Petersons Pool Hall
Railton Road, Brixton, London

Looking deep into his eyes, he wonders if he'll bottle it. No sign of panic though, seems steady enough, maybe he can do it. 'All you got to do is get the bag,' Devon confirms. 'Just open the door, reach under the seat and take it.'

'Then head straight back here, yeah,' Paul adds.

Devon looks sideways at Paul, then back to Delroy. 'It's no problem dred, just be cool.'

Nodding, Delroy gets up and heads for the door.

A dancehall vibe surrounds the Pool Hall, which is unusually busy with rude-boys smoking weed, drinking beer and swapping stories about the trouble earlier. Looking around, Devon spots faces he hasn't seen in ages, such as Hammerhead from Lewisham, and a couple of old school friends too.

'Like a mini-Super, a carbon copy,' Paul ponders, watching Delroy disappear through the door and head toward the taxi office and the parked-up Dolomite.

'Yep, brave as a lion, stupid as fuck,' Devon agrees, his thoughts spiralling toward Super who, less than an hour ago, had the shit beaten out of him by a group of rampaging Beasts. 'Probably in a cell now, enough cuts and bruises.'

'Or in the hospital,' Paul sighs, his words trailing off.

Meanwhile…

Delroy strolls the short distance along Railton Road toward the Taxi Office and what remains of Pauls car. The windscreen is smashed in and the passenger door and front wings dented and buckled. Groups of rude-boys and pickney-yout are still hanging around while Babylon have grouped together at the far end of the Road, maybe a quarter of a mile away. The atmosphere's tense and dry as both groups watch each other, waiting for something to happen. Deep breath, swallowing hard, he looks around before tugging at the door. Pulling hard, it creaks open before gingerly feeling under the seat.

Thirty seconds later…

Arriving back at the Pool Hall, he makes his way around the two American sized pool tables toward the back. Triumphantly, much to the surprise of Paul, he places the white plastic carrier bag in the centre of the table.

'Rudie, well done!' Devon grins, patting him on the arm.

Delroys face beams.

In the process of thrashing Ashley on the far side table, Marlon looks over through jealous eyes. I should be there with my brother, he thinks.

'Your shot mate,' Ashley prompts, noticing Marlons stare.

Then, Marlon spins around as a couple of Jam-Jars race by heading south, sirens and bells blaring.

Suddenly, the overhead lights go out and the Pool Hall is plunged into darkness. Silence descends and the party vibe grinds to halt.

Everyone looks at each other.

What the fuck?

'Babylon dem come,' comes a yell from the front of the hall as the front door slams open and a dozen or so Officers steam in, truncheons drawn. In a flash, the place is a scribble of chaos with rude-boys yelling, some running outside while others scuffling with the Officers.

Hit in his shoulder with a rogue truncheon, Ashley screams out while Marlon is pinned onto a table by a rude-boy who has a Police Officer on top of him.

Pauls eyes meet Devons. 'Fucking hell, the weed.'

'T'cha, get rid of it, it's cursed, man,' Devon yells, flinging the bag into a dark corner before receiving a punch in the face from an older looking Officer.

The Pool Hall empties as everyone streams out. It's utter chaos, rude-boys engaging in toe to toe battles with Babylon while young kids flood into the newsagents next door, exiting with handfuls of sweets and bottles of Rola-Cola.

An eerie roar erupts from the now massive crowd gathered outside, it's madness. Instinctively ducking, Devon hears a massive smash and, spinning around, he sees the plate glass window of the Pool Hall explode and a rude-boy land on the pavement dazed, blood pouring from his head. Looking north toward Atlantic Road he sees a couple more SPG vans parked up, one in the middle of the Road with maybe a hundred youths and a dozen or so Police battling around it. Bottles and bricks are launched as the Police charge indiscriminately.

Then…

Something enters his peripheral vision, alerting his senses, triggering his fight-or-flight instinct. Through the crowd he sees a guy with a black jacket and an ultra-short crude-cut heading toward him. He looks pained, anxious, angry and scared, he's a troubled soul.

Skinheads, shit.

The Troubled Soul runs towards him, apparently not dodging trouble, but trouble dodging him. He freezes, his eyes drawn to the bottle in the Troubled Souls hand. With the threat of a bottle over his head, his natural instinct is to run, but he can't.

Then…

Time slows down.

The intense roar of the rampaging crowd begins to blur and echo. Sprinting fast, the Troubled Soul reaches into his pocket and pulls out silver Zippo lighter. With that, time starts to stretch and slow down even more…

In slow motion…

The Troubled Soul strikes the lighter on his chest several times and Devons stomach churns with every movement. Eventually, the rag poking out of the neck of the bottle ignites.

Then, time stops.

Reality freeze-frames.

In that single moment, a grain of sand on the urban beach of eternity. Their eyes meet and Devon sees infinity, the actual end of time. At last, he's met his nemesis, a messenger from the Devil himself, come to take him down to the lake of fire. He isn't scared though, not even surprised, it's oddly normal, like it's somehow meant to be. He never thought it would end this way though, he imagined his fate would resemble a Hollywood movie with a dramatic finale set-piece shoot-out, like the one in Taxi-Driver with Robert DeNiro going down in a blaze of glory.

His end isn't meant to be this way.

Not like this.

Not by a petrol bomb over his head.
Not here, and not now.
Then.
Time speeds back up…
In a flash, barging Devon out of the way, the Troubled Soul flings open the door of a parked Jam-Jar. A quick look around and he launches the lit bottle inside before slamming the door shut. Turning, he looks back toward Devon.
Vision zooming into a long dark tunnel, the Troubled Souls gaze burns into his cornea, he's somehow familiar, like he knows him, a long-lost friend, a brother or something. The Troubled Soul slowly nods, then smiles before setting off down Railton Road.
Shaking his head, Devon blinks.
Is this for real?
Did he imagine it?
Back in the real-world the noise, anger and violence engulfs him once again. The inside of the Jam-Jar is now burning dark red and the windows begin to blacken. Grabbing Delroy then Ashley, he pushes them toward Paul who's now at the other side of the Road. 'Where's Marlon?' he yells.
'Dunno, still in the pool hall?' Ashley looks around.
'He'll be alright,' Paul says, grabbing Devons shoulder.
'Big enough to look after himself,' Delroy adds.
Devon looks over his shoulder, over the burning Jam-Jar and through the smashed window into the Pool Hall. 'Wherever he is, he's not in there, so fuck it, lets go.'
'Leave, you mad?' Delroy screws up his face. 'This is it, what we've been waiting for Dee.'
'What?'
'T'cha, I'm not going nowhere, this is it, this is our time,' Delroy nods, excited by his train of thought.
'Leave him Dev,' Paul urges, pulling at Devons arm.
'Ash, you standing with us?' Delroy asks.
Ashley looks both ways up and down the road. 'Delroy, come on mate, this is madness, we got to go.'

Shaking his head, Delroy jogs toward the roaring crowd, now formed into a single entity in the middle of the Road.

'Delroy, come-nah-man,' Devon shouts after him.

'See you pussyclats later,' Delroy yells as he's consumed by the sea of angry, shouting faces.

Five minutes later…

Paul and Ashley follow Devon north toward Coldharbour Lane and the centre of Brixton. In the distance, they hear several loud popping sounds before an enormous explosion. Devons shoulders fly up as he swings around. Looking back down Railton Road, orange-red flames lick through the shattered windows of the Jam-Jar as thick black smoke mushrooms into the air. Beyond that, he can see the large crowd cheering, jeering and roaring.

Continuing north toward the town centre, they pass an old Triumph Herald tipped onto its side. A crowd of youths have gathered around and are poking and probing at it like it's a wounded animal caught in a snare. 'Keep walking man, this is crazy,' Devon whispers. Slowing their pace, they approach a mass of Jam-Jars, SPG vans and several dozen Officers in a line, proceeding along in the middle of the road. Looking toward the Officers then back to the growing crowd further down the road forming a silhouette in front of the orange tinged smokey-grey background, Devon realises they are in the no-mans land of what has become a war zone. 'What the fuck's happening,' he says. 'And where the fuck is Marlon?'

Saturday, 11 April, 6:05pm
Corner of Atlantic Road and Railton Road
Brixton, London

The Rastafarian and the Reverend stand side-by-side. To their left several hundred angry youths and rude-boys while to their right, blocking the southbound approach from the town centre, two rows of SPG vans each nose to tail with around sixty Officers in front. The Reverend holds a cream and grey megaphone given to him by the young Police Inspector standing fifty feet behind him.

'Please listen,' the Reverend yells into megaphone. 'This will achieve nothing, go home, look after your own tonight.' His words are drowned out by the violent hum hanging in the air. Turning to the Rasta, he shakes his head. Taking hold of the megaphone, the Rasta tries reasoning with the crowd too, but his pleads are greeted by several half bricks thrown over his head into the Police cordon.

Quickly realising reasoning with the crowd isn't working, the Young Inspector approaches. 'Thank you, erm, for trying,' he says, raising his voice above the noise. He shakes their hands before relieving them of the megaphone.

'God forgive them,' the Reverend shakes his head as he heads back behind the Police cordon.

The sun sinks into inner city landscape…

The crowd, resembling a plague of locust, edge slowly toward the Police line. Random youths step forward to launch a brick or two before being consumed back into the heaving mass. At the same time, a group of middle-aged men with note pads and expensive looking long-lens cameras stand watching as an Officer is floored by a house brick. Blood streams as two other Officers run to his aid, lifting him to his feet, then back to the rear of the cordon.

'Hold steady,' the young Inspector yells as more missiles crack against the mesh covered windows of the SPG vans.

As the crowd gains momentum, the Young Inspector darts to the control van at the back of the cordon. Using his radio, he contacts the second cordon located a quarter mile north, at the corner of Coldharbour Lane, just before the main shopping precinct. 'This is, um, Inspector Cummings. We erm need more men, send more men!'

'Aye, okay Cummings, sorry… Inspector Cummings,' crackles a thick Scottish accent back through the radio.

John shakes his head, surely not?

'Be right there Johnny-boy, you crack on, we'll be there soon-as pal,' comes the voice again, almost singing.

Donnie?

Really?

Thank god, he thinks, quickly followed by a disheartening thought that if he's grateful for Donnie, then they are indeed in trouble.

Looking past his men and as far as he can see south along Railton Road, he sees a sea of anger and violence. Shops and houses are smashed up, parked cars turned over and burnt, garden walls kicked over with the bricks and masonry used as missiles. The drills at Hendon haven't prepared him for the gut-wrenching feeling deep in the pit of his stomach at the thought of an entire community literally ripping the wallpaper from its fragile existence. Breathing deeply, he looks around, his men are exhausted and in need of rotation. Many of them, like him, have already worked for fourteen hours straight, many of them even more. With the darkness of the night approaching, he knows they will be thinking about their families and loved ones, as he is, with him pondering why he joined the force in the first plave, and why he volunteered to leave the safety of Operations Command and join the effort on the front line. Right now though, they have work to do…

Standing behind the two rows of Officers, scanning the crowd he swallows hard, he knows what must be done next. Without the support of the mounted division and their ten-feet tall horses, the riot control drills at Hendon suggest they must seek to contain the breakout, then gain control of the area and disperse the perpetrators. His university studies suggest mass-disobedience is associated with herd-mentality and group-think, thus, deviance increases with scale. His strategic response to this is simple, reducing the size and density of the crowd will exponentially decrease deviant behaviour.

'Present arms,' he yells as the unmistakable sound of oak slamming against perspex rings around his ears, the noise deliberately intimidating. Simultaneously, guilt tugs his inner core, he doesn't want to fight these people, of course not, quite the opposite in fact, he genuinely wants to help. However, his men, one and all good honest coppers, are currently subject to the most horrendous violence, and the crowd refuses to listen to reason.

Another deep breath, he closes his eyes.

'Charge, charge, charge,' he bellows before blowing his whistle in three short blasts.

The Officers charge.

Truncheons swing.

Heads crack.

To his right, he sees a large Scottish thug dressed in full uniform stomping through the crowd. Bodies fly in all directions as he punches, kicks and head-butts everything in sight. With that, the crowd splits into two and the majority back away. 'Aw-hay Jonny-boy, let's go,' Donnie yells.

Before he can acknowledge his old friend, a sense of panic washes over him. Ducking instinctively, he hears a sizzling sound whoosh passed his head, a smash then a boom, the unmistakable sound of a petrol bomb igniting. Spinning around, he sees an Officer surrounded by fire, tackled to the ground by a colleague and the flames dampened down. In between the SPG vans, more and more shield-bearing Officers appear. In line with standard operating procedure and the endless drills at Hendon, they form two lines, one in front of the other, thereby creating a seamless wall of plastic to contain the egress.

As the wall edges forward, it's met with a barrage of fists, boots and screams. Allowing respite, John establishes a rotation of men at the face of the wall every couple of minutes. The strategy is working, but, for how long? He glances at his watch, the very same watch his mother gave him for his eighteenth birthday and his mind drifts… Melancholic thoughts morph into the stomach-churning realisation that he'll have the whole night to contend with. Thoughts of the Army spring to mind, knowing the very same thoughts will, no doubt, be crossing the minds of the Swamp 81 Operations Team, the very same men who devised and approved this nightmare plan. He quickly dismisses the thought, no way the Government would approve the deployment of troops on the mainland, unless emergency powers were approved by Parliament, plus the political fall-out would be immense.

As the night unfolds, additional Officers are seconded from neighbouring forces, and, within a matter of hours, around a thousand Officers are deployed into an area less than a square mile, commonly referred to as "the Frontline".

Saturday, 11 April, 9:18pm
Railton Road,
Brixton, London

Having left the troubles a few hours earlier, Delroy heads south to Herne Hill in search something to eat and to look for Marlon and the others. Portion of chips and a can of Lilt later, he decides the pussy-holes must have stayed in Brixton or fucked off over to Greenwich to see them fit girls they keep going on about. Heading back to the Frontline, he finds the main roads blocked-off by Police, so makes his way over the railway tracks, through back gardens and in and out of alleyways. Eventually, dipping below the low railway arch on Shakespeare Road, he stops at the corner of Railton where he's greeted by a scene of complete and utter devastation. No sign of any Police, only a few locals, mostly older folk busy sweeping up while a few Mommas huddle together, crying. He spots an old man with greying hair and a burgundy cardigan poking around in the rumble taking pictures with an old cine-camera. Swinging his camera around, spotting Delroy, he slowly lowers it. 'What'am my youth,' the Old Man says, approaching with a kind smile. 'You all-right, pickney?'

'Yeah man, I mean Sir, what happen here?'

'All dem' crazy-bad-man-and-yout tear up the street an head to the market and shops, looting and robbing and ram-shackle da-place,' the Old Man says shaking his head.

'Shit-man.'

'T'cha, language-nah, boy.'

'What, yeah, sorry-Sir, sorry.'

'Man gone mad yah-naw, fighting and steeling. Lord God told of the day when Satan and the horseman walk upon…'

'Right, right,' Delroy interjects, not wanting a lecture on fire and brimstone. 'So, they all head up town, what about Babylon, I mean the Police?'

'They just as bad, smashing and charging and ting. Listen, you look like a good boy, where-you-a-stay, where your momma or daddy?'

'Momma at home, not seen my dad in time though.'

'Listen, go-nah, head back to your momma and take care of her,' the Old Man pleads, placing a caring hand on Delroys shoulder.

'No problem, no problem, will do, thank you, Sir,' he says, lying, no way he's going home. Waving bye to the Old Man, he sets off toward the town centre. Passing Leesons Road he sees the Windsor pub ablaze with no sign of any fire engines. In front of the pub, a small crowd are battling with several rows of riot shielded Beasts. He's not scared or even shocked, this is normal now.

Then…

A solitary figure splits from the fighting crowd and makes its way slowly toward him. Readying himself for a tear up, his heart thumps. About six-foot tall, he recognises the dip of the shoulder and sway from side to side. Closer still, he knows the hair and toothy smile. 'Bom-ba-clat, where the fuck you been?' he says as they embrace.

'Here, all day,' Marlon whispers. 'It's madness, Beast are rampant, we not much better.'

Delroy looks his cousin up and down.

Looking a mess and completely exhausted, his hair's partially white from soot or ash or whatever, and his leather jacket and once yellow t-shirt are stained blood red. 'Shit man, look at you, you alright?'

'Yeah man, cool, cool, of course.'

'You sure brother, you look like shit.'

'I'm safe man, safe, anyways, you seen Devon?' Marlon looks around nervously.

'Left them hours ago, not long after the pool hall ting.'

Marlon turns and sets off toward Brixton town centre.

'Wait up then,' Delroy follows.

As they walk, weaving in-between several skirmishes they hear a distant roar of what must be the main riot. 'Look at all them watching,' Marlon nods toward what looks like a film crew interviewing several rude-boys busy gesticulating into the lens. Progressing further north toward the town centre, they notice more and more locals standing around on the pavement, watching the fighting as it intensifies. 'I hear the town hall got stormed,' Marlon sighs, without breaking stride.

'Yeah man,' Delroy agrees, keeping pace with him. 'I hear the Police Station got petrol bombed.'

'Things will never be the same,' Marlon shakes his head.

'They can't be sus-stopping us no more,' Delroy nods.

They pass a solitary SPG van lying lifeless on its side, charred and burnt out. Meanwhile, groups of youths walk in the opposite direction with new, clean clothes, mostly not fitting right. They have their arms full of small electrical goods including irons, toasters and kettles and one guy in particular, smiling like a Cheshire-cat, is pushing a shopping trolley full of what appears to be designer leather jackets.

'Fucking hell man, we must have taken over the town centre,' Delroy puts his arms around his cousins shoulder. 'Let's get up there get us some goods too.'

'Need to pass by mine on the way,' Marlon nods slowly.

Turning left onto Saltoun Road, the noise of the riot dims and an almost eerie stillness surrounds them. Marlon can't understand it, less than two hundred yards from the riot, his street and more importantly his house is fully intact and completely fine. Looking through his front window, it's all locked up and in darkness. Momma must have taken the money Devon gave her earlier and got a taxi to Tottenham to stay with her cousin while Pops must still be at work, or maybe gone up there too. Satisfied his family are safe, they continue toward the town centre, finding themselves on Brixton Hill.

Stopping abruptly, Delroy grabs Marlons arm. 'Hold up,' he says, nodding toward a battered old brown Ford Cortina approaching, moving slowly with a menacing calmness.

'No way,' Marlon whispers, his jaw dropping. Crouching down he squints, trying to get a better look.

Shit, it's him.

Kingys in the passenger seat staring straight ahead, unaware he's being watched. The driver, an overweight middle-aged man with greased back greying hair and a beige trench-coat grips the steering wheel with his left hand, with what seems to be a CB radio in his right.

'Mother… fucking… rat-boy,' Delroy sings. 'Riding with Babylon, what the fuck?'

'Hush-nah man,' Marlon whispers, watching the car pick up speed as it passes. 'He's a snake, I can't believe it.'

'I fucking knew-it,' Delroy nods. 'From time I knew, told you so, remember?'

'Yeah, yeah, just settle man.'

'Hear me know, dat-bwai is a dead man when I catch up with him,' Delroy grabs Marlons arm.

'I can't believe it.'

'Believe it, he's fucking dead.'

Continuing into the town centre, the rioting has all but stopped. Along the High street, lots of Police stand around a large dark green and cream coloured single decker bus, some are changing clothes while others are drinking tea from polystyrene cups. Slowing their pace, they eventually stop under the tall railway bridge, looking toward the smaller bridge to the right and the "Welcome to Brixton" sign.

Marlon laughs out loud.

Delroy stares at him. He's odd, too quiet, too distant, not his normal big-mouth know-it-all wanker self. 'What'am Marlon, what's so funny?' he asks tentatively.

'Look-nah, what a welcome we bring,' Marlon sighs, his laugh subsiding.

Then.

They spin round at the sound of screeching tyres ripping against the tarmac.

SGP van, shit.

The back doors swing open and four Officers jump out. 'Oi, stay there!' one of them shouts.

Pushing Marlon to the side, Delroy readies himself.

Smash.

Rugby tackled by the Officer, they stumble back, landing together on the floor. Within seconds, another two Officers are on him.

Fists clenched, fighting the urge to run, Marlon looks toward Delroy taking licks from the Beasts, screaming and shouting and getting mashed up. Tired of ducking and diving, running and hiding and looking over his shoulder, he has to make a stand right here, right now. 'Come on then!' he screams.

The remaining Office, younger than the others, moves into a fighting stance. 'Get back,' he shouts, raising his truncheon.

Pausing, Marlon becomes aware of his situation. He glances toward Delroy who's now on his feet bent double with his wrists pushed high in the air behind his back, being led toward the van. 'The Beasts done get me, man,' he wails.

Marlon looks back toward the Young Officer, now facing him side-on with his truncheon above his head. He's sweaty and dirty and breathing sharply. He looks scared, like he wants out, out of the uniform, out of Brixton and out of this predicament.

'Pussyhole,' Marlon yells, feeling the adrenalin building. He feels invigorated, fresh, new. Weeks of worry, avoiding Peckham-bad-boys and crazy psychopath chip-shop owners has come to an end. This is it, his time to make a stand. 'Me and you, right here.'

The Young Officer doesn't move, fear fills his eyes.

Marlon steps forward. 'Come take me then Babylon, take me if you can.' He feels fearless, ready, primed.

Stepping back, the Young Officer raises his truncheon further above his head.

Looks over the Beasts shoulder toward the SPG van in the distance he sees Delroys screaming and struggling as he's thrown into the back and the doors slammed shut.

'I'm right here,' Marlon says, nodding and smiling.

The Young Officer stares, his eyes glazed, uncertainty scribbled across his face.

'Simon,' comes a shout from the van. 'Let's go.'

The Young Officer hesitates before standing upright, pointing the end of his truncheon toward Marlon. Maintaining his stare, he tentatively steps toward the van before climbing into the passenger seat.

The engine roars and the van pulls away.

Marlon can't quite believe it, the Beast backed down.

'Oi, you, pick-en-ey, halt nah-man.'

Shit, what now.

Swinging around Marlon's confronted by a rude-boy wearing a brilliant-white, nineteen-seventies-style bell-bottomed suit. Two lads flank him, one carrying a half empty bottle of brandy, the other a cassette player.

'Fuck-ing-hell?' Marlon whispers out loud, over pronouncing every syllable.

Arms wide, Devon spins around three-sixty, giving a twirl of his new suit before running toward Marlon. Instinctively, they embrace before quickly shrugging each other off. 'You're safe then?' Devon nods, gently punching his arm.

'Safe, that's one word for it.'

'So, Delroy in chains, wha-gwan?'

'We just walking, and they shank us.'

'Mate, what are you like?' Ashley places his arm around Marlons shoulder. 'Wanting to take on a whole heap of Beasts, we saw you from over yonder.'

'They mash-up Delroy, what else could I do?'

'Err, try using your head,' Paul adds in. 'Maybe not

fronting up to a wagon-full, anyway, where'd you get to?'

'Dunno, after the Pool Hall, I see Claude and tagged on with him for a while,' Marlon wipes a tear from his eye. 'Got surrounded near Leesons Road, Babylon everywhere,'

'Crazy innit?' Ashley swallows hard, he's never seen his friend in such a state.

'Enough troubles man,' Marlon continues. 'Not just Babylon neither, everyone's fighting everyone, man against man,' Marlon wearily shakes his head. 'You lot been shopping then?'

'You like my new garms?' Devon dusts down his collars.

'Bit bright, man,' Marlon theatrically squints, raising his hand to avoid the dazzling whiteness.

'That's more like it, come nah-baby brother,' Devon smiles, placing his arm around his shoulder.

Sunday 12 April, 1:33am
Divisional Operations Centre,
Lambeth, London

At the end of the large meeting room several radio operators sit glued to receivers taking information from each of the four Stations within the Borough. The ultra-bright lights hanging from the ceiling beam through the fog of cigarette smoke illuminating the oversized table littered with half drunken cups of tea and overflowing cigarette trays. A map of Brixton is stretch out with red lines sketched on showing what is now being referred to as "disturbance zones". Several dozen small red circles represent properties gutted by fire and blue triangles represent commercial properties which have been burgled or looted. Then, the two wooden doors at the other end of the room swing open as several Divisional Commanders as well the entire Swamp Operation team enter and take their seats before Jenkins calls the meeting to order.

'Gentlemen, safe to say the operation hasn't gone to plan tonight, but, what's been done, is done,' he says, abruptly and to the point. 'Status update, Commander Crow?'

'Er-hum,' Crow clears his throat and pushes his chin through his tightly button shirt collar. 'We have around… fifteen hundred Officers deployed with… another thousand or so on standby.' Pausing, he scans around the room. 'I've witnessed… a highly credible presence in… and around all the key locations… we have gained full control… majority of the unpleasantness has now ceased.'

Making some quick notes, Jenkins nods and looks toward Assistant Commissioner Warren. 'George?'

'Sir, twelve vehicles unaccounted for, a fire-tender has been damaged beyond repair and a couple of Ambulances are out of action, smashed windscreens mainly.' Warren sighs, removing his glasses, closing his eyes and pinching the bridge of his nose.

'George, this isn't easy for any of us, please continue,' Jenkins prompts.

'Regards the "unpleasantness", fifty-two arrests, mostly public order offences and looting. However, I'm afraid we have two serious incidents…'

'Go on,' Jenkins urges, growing impatient.

'Two suspects held on suspicion of rape, and we arrested another suspect just east of Acre Lane for threatening an Officer with a hand-gun, attempted murder if we can get it.'

A rumble of titters fill the room.

'Fifty-two… that simply… cannot be right,' Crow growls through gritted teeth, the lines on his forehead deepening. 'With my own eyes I saw… hundreds rioting, if not… thousands.'

Ignoring him, Warren continues. 'Seventy or so members of the public have been taken to hospital, around two hundred Officers injured with further forty to fifty in hospital.' Warren notices Crow shaking his head. 'All in all, tonight has been an unqualified disaster, put us back years, if not decades.'

'George, perspective, please,' Jenkins pats the air. 'None of us are proud of what's happened here tonight, but we're all here for the same reason.'

Warren nods, his eye lids closing.

Inhaling deeply Jenkins looks toward John. 'And the civic perspective Inspector Cummings?'

John wipes his left hand across his face down to his chin. 'Sir, I accompanied the church leader, Reverend Johnson and a community leader known as "Bones" as they addressed a large swathe of rioters but with, erm, little effect.' John sees Crow theatrically raise his eyebrows, damn him, he's not about to be put off his stride by a caveman. 'They have, um, opened up the community centre to cater for those displaced.'

'John, thanks,' Jenkins smiles. 'And the Security Services?'

Giles, the young civilian sporting brown corduroys and a cream woollen jumper pushes his glasses with his index finger. 'I'm pleased to say we have taken several high-quality targets including a suspected importer and distributor of marijuana, a suspected opiate distributor with links to the middle-east, along with a serious player in prostitution and people-trafficking. We feel the timing is right to allow low-key snatch operations to arrest others known to be near the centre of much of these events, far right anarchists and agitators plus a few loosely associated with Ulster. We have already passed Crow and Warren a list of possible targets.'

Jenkins looks at Crow, then Warren, who both nod. 'So, Giles, let's be clear, you're suggesting by sun-up we will have arrested the perpetrators?'

'That is my understanding, yes.'

'And, what about these "crime overlords" you mentioned before, the heroin dealers?' Warren urges, sitting back in his seat, tongue firmly in cheek.

'Good question, we have several suspects who we believe will provide good information on trafficking routes and money laundering operations. I understand we have confiscated a significant volume of illegal substances, including heroin, also several firearms.'

'Very good. I have a briefing with Armstrong at Downing

Street in an hour,' Jenkins stands up. 'Suggest we get together again at six-hundred hours.'

Sunday 12 April, 2:15am
Kennington Park Road
London.

With no traffic and the open road ahead, John presses the clutch pedal of the Ford Escort Mk2 and pushes the gear stick into forth.

The Engine roars.

'Where did we go wrong?' Warren askes, wiping the condensation, staring blankly out of the passenger window.

John shakes his head. 'Not sure, Sir. Suits everyone though, doesn't it?' he continues.

'What on earth do you mean?' Warren raises his voice.

'It's just, very convenient, isn't it? The informants allow us to arrest the dealers and, with the unrest, we get to arrest known troublemakers too. The council get the squats cleared and the locals get to vent their anger. It, um, tidies things up nicely.'

'Tidies things up?' Warren looks deep into John. 'Listen John, last night was nothing but terrible decisions made by incompetent and blinkered fools.'

'Really?' John says, struggling to hide his sarcastic tone.

'You're your own man, John, intelligent too, but really, could all this really be orchestrated and planned?'

Johns mind races with thoughts of invisible hands and political manoeuvring. He remembers the visit to Jenkins office just before graduating and seeing the then unknown Giles Askwith-Parsons waiting in reception. Tired and suffering with fatigue, he can't quite piece all the pieces together accurately, but, he knows somethings not right.

Couple of minutes later…

They approach a roadblock at the north end of Brixton Road. Spotting Warren, the Officers standing in front of the pander-cars wave him through. Two minutes later, they pull into the car park at the rear of Brixton Police Station.

'And, here we are John, home sweet home,' Warren sighs, clambering out and stretching his back.

'Very good Sir,' John agrees. Hearing the faint sounds of dub-reggae flowing from the suburbs, he looks out over the perimeter wall. Although the middle of the night, he can make out the silhouette of black cloud hanging high above South London, illuminated by the orange glow of fires burning below. 'Welcome to paradise,' he whispers.

Sunday 12 April, 2:35am
Loughborough Estate,
Brixton, London

The fifth-floor two-bedroom flat is rammed with sweaty, jubilant revellers. The party is swinging with everyone cheering and whooping, gyrating and mingling. Spliffs are passed around along with bottles of brandy and wine, liberated from the town centre shops. With the goodness from the five-skin filling his lungs and the baseline of The Gongs "Redemption" thumping into his chest, Devon sways as he feels the vibe. Spinning around, he sees rude-boys and hot-girls coming together in a seamless celebratory mass, hugging, dancing and drinking, sharing kisses while rubbing and grinding. Completely at ease, feeling safe and protected, he bobs his way through the room. Smiling to himself, he scans across to Paul who's standing next to the six-foot tall speaker system laughing and joking with a half-dressed light skin girl with striking green eyes. The sound controller switches-up the delay dial on the echo chamber and proceeds to mash-up snare drums with trumpet stabs. Standing next to him, a rude-boy dressed in army uniform clutching the microphone clears his throat, preparing to toast over the next baseline heavy tune.

Turning back around, he sees Claude who, after a firm handshake followed by a brief hug, tells him how Crissy got arrested outside the Windsor late in the afternoon, and about Snakehead going missing around eight in the evening. He goes on to tell him about the council bulldozing parts of the Frontline, with the Windsor Pub going first. As Claude leaves for another party in Stockwell or Clapham or somewhere they promise to meet up later in the day.

Looking out to the balcony, Devon sees the orange glow of a joint being passed between Marlon and Ashley. Dipping through the doorway he steps out into the cold night. The dark sky twinkles with more stars than he's ever seen before while the horizon is illuminated with the glow of fires and blue sparks of Babylonian lights racing here and there.

'Alright Dev,' Ashley smiles, passing him the joint.

'So,' Devon nods. 'Beasts got what they deserve, yeah.'

'What they deserve?' Marlon sighs. 'Nah-man, you don't get it, this place is fucked brother, fucked.'

'Nah-man, we've risen, things will be different now.'

'Completely different,' Ashley agrees.

'We've ripped London apart, Beastman get mash-up, pickney get mash-up, stabbed-up too. Houses, cars, shops and the whole Frontline get mash-up,' Marlon blurts, tears welling in his eyes. 'And for what?

'They all get mash-up,' Ashley agrees, worse for wear he's slurring his words.

'Lickle man, you did your fair share of rampaging too-yeah,' Devon places his arm around him. 'You-been fucked about by Babylon from time, you don't have to feel nothing for them, nothing.'

'Been fucked around-mate, he's talking sense,' Ashley shakes his head, retaking the joint from Devon.

Marlon stares at the balcony floor.

'You just tired dred,' Devon says, standing back up and rubbing his hand over Marlons head.

'True-say,' Ashley agrees. 'Just tired innit.'

'Now listen, I'm gonna get pissed and get me some with little-miss-green-eyes through there,' Devon squeezes Marlons arm, giving Ashley a wink before disappearing back into the pulsating crowd.

Looking out from the balcony, Marlon spots more and more youths walking toward the tower block. He beckons the joint from Ashley before inhaling deeply. He nods as the *"when I was a youth"* vocals bounce along with the rumbling baseline while the echoing piano stabs echo around his exhausted, weed massaged brain. 'You know what?' he says. 'I've had it with this place.'

Ashley looks up. 'Eh?'

'Dis place, this fucking shit-hole.'

'Yeah man, its dry, let's go somewhere else then.'

'Not right here, right now man, I mean Brixton, London.'

'What you on about?'

'Been thinking, soon as my exams are over with, I'm off.'

'Off, where?' Ashley asks, his voice breaking slightly.

'Look at this place, burnt-up, smashed-up, it's fucked man, fucked. Enough people got hurt tonight and true, most deserve it, but some just got caught up. Man can't live like this with all the tribulation and aggravation, looking over our shoulder all the time.'

Silence separates them for what feels like an age.

'Where will you go?'

'Got an Auntie in Birmingham, might head to Manchester or Leeds maybe. Brighton even, things were controlled down there.'

Ashley stares at the Balcony floor for a few seconds, then looks up, tears filling his eyes. 'What will you do?'

Marlon turns to the smouldering cityscape in the distance. 'I don't know, but life has to be better than dis.'

# R I O T

## PLAYLIST

1. "Funky Town" by Lipps Inc.

2. "Don't Stop Till You Get Enough" by Michael Jackson

3. "Brick in the Wall" by Pink Floyd

4. "Can You Feel It" by The Jackson Five

5. "Call Me" by Blondie

6. "Fantasy" by Earth, Wind & Fire

7. "Reward" by The Teardrop Explodes

8. "The Force" by The Real Thing.

9. "Fade to Grey" by Visage

10. "Ant Music" by Adam and the Ants

11. "Cars" by Gary Numan

12. "War of the Worlds" by Jeff Wayne

13. "Skinhead Moonstomp" by The Specials

14. "Rudie" by Gregory Isaacs

15. "Air Tonight" by Phil Collins

16. "No Future" by the Sex Pistols

17. "Love will tear us apart" by Joy Division

18. "Jah Children" by Aswad

19. "Dub Station" by Yabby You & Michael Prophet

20. "Bankrobber" by The Clash

21. "Vienna" by Ultravox.

22. "Walking on the Moon" by The Police

23. "Hawaii-Five-O Theme" by Morton Stevens

24. "Geno" by Dexys Midnight Runners

25. "Too Young" by The Specials

26. "Baggy Trousers" by Madness

27. "Living Dub Vol One" by Burning Spear

28. "Lip-up Fatty" by Bad Manners

29. "Redemption" by Bob Marley

30. "Hard Times" by Pablo Gad

## EPILOGUE

### Chief Superintendent John Cummings

Served in various senior roles within the Metropolitan Police, featuring in a BBC fly-on-the-wall documentary "Policing London' before leaving the Met and becoming a political and social commentator. Nowadays, he is a regular or various radio-phone in talk-shows.

### Constable Andrew Jones

Transferred into the vice squad late 1981, then, some time later is discharged from the Metropolitan Police for impropriety and questionable behavior with an informant. Current location unknown.

### Sergeant Donnie MacDowell

Shortly after the disturbances in Brixton, made sergeant within the Special Patrol Group before transferring the SO19 firearms squad. Now serves in the SO14, the Royal Protection Unit.

### Sergeant Smith

Remained as lead tutor at Hendon before retiring with full honors in 1986. He now volunteers at a local Scouts group and, sharing the same agent as John Cummings, acts as a consulting advisor on Police matters for various authors, writers and television production crews.

### Commissioner Armstrong

Supported the rebuilding of the Metropolitan Police throughout 1981 to 1983, including the establishment of the Independent Police Complaints Authority. Received a Knighthood by Her Majesty the Queen in the 1984 New Years Honors list.

**Deputy Commissioner Jenkins**

Elected to take early retirement late 1982 due to sciatic nerve damage. Nowadays, enjoys spending time with his three granddaughters, gardening and lowering his golf handicap, (currently 8).

**Assistant Commissioner George Warren**

Appointed expert witness for the post-disturbance Scarman Inquest, specifically focusing on the planning and execution of Operation Swamp 81, before moving to a leadership role within the Metropolitan Police wide improvement task force.

**Commander Crow**

After leading a restructure of the Special Patrol Group immediately after the disturbances, early 1983 he transferred to Hendon as course leader. Has written several academic books on deviant behavior and also a prize-winning novel about a private investigator in New York City.

**Detective Chief Inspector McCrudden**

Mid 1981, accepted a Commander position in Belfast responsible for offshore missions including the interception of weapons bound for the provisional IRA. Achieved a commendation from Her Majesty the Queen for seizing several Belfast-bound shipments of assault rifles and plastic explosives, believed to be from Libya.

**Detective Inspector Collins**

Late 1982, was subjected to an internal investigation of wrong doing associated with mistreatment of informants. After union advice, decided to take voluntary redundancy in 1984. Current whereabouts unknown.

**Giles Askwith-Parsons**

Featured as an expert advisor in the post disturbance Scarman Inquest. His employment record since then is highly redacted and classified as "Top Secret", but he is believed to have led an analyst function within Government Communications Agency.

* * *

**Devon Walters**

Moved in with the love of his life, Shirley shortly after the uprising, having their first and only child, Tyrone, in 1982. Goes on to own and run a pirate radio station and become a nightclub promoter.

**Paul Richardson**

After the uprising, focused on his career in financial services and, in March 1986, made his first million-pound bonus as part of a large property re-financing deal. Currently dating a budding singer based in Bromley, Kent.

**Winston "Super" Cottbed**

Relocated to Tottenham late 1981, securing a steady job providing security at several nightclubs in Hackney. Convicted of the murder of a Police Officer during the 1985 civil disturbances in north London and is currently serving an indeterminant sentence at Her Majesty's pleasure in Wormwood Scrubs prison.

**Shirley Bullbrook**

Moved in with the love of her life, Devon, shortly after the uprising, giving birth to their first and only child, Tyronne, in 1982. Currently runs a mother-and-toddler group every Friday morning at the local community center in Deptford.

**Sammie Maclean**

Dated Paul Richardson for about a year then, mid 1982, married a soldier who, shortly after, was posted to Cyprus where she worked in a bar before eloping with a young bartender named Christos. Current whereabouts unknown.

**Chantelle Bannerman**

Lost touch with Shirley and Sammie shortly after the uprising, becoming a traffic warden. Currently residing in Bexleyheath, Kent, she is happily married to Trevor, with twin daughters. She has been tea-total for several years.

**Claude Williamson**

After the uprising, embarked on a brutal war to gain control of the drug trade in south London against Snakehead and his crew of "yardie" gangsters. Suffered life threatening injuries in 1985 when thrown off the roof of a tower block in Peckham.

**Cristobal "Crissy" Campbell**

Arrested on the night of the uprising and remained in custody for 7 months, before a lengthy criminal trial. Found guilty of importation of drugs and money laundering before being deported and is serving an 18 year sentence in the South Camp Correctional Institute.

**"Snakehead"**

After the uprising, embarked on a brutal war to gain control of the drug trade in south London against Claude Williamson. Claimed to be responsible for the rise in "yardie" based gang-warfare currently terrorizing communities across London.

**Kenneth "Kenny" McCoy**

Found guilty of a string of offenses including firearms charges and sentenced to 8 years. Currently incarcerated at category C open prison HMP Highpoint, just outside Cambridge, where he is studying for a criminology degree.

**John-Michael McMahon**

Shortly after the uprising, joined various political parties and was an active protestor for anti-immigration policies. Late 1982, became a founding member of the English Nationalist Party. Currently a regular contributor to various anti-establishment magazines.

* * *

**Marlon Walters**

After the uprising, continued his studies where he achieved good grades and, after spending the summer in Leeds, enrolled onto a sound engineering course at Tottenham Technical College. Currently works part time in a record store in Dalston and deejays on local pirate radio.

**Ashley Richardson**

After leaving school was offered a YTS position at Crystal Palace FC where he made 33 appearances for the B Team scoring 7 goals. After a serious accident receiving multiple leg and back injuries, was released from Palace and is currently employed as a regional manager for McDonalds.

**Delroy Collis**

Left school shortly after the uprising before his end of year exams to became a courier for Snakehead, moving drugs and cash to and from the Netherlands before, a few years later, relocating to Miami Florida where he operates guided tours of Biscayne Bay.

**Gladstone Walker**

Remained close friends with Marlon Walters, attending the same college on the same sound engineering course. Currently deejays on local pirate radio and holds a Thursday night residency at Astoria nightclub on Oxford Street in Londons West End.

**Andrew "Kingy" King**

Placed into the Witness Protection Program after testifying in several high profile "yardie" deportation cases, including the case of Cristobal Campbell. Believed to have started a new life in Edinburgh, Scotland.

**"Yellowman"**

Has not been seen since the night of the uprising. Rumored to have been subject to a brutal gangland revenge killing with his remains being buried in the foundations of a tall office block in London Docklands.

**Stevie Gentle**

Arrested on the night of the uprising and charged with disturbing the peace. Served 3 months in Feltham Young Offenders Institute before, on behalf of Snakehead, gaining control of the main drug dealing gang on the North Peckham Estate. Currently engaged in an escalating turf war with Turkish gangs.

**Ernest "Junior" Thompson**

After a lengthy recovery from stab wounds to the chest, relocated to Berkshire, gaining a scholarship at the Red Coat Independent School, achieving excellent academic results. Currently studying politics and philosophy at Oxford University.

## MORE FROM THE AUTHOR

### **"R A V E R"**

the sequel to Riot.

Illuminated by high frequency super-bright flashes, strobing freeze-framed hands punch the air as the tie-dyed dungaree ravers chant "ah-seed" to the never-ending four-four kick drum and acid-house squelches. War of the Worlds style, the pitch-black countryside is ripped apart by two high powered light-sabre green lasers sweeping toward the brightly lit big wheel and spinning waltzers. Scanning across the multi-coloured silhouetted horizon the euphoric rush caresses his spine, tingles his skull and a sense of love fills his heart. Alive like never before, he's loving life and loving everyone. He's lived a half-life, surreal and unreal and make believe, an urban daydream clouded by hazy chemical cocktails. Eyes closing, his thoughts drift to the night-time darkness. Mind splintering, he's faced with black-and-white snap-shot pictures of tower-blocks and skinheads, riots and Police brutality. Nostrils flaring with childhood smells of ginger-bread spices, stewing tea and curried goat, guilt, remorse and regret creep slowly from the shadows of his mind. Fight the darkness, fight the fear, get back on the up from the down. Squeezing his eyes tightly shut, the "move-your-body" metronome echoes around him and once again takes him higher.

That was then, this is now…

Knock-knock. No answer.

Looking over the open walkway around the estate, he hears the opening bars of that Guy Called Gerald track echoing from an open window in the other block, "ahhhha-ha-yeah, voodoo-ray, voodoo-ray." A smile curls at the corner of his mouth. He remembers moving thirty thousand ravers to that very tune just a few of weeks ago.

He knocks again, harder this time. Still no answer. Looking through the window, he can tell someone's inside. Facing the door he smashes his foot against the lock. Bursting open, the door slams against the inside wall before bouncing back. Turning away he covers his mouth as an unbearable smell burns his nostrils. Edging in, he can just about see through the kitchen door, three-quarter closed. Eyes dart to the balcony door, smashed and bloodied. Slowly pushing the door ajar, he scans the torn apart room. Signs of a struggle. He spots a pile of papers on the table, chewed up with scribbles all over them. Beyond that, past the table he sees the body on the floor…

Printed in Poland
by Amazon Fulfillment
Poland Sp. z o.o., Wrocław